The Birthday Gift

The Birthday Gift

ANTHONY SCOTT

Matador
9 Priory Business Park
Kibworth Beauchamp
Leicestershire LE8 0RX, UK
Tel: (+44) 116 279 2299
Fax: (+44) 116 279 2277
Email: books@troubador.co.uk
Web: www.troubador.co.uk/matador

ISBN 978 1784620 103

British Library Cataloguing in Publication Data.
A catalogue record for this book is available from the British Library.

Typeset in Palatino by Troubador Publishing Ltd
Printed and bound in the UK by TJ International, Padstow, Cornwall

Matador is an imprint of Troubador Publishing Ltd

For Karen: Matyamou, Karthiamou, Psychemou

"Men's wretchedness in soothe I so deplore,
not even I would plague the sorry creatures more."
Mephistopheles
Faust, Part 1 1808
Johan Wolfgang von Goethe

Chapter 1

Porthmeor Beach, St Ives

September 2009

The early evening sun danced and dazzled on the sea as it reached its crescendo, its fine and final act. All afternoon the energetic waves had been driving higher up the beach and crashing on to the brave souls still in its water. Each person waited for a fresh wall of excitement to arrive and in turn screamed with delight at the sheer exhilaration of being so vulnerable to the elements. And now, at last, this final fling, this royal dance with the high tide to which demons and angels would thrillingly ride.

Summer was almost over and despite it being a Saturday evening there were very few people now still out, a fresh westerly breeze being less than inviting to stay on for the closing movements. Viewing this theatre of ballet on the waves was The Beach Café which sat nestled under the protective arms of the Tate Gallery and looking out on to Porthmeor Beach and this oncoming onslaught of the cool, blue sea. Tess sat huddled up on its open balcony, armed with a bottle of cool Chilean Sauvignon Blanc and two thick jumpers as she watched her precious son and equally precious elderly father laughing gamely like two small overexcited children. Her father was now eighty-five years old and yet he had insisted on keeping his birthday ritual of whatever the weather he would take to the Cornish sea at high tide and celebrate that he was still alive!

'Grandad!' shouted Noah over the thick roar of the waves,

1

laughter filling his face, 'Are you OK? Have you had enough?' Noah was under strict instructions from his mother and grandmother to keep Joshua in the water for the shortest time possible. Joshua responded by letting out a loud roar of excitement as he tried to walk back deeper into the sea. It was his answer to his grandson's question, his cry to the sea and to life itself. He had in fact only just got up from a huge and powerful wave, a wave that had knocked them both easily over into the waiting harsh mixture of sharp pebbles and gritty sand that gathered only on this part of the beach for high tide.

Noah marvelled at his grandfather's willpower, that at his celebrated age he would still brave the elements of a cold September evening in the sea. Left to Noah he would have understood if his grandad had chosen to give today a miss. It was, after all, far from an Indian summer with the weather laced by a stiff, cool wind that carried more than a hint of rain. Still the old man was an indomitable old so-and-so and this year, despite being dogged by illness for most of it, Joshua had been as determined as ever to make it down to the beach that his house overlooked, the house that he had lived in for over fifty years. Here, as ever then, he would face the sea head-on before his birthday party. Far be it from his adoring grandson to not accompany the brave Joshua Spearing into the Atlantic Ocean and Noah did so with great pleasure and honour.

Noah was protected by a full-body wetsuit, which kept him relatively warm and took the sting out of the waves as they showed no mercy and smashed down on them. He was also twenty-four, an experienced surfer and he was wearing a well-toned body that was used to the sea the whole year round, and yet despite all these pluses in his favour, even he was struggling to keep his balance. At this part of the beach, when the sea reached so high that it threatened to push higher than it had ever done so before, the waves crashed with immense power and the difference to being out in the surf was that here there was only hard beach to fall on to, no depth of sea to crash into and recover. Each time now that Noah and Joshua fell, the sea was angrily meeting with defeat at the hands of the slope at the top part of the beach. Here the hard beach now had the upper hand against the sea and it sent its old foe back at full speed with a glint in its eye and a two-fingered salute. The waves, like an undeterred kitten who was determined to play with anything it shouldn't, would simply fall away, recuperate and try again with as much vigour and steam as they had done the last time. The effect on those hardy souls to still be in the water was that as one wave hit them and knocked them backwards, the last returning wave moved their feet in the other direction. You left the sea inevitably battered and bruised having been used as a pawn in the game between wave and shore.

As another shriek of laughter emanated into the early evening sky, Tess blinked her eyes and took a mental photograph of the scene before her. Tess took photographs with her eyes all the time and sketched them later in her studio as a keepsake and inspiration for her wider work. Her life, memories and moments, lay scattered around her studio and house as a constant reminder of what had mattered to her and her need to live and live some more. This was her gift.

As grandson and grandfather took another tumble, a fresh blast of sea having again battered them to the ground, the two of them continued to giggle, the hilarity of the situation taking over and making them oblivious to the cold and the danger of the sea. Noah pulled himself up once more and as gently as he could manage in an angry sea, helped pull his grandfather up again. Joshua wore only long trunks that now clung to him and made his old, reducing frame stand out even more. The trunks were a faded red colour clinging from high above his waist down to the top of his thighs.

'I must borrow those trunks some time, Grandad!' shouted Noah with a huge grin.

'Yes, you must, you cheeky bugger! They will help you with the ladies! They were all the rage once you know.'

'In the 1920s?'

'The roaring 1940s and 1950s of course when your old pops was an international playboy!' called Joshua without a hint of irony. 'I have a choice of colours you may be interested in!' offered Joshua with a hint of mischief in his eyes.

Noah laughed and as he did so he got a mouthful of water as another surge of the sea pounded into him causing him to choke.

'Come on, Grandad, let's get to the safety of dry land! I know you could stay in here all night but I've had enough!'

'I've beaten you again eh, Noah?' Joshua laughed brightly, proudly, accepting that the time had indeed come to return to dry land. He was exhausted and knew his body would scream at him later and for days to come, yet he was buoyed by the energy of being with his precious Noah in his old friend, the ocean, on the glorious Porthmeor Beach.

Noah put his arm around his now-thinning grandfather's shoulders, shoulders that had once eked with immense muscle and power, and led him out of the sea to their waiting towels, thick and luxurious and purposely brought down to ease their anticipated aching limbs and warm them up as quickly as possible. Natalya, Joshua's beautiful Russian wife and Noah's dear grandmother, had even packed several hot-water bottles, which were gratefully grasped tightly now. The two men looked up to the café to catch the eye of their precious Tess who in turn waved exuberantly, hugely relieved that at last her father had left the sea without, it appeared, having broken anything. Noah made a face of exaggerated expression as he sort to show his mother just how cold he felt. Joshua stood and simply laughed; the air and its effect on his skin making him feel more alive than he had done for some time.

'God, that was good, my boy!' he said. His year had been one of dreadful life-stripping illness and he had often thought he might not even see this day. Now that he was here, that he had made it, he was determined to enjoy every moment. Life he felt was faint and uncertain, yet never truer than shared with the loved ones of choice.

Tess, from the safety of the café, smiled. How many times had she seen this now? From the moment that Noah could stand, her father had taken him down to the sea and together they had filled the air with screams of laughter. They would normally outlast anybody else in the water, be there for ages and come out so cold, their skin misshapen by being so long in the sea, their very physical being so sapped of any strength that they had taken into the surf with them, and yet they were both so bountifully happy. It was the same today, with only surfers safely out at sea in deeper water and away from the madness of the shore, outlasting the two of them. They had a

4

very special relationship, grandfather and grandson. They always had. It was a connection that transcended any other that either man had known and, despite the other children and grandchildren that Joshua had, it was his connection with Noah that was his strongest link with anyone. They were so close, and for this Tess was very thankful and happy.

Click; her camera on her phone taking a memory that she would transfer to her desktop in her studio later. Tess was an artist. She painted abstract pieces that followed a theme. She would close her eyes and the colours she wished to concentrate on would flood into her mind, colours that she had been breathing in throughout her days in and around St Ives and were as natural to her as the colour of her skin and the contours of her face.

She filled her glass again, took a large, grateful sip and let the earthy texture of the depth of the wine fill her throat. As she did so she looked out longingly to the immense and unfathomable emptiness of the sea. The wind blew forcefully across her face, her hazel eyes protected by her large sunglasses, her long, strawberry-blonde hair which over the years she had dyed almost every colour possible, was now being lifted from her neck, its cool touch moving around her exposed skin and making her feel sensual and free. God, she loved this place, the ocean, the exposed coastal paths, the history of a piece of land that knew what it was like to see nature roar. Somehow the very act of being in St Ives made Tess feel stronger than she felt anywhere else. Why? It was difficult to analyse it and she had tried to because every time she went away she just longed to be back and this was not always healthy for her. It was more than the fact that it was home; rather, this was the place where she felt most alive, where she walked its streets and paths and could almost feel the electric of the place run through her veins. Here she was plugged into the actual landscape, truly wired up to nature's cabling and set free by it. Tess had no reason to question its magic, its enchantment, its unquestionable allure for her; she just connected into its energy source, welcomed it and emptied out its effect on to her canvases and photographs.

Noah and Joshua were now at last walking up the beach, speed now at last apparent as the allure of the café pulled them closer to her and sustenance, and warmth! They had wiped away the cold sea from their still very cold skin, and pulled on layers of flannels and fleeces to combat the feeling of ice that arrives as soon as the fresh air meets you after you leave the sea, yet its cold was not about to leave them that easily. It was now, despite Natalya's welcome hot-water bottles, simply refusing to leave their bodies and Joshua's chattering teeth were causing Noah to grimace.

'Three large coffees please, Sylvy!' called Tess to her best friend who ran the café. 'We'll have them inside too and warm these brave souls up.'

'Warm chocolate brownies too, sweetie?'

'Oh yes. Why not?' Tess made her way past the bar just inside the door and to the far table by the western window.

'He's amazing isn't he?' said Sylvia as she busied herself getting some glorious fresh coffee flowing, the beautiful smell of fresh beans filling the air, 'I mean, how old is he?'

'Eighty-five today.'

'Eighty-five today! I mean, God, eighty-five. He's got such spirit, such strength. I want what he's taking, Tess. Find out what it is!'

'Fisherman's Friend,' laughed Tess, thinking as she did so on Sylvia's words. Her father had always been such a character, a larger than life personality that had filled her world from the moment she was born. Everyone in St Ives knew him and Cornwall itself held him in the highest esteem, proud to count him as one of their own. People, important people, had always come from around the world to see him, and Tess had grown up with this as a simple fact of her father's life and therefore her life too. Joshua Spearing's life in the armed forces in and after the Second World War, and then straight into the limelight of public service, this very life had thrust him into the public eye and he had revelled in it. The high rank he had achieved in Her Majesty's Armed Forces was a precursor to the heights he would reach in public life as a Conservative Member of Parliament and then a Lord. He had connections everywhere and stories to captivate any audience. Yes, people came to see Joshua Spearing. They always would. He had a presence about him, a mystery and an allure that held his audience captive and refused to let them go. When

6

Joshua Spearing spoke, people listened, and to those dearest to him, their very lives were built on him as a huge part of their foundation.

'Come on in you two,' called Sylvia to the two bedraggled bathers who had arrived at the door, 'Red-hot coffee is on its way to warm you up and get you ready for your party young Joshua!'

'And please add a little drop or two of magic, Sylvia. Push the boat right out! It is after all my birthday,' he replied as he sat at the table to the left of his daughter and away from the draft of the still-open door. Tess leaned over to her father and kissed his cold right cheek. She put her hand to his cool and reddened face and cupped his smiling complexion hoping, as she did so, to never let it go.

'What are you like, Papa? You're freezing. You are a brave old thing.'

'There is no such thing as bravery, Mother, only degrees of fear!' declared Noah having left the bags of excess towels and water-bottles by the door and now coming and sitting himself across the table.

Tess laughed at what she thought to be a quote and took in the sight of her son, his blonde unruly hair even more all over the place than normal.

'Let me guess, Shakespeare?' she asked.

'Wainwright!' declared Joshua proudly. 'You're getting to be quite the scholar my boy.'

'Boredom can achieve great things, Grandad.'

'That it can, that it can,' Joshua replied, gently laughing as he did so before a deep cough arrived and wracked his chilled and frail frame.

Steaming black coffee and sumptuous rich brownies with double cream arrived and Sylvia, with nothing but an empty café to attend to, sat down with her friends.

'So how was the sea, Joshua?' she asked.

'Sylvia, it was glorious! You should have come in. I would have been delighted to see you in your bathing suit! You do look delightful in a swimsuit, my dear, and I really wish summer would continue for longer so that I could see you in it more often.'

'Now come on that really is outrageous!' cried Noah.

'Not at all, my boy. An active mind keeps the enemy at bay.'

'And we all know that you have an active mind. You're a very naughty old man!' laughed Noah, impressed as ever by the cheek of the older man while his mother just rolled her eyes.

'Yes indeed, but further, and to my defence, I would add that it is my birthday and if you can't be extra cheeky on your birthday, when can you be?'

'True enough,' responded Sylvia, 'Cheekiness clearly in your case keeps the heart younger.'

'That it does, young lady, that it does. Now then, Tess, is it far later than it should be?'

'It is, Daddy, and we have as you well know a very special party to attend,' Tess said, hearing her mother's list of warnings that she had left the house with. Make sure he didn't stay in the sea long – failed. Make sure he didn't get too cold – failed. Make sure you didn't go in the café – failed. Make sure you get him back up here by six. It was quarter-past already - failed.

'We do, my darling! Natalya will be so excited! She loves her parties, damn, I love our parties! So fine to get the music on, eh? Sinatra, Cole, Sammy, Armstrong, Getz, Henderson! My God! What joys, eh?'

They all smiled knowingly at this as they knew the house on the hill would later roll to the sound of jazz that would spill across the landscape like a coating of snow.

'She will love to get you back in one piece to enjoy your party,' said Noah, delighted to see his grandfather in such high spirits.

'Yes she will, she will indeed. She had been rather less than enthusiastic of my trip to the sea tonight.'

'The arctic conditions bothered her did they, Grandad? Never gave me a second thought! I for one couldn't wait to come down here, get hit by wave after wave of a far too enthusiastic sea, and in turn see my own skin actually turn blue. Marvellous. Good for you!'

'You have been ill, Papa,' Tess said, taking her father's hand in to her own, 'very ill. You are not twenty-one.'

'But my eyes tell me I am, little one.'

And they did. Joshua Spearing had bright blue eyes that shone with piercing brilliance from a body that was coming to the end of its time.

'You have pretty eyes, Papa, pretty eyes that tell me you can be as young as you like.'

'Exactly my dear! And so, Sylvia, how about us arranging a further trip to the sea before we go?'

They all laughed.

'New Year's Day as always,' she said, 'though I suggest winter wetsuits for us all.'

'Wetsuits? Nonsense, young lady. I have worn trunks in the sea all my life and trunks alone and I do not intend to succumb to the trends of the youth at this late stage in my swimming career!'

'To be fair Grandpa I would very much like to see you in a wetsuit,' said Noah, causing uproarious laughter around the table.

'Joshua, you must. A wet-suit! The whole of St Ives would turn out to see you in it. It would be a blue ribbon day for the café. Imagine!'

The table now laughing even more as Joshua held out his hands in mock indignation at the very thought of him succumbing to protection from the sea!

'Now, who's coming to your fabulous party tonight?' asked Sylvia, keen to know the people she would be seeing later.

'Well most of them are already there waiting for His Royal Highness to return! Just family and a few score of close friends, like you of course,' Tess replied, recalling as she did so the fallout between her parents when Natalya had insisted on seriously cutting back numbers for this year's party. Every year for as long as Tess could remember, they had been celebrating her father's birthday with a huge party at Porth-Ia-Chy, the family home that sat high and majestically on the hill overlooking Porthmeor Beach. However, Joshua had suffered appallingly all year with an illness that had eventually been traced to a rare blood disorder for which he was now getting treatment. He was noticeably thinner and far less able to keep as active as he had been used to all his life, even still in these late autumn years. Joshua had seemingly taken the change illness had wrought on his physical self within his stride. He made it clear that he was not going to worry about things he could not influence saying he would leave that to the doctors and he encouraged anyone who asked of his health to do the same. The effect on those close to him was far more profound. Tess and her mother in particular had been very upset by the changes in Joshua, fearing what was to come and feeling unable to do anything about it. Noah, caught up in his grandfather's laissez-faire attitude, chose to ignore the changes in him, preferring only to see Joshua's glowing smile every time he saw Noah and revelling in the time they spent together.

When the conversation came round then, months earlier, to a large party, Natalya was clear that this was simply not going to happen. She had decreed that they would invite family and a few close friends only. Joshua sulked for several days and then invited several more friends anyway. Both were therefore given a partial victory of sorts and they settled at that with the air of illness changing their lives forever hanging over them in its dark cloud of unknowing.

Two hours later and Lord Joshua Spearing, dosed with painkillers and his long list of medication and warmed by his favoured red-hot bath, appeared at the top of his grand staircase with his beloved Lady Natalya on his right arm. Charged glasses ready and waiting were lifted and cheers arose from the collection of happy faces below as spontaneous applause broke out to be greeted by a wave and a cheeky grin from the star of the show. Towards the back of the throng of people, Tess choked back tears as she fought the inevitable fear that this could be one of the last of her father's big birthday parties. He was a man destined to host such events, relaxed in the attention, indeed soaked it up and enjoyed every last minute of it, never more alert than when in the limelight. It was strange then that she, his beloved and youngest child, was so different to him, Tess, the girl who hid from all attention and would go to virtually any lengths to avoid it.

Porth-la-Chy, the house on the hill, seemed to actually come alive itself when people filled its rooms. The back of the house had huge Victorian windows that opened out on to the majesty of the western sky, a sky that was now darkened with a hint of a red glow suggesting tomorrow's weather would be fine after all. The property had been designed by the renowned architect, Henry Sam Jones, an associate of the great William Burgess, and his work had been done to produce the house to which he would retire by the sea having spent a life designing and building great properties across Europe. It was a grand house, out of character for the area in which it sat, and inevitably despite trying to hide behind tall trees, it still stood out high and mighty as it overlooked its friend, St Ives town.

Exquisite tall ceilings and Natalya's fine taste of décor created a house of immense taste, glamour and interest. Fine and classic wall colours, long, rich drapes and chic expensive furniture intoxicated the eyes. The backdrop to every room was the owners' shared lifetime hobby of collecting pieces of art. It was a heady mixture of international and local artists, both old and new, and there were extensive treasures to be enjoyed. Some of the pieces were obvious and very much on show, while others were more hidden and needed, if they were to be found, to be sought out. Natalya had done this on purpose, placing for example a Naum Gabo sculpture to be sat quietly in a corner where it settled happily next to a small sketch of Frances Hodgkins by Cedric Morris before he painted her portrait. Then a small Bernard Leach bowl lay at the back of a shelf, its treasure rarely uncovered, and a private secret that Natalya smiled at often. Here in most rooms was a labyrinth that if you followed it, took your time, led to treasure: real, sublime, artistic, gold.

Other pieces were plain to see. One of Tess's favourite paintings, a sumptuous Cumbrian landscape painted in bright, inspirational colours by Winifred Nicholson, greeted visitors as they walked into the grand hallway of the house. Natalya had chosen this piece on purpose as she considered that it could not fail to lift the spirits of any visitor. It didn't fail. Even a person entering the house that was normally totally uninterested in paintings, would smile at the glories of this celebrated Nicholson treat. To the right in one of the reception rooms an early Marianne Stokes' landscape graced a whitewashed wall, while opposite it by way of total contrast a huge Seb West piece of Porthmeor Beach brought colour and form. Several abstracts from Betowski, Blow and Wilson filled the opposite reception room with an explosion of colour, vibrancy, hope and intrigue.

The darkly-painted dining room held special treasures with highly significant European avant-garde pieces on show. Here Alexander Archipenko, Vadym Meller and Kazimir Malevich all satisfied Natalya's desire to have a room dedicated to an art movement that she remembered from her childhood and fully understood. It was also her way of making all guests to Porth-la-Chy begin to understand the Russian lady who ran the house. She may have left Russia, but she had always been determined to ensure that her roots stayed with her and touched the lives of those around her, and she had achieved just that.

So here, in Porth-la-Chy, as the jazz music kicked in and the party filled out across the house, everything had its place; the hosts and their guests, the outlook and position of the building, the beautifully-chosen furniture, the colours on the walls and the stunning depth of art that adorned it. No wonder people had willingly flocked here for many years and not only to see the great Joshua Spearing and his beautiful Russian wife, but also the dazzling wealth of treasures on show at the house.

At one o'clock in the morning, as the guests who were not staying over had left and most of those who were staying over had retired, Noah made his way to his grandfather's study. Joshua had asked him to do just that when they had dried themselves off after their dance with the waves earlier.

'Why?' Noah had asked.

'Because I have something for you.'

'What Grandad?'

'Something that can wait until 1am tonight young man! Patience is what?'

'Dependent on your position of need,' Noah had answered happily.

Noah now knocked very gingerly on the large, heavy oak door, the sound echoing around him and making him feel very aware of himself in this house at this time. Behind him the magnificent old grandfather clock clicked with the same strength it had always had. Tick, tock, tick, tock, its steady reliable hum filling the hall. Noah, reassured, knocked again but with more purpose.

'Come on in, dear boy!' called his grandfather from deep inside the room.

Noah pushed down on the weight of the handle, something he had first done many years before as a little boy and something that for some reason he remembered clearly now, the feel of the handle and size of the door that had seemed so immense to him, a little Cornish boy.

'Surprise!' said Noah as he put his head around the door and peered into the half-lit study.

Joshua stood by his desk, which sat in front of large French doors that in turn opened out on to the side of the extensive and botanic wrapped-round gardens. He motioned for his grandson to come forward and sit down at the desk and, as he did so, Joshua turned and sat himself down behind the rich mahogany piece that he had bought especially for himself fifty years earlier.

'This is a bit formal isn't it, Grandad? Are we having an interview? You know how rubbish I am at them!'

Joshua laughed.

'No, not an interview dear boy, but I wanted this bit to be a bit formal. It's important.'

'Oh?' replied Noah, hearing the serious tone of his grandfather's voice. Something of gravitas was coming.

'I have for you a special present that I have been saving for some time, for almost a lifetime in fact.'

'But it's your birthday'

'I know, and therefore this is my birthday gift to you.'

'Oh. OK,' replied Noah with uncertainty laced through his voice.

'Allow me, if you will, the indulgence to tell you a short story,' began Joshua, pouring two whiskies out from a heavy crystal decanter for the two of them as he began. 'Your mother was such a gift to me. The daughter of my beautiful Natalya and a joy from the very moment she came into our lives. You know much about me Noah due to the hours and hours of tales I have regaled you with, but there is much you do not know, at least not from me! You see, before Tess, before you,

13

Natalya and I had another life, a life full of episodes that had consequences.'

'You mean your first family, Grandad? I know all about that!' Noah was referring to Joshua's first marriage and family. It had broken down initially with a temporary separation from Cynthia and then the painful end that had soon been followed by Joshua finding his new love, the beautiful seventeen-year-old, Natalya Portichenko. The pain of it all, and in particular the young Russian beauty, in so short a time had caused Cynthia and many friends and family to be unable to forgive Joshua and indeed many supposed the girl was the reason for the break-up. Whilst this was not true, the rumour mill was in play and there was nothing Joshua could do to stop it. The mess that this had created had been something that had made his relationship with his children from his first marriage very difficult, indeed tortuous. Time had gone some way towards healing the pain of the break-up with all of them having visited their father, though some more than others. Only dear Gracie and her family were at Porth-la-Chy on this night, the others having sent their apologies, apologies that in Alice's case meant she had only ever been to the Cornish house once, years earlier, on a visit that had ended with huge arguments and broken glass. There were deeper waters here and Noah knew he did not understand them. In truth he considered all family politics ridiculous and all-consuming. His own simple family life caused no such frustrations and he was glad for that. He had never known his father and had no interest in doing so. Rather, he had his precious mother and grandparents and that was fine by him.

'Yes, of course, you know all about the great heartache with Alice and, though to a lesser degree, Edward. But there's more, much more you know nothing about, though this is not the tale I will tell this night.'

Now there was intrigue! Noah's mind thought about racing ahead but then held itself in check as he realised he needed to really concentrate. His mind could race all it wanted to later.

'No, my point, particularly on this happy occasion young man, is that at one moment in my life I was adrift and I made choices that set me on a path that caused upset and pain and, the truth is, if I could have my time over I would do things differently. And yet God, in his infinite wisdom, chose to look past my mistakes and bless me with a second chance and he gave me my precious Natalya out of a difficult situation. She is still a Russian beauty now is she not young man, but then, oh then, she was a slayer of men's hearts. I simply saw her, with wanton eyes afresh and she won me over with one blink of those big Russian eyes.'

Noah listened intently. He heard the words and tried to store them, knowing they would need to meet close interrogation with his mother later.

'And then we found Cornwall and St Ives, and Porthmeor and Porth-la-Chy, and then, oh yes and then, we had dear Tess. She has been a daughter that has brought me such joy that I have been so thankful for, joy enough for any man and then, miracle of miracles, Tess gave me you.'

'Ah, we get at last to the real blessing, eh?' Noah cheekily offered.

Joshua smiled so warmly at that point, with such an ease of immense happiness, that Noah actually felt a tear pull at his eye. It was true that for whatever reason, he and his grandfather had always been extraordinarily close. Joshua had been so involved with his grandson, in part taking the place of the father he had never known, but it was more than that. Joshua and Noah were totally connected. It was that simple. You could analyse it all you wanted but the fact was that this was what it was. There was an ease of being between these two men that crossed over the boundaries of age and circumstance and made the two of them as one in spirit.

Noah noticed suddenly that Joshua was actually crying, silently, with tears falling down his cheeks, and he got up to go round and comfort him only to be stopped by the old man lifting up his hand and directing him back to his chair.

'No, Noah, I'm fine. You stay there and let me continue.' Joshua pulled out a large white handkerchief, blew his nose at an extraordinary high-pitched volume, wiped his eyes and sat up straight, ready to go on with a script that he had prepared years earlier. 'I've been saving this up for a long time now young man, so you had better let me finish while I still can.'

'All right, Grandad, take your time and don't worry. Cry all you want for me. Perhaps I might join in?'

Joshua smiled, his eyes twinkling with a mixture of merriment and sorrow in the half-light of the study.

'Many years ago, before Tess, before Cynthia and before Natalya, I was presented with something glorious, something that came into my life through circumstances that you will never know about. They were incredible times and as a result amazing things happened even to the most normal of people.'

'You were never one of those,' said Noah, unwilling to hear even his grandfather describe himself as normal.

Joshua just smiled, happy with the adoration he felt from his Noah.

'Amazing times I say and they led to opportunities and connections that a young man could only dream of. I lived that dream and through it I was given a gift, a wonderful gift that now I want to give to you.'

Noah sat glued to his seat, suddenly aware of the fact that his mouth was open and dry from a mixture of the whisky and the excitement in the air. His heart in turn was beating frantically and there was nothing to do but let it continue its march. He watched his grandfather stand, walk to the side of the desk that had been hidden from his view up to this point, and, the drama complete, pick up a parcel wrapped in simple brown paper. The parcel looked like the shape of a mirror or a picture and his grandfather came around the table and gave it to him.

'It is very precious, fragile and extremely valuable so please be very careful with it.'

Noah nodded.

Joshua continued, 'I want you to know that this gift is a sign of my respect for you and my love for you. Please promise me that you will keep this safe and private. It must be that way, Noah, just you, yes? This is my gift to you, only you I repeat, and it is our secret passed down through the generations. One day you will do the same. So, you understand?'

Silence filled the room like a gas that had been let in through the windows and Noah suddenly realised his grandfather was waiting for him to respond.

'Yes, sure,' he replied hastily, not because he had time to think it, but because he knew it was what his grandad now needed to hear. 'It's our secret, though it's pretty obviously, I would guess, a picture of some sort, unless it's an unusually-shaped pet?'

'Yes, my dear boy,' replied a smiling Joshua, coughing heavily as he did so, recovering, and then adding, 'It is indeed a painting of some sort and that is all you need to know for now. The rest will become clear in the fullness of time. I have not known what to do with it, though I have treasured it and kept it close to me for all of my adult life. I also know that you are the best person to have it. Please, though, promise me further that you will not open it until after I have gone.'

'Why, where are you going?' asked Noah quickly, the answer immediately forming in his mind as the words shot out across the room.

'I am dying, Noah.'

Chapter 2

Discovery, St Ives

March 2010

The sun did not shine that day down on to a solemn Barnoon Hill as Joshua Spearing was laid to rest in a closing burial service under the gaze of a dark St Ives sky.

Two hours earlier the family had seen pomp and ceremony in the celebration of his life at the magnificent Truro Cathedral. There had not been a spare seat as Bishop Winfred-Jones, a fine man and a personal friend of Joshua, had conducted sombre proceedings with a dignity befitting the death of a great man. The Cathedral of the Blessed Virgin Mary in all its gothic revival glory had never had a better match than in this ceremony on this day. The setting of the building, a great Victorian take on a classic medieval design, tricked the congregation into thinking they were in an ancient building befitting the deceased's stature, when in fact the building had been built on a new site towards the end of the nineteenth century. And so as each mourner sat and considered the ancient building in which they thought they were sitting, so they considered the life of the highly-regarded Joshua Spearing assuming he had always been a man of the most magnificent calibre, of great dignity and of unquestionable character. He had not, though, and it was probable that nobody, quite literally nobody, in that service knew this.

The cathedral had hummed with the beauty of Claude Debussy's *Quatuor à cordes en sol mineur* played with passion and poise by the French Quartet, *Quatuor Ebene*, who Joshua had discovered for himself on BBC Radio 3 and had instantly fallen in love with. For twenty-six minutes and ten seconds the gathering was as silent as a religious order as Debussy's dream of what a string quartet should sound like came alive. It was an undulating movement of music filling the air and pervading feelings of peace and unquiet at the same time, wave upon wave of musical genius. John Wesley looked down from his magnificent Victorian stained-glass window and refused to change his expression no matter the temptation to do so as the three sisterly spires willingly allowed the sound to reverberate around their spaces, taking each note and amplifying it still further through their antechambers of worship.

Contemplation was stark and focussed as Noah gently held the hand of his mother, his thumb softly stroking the back of her hand, as in his mind he went back to the last time he had been in the Porthmeor sea with his grandad. Had it really only been six months earlier? It had been a day when the sun had shone over a late autumn eve and the two men had been lost in the power of the moment. The music in the cathedral washed over Noah as in his mind he bent down to lift Joshua out of the sea and whisper in his ear, 'I love you.'

Now, at Barnoon Cemetery on the stunning burial hill overlooking Porthmeor Beach, the seagulls provided the music as the poem *The Tollund Man* by Seamus Heaney drew to a close, read as it was by Joshua's good friend Arthur Symons, local poet, seasoned personality, and part-time gallery owner.

'"… Something of his sad freedom
As he rode the tumbril
Should come to me, driving,
Saying the names

Tollund, Grauballe, Nebelgard,
Watching the pointing hands
Of country people,
Not knowing their tongue

Out here in Jutland
In the old man-killing parishes
I will feel lost,
Unhappy and at home."'

Noah had mouthed the words as they were read out from the Irish poet who Joshua had impressed upon his grandson from a young age.

'Seamus Heaney gets to grips with what is real, young boy,' his grandad had said earnestly, 'You read his work and you touch what he describes, you taste what he writes and you feel what he presents.' And Noah had done just that, every bit of it. He had majored on Heaney at university and his words were now as easy to recite as to breathe.

Joshua now made his last journey on this earth, gently lowered into the grave that he had chosen years before. It was a beautiful spot, high up the graveyard and overlooking the ocean, the spot not too far away from the greatly celebrated St Ives painter, Alfred Wallis.

Natalya, who had been amazingly stoical throughout the day, now crumbled and fell heavily on to her knees by the side of the grave, the earth still very wet from the heavy overnight rain that had now cleared to give a blessed dry afternoon.

'My love, my sweet love, *Ja teb'a l'ubl'u, Ja teb'a l'ubl'u!*' she cried in a heavy Russian dialect that came from her childhood voice as it flooded out from her in her absolute agony of dreadful loss. Her husband was gone and she was now to be without him for the rest of her life. No feeling could ever match this ripping away of a person to whom you had lived your life. It is a cruelty of nature and a truth we must all face. Tess had instinctively dropped to her mother's side, kneeling with her as silent tears flowed down her own cheeks and on to the sodden Cornish earth beneath them.

'Mama,' whispered Tess over and over as she stroked her mother's neck and felt, from somewhere, an inner resolve to keep herself together. She knew she would come back to this eternal resting place many, many times and her agony, her loss, would be for her and her alone.

Seven hours later and tucked into the corner of the public bar of the ancient Sloop Inn, faces from the past gazing down at them from the photos on the walls, Noah raised his sixth pint of Guinness to once again toast the memory of his beloved Grandad. Flora, Noah's dear friend of many years who he very much wanted to be on much closer terms with but he had no idea how to tell her, joined the toast, raising her sixth glass of Spanish red wine and feeling quite wobbly and drunk as she did so. It was just the two of them together, exactly how Noah had wanted it.

'He was a wonderful man, Noah,' declared dear Flora.

'Yes, he was!' slurred Noah, 'Yes he was!'

'A grandfather to be proud of.'

'That he was. You've got him, the essence of the man.'

'A man, though, who it has to be said had big ears.'

'True enough, Flora,' snorted Noah, 'true enough. You couldn't but notice his enormous ears.'

'He never tried to hide them,' added a laughing Flora.

'No indeed. Why would he? Magnificent beasts of ears any man would have been proud to own! Probably very good for hearing I would have thought, though he was a little deaf. Still, great ears!'

'A little hairy, though,' added Flora in a serious voice.

'Too hairy for ears,' smiled Noah as the beauty and hilarity of the easy banter between two special friends flowed, soothing his pain as it did so.

'Trimming would have been easy,' added Flora easily, comfortably.

'With so many trimming options.'

'So many indeed!' snorted Flora, laughing into her glass at the absurdity of the idle chatter.

'Yet neglected.'

'Anyone could have done it.'

'We were both guilty,' said Noah, sitting back in his chair and nodding his head at his own guilt.

'And yet they were his ears.'

'That they were. Grandad had, I think we are clear on this, hairy, big ears.'

'But a big heart.'

'Aye, indeed, a heart that touched a county, and do you know?' began Noah, only to be caught off guard as he did so because Flora, who had dropped her bracelet that she had been absent-mindedly playing with for the last hour, now bent to retrieve it and through no fault of her own revealed her rather beautiful breasts for a few seconds. Thankfully for Noah she was wearing a bikini top because had that not been the case it would have rendered him speechless for an extended time that would have become uncomfortable for them both.

'Yes, cute nose?' asked Flora, blissfully unaware of the discomfort her less than graceful reveal had caused her dearest friend to feel. Noah gathered himself together.

'Cute nose, you say?'

'Yes, cute.'

Noah considered the term cute. Was this in any way able to cross the divide he wished to cross to cause Flora to see him as her man? Cute was how he considered you would describe a small puppy or a soft and furry kitten. You could love a kitten, though! On balance he considered cute was not a mandate for everlasting love. Something more substantial was needed!

'Not dashing, then?' he ventured in a voice that came out far too needy.

Flora laughed far too hard for Noah's liking, pulling the laughter back only when she saw the light in Noah's eyes die a little.

'Noah, of course you are delightfully beautiful, but no, your nose is not dashing. You're not a dashing sort of man!'

Noah let these words settle for a moment, his alcohol-infected brain confusing him still more. He knew he looked like a local, and that "beach bum" would always be more accurate to describe him than a classically dashing Fitzwilliam Darcy, but even so, it would be nice to be at least a little slightly dashing.

'Not even my ears? They do have a certain *je ne sais quoi* about them don't you think?'

'Noah, no! Not even your ears, although I will grant you they are, as your grandad's, fairly flamboyant ears!'

Flora leaned forward and stroked Noah's left ear. He smelt her gently-perfumed hand. He breathed it in deeply while muttering, 'Flamboyant ears indeed!'

'And my arse?' he asked hopefully.

'Well, maybe your arse. Rotund and peachy, yet firm and athletic!'

Now they both laughed.

These two dear friends had pretty much grown up together. They had been best friends from the moment they had met as babes, their houses on the same road and their mothers being really close too. When age allowed, the two children would walk down the school lane together holding hands and gathering adoring looks as they did so, their parents' eyes burning love into the back of them. They had remained extremely close throughout all their school years with Noah eventually being the one to move away to Bath University to study English Literature, a choice that had been mapped out by Joshua as soon as it was clear that his grandson was as hooked on literature as he was himself.

Flora had not left her precious St Ives seeing no reason to do so. She was happy here and always had been happy here and so she saw no benefit in leaving other than to travel which she did when she could or felt the need. She had an ease of purpose about her that Noah craved for himself for he felt no better happiness, no more settled stillness in himself, than when he was with her. So much activity happened in his head that he wished he could ask it all to form an orderly queue so that he could deal with each item when he was ready. Instead his mind raced ahead on Grand Prix terms and he constantly felt he was on catch-up. And yet with Flora, he felt an extraordinary calm. He became lost in her and his love for her. As she talked he watched her lips move and was entranced.

Noah had returned to St Ives after university and joined the staff of the St Ives School in Higher Tregenna to teach English. He had been attracted to teaching during his time in St Ives, inspired by an elderly English Literature teacher, Bill Jones, a man who let words flow so easily from his memory into the classroom before him. The man had an energy and a pure delight in his subject that was electric. He would take his young students on walks around the school and town, reciting words of literature as he did so, regaling them all with some inner-knowledge of the poet or author. Some thought him mad. Noah knew him to be a genius. Shortly after Noah had left for sixth-form college, Mr Jones died suddenly and it had a profound effect on the young Noah as he was seeking to find his place in the world. The thought germinated then that after getting his own degree he could come back and try to replicate the man and here, several years later, he was back to do just that.

Flora had left school at sixteen and worked full-time ever since with Sylvia at the Porthmeor Beach Café, having worked there when she had been at school, at the weekends. She simply loved it, the buzz of the place, the easy banter with locals and tourists and the constant light that streamed into her day from the Cornish sky. The very fact that she was next to the ocean all day, her thoughts embraced by the intoxication of her surroundings, fulfilled her and gave her the blessing of contentment. In her spare time she busied herself with every short course going from painting to pottery, poetry to building. If there was an option to learn something in St Ives then Flora was one of the first to sign up.

Flora began to tell Noah a story from the previous day when a man and woman had been in the café and they had been regaling her and Sylvia with a story of their trip to Canada, and of how they had met someone from St Ives even there in the most unlikely of places!

'Isn't it just amazing', she was saying, 'that you can go to the other ends of the earth and find someone who grew up where you grew up?'

Noah, who had been aware of words falling down around him, let his eyes tell Flora he was listening while his brain again wrestled with the fact that he had begun to realise more and more that he adored her. It had happened pretty much as soon as he had got back to St Ives. He had always known that they were very close, but as friends. They had never had awkward moments when they were growing up together that he could remember, never crossed the line where there became moments of embarrassment as they became aware of each other as teenagers growing into adults. Rather, they had been there for each other as they had made the tortuous journey into teenage relationships. How often had they ended up at each other's house late at night to get an update on one another's life, never once swaying into wondering if they were destined for one another? They were simply best friends, that was all, and that had been perfect and enough.

When Noah had been in Bath studying, he had forged his own life away from Flora, seeing her lots when he had holidays at home in St Ives, but never asking her to come and visit and in turn she never asked to come. Why would she? They were friends, extremely good friends, but that was all. Time away had meant that they had grown apart a little, the inevitability of new friends, new connections causing a small gap to grow. Noah had thought about that a lot of late and wondered why they had allowed this small distance to come between them. Had they realised that they needed to make their own lives without one another? Had they known that in fact their closeness often suffocated new relationships before they could even begin? Possibly so, and in Noah's absence from St Ives Flora's relationships had indeed flourished to the point that she had now been with her boyfriend, Jake, for four years. Jake was, much to Noah's bemusement, very dashing indeed. He looked a million dollars and was actually worth that and more on the back of running, with his dear and extraordinarily wealthy father, his family-owned surf shops in St Ives with their own label that he was actually, apparently, exporting across the world. The worst of it was that Noah actually quite liked him having been at the Truro sixth-form college with him. Jake was witty, warm, kind, focussed and a hunk of a man and no doubt perfect for Flora. Bastard.

As soon as Noah had arrived back in St Ives and settled down in his new house and new job he had begun to feel keenly the "loss" of Flora. It wasn't just the missing of her being there all the time as she used to be when he lived in St Ives before university, it was the fact that he had realised the unmistakeable truth that he loved her. When he thought of St Ives he always thought about him being there with Flora. He realised he had allowed years to go by and in not making the more obvious move, he had probably now lost out on the most important thing he actually needed. When he went to Jake and Flora's fabulous apartment in the east of the town and saw numerous happy pictures of the two of them, their smiles a testament to what he was missing out on, he felt his insides pulled and twisted and a feeling of loss take him over. In fact, as he thought of this now, a fresh morose emotion slapped him around the face.

'Are you listening?' asked Flora, seeing a glazed expression sitting clearly over Noah's face.

'What? Erm, yea, of course I am. It's remarkable!'

'What is?'

'The connection, you know? Canada and all. Wow!'

Flora tutted and waited. She loved seeing Noah. He made her laugh in a way only he could. No one had the effect on her that he did. He was unique and his lack of confidence was hilarious given the talent he had. Noah was a writer, already the author of a hundred or more unpublished poems that had moved her enormously when he let her read them. In many ways Noah was the opposite of her boyfriend, Jake, and she felt so lucky to have them both in her life, and for them both to like each other too was perfect.

'I think I'd better go home now,' managed Noah, his eyes beginning to close as the tiredness and the sadness of the day had caught up with him. The crowning sadness of his thoughts around Flora and Jake had been his call to close the evening and make his way back to his delightful old, stone whitewashed cottage which was only a few hundred metres away, tucked secretly away behind Island Square. He had bought it as soon as he had come back to St Ives, with his Grandad kindly giving him the deposit he needed to get the mortgage.

'Yes,' smiled Flora who suddenly felt very tired herself, 'I think you better had,' seeing clearly how tired and sad Noah suddenly appeared. 'You have had the day of all days. Oh Noah, I am so, so sorry for you. It is the greatest of shocks for you.'

'That it is,' replied Noah, his voice now tailing away with pain.

'But it's been an amazing day, Noah, so many people to celebrate him!'

'Yes, a day to mark a great man. Will you give me a hug please?' Noah asked, all the emotion clear to see in his eyes.

Flora stepped quickly around the table and they held each other for several moments, she feeling the hurt of her precious Noah, and he comforted in the arms of his private love.

'Are you staying over with me?' asked Noah with a smile on his drunken face as they fell onto The Wharf.

'I think Jake would rather I go home,' replied an amused Flora, fully aware that from time to time Noah would flatter her to the point that people might even be tricked into thinking he wanted her. She was not so easily fooled! 'You can come up and stay with Jake and me tonight? Better than being on your own?'

She lived with Jake in a penthouse apartment overlooking the whole of St Ives up off Talland Road. It was brand new and contempoaray and extremely cool. Noah hated it as he pointed out to them both willingly every time he visited them. It had, according to Noah, very little going for it. It was on the wrong side of town, i.e. not his side, it was pretentious in its pomposity that had no place in his St Ives and it had glass all over the place which he declared was simply not traditional for his town. 'Don't be silly,' Flora had reprimanded him. 'Don't be a dick,' Jake had kindly added.

'No, thank you,' replied Noah, 'He's not my type! I tell you what, though, I should walk you home!' Noah now gallantly declared as he offered an elegant bow that led to him catching his forehead with a little force on the back of a quayside bench. Flora laughed.

'There, you can be dashing after all! Now don't worry about me. Go home. I shall text you tomorrow morning, OK?'

'Yes. I guess. If you're sure about not staying over? I have croissants and honey?' he offered in one last effort to win the lady for the night. He looked at her, making his eyes as big and hopeless looking as he could. She simply looked back at him with a small determined smile that told him to stop being silly.

'OK,' he said softly. 'Thanks for tonight.'

'For what?'

'For being with me. I needed that more than you know.'

'Don't be silly. I am always here for you.'

'Are you?'

Flora twisted up her nose in a questioning manner and Noah just lifted his shoulders up and down in an "it is just me being silly" response.

'Come here,' she said, arms wide open as she did so.

The two of them gave each other a final huge hug, Flora eventually prising themselves apart after Noah made no attempt to let go. She stood and looked at him, his hair that desperately needed cutting and was now growing in all directions in wild and wondrous ways, his ill-fitting suit now creased beyond repair, his black tie borrowed from a friend, now long gone and missing in action.

'Goodnight, Mr Spearing. You have been a delight.'

'Goodnight, Miss Trembath. I shall love you and now leave you to your wares.'

Noah again bowed extravagantly and this time felt his insides begin to wretch. Thankfully he kept it all together allowing Flora to pleasingly disappear along Fore Street before being violently sick over the side of the harbourside.

Noah held the debonair pose of hanging on to the rails for dear life for a few minutes as his body decided whether or not to torture him again. Thankfully it decided against it and his head gradually came back into focus allowing him to stand upright. He looked across the harbour that lay stretched before him in his own private show. It was a still night, the sea out now and the few boats that rested in a winter harbour sat waiting and resting against a blessed St Ives night sky. High above, the stars were shining brightly, their beauty surrounded by a bright and waxing quarter moon that to Noah had never looked as amazing as it did so right at that moment. The air was speaking to him.

'Goodnight, Grandad' he whispered into the night sky, waiting a few moments more as the words made their way into the heavens before he turned to make his short climb up to his house. Round the back of Café Pasta and up to the safety of Victoria Road, Noah arrived home and went straight into his kitchen for a huge glass of water which he quickly sank, and poured himself another one. He placed this on his lounge coffee table, a lounge now blessed with a view across a harbour that was bathed in near-perfect moonlight, and he sat himself down feeling suddenly remarkably awake, alert almost. A thought shot across his mind, one that he had been putting off for six months now. The picture.

Joshua had asked Noah two things with regard to the birthday gift. Firstly, he was not to share what it was with anyone. Noah had no idea how he was supposed to do this but by simply hiding the surprise in the roof he had not had to worry about it. Opening the thing would open his urge to share whatever it was with someone, someone probably being his mother and almost certainly being Flora too. Secondly, Joshua had been clear that this was something to open after his death. He had died ten days earlier but still Noah had been nowhere near the gift. It had not felt the right time. Now, the night of the day they had laid him down to rest in his grave, now felt the right time.

Noah went through to the landing and got a chair and strained to open the loft hatch. Noah was not blessed with height, being 5 feet 9 inches tall, and the chair, a simple old and battered, wooden dining chair, was not blessed with height either. With hindsight the stepladders in the outside shed would have been the safer and smarter option but drink has a strange way of blinding the obvious and making you think the impossible was possible. Therefore, the assent to the loft meant immense and painful arm muscle was required for the final climb into the dark and windy roof space. Had this been the middle of a normal day then Noah, blessed with upper-body strength gained from hours of surfing, and a slim muscular body to match, would have more easily lifted himself almost jauntily up through the hatch. Six pints of Guinness and three glasses of whisky, though, were never going to help the climb and as he pulled himself up into the darkness he felt his head telling him he was going to fall down. Amazingly he didn't, falling into the loft instead with the dust and darkness settling around him and calling him to stay awhile as he worked through a long line of sneezes brought on by the dust.

Eventually Noah managed to stand up, carefully balancing on a beam and shining the torch that he had cleverly remembered to carry up with him by grasping the string tied to its end in his mouth. The torch now shone gingerly into the corners of the roof space where there, in several black bin-liners wrapped around his gift by Noah in a moment of common sense to keep any damp away, his prize awaited. With the dexterity of a cat with a dizzy spell who had used up all nine lives long ago, Noah succeeded in retrieving the painting and not putting his foot through the ceiling below, and, returning to the hatch, he gently lowered the painting by acrobatically hanging out of the loft and letting it drop gently on to the chair. It landed with a little bump and mercifully, after threatening to fall off the chair, retained its balance and stayed put. Sadly Noah did not do the same, his grip failing him as he fell out of the loft and hard onto the floor below. He was cushioned by a mixture of landing on his bottom and the drink which had the merciful effect of numbing the immediate pain. The bruise would be hideous but that would be the full extent of the damage.

He stood up, stretched himself out, and picking up his mysterious gift which had still been happily resting on the chair in a didn't-I-do-well? fashion, the two of them made their way back into his lounge where, placing the painting down by the sofa, he turned to his stereo and turned on his iPod. Choosing the music for this occasion would have been too big a task for a drunken Noah, but thankfully he had had six months to think of this and he knew exactly what to play.

The room warmed up to the sound of "The Bends" as he walked back to the sofa, sat himself down, and began to unpeel the bin-liners, all ten of them. 'Better safe than sorry,' Noah repeated to himself as he carefully unwrapped layer after layer, each one raising his excitement levels as he became more acutely aware of what he was doing, the moment he was now facing. Eventually he came to the brown paper that would be the last obstacle before knowing exactly what Joshua Spearing had given his grandson.

Noah paused. It had remained a quiet night with still virtually no wind outside and all around him quiet, save for the majestic Radiohead now moving into "High and Dry" territory.

"*Two jumps in a week,*" declared Tom, "*I bet you think that's pretty clever don't you boy?*"

Noah leaned back in his sofa, and listened to a song that he had discovered years earlier in his teens and one that still beautifully haunted and moved him today. In it Noah remembered a thousand thoughts and hopes and dreams, and tonight he remembered Joshua, his dear and precious Grandad who would never, ever leave him.

'So let's see what all this is about, Grandad,' he said to the air as it listened and watched him.

Noah leaned forward and gently ran his finger under the Sellotape that held the top frame. It came undone easily and he eased the fold of the brown paper backwards and away from its prize. He then repeated the exercise on the bottom of the package and then placed it on its side on his coffee table. As carefully as his trembling hands would allow him to do so, he pulled the join on the back of the package away and now opened the paper to reveal an old piece of gold-encrusted wood that was clearly the frame at about 90 by 70 cms in size. He took a deep breath, and tenderly turned the frame over to reveal an ancient-looking painting, in oils, of a young man looking calmly straight back at him, dark reddish hair falling down both sides of his face as a start of a smile and glint in the eyes suggested there was something secret between the artist and his subject. A blue sky filled the window in the top-right corner of the painting, and yet the young man wore a thick-looking fur draped over his shoulder and a beret of sorts, which was either being worn for decoration, fashion or the cold. It was hard to tell which but Noah guessed at fashion or possible humour. Those eyes, so expertly painted, held Noah's gaze and yet, as Noah's eyes closed and reopened, the young man's eyes did not blink. They were open for all time.

Noah studied the painting, looking for something to stir in his memory from his art days at school. The style was traditional. There was certainly nothing contemporary in this piece indicating, Noah thought, that this could be very old, maybe even valuable. He thought it an odd painting in many ways as Joshua and Natalya didn't have anything else like it in the house that he could think of. The painting was, well, normal. It was simply a beautiful piece painted with absolute symmetry and grace. It seemed to be feeling its age with the varnish bowing to time and the oils now noticeably cracked. A job for restoration was in need! Maybe old John Ryan, art teacher at the school since the Middle Ages, would be able to do it? Then Noah reminded himself of his Grandad's words that this gift was between the two of them only and no one was to know about it. How peculiar! What was it about this painting that caused such secrecy, such a hidden gem that was now being allowed to deteriorate because no one could know about it? It made no sense to Noah at all and he decided he would need to give serious thought to what decisions he made.

The first decision Noah now made, though, was to go to bed. The sudden attack of being wideawake left just as soon as he had opened his gift. He was now desperately tired, aching and exhausted. He needed sleep. Once in bed and just before his friend of slumber arrived, Noah made his second and third decisions. Firstly, he decided he would in due course tell Flora. He had to tell someone because he needed advice and she was the only person he felt he could tell and she would not feel burdened with the news. He knew Tess would be confused by the gift and by the secrecy of it and, while he knew he would tell her in time, with the hurt and grief of losing her father taking up her every thought, now was not the time. Secondly, he knew he needed to find out about the painting. Who had painted it? Was it ten years old, a hundred years old? Where did it come from? This history would hopefully tell Noah something more about his Grandad and that was worth searching for.

Then, just as Noah had got on to a roll with his thought processes, they decided to all turn off, and he went into a deep, deep sleep where he was visited by dreams and visions of the sea and of a girl he thought he recognised.

Chapter 3

Tess in Therapy

'I think the basic truth, the deep-down unavoidable malaise in my head, is that I have always had such a strong sense of self, myself, do you know what I mean, Robert? I have so much inside me that refuses to come out, that can't come out yet, that might even be best if it never came out! I mean, Christ, I'm a walking lunatic with the touch of an angel.'

Robert smiled.

'Yea, I read that once. Good, isn't it? Write it down, Robert, you could use that in one of your lectures at Truro. Say you made it up and get five brownie points! Somehow or other it appealed to me. You've been asking me what "self" means to me and that is what I have spent my life to this point asking and the main reason why I am unable to commit to anyone or anything else because I will keep on asking it, again and again. It's like a quest, you know? A personal crusade, peculiar to me, to me alone, and only I can fulfil it or maybe fulfil it. Maybe not. I swing rather between the two.'

Robert looked over his glasses at her.

'You're very good at that peering-over-your-glasses thing you know. It becomes you. Was that a syllabus at university? I imagine they took peering very seriously. I mean, peer too hard and you scare your patient, not peer at all and the patient thinks you are thinking about your dinner!'

Robert offered a gentle smile but no comment. He waited. He was good at that, too.

'Anyway, I know what you are getting at and yes, I do commit to my art by way of committing to finding the very core of me. It is a hundred per cent of what I do, although I know that this just gets at the truth of what is in me at any one point in time. And this changes, you know, over time, like the changing face of the landscape that I try and capture. My art is not extraneous, of course it's not, how could it be in any way separate to me, the core of me, the be-still-my-beating-and-bleeding-heart part of me? I mean it is, technically, separate from me; I produce it and it stands alone, but it is me.'

She waited. The room waited. This conversation, that she would have with herself time after time, this room listening, these walls with its ready ears to do nothing but be a safety net for her.

'And so your art?' Robert asked, feeling a need to nudge Tess on her way.

'It stands for me. It helps me on my search.'

'The one you've been talking about?'

'Yes.'

'And others see this?'

Tess sighed. The ever-charging drain on an artist, the simple truth of whatever they produced would be poured over, by anybody who cared to look, some with a simple glance and others with a full-on magnifying glass and a light armed with a thousand bulbs.

'Yes. Of course they do, Robert. It is the inevitable lot of an artist. You know this brain that we have is remarkable isn't it? I function so many thoughts and ideas and I commute them all the time, working them through my mind and coming up with plans and strategies and aspirations and next stops and so much other magical and messed up stuff. Well, of course, you know! You've studied the subject for years and now you have to listen to it all from every poor creature that comes over your doorstep! And yet before, that is before I really got lost in my art, I was just lost in myself because I didn't have my own identity, just my ideas. Before seems like a prison, Robert. I hated it. I had it all inside and nowhere to go.'

'So there's a release here?'

Tess smiled. A release, ah yes!

'Yes, yes there is. Now I use my canvas and my camera to get it all out, to truly use this outlet and that, that is what "self" means to me. I sometimes wonder how my friends and the people who kindly buy my work cope with me and then I realise they're not. In fact, they are using me.'

'Using you?' asked Robert, trying very hard to keep his voice soft and level. This was a new turn of phrase for his client and would need many hours of investigation.

'Yes. Using me. I see that appals you.'

Tess waited. Robert would not be drawn and he waited now, easily falling into his role. Tess relaxed and explained.

'OK. Sorry. I am not saying "used" in a nasty "using me" sense. Well, some of them do, of course. No, they plug into me when they need me. They use me to help them see they can have a life away from normality. Not everyone obviously, but most.'

'Most?'

'Well, not Sylvy and Noah and Mum. Though sometimes they all do as well.'

'So, everyone then?'

'Yes, I guess, yes,' mumbled Tess, tiredness now beginning to fill her up, affecting the balance in her neck and causing her to feel quite tight. Almost always she would leave these sessions with Robert utterly and totally exhausted. 'Everyone. Everyone uses me. I have come to see that this is the journey of any artist whose work is on show and who crucially exhibits anything of themselves. It is my destiny and I fought it for a long time but I can't have the journey to finding my true self that produces the art and not have the knock-on effect of people studying it.'

Robert thought of asking why she even put it on show if this was an issue for her, after all money was not and had never been an issue for her. This was not the time to go down this route, though. That would do for another session.

'And, assuming what you say is real, do you mind?'

'Yes. But also, no. God Robert, you do realise I can never just give a straight answer can I? This is why I am here.'

She looked over at Robert, the truth in her words tiring her still further and making her seek an acknowledgment, which he duly did with a warm smile, a Robert smile.

'Look, what I mean is that my work gets me out of my head. For that I can be thankful, I can be very thankful indeed. You're lucky, Robert. You see the screwed-up Tess who has

35

been able to get a lot of her shit out on canvas. Imagine the one before! You could have written books on me!'

Robert let out a little snort at that. Tess, pleased as ever when she got a response out of him, went on.

'I am now able to complete my journey, my mental trip, transferring what is in here,' she said, pointing to her head, 'to my art. This completes me, though it doesn't take away the inevitable feelings that come with putting yourself on show. How can it?'

The two of them waited some more, allowing the words to settle and waiting for what would come next.

'Are we all not on show, Tess, for bits of us to touch others?'

Tess meandered on this for a few moments.

'Yes, I suppose we are, though because I'm an artist there is more of me on show to people.'

'Through your work?'

'Yes. But also through me. Because of who I am, I am on show all the time.'

'So you see yourself as some sort of conduit?'

'Yes. I guess I do. A conduit. Why not?'

'And this is your lot?'

'Yes.'

'For what purpose?' Robert asked, his words always delivered in short, easy questions.

'What do you mean, what purpose?'

'Why is this "your lot"?' asked Robert.

Tess laughed.

'To be free!'

'Free?'

'Yes, not constrained by the ordinary, the nine to five dripping normality of a world-made timetable of how to live your life.'

'A free spirit maybe?'

'Well, put like that I sound like an arse, Robert, but yes, maybe,' smiled Tess. 'I just mean that I have chosen the path that has kept me free from convention and people crave that too. You know that as much as anyone. You too have plugged into the free-spirited Tess when you needed me.'

Robert nodded. Their relationship, intense fling really, had

36

been brief but full of fire and passion. He could not hope to keep up with Tess but for a while she needed his stillness and he needed her fire. It was against all his better judgement that he ever took up with a client and in his twenty years of practice it had only happened twice before, and one of these was now his wife. With Tess it had been an absolute animal-like attraction that almost needed to burn out so that they could get on with the actual business of therapy. It lasted a month then they both filed it under "necessity dealt with" and moved on. That had been four years before and there had never been any hint from either of them of ever needing to cross that line again.

'I am me. I am no one else. I am not beholding to anyone. That is me!' Tess spoke now with an authority, a voice full of conviction and a solid grounding in the belief of what she had said.

A seagull called in the air outside somewhere, its comforting voice warming Tess and making her smile. Her flying friends' magnetic call never failed to have this effect on her.

'I think I have often fought against myself, sort to place myself within convention only to find it stripped away what was the very essence of me, nullifying me, neutralising me. I am not a bird to be caged, no matter how beautiful that cage might be, how decorated it is and how comfortable it is. No, this is not for me. The fact that I know other people, most people, if the truth be known, can live like that, well that's fine. It's not me though, not the life for me and not one that I will ever live again. I have been there and it took away the very heart and soul of me. To be in a world where you survive by looking forward to transient moments, you know, temporary fixes, well that would be the death of me, the dripping tap of the joys of life when, in fact, I crave constant running water. No, I have my way now.'

'Your way alone?'

'No. I am really not that conceited, Robert! I obviously know I am not unique in this and certainly there are many far more practiced in this than I. There are many like me. We are not alone Robert. I know this sounds like I am talking about aliens but bear with me!'

Tess laughed. Robert smiled.

'Look there are many who came before me and many who will come after me. This life I have chosen spells freedom for me as it did for them. It's actually the only way we know how to live. I say we! I make it sound like a movement, don't I? The "Free Love and Life Sad Bastard Brigade"! Write that down! I might use that later. There's an exhibition there in itself not to mention an album title if I ever form that rock band!'

Robert raised his eyebrows but managed to stop the question. With many clients, finding the way in was the hardest thing with these sessions. With Tess it was the opposite and stopping himself go down one of many avenues she opened up was always his challenge.

'I know I am not alone,' continued Tess, aware of Robert biting his tongue, 'Here in St Ives, for instance, there are many of us free-spirit types, probably the majority of us are in therapy with you! So many of us are here in my beautiful Cornwall where the walls don't feel like walls anymore. I may sound like an arse, Robert, and I know I am an arse too, but it turns out I am not that unique after all, doesn't it, and for that I am very grateful.'

Robert rolled his eyes at this in an "at last!" look. Tess saw him and smiled.

'Yes, I know. Even I can make progress, Robert. I just know that now I am at peace with me and how I am and what I want, and most importantly of all, is that life for me now, living the way I do, is OK. No, actually, it's better than that, it's good. I mean, sure, I sometimes miss, no I often miss, the touch of a lover with me when I need it but you know the fact is that I missed my head space when Mr Loverman was always there.'

'Your dilemma then?'

'Yes, my dilemma. For a long time this was chicken-and-egg for me but once I came to a peace, a place in the road that saw me make my decision, I was happy. I want me first and ultimately that is the creation you see before you. I mean, you know, why do we have such a one-size-fits-all approach to life? It does my head in, angers me to be honest and really confuses me. Look, we live in this vast space, you know, the universe, with all its galaxies and great unknown, and yet we live here under such set rules based on minutia. I ask why all the time!'

'Why?'

'Because I don't understand it for myself. I struggle to fit in to my day-to-day normal existence at the side of the extremities that actually exist. Normality versus exceptionally fantastic, I mean, how do you possibly balance that? The simple reality for me was that for many years it confused me as to how I should be living. I think, really, most people have a sense of what is normal for society and that helps them basically be able to make sense of it all but for me that just actually stripped away the very core of me.'

Tess stopped talking and tried to connect what she was saying, to find a line that would join the dots in her over-charged head.

'So you are finding what is normal for you?' asked Robert, his slow laconic words guiding this vessel before him.

'I am, Robert, yes I am. I know it is the main reason that I have not been able to settle down with just one single, finite person. How could I? How could this man possibly be all I needed to sense, to know? Add to that all his troubles and his inevitable need to have me carry them for him? No, to have another person, their life, no matter how precious or important to me, be the sole viewpoint for my love and my inspiration? Well, I could not live like that. I have tried it you know! Well, of course, you do know. It will all be in those scintillating notes you take that one day, young Robert, could make you a lot of money, though let's be clear, I do want a share of all royalties and final say on who plays me in the film!'

Robert nodded his head.

'Living my life for me alone means there is much more head space and that is scary for most people.'

'And not for you?'

'Well, I can't say I don't have my moments. Again, you know that. But somehow breathing in the space I create for myself is a release for me. I crave my space. It's what I want most of all and I have come to realise that it is what I need to survive, to grow even.'

'And is there a sense of loss?'

Tess nodded.

'Yes. It's real, it's tangible and it hurts, often. I can't lie to you and I have stopped lying to myself. That's the truth and I have spent years dismissing that, too.'

'And now?'

'I embrace it. I use its energy; make it my companion, my workmate. You see it in my work.'

'I know you do.'

'You do?' asked Tess mischievously, knowing Robert had offered an opinion which was something he was careful to never do during a session. He just looked back at her, nodded as if to accept his error, and waited.

'I wonder,' he asked, a minute or so of silence having passed, 'where does Noah fit in to all this?'

Tess closed her eyes and pictured her son as a bump, as a baby, as a growing boy, and as he was now.

'Noah's grown up, Robert, and so have I.'

Silence. Time waiting and yet not waiting at all.

'Has he?' It was a simple question yet one that Tess knew she did not really have the answer to. Her son, her one and precious child, just how stable was he?

'I think so,' she answered truthfully. 'Do you?'

There was no reply. Robert was not here to give answers, rather extract the depth of his patient into the light.

'Do you know I only ever think of the fact he has no father when I come here?'

'And?'

Tess swallowed hard. This would hurt.

'And I think that he has never needed one because he had Daddy. And now Daddy's gone… ' She caught herself. Tears came at the very mention of Joshua but she stopped short of literally sobbing. There had been plenty of times since Joshua had left her when stopping her emotions, wave upon wave of hurt upon hurt crashing over her like a never-ending incoming tide, had been impossible.

'It's OK, Tess,' said Robert, passing over several tissues, 'take your time.'

Tess wiped her now red eyes, mascara smeared gracefully around her eyelids, and blew her nose.

'As you well know his father was a one-night stand that I easily forgot save for the beauty that it left me.'

'We've never discussed this past this point have we, Tess?' It had been a delicate matter ever since they had started these sessions and Tess had never got past saying the moment that Noah had started his journey had been on the back of a mistake. Robert threw this question out now, wondering if this day would be the time when more would come out.

'No, we have not. Look, the man was an idiot and I was taken with his charms under the influence of a Mr Jack Daniel's. I considered telling him once when I saw what he had become, the business empire he had built, but I knew he was still an arse and my precious Noah never deserved him.'

'And Noah does not know this?'

Tess paused. Only Sylvia knew the truth about Noah's father, about the night that saw her scarred, the night she saw how black were the depths that mankind could sink to, about the night that gave her hope when she thought she had lost all hope.

'Noah will never know it, Robert, and that's enough about this, please. Let us never talk about this again. Just know that this man is not fit to know and that I did what I had to do.'

Tick, tock. Tick, tock. The old mantelpiece clock resting grandly over the fire, its easy heartbeat letting the sound of the room breathe in and out.

'This gives you peace?' asked Robert at last.

'Yes, this gives me peace,' replied Tess, the truth passing her lips and making her smile.

'And Noah?'

'Has peace too,' she replied instantly.

She had told Noah as soon as he had started asking, that his father was a one-night stand.

'A what?' Noah had asked, his hair all over the place, chocolate from the Curly Wurly bar he had been chewing on coming home from school, all over his face.

'A person I slept with for one night and never intended to sleep with again,' Tess replied in haste and, seeing the poor boy's confusion matched her own, she picked him up and sat him on the edge of the kitchen table to wipe his face free of chocolate.

'You see Noah, sometimes in life people make mistakes, just like when you left your school shoes outside one night and it rained and they got ruined, remember?'

41

Noah nodded.

'Well, can you remember we talked about how babies are made?'

Noah couldn't forget. It had been the night before he started school and Tess had decided it was best coming from her first. The fact that she used two of Noah's cuddly toys as models had caused them both to laugh a lot during the whole demonstration.

'Yes, Mama. With elephant and blue bear,' Noah smiled. Tess laughed. Sylvia had nearly died laughing when Tess had recounted the story later that night.

'Well, Noah, Mama and a man had sex and you came out of it. Mama and this man were just having a bit of fun, but Mama did not love this man. Anyway, this man went off to join the army and he died.'

The last bit about Noah's father dying just came out. Tess had never intended it to. Somehow, though, the line, the lie, seemed best. Noah must never know the real truth and anything else would also be a huge lie. It was a story, all of it from start to finish, that only Sylvia could ever know, so when Robert asked did Noah have peace, Tess could reply in all honesty that as far as she was concerned, he did.

'Well, that's time, Tess. You will call when you're ready?'

Tess smiled.

'Well, you know me. I can't give you an actual time!'

She stood, kissed her analyst on his cheek and stepped out of his room into the light of the day.

Chapter 4

Natalya's New Arrival

Natalya Portichenko married Joshua Spearing, the beautiful, dashing and highly exciting officer from that exotic creature called England, in the late summer of 1960. Joshua was her dear father's good friend and the match was therefore approved. She never changed her surname, rather keeping it to in turn keep her company in their new home of St Ives, a seaside town in the far south-west of Cornwall. This place was surely one of England's best-kept secrets, a place that shone so brightly under the burning sun which played with the blue sea that in turn surrounded St Ives. The effect was magical and had caused the streets to flow with a rich tapestry of artists and fishermen, galleries and inns.

Marrying Joshua all those years ago remained a dream-like day in her mind, all sepia now with faces of friends and family etched clearly in her mind's eye. Even today, when she listened hard enough, she could hear the laughter and constant chatter of her family and friends lost in the beauty of that moment, so excited to be involved in her big day. They were, of course, fabulous times never to be forgotten and her eager replaying of moments in time meant that she never would.

Joshua had been her father's friend, a warm and strong connection made during the war that had led to a friendship that far from ending had in fact grown and grown. The Englishman was like no other man she had ever met; fiercely attractive, hugely entertaining, incredibly bright and unmistakably interested in her.

In fact, when Joshua Spearing had first met her she was just a little girl. Natalya often smiles as she remembers him coming back to their home in 1960 and meeting her again after a gap of ten years. The little girl had grown up into a seventeen-year-old beauty and she saw Joshua's breath almost disappear when she entered the lounge to meet their esteemed English guest to ask if either he or her father wanted tea. Their eyes had met, the hearts had somersaulted and within three days they were sleeping together. This was not normal behaviour for either of them and they felt initially ashamed, skulking around the house at night for fear of being discovered after all were asleep, their movements as quiet as wee mice. And yet Natalya's father had guessed almost instantly what was happening, saw the look between the two lovers and confronted Joshua on his feelings one evening. Joshua, at that time recently and painfully divorced, acknowledged everything and to his immense surprise and pleasure Caspar Portichenko encouraged the two of them to see what they really felt for each other.

'Mother Russia is not the old lady I knew. She was once proud of our heritage. She lived and breathed this great country. She has changed now though, Joshua, beyond all recognition, nothing like the proud country we fought so bravely for at your side during the war.'

Joshua had nodded gravely, knowing only too well the vice-like grip the intelligence services had in this communist state.

'You know what it is like now in Russia, even here in the quiet countryside where we are far away from the everyday claustrophobic powers that be; there is nowhere to be free. I don't want this for my Natalya, my legacy and, God willing, my grandchildren. No, if the two of you have something, truly have something above the somersault song of lust, then please take her with you and make her happy. I know you my friend, you know that, and most importantly I have trust in you. We met by chance and here, my friend, we are. It is a wonderful thing that we found each other, yes?'

Joshua nodded appreciatively. From the moment he had met Caspar he had smiled. The man exuded warmth and made you feel several inches taller just by being with him.

'Yet the very fact that you are here, Joshua, is clearly fully noted by the state. It is a miracle you wander here so freely and you know that it is only my position in the party and their desire to know as much as they can about what you are actually doing here that keeps them from being here now to take you to the nearest airport.'

'I don't know how you continue to live under this regime, your people too, how do you put up with it?' Joshua replied, a look of warmth passing between the two men.

'You know, Joshua, I live a charmed life really. The party gives me liberties that most will never know in their lifetime, yet I ask you, what true liberty do even I have, eh? It is not like your freedom, like the freedom you can give to my Natalya. You have always been a free man, if only in your head, eh, Joshua?'

'Well, yes my friend, I feel free, yet I know that should the state ever call on me I am there for her.'

'And there, right there, that is the difference. You English, you make that choice, yet I have that choice made for me. I think about these things all the time, my friend, the choices made and how little influence I ultimately have over being able to make my own. The people around me, those that I love deeply, well, what true choices can they make, eh? It is food for precious thought and I do so enjoy thinking, my friend! You see, thinking is the one precious luxury that no one can take away from me until they take my life.'

'I would try not to think too much about some things, Caspar. It can be too depressing.'

'Ah! There you have the difference between those of you from the so-called free world and us proud Russians. You should know this with your Russian heritage, Joshua. You brood over problems and it builds up into a mothball of depression that will eventually disable you and render you useless. For us, we thrive on brooding! We say bad mood, bring it on! I want you to come into my life and have that discussion with me today! We are never happier than when we think on a scale of deep and brooding depths. It is in our national psyche, in our very blood!'

'But they are still problems, old boy!'

'Yes. But you fear them because you fear they will embrace you and weigh you down.'

'Indeed I do!'

'I, on the hand, welcome them as a set of issues that I ponder over and over again, thrilled to mull them over again and again in my head.'

'Which is why it is a well-known fact all Russians are hopeless drunks!'

Both men laughed raucously at that, raising their glasses in a happy drunken toast. Silence then fell over them and Joshua leaned over the table and patted his old friend's arm that rested by his side. It was early summer and the evening was blessed with a warm sunshine that touched the two men's faces. They were sitting at the side of Caspar's old country house with a bottle of cognac between them and two glasses that had already been emptied and refilled several times.

Joshua looked across to Caspar and took in his friend's profile afresh. He had aged, more so than Joshua had. The strain he was under was clear. It was sixteen years earlier, with Joshua then a young and highly capable twenty-year-old officer, that the two men had met in a series of secret briefings of high-ranking officials at the Yalta Conference in the Crimea. Caspar, then a well-heeled and highly intelligent twenty-five-year-old officer with perfect English learnt studiously at the best schools in Leningrad, was there in a dual role. Ostensibly he was there as a translator, but in fact his real role was that of spy. He was to befriend as many of the allied party as possible, get them as drunk as possible, and find out as much as he could about anything that he could. His command of the language together with his good humour and amiable character, mixed with his fabulous ability to drink vodka without it affecting his brain, meant he was able to mix with the allies very well indeed.

And so it was that over the course of the conference Caspar Portichenko was the life and soul of every out-of-hours event, mixing very well socially and able through this process to gather all manner of information for his commanders. Caspar revelled in the assignment, laughing as he did so at the allies he met, so drunk in their own self-importance and so keen to tell a young Russian officer from Leningrad why their blessed western values would prevail. Caspar's work here helped as much as the work on the battlefield, his information gathered going to the very top of the Russian chain and ensuring that the young Portichenko was recognised at the highest political levels. He was a young Russian on his way up the food chain and his intelligence gathering would help ensure that weak western values would never rule the Eastern parts of Mother Russia's growing Europe.

The young Joshua Spearing had a Russian mother who had fled with her aristocratic parents from St Petersburg to settle in London following the revolution of 1905. The need to leave had followed the awful Bloody Sunday that had seen violence on an unprecedented level reach all levels of society. The Russian heritage was held proudly in his family and remembered well despite the fact that the privilege they had known in Russia quickly became an English upper-class privilege that they had walked so easily into in an English country life. Anya Medvedev was a young Russian beauty and Joshua's father, the eldest son of a renowned English family of great wealth, fell into a great love affair with her, and that in turn had born the young and extremely privileged, Joshua Spearing, several years later.

Joshua had been hand-picked out of Oxford University where he was studying law, for the Special Forces and was here at the meetings in the same capacity as Caspar Portichenko. They were both so good at what they were doing that they both figured out fairly quickly who and what the other one was and just how good they both were. Both, years later, now remembered differently who was first to challenge the other on being a master spy. Caspar clearly recollected them being up rather late in a crowded bar and Joshua laughing off the suggestion while doing pretend secret waves to others across the room. Joshua remembered they were walking through the grounds when he caught Caspar out with a question that he should not have answered. Either way, they knew about one another, and rather than pulling them apart, as it clearly should have done, they felt very at peace with one another, spies abroad, yes, but equally people, flesh and blood, who recognizing a person they really liked, was prepared to befriend that person. Their shared Russian heritage made it easier for them to have an immediate bond, particularly the St

Petersburg connection, but they did immediately warm to their characters and fell into an easy walk with one another.

Both took the friendship back to their bosses and dressed it up easily as a contact, and both were encouraged to build on the contact, which, of course, suited them both nicely. As a result they spent more and more time with each other, often outlasting all in the bars at night and speaking to one another in Russian in the corners of the hotels the allies were staying in. They had in common a cheeky smile, an appetite to truly learn of the other's country and a hunger to climb up their own prospective career ladders. In turn they exchanged useful bits of information that would help the other impress back at home. This continued throughout their professional lives and it did help enormously, both benefiting from coups of news that got them noticed as they clambered up their respective vocational calling. At Oxford a senior tutor had advised Joshua that "politics can be a dirty business but it can also be joyous too" and here with Caspar was the very proof of that.

Trust can sometimes be earned over time, often over a long time. Occasionally time is a luxury you do not have and opportunity, and the trust to take it, has to be instinctively seized. It happened like that for Caspar Portichenko and Joshua Spearing. Now, many years on, Caspar was entrusting his young and beautiful daughter into his friend's hands. He knew he could trust him having trusted him over all these years with his life. Wrong information fed over the years to Caspar would have had him killed. He had therefore already entrusted his very life to Joshua for all these years. Now, he would entrust his youngest child, his beloved Natalya, to him too.

'You have done well, my friend! Your life, your beautiful family, this fine house!' said Joshua, raising his glass in honour of his host.

Caspar smiled and took another thick and luxurious Cuban cigar sent from their new best friends in South America from the open pack on the table, offering one for Joshua as he did so. Lighting them both and then resting back in his comfortable, leather, battered garden chair, he inhaled deeply as he took in the noises of the night that were beginning to descend.

'We have done well,' he declared in his thick and heavy voice.

'Yes,' replied Joshua, a huge contented smile filling his sun-kissed face, 'so we have.'

'The war, my friend, still seems like yesterday here in Russia. We live it and relive it.'

'Of course. So do we!'

'Really?' replied Caspar with genuine surprise, 'You seem to have moved on so much more than we have, done so much, protected so much. We, on the other hand, are stuck in the old days, just as our communist masters dictate it must be and for even saying that, well, you know the dark consequences of opinion in this country, Joshua.'

Joshua nodded. He had nothing else to add. Living in this country's heavy shadow was a feat he simply could not do.

'But I revel in your life, Joshua, and as you see,' at this Caspar cast his right hand across the lands in front of him, 'I don't do too badly and now we have new friends to cultivate.' Caspar pointed to the rich cigar smoke that was filling the air to signify the Cubans, 'I sense many a fine trip to sunnier shores.'

'So you will stay?' asked Joshua, afraid of what the answer might be but unable not to ask it. If Caspar wanted to escape the grips of his masters it would be the help of Joshua he would seek.

Caspar smiled and inhaled more smoke as he pondered on the question.

'I will stay. I am not one for leaving, my dear friend. I have too many, how do you say, roots here. To leave it all would be too much for me to bear. You know, as much as I despise so much that is around me, I live for it too, it is my communist blood. I do not like the system that over-analyses everything we do, and yet I respect the system that is so focussed on its one goal. I look to the West and see what you do so well and yet I also see such disorganisation in a free-speech society that sees idiots allowed to rule. Here half of your Cabinet would have disappeared a long time ago!'

They laughed at that heartily.

Caspar went on, 'I love my country, love that it tries to make a difference; that it believes we have a way to make life better for all. I know we fail badly too but without a belief in the core of what we do, well, I would then be a traitor. Does that make sense?'

Joshua nodded. He knew all about living for a state you believed in in spite of often the illness at the centre of the apple.

'So I stay, and my dear beloved daughter, well, she goes to look after you and keep you and our secret and sacred treasure safe.'

'I'll drink to that!' laughed Joshua and they chinked their glasses and drank more cognac. It was a good night.

Joshua Spearing had enjoyed this trip to Russia like no other. His one-month trip had become a three-month one. His visa had stated he was working with the British High Commission on building ties between the two great countries. Caspar, now high up in the Leningrad governing echelons, ensured the visa was upgraded. Caspar had done well on the back of the restructure of Leningrad after the war with huge building reconstruction and an unprecedented inflow of millions of people. There was much money to be made with a man well placed to do so, and Caspar Portichenko was certainly well placed to do so. He lived with his family in this beautiful *dacha* in the countryside just outside of ancient Novgorod. Here the residents were blessed with esteemed old buildings and Caspar had easy access back to Leningrad and a select set of apartments reserved just for him and his family. In Soviet Russia it was a life so few could and would ever enjoy. Caspar, though, knew and appreciated the frailty with which he enjoyed his life, knowing that one slip could prove fateful and see all his cards so carefully stacked come tumbling down. It was truly living life as playing a game of poker with the stakes as high as they could ever be. One wrong move, as he had seen with so many other unfortunate souls, and it would all end. He knew, therefore, that his youngest daughter marrying a British high-ranking spy would either be seen by his bosses as suicide or ingenious.

This night, the two men drinking in the countryside around them and smelling the smug scent of satisfaction, followed a conversation Caspar had already had with his hierarchy. The marriage of his youngest daughter to a fast-rising English agent involved in the Foreign Office of a vital rival nation was approved. In truth Caspar had been told he had made the ultimate sacrifice for his party and that the rewards would be in kind. Nikita Krushchev himself had phoned to congratulate him and that was something that would happen probably once in a lifetime. Yes, this night, a fair evening in the still of a Russian summer, was an evening to be savoured. They had done well.

Now, all these years on, Natalya was, for the first time, without her special Joshua. A deep sadness went to bed with her, woke up with her in the dead of night and accompanied her throughout the long days. Her precious daughter, her dear friends, her interests, and even her treasured grandson could not dispel her aching heart. There seemed nothing that could be done and Tess in particular had found herself at a point of despair as she had tried so hard to help her mother rise above her grief. And then some wonderful news had arrived. Natalya's brother's only son, Mikhail, had called to see if he could come and stay and bring the thoughts and good wishes of all her family in St Petersburg. Natalya had almost skipped down West Place to her daughter's house to tell her the news in person. She was so excited and her joy leapt off her and blessed all she would meet. Yes, a real life Portichenko was coming here, to Cornwall, to St Ives! One of her own family from her precious Russia, the son of dear Uncle Anatoly who she had missed so much when she had left all to be with Joshua. At last, today, she would see Anatoly's son! Tess was collecting him from the local airport at Newquay this very morning, and for the first time since her precious Joshua had left her Natalya felt a warmth, a surge of joy, rise from deep inside her.

Tess waited in arrivals tired out from a succession of late nights that had fallen into early mornings as she had worked tirelessly on her new project for a gallery show in Newlyn. The project had not been without its challenges and Tess had felt particularly worked up around timings and numbers of paintings required. It was all well and good her work being liked but the strain it placed on her to produce was sometimes far too heavy a burden to carry. Exhausted, a strong black coffee was trying its best to coax her out into being at least awake, but it was a struggle. She could have done without a trip up to the airport but her mother was so excited and what else could she do but offer to be taxi driver to her long-distance cousin? Tess had half offered Noah in a moment of weakness but Natalya had been insistent that it should be her daughter, Tess, that should be the one there to meet him.

Now, sat here in arrivals with moments of peace she had craved hours earlier but was now loathing time lost, Tess had no idea as to what to expect of this man called Mikhail Portichenko. He would walk through into the arrivals lounge and, seeing his name written in large black letters on a piece of card that Natalya had drawn up and proudly handed over to her daughter before she left that morning, he would walk towards her. Tess found herself feeling strangely nervous and giddy, almost schoolgirl-like, as she sat fidgeting with her hair and steadily biting her nails, a habit she had failed to shake despite her nails often being covered in paint. In fact, she was now so used to the paint taste she liked that as well! Since her mother had told her of their guest who was coming over for a month, a whole month, Tess had found herself, against her better judgement, daydreaming of the type of man he could be. She had imagined all sorts of images and scenarios ranging from a Russian gangster to a Russian millionaire oil baron. She and Sylvia had shared lots of ideas over many glasses of wine and her friend had decided he would definitely be a hunk of a man with a wonderful personality like Doctor Zhivago from the film they had watched as girls. Natalya had then unhelpfully told Tess that this potential dreamboat was a long-time civil servant and all glamorous thoughts sadly fell away as she put him down to be middle-aged, fat and bald with unfortunate pimples. Unkind but better to be prepared than disappointed she concluded.

It was, therefore, to her great surprise that she was snapped out of her daydream to see a very friendly face, and a rather attractive one, belonging to a Russian man standing in front of her with a huge grin on his face and pointing at his name on the card that was lying on the floor by Tess's feet.

'I assume that is me?' he asked, a pleasant accent written across incredibly good English pronunciation, as he looked at his name on Natalya's home-made name card.

Tess smiled awkwardly and jumped off her chair, catching her foot in her skirt as she did so and falling into Mikhail who immediately caught her and helped her to her feet.

'I'm so sorry, Mikhail. I was half asleep, you know, late night and all.'

'Ah, burning the candle!'

'Yes, you could say,' replied Tess, amazed by Mikhail's English.

They shook hands formally causing Mikhail to laugh and place his arms around Tess and give her a huge bear hug that went on for far too long and was far too tight. Tess was initially aware of the tight body that was hugging her and she would have, in other circumstances, happily surrendered to this, but with the hug going on with copious amounts of patting too, she quickly lost the desire to enjoy the body she was locked into and rather, just felt acute embarrassment. She looked around the airport to see who was watching and was disturbed to see several people were and she could have sworn some were even pointing. Desperate to say something but at the same time not wanting to upset her cousin, she was at last mercifully released as Mikhail finally stepped back and looked Tess up and down, as though inspecting her. Tess gave him a hard stare and he in return gave her a hard stare, mixed with a big smile, back.

'You look nothing like me!' he declared, happily, Tess noted.

'Yes, well, you are Russian. That's another country, Mikhail, a long, long way away. People there look quite different to the English you see here.'

'But you are one of us!'

'What?'

'Russian!'

'Well, yes, I guess I am,' she conceded having given her lineage little thought since she used to dream of it regularly when she was a teenager desperate for romantic adventure. 'Good point. Maybe if we look at each other after quite a few drinks we will look more alike. Now come on, let's go,' she said, helping Mikhail with a bag and leading him out towards the exit signs.

'I'm so sorry, Mikhail, once again, for not being ready for you.'

'It is no problem,' replied Mikhail as they walked towards the exit, 'My aunt tells me you are an artist so I suspect you are often lost in your thoughts, yes?'

'I guess I am,' replied Tess, lost in her thoughts now as she immediately calculated why she liked this man and why she suddenly seemed so determined to not like him. He was most certainly not what she had expected.

'Your flights were OK?' asked Tess quickly, looking to regain any initiative she could.

'Yes, fine. Most pleasant.'

'Pleasant!' replied Tess, who hated flying with a passion and would describe even the shortest flight as purgatory.

'Cool?' replied Mikhail, wondering if he had got the meaning of the word pleasant in the wrong place in a sentence. He would look that up later but for now he was concentrating on making as good an impression on his cousin as he could.

'It is very nice to be here, Tess!' he declared, a big smile filling his happy face.

'And you like our little airport here?' Tess asked, admonishing herself as she did so inside her head for liking this Russian too much already.

'I do! It is very, how you say, cute!'

'Yes. That's a good way of putting it. Cute indeed. We've not had it long. It's been a revelation for us. Soon we shall have cars!'

Mikhail looked confused and then saw the smile on Tess's face and realised he had heard a joke. He laughed late and very hard as though Tess had told the joke to slay all others. He laughed and laughed, leaning with one arm on to Tess's shoulders as he tried to come to terms with the most amazing joke ever shared in Christendom. Tess smiled awkwardly, people looking at the loud, laughing man as they finally walked out of the airport and into the waiting sunshine.

'Soon we shall have cars!' repeated Mikhail to himself, causing him to laugh hard once more.

Tess wondered if she had collected a lunatic as she led the way towards the car park and her trusted black and scratched and bumped and rusting VW Golf that had not let her down for fifteen years now. As they walked Mikhail kept up a running commentary about his trip, the flights, the people and the airline food. Tess had decided by the time they reached her car that Mikhail was probably a little mad, clearly a tourist who had never been on a plane before, and his incessant chatter would be hiding some deep underlying problem that would probably manifest itself over the month ahead. Just her luck to have a very nice-looking Russian cousin who turned out to be as fruity as one of her mother's legendary fruit cakes.

'Your Golf!' declared Mikhail with wonder in his voice as though he had just discovered cheese. They had finally arrived at Tess's car, much to her relief to finally get herself and the mad Russian out of the public eye. Sadly as she lifted the boot she discovered she had taken nothing out of it from her trip to an art class from the previous day. She swore under her breath, a bad mood falling hopelessly upon her, as she emptied / tipped the contents of her boot into her back seat that was mercifully clear of anything other than several coats, some of which had probably been in the car for years.

Mikhail seemed oblivious to the boot blockage as he recited his knowledge of the VW Golf.

'Built since 1974 and a follow on from the Beetle, nice car the Beetle. Did you know the nameplate Golf derives from the German for Gulf Stream?'

Tess turned and smiled at this, hoping she looked slightly interested and not in fact so bored that she had not heard a single thing he was saying for some time now. She turned back to the car and continued to fling paper, card and bags over the now full back seat as Mikhail went on with his overview of the German masterpiece.

'Fascinating fact that, yes! You see, this Golf is part of a huge worldwide success story. I am not surprised you drive it. Aunt said you had a Golf. I was not at all surprised, not at all surprised! The world's third best-selling car ever and needless to say VW's best-seller. Imagine that!' Mikhail delivered these lines with incredible gusto and excitement. He really was enjoying himself being in Britain and with this very pretty and lovely young Tess to pick him up and take him on a journey to meet his often talked about Aunt Natalya who he had not seen for far too long. He was so excited, aware he was babbling nonsense, but unable to stop himself and blissfully unaware that he was boring his current host rigid, though he had noted a distant mood which he had immediately put down to nerves on her part.

Tess eventually cleared her boot and crammed Mikhail's luggage in, and the two of them got into the car.

'This is the Mark 4 is it not?' asked Mikhail, in a friendly open voice of sweetness and happiness as he manoeuvred his body into the seat in a manner of a man enjoying seating himself in a seat of great luxury.

'I have no idea,' replied Tess, in a voice laced with boredom and frustration as she backed into a curb at speed causing them both to be thrown forward in their seats and Tess, who had been leaning forward anyway, to bang her head on the driving wheel. Mikhail leaned over and gently pulled her head towards him to look for any damage. Tess felt her head in his vice-like grip while at the same time hearing a buzzing in her ears and a chorus of horns telling her to get a move on from the now blocked exit road out of the car park.

'I'm fine,' she replied gruffly, pulling her head away from Mikhail's soft hands and feeling a pain rebound across her temples as she did so.

'Oh, good! A quick healer and a strong spirit. Typically Portichenko! That, my pretty, artistic cousin, is a family trait. Pain does not stay with us for long.' Mikhail almost sang these words out, settling back into his chair as he did so and looking out at the road before them, humming a happy tune that went up and down like a bird on the wings of a perfect summer's breeze. They reached the open road and Tess, feeling a sudden urge to cry, apologised.

'I'm so sorry for being a little grumpy back there.'

'Grumpy?' replied Mikhail, as though he had not noticed, which of course he had but as always he had used his normal diversionary tactic of music to fill his mind. It rarely failed him.

'You need not apologise to me. I am a guest and I am more than happy that you have taken time out of your busy artist schedule to come and get me, your distant and extremely excited and, no doubt, idiotic cousin.'

Tess's heart crumbled at that. How petty and silly she could be at times! She counselled herself accordingly and made a mental note to ensure her next session with Robert would concentrate on this. Tess placed her left hand on Mikhail's arm, squeezing gently and then patting it twice.

'It is lovely to have you here, really lovely. I can't tell you how much Mama has been looking forward to seeing you. I can honestly say your news of your arrival lifted her out of oblivion. I could not be happier that you are here, truly. It has been a stressful time and you, my dear cousin, are most welcome.'

Mikhail smiled broadly at that and launched into a song in Russian that broadly translated, which he did after he had finished its sudden burst, that happiness was in the air and would breed and multiply like rabbits. This made Tess laugh a lot.

'That can't be a song!'

'It is!' replied Mikhail, laughing as he did so. 'It's a traditional song and your mother will know it well.'

Tess smiled at that. Mikhail was bringing her mother's childhood back to her and this would make Natalya so happy.

'OK,' said Tess in a friendly let's-make-friends-again voice, 'What car do you drive?'

Tess asked this question certain that a bumbling Russian civil servant, cute though he was, would no doubt be driving some clapped out old Trabant. Not that she cared about what one drove, it was just her natural assumption.

'Oh, just a runabout. You know.'

'No, I don't know,' replied Tess, suddenly intrigued by the vague reply.

'Lovely day, is it not?' chirped Mikhail, gazing out at the fields stretching out around them across the glorious day that now shone across them as they reached the A30 and began their descent to St Ives.

'Of course it's a lovely day!' declared Tess who knew a diversionary tactic when saw one, 'It is nearly always a lovely day in God's country.'

'God's country?' asked Mikhail, a little confused by the assertion.

'Cornwall is heaven,' replied Tess.

'Ah, you think your little patch of England the most special, eh? Well I admire that. I really do.'

'It's true! I've been everywhere and always this place brings me home.'

'Yes, well I see its beauty,' he said, looking at the views of the open fields being touched by the warm April sunshine that lifted fresh greens and pointed towards the summer to come.

'And your car is?' asked Tess, pulling her interesting cousin back on track.

'A black one.'

'A black what? A Trabant?'

Mikhail laughed, snorted even as he did so.

'Not quite. Look, it's not important, dear cousin!'

'It is to me given your in depth, and may I say, extremely informative overview on everything that is the Golf,' replied Tess with a smile on her face. His cute song had endeared him to her.

'OK. Well, and this is just me telling you, not for general consumption, it is a Maserati GranTurismo. I've had it six months now and it is a beautiful car and I am very lucky to have it. A stunning sports car on show at the 2008 Geneva Motor Show, where you may have seen it on TV, and it turns heads wherever I go.'

Tess took in this information not knowing exactly what a Maserati GranTurismo was, though it sounded Italian and expensive. She therefore asked the obvious question.

'Is it Italian and expensive?'

Now Mikhail really laughed for quite a while. Tess let him enjoy himself and concentrated on driving slowly on purpose in the outside lane to annoy some lunatic tourist, no doubt, who was driving way too close to her car and was now stuck behind her and a lorry on the inside lane as they crawled up an incline in the dual carriageway.

'Yes,' spluttered Mikhail as though Tess had just told the second-best joke ever, 'it is both Italian and expensive.'

'And I thought you were a civil servant, a Russian one at that.'

'That I am!'

'And yet you drive an expensive Italian sports car?'

'Ah, I see! You think I am a mob criminal now you find I drive nice car! I knew I should have stuck with the Trabant cover!'

'Not necessarily a mobster, Mikhail,' replied Tess, finally pulling into the inside lane and giving the passing driver a raised one-finger salute as he angrily pulled past her, 'Though for all I know, and care really, you may be. You are here to cheer up my mother so tell her what she needs to hear and drive what you like.'

As Tess said this she was surprised by just how severe her voice had become. All Mikhail had said was that he drove an expensive sports car and the effect on her had been so negative. She didn't even like cars! She felt Mikhail's eyes on her.

'What are you looking at?' she asked quickly.

'You, Tess, just you.'

'Why? And also, by the way, please don't.'

'Because when I saw you I thought you were very pretty, but now you are mad I think you are extremely beautiful.'

Tess heard the words, similar words that she had dismissed many times from men trying it on, but words that in the cold light of just her and her cousin in the car having met for the first time, caught her out.

'You see,' Mikhail went on, 'I admire honesty, more than anything. In Russia we have become adept at sharing the truth carefully. Here you obviously have no such issues. I drive a very nice car because I can. I am very wealthy in my own right, Tess. My father, your uncle, was very rich indeed and it all became mine when he died. I am therefore ridiculously wealthy and have everything I could want, that is materially I have everything I want. I chose to be a civil servant as my job many years ago because my father told me I needed to do something useful. As a result I went into the civil service in the branch of arts heritage after university, having studied Art History and becoming pretty engrossed by it all. I now work within the arts and culture team at St Petersburg overseeing, amongst other things, the most famous and most wonderful Hermitage Museum, which you will no doubt know all about. My day car is in fact a VW Golf that is even a little older than this fine specimen. I live two lives and I enjoy them both tremendously.'

Tess had listened to this overview and found herself unsure to know what to say. He had once again made her angry and then ashamed in the space of a few short minutes. Whatever he was doing to her he was clearly able to dictate her emotions, which she was not very happy about, but she was immediately fascinated by. This man, her own distant cousin, was obviously very interesting and time would tell just how genuine or not he actually was. Sylvia, who was nearly always a wonderful judge of character, would help enormously.

'Is this the point where I tell you about my Maserati?' offered Tess with a wicked glint in her eye.

'Yes,' replied Mikhail, happy to see Tess confused by him. He had grown used to people not knowing how to place him. He knew he was something of an enigma. He was sure Tess would work him out for herself if she chose to do so, and he hoped she would very much choose to do so because he found her quite delicious.

Within twenty minutes Tess was driving towards town and Mikhail was left speechless by the azure sea stretched out before him in the bay, the sky seeming to bounce off the very surface of the water causing him to shield his eyes.

'Is it always this beautiful?' he asked, his voice stilled by wonder.

'Just most of the time,' replied Tess, a happy smile written across her face.

Down Tregenna Hill towards the centre of the town and then turning a sharp left at the NatWest Bank and up The Stennack.

'What a busy town!' remarked Mikhail seeing tourists and locals try and negotiate the thin pavements while avoiding the traffic.

'You should see it in the summer. This is a breeze compared to then!'

Out at the top of Bullans Lane and then right towards the huge drop that is Porthmeor Hill. Mikhail laughed nervously as they took the tight left bend at speed and he saw the ocean below them, the waves firing in, the beach covered by its high-tide coat.

'Don't worry, my dear cousin, these old VW brakes have never let me down, at least not yet anyway!'

And then no sooner had the fairground ride started than Tess was turning off left and heading down on a much softer incline to Carthew Way that led through to home, Porth-la-Chy, which looked as magnificent as ever, aglow in its position on the headland. It all took Mikhail's words away as silence had eventually descended upon him. Along the gravel drive and parking up, Tess turned off the engine and said simply, 'Home.'

Natalya, who had been waiting by the door doing nervous little jobs as she tried to still her mind, now ran at a pace she had not managed for a long time out of the front door and took hold of her nephew and gripped him hard.

'Mikhail! Mikhail! How fabulous to see you my dear, dear boy.'

They hugged tightly, speaking quickly in tender Russian as they did so.

'Now, stand back,' said Natalya.

She looked him up and down, like studying a piece of art, making small agreeable murmurs as she did so. Tess watched it all as she got out Mikhail's bags, amused by her mother and fascinated by what the next few weeks would hold for them all. Mikhail simply stood and waited, a huge grin on his face as he felt the full magnitude of an aunt in awe of him.

'You look like your father a little. You look like your mother a little less. You look like yourself a good lot more!' Natalya's words escaped into the air with such joy as the old woman stepped forward and got hold of each of Mikhail's cheeks and squeezed them hard.

'You look after yourself, that much is certain, Mikhail,' she went on, 'and that is very good! A fine figure of a man. Isn't he a fine figure of a man?' declared Natalya, turning to her now beyond embarrassed daughter who refused to answer but managed a little curtsy that made Natalya tut and Mikhail laugh. Natalya, seeing the smiling cheeks of her nephew puff out, chose the moment to step forward and squeeze his cheeks hard as though he were some young boy and not a man of forty-four years old.

'Unlike my daughter, who eats badly, sleeps badly and in short, lives...'

'Badly?' offered Tess, attempting to carry all three of Mikhail's bags only for him to see her stumble into the laurel bushes and rush to her side to help pull her back up and take the two large suitcases off her.

'I was fine, thank you!' Tess said abruptly. Mikhail just laughed and walked after Natalya towards the house listening to her declaring the virtues of good cooking and how the dinner she had prepared for the three of them would underline her point.

Into the large hallway, its welcoming bleached whites married with the colours of paintings making any visitor feel immediately at rest.

'What a beautiful house!' declared Mikhail, immediately intoxicated by the peace he felt all around him. Natalya simply smiled and carried on through to the kitchen shouting instructions as to what to do with Mikhail's luggage to her daughter. Mikhail was caught in two minds as to whether to follow his aunt or stop to help ensure Tess would not once more fall foul to the weight of his cases. Tess gave him a forceful nod that sadly reminded her of the earlier bang to her head, the nod telling her cousin to follow her mother and she mouthed the words, 'Don't mind me!' in exaggerated fashion. Mikhail simply smiled back at his slightly older cousin and gave her a cheeky thumbs-up.

As Mikhail disappeared into the kitchen Tess wrapped the handle of his large and exceptionally heavy holdall over her neck and took one case in each hand. She made it halfway up the stairs to where the stairs turned and she gave in, deciding instead to carry each item up on its own and dropping them on the floor of the largest of the guest bedrooms. Minutes that seemed like hours later and the last item duly delivered, she looked at the pile of bags and cases and considered opening one or two or all three of them and then dismissed the idea as too naughty even for her.

She then walked over to the huge bay window that majestically looked across the beach laid out below her. No matter what the day, the month, the weather, there really was no better view in the whole world for her. Ever changing, ever new, and ever true. St Ives was her everything and the main reason that her life had ever made sense.

'Tess!' called Natalya in almost theatrical tones from the bottom of the stairs, 'Dinner is served!'

Tess mimicked her mother's voice in a childish manner that made her smile to herself as she walked towards the door, stopping briefly once more to consider having a quick look in the holdall and noticing as she did so that it had a lock on it. She looked across to the cases, which also had locks on them, proper locks too she noticed and not the cheap type that if she ever remembered to buy any she would almost certainly buy ones that were accessible with a good hairgrip. Defeated, she walked down the stairs to have dinner and listen to her mother tell her just how wonderful this new man in their lives was, something she knew she would have to get used to for many years to come.

Chapter 5

Portrait of a Young Man

'So, what do you think?' asked an over-eager Noah, relieved that he had at last been able to share his secret with the one person he thought he could safely share it with for now, Flora.

'It's nice. You know, nice colours and all. Perhaps a little ordinary for your tastes but of course it was a gift so...' offered Flora, not sure what she was supposed to say about the painting that rested on Noah's floor and which she would not have even noticed in a shop but here, in Noah's house, it rather stood out. The paintings and prints that already adorned his whitewashed walls were all abstract, bright colours catching lots of the area of Cornwall on canvas. None were traditional in form as this painting clearly was. There was further the added complication of this being a precious gift from the man Noah had loved more than any other and so to say the wrong thing at this point would be a tortuous error!

'But wonderfully painted,' she added, with as much enthusiasm as she could. 'It is an original I take it?'

Noah nodded his head vigorously and then regretted the action as he had drunk too much the previous night. He had been out with his dear friend Sam when a quick pint turned into a four- hour session that had culminated with a late-night dip under a starlit sky. The sea had been freezing and his wet clothes all lay in the downstairs sink, the cloth heavy under the touch of the ocean, waiting to be washed free.

'So, great! Shall we go out then?' asked Flora, rather bored already in looking at a painting of a boy who could well have been a girl from the Middle Ages, dressed to the nines and holding a quite ridiculous and rather pompous pose.

'You see, I have a problem,' replied Noah having seemingly not heard the request to go out.

'Really?' asked Flora trying hard to stay patient.

'Yes. You see, this painting, this precious piece of art, was a very private gift from Grandad. He told me I was allowed to tell no one.'

'Yes, you said that while having me swear to death after hideous torture before bringing me into the room and yet note, here I am.'

'Indeed, but you don't count.'

'You mean I'm a no one! How dare you!' Flora threw her hands in the air for added dramatic effect.

Noah smiled. She knew the answer to that already.

'You see, we need,' he went on.

'*We* need?'

'Oh yes, *we*, always *we* Flora, the Salander and Blomkvist of St Ives! That is if you don't mind? I mean, far from me to be presumptuous!'

'Of course I don't, Mikael,' returned Flora with a huge and generous smile added for good measure as she laughed at the thought of her playing the part of the gothic Scandinavian.

'Well, Lisbeth, we need to do some digging about this painting. I want to find out what it is, who it is by, what is its history!'

'Yes, sir!'

Noah gave Flora a let's-concentrate-now look and continued.

'This gift was given to me privately and I think I need to understand it fully to understand the true extent of the gift.'

'What do you mean?'

'Well, as a starting point, I mean the phrase 'tell no one!'. It's like something from a mafia movie or something.'

Flora heard Noah's words and shuddered a little. It was rather strange that this painting, this very old looking and not at all to her taste painting, had been such a hidden secret and one that on passing it on to the next generation, Joshua had felt the need to tell his beloved grandson to tell no one of its existence. Maybe it was a gift from a lover and almost definitely it was a secret that if they discovered it, it would lead to pain. Counsel was needed.

'Noah, we are talking about your Grandad here. The man you love more than anyone else in the whole world and he specifically told you to keep it all a secret for a good reason no doubt. I honestly don't think any good can come from looking for its past, whatever that might be. Are you sure you want to know its secrets, Noah?'

Noah nodded.

'Yes. I'm sure. I know what you are thinking and I've thought that too but if it's only you and me then I'm sure we can carry the burden, eh?'

Flora smiled and thought momentarily for his sake about agreeing and then simply said,

'I don't know, Noah. Seriously I don't. It depends what it is, doesn't it? Is that a risk you want to take?'

Noah looked straight into Flora's eyes.

'I've thought of very little else for quite a while now and yes, it's a risk I want to take. Having you there makes me braver, that's true.'

'OK then. I'll gladly help you. OK?'

'OK.'

Noah walked up to Flora's side and the two of them stood taking in the piece, looking for a clue that might magically jump out at them.

'The window view looks pretty hot,' offered Flora.

'Yes. European maybe.'

'Yet he wears a thick animal fur.'

'Only on one shoulder, though.'

'So you are thinking he is fashionable?'

'Yes,' replied Noah, 'and rich.'

'The walls look European too and Mediterranean.'

'Why?'

'Well, they look terracotta washed, not at all English!'

'Flora, you are a genius!'

'Yes! I'm enjoying this. I sense a new career in the offing! He is rather pretty in a young man sort of way, classic I'd say, if I knew anything at all about this sort of thing.'

'Mmm,' agreed Noah. 'I wonder what his name is?'

'Francesco!' offered Flora immediately, a wonderful tint of Italian over the name.

'Yes, that would work. Or maybe Federigo.'

'Or Antonio!' laughed Flora.

'Ah yes, Antonio. That's my favourite. Let's call him that!'

Noah found his mind wandering as the scent from Flora's neck touched his senses. Flora in turn smelt the lunch being cooked at Olives in the square and her stomach felt the need to go and eat.

'Why don't we go and have lunch at Olives and chat?' declared Flora, snapping Noah out of his reverie for Flora's intoxicating aroma.

'That, my dear Flora, is an excellent idea. First let me put this back in its hiding place and you can help me by holding the ladder!'

'From art historian to ladder holder! My star has fallen!'

'Your star, dear girl, will never fall. It may lean a little, admitted, but never actually fall… '

Flora smiled widely. She always did when she was with Noah. He made her feel so happy and treasured. He was the most dear of friends.

Ten minutes later and they were sitting outside Olives at a table at the bottom of the steps that went up to the café and the ever-open door from which floated the mouth-watering smells that were cooked freshly each day. Here they waited for their eagerly placed order to arrive as a gentle sun touched their faces, a light breeze allowing the gulls to ride on the waves of the sky.

Flora now felt hungrier than ever, the need to eat always catching her out and filling her with the enormous desire to devour her food ravenously. Noah would watch her eat and smile, Flora catching his eye and asking him what he was smiling at, only for her friend to smile back.

'I am sure I read recently that there's a site you can type details in such as a painting name and the site will tell you the painter,' offered Flora, aiming to let Noah know she had been thinking through solutions and not just her lunch. The sun gently touched her face as she twisted her nose into the air to catch its warmth. It was an amusing pose and Noah mimicked her causing her to laugh and throw back a turned-up nose.

'If only we knew the painting's name then! I guess we could guess?'

'Of course we could. *Man in Silly Hat and Overthrow* would be a good name!'

'True,' laughed Noah, 'he does look a little odd, though it was clearly a fashionable garment when it was painted.'

'Not that you know that.'

'Ah yes, true. He could have been a man with no friends and a hideous dress sense!'

'Or,' added Flora, 'a fashionable model leading the world's choices, just like you would claim that garish jumper you are wearing is fashionable now?' asked Flora, pointing to Noah's red and white striped jumper that he loved dearly.

'It is! It's just that you don't see anyone else wearing them and that makes me a trendsetter!'

'That makes you many things, Noah, and it is not necessarily a trendsetter.'

Noah smiled, then thought about Jake and all his trendsetting surf wear and stopped smiling.

'Keep smiling. That's the rule. You know you can never stop smiling when you are with me,' said Flora, putting her hand on her friend's and stroking the back of his hand. She loved his hands, so soft with light blond hairs touched by the sun.

Noah looked at their hands, together, on the table, touching softly and all the happier for it. He looked up into Flora's eyes, slowly, purposely.

'Marry me?' he asked, a question he asked on a regular basis on the premise that eventually she would accidentally say yes instead of laughing as she always did. Once again she did not fail to oblige.

'You are funny!' she laughed out loud.

'Yes I am, a comedian of the highest honour. I should do a tour, *Spearing Knows Best!* What do you think?' he asked, large eyes hiding his deepest thoughts for Flora.

'Would you like to be married Noah, really? Imagine the domestication, the routine, the same everyday with the same person. At the moment you do get around a bit, don't you?'

Noah offered Flora his how-dare-you look.

'You couldn't really cope with someone normal like me

every day. Boredom is not an easy best friend, Noah. It finds a way to make the interesting mundane and I wouldn't want that for you.' Flora had spoken without hesitation and had got halfway through the sentence before regretting where she was going. Talking about relationships had never been their thing, a subject best avoided between the two of them. For Flora all she knew was that she was with Jake now and he, Noah, was quite free. Over the last few years Noah had enjoyed several girlfriends, none of whom had mysteriously been able to develop a long-standing relationship with him and she had found that fascinating, telling Noah that it must be the small detail that was putting them off.

'Like what?' he had once asked, only to be met with a long list of bad hair, random socks around the house, old neighbours who always entered the house at any time they wanted, eclectic musical tastes, far too cheerful for his own good, humour that often left you unsure whether there was a touch of madness there, a certain touch of English eccentricity and an over the top desire to be friendly. 'Shall I change then?' he had asked and Flora had answered instantly no. The truth was she liked him being just the way he was and most certainly she liked him being single and, as selfish as she knew this made her, it suited them both. In Noah she saw the most interesting man she had ever met. He said things the way he saw them and took his own step, not at the behest of the flock. She loved him for that alone but never seriously considered the two of them being together other than as dear friends. It was perfect that way and they had never crossed the line to be any closer other than in Noah's very regular comedy attempts to suggest betrothal.

'Well, I would survive the boredom if it meant looking at you while you slept and drinking in the very sight of you,' replied Noah in a typical mixture of humour and words, words delivered with a huge grin that meant you could not be sure if he actually meant them.

'I'll marry you then,' Flora replied, her brain stuck on the beautiful last few words she had just heard, 'If you promise me one thing.'

'Yes?' asked Noah, an excited glint in his eye.

'To burn that jumper.'

The spell was broken.

'Ah! This I cannot do, young lady!' Noah declared in comedy enraged tones. 'You ask too much of me! My house, take it. My car, why not? Even my surfboard, my dear and precious charge, could be yours! But my jumper, my precious and trendsetting jumper, that has lived with me through plague and famine, this, this I cannot do!'

Together they laughed as their lunch arrived. For Flora a Greek salad ladled luxuriously with milky-white Greek feta cheese, shiny black olives and drizzled in fresh virgin oil. For Noah a more straightforward choice and personal favourite of beans on thick and heavily buttered brown toast with a round of salad on the side, heavy in red onion. It wasn't a choice on the menu, rather a meal made for a loyal café regular.

'Yuk!' said Flora, looking at Noah's lunch.

'I know. Yummy, eh?' he replied as he lathered his food with brown sauce. A couple on the table behind them laughed as Flora made eyes at them and shook her head in a you-can't-take-him-anywhere look. Noah, like a pig in muck, happily ploughed on regardless.

'Do you think', asked Flora, starting to make her way greedily through her lunch, 'that you will stay in St Ives now?'

Noah, swallowing a divine mouthful of beans, was surprised by the question.

'Why?'

'Well, you've been away and often that means people either stay away or find it easier to go away, you know? Where do you stand now?'

'Ah! You're worried about losing me, aren't you?'

Flora just flashed Noah a smile that said he was right but she wasn't going to give him the luxury of telling him so. Noah thought about teasing her some more and then realised it had probably not been an easy question to ask so he gave a serious answer.

'Apart from holidays or necessities, dear Flora, I do not believe I will ever leave this county again. Whether or not I stay in St Ives is a different matter, but Cornwall is just too precious to ever consider not living here. It's about the surf and the light. Where else could I get that? And then there's Mum and Grandma and my memories and, well, I'm going nowhere. What about you?'

In asking this question Noah tried to be as calm as he could. He had long suspected Jake would not only marry his precious girl, but also whisk her away to some distant part of the globe. He had often heard him talk about conquering Australia, taking overseas his brands to be enormously successful over there. They were already exporting and there was talk of opening a shop on Australia's famous Gold Coast, on Kirra Beach.

'I'm like you, Noah. I can't leave, but I will travel.'

'For long times?'

'Maybe. Though I'd miss the café so it couldn't be overly long.'

'And me?'

'Of course you.'

'What about Jake?' asked Noah, again careful to not show an over interest in his voice.

'Jake?'

'Well, I'd heard he plans to open up in Australia.'

'Had you indeed! Where did you hear that piece of hot gossip?' she asked with an injection of fire in her voice.

Noah paused.

'Around,' he answered, softly.

'Really?'

'Yes,' he said, quietly.

Flora ate, her words gone for now.

'Well, has he?' Noah asked, his voice still quiet.

Flora carried on eating and simply answered whilst doing so.

'Yes.'

'And he plans to live there?'

'Yes.'

'Really!?'

'I did just say yes!'

'And you will go with him?'

'Not to live, no.'

Noah raised his eyebrows without meaning to do so.

'And he knows this?'

'Yes, of course,' replied Flora, looking up purposely to answer with spirit whilst looking directly in Noah's eyes, 'And you can stop the amazed-face look now as well if you like.'

71

'Oh, was I? Sorry. I'm just surprised.'

'Well, don't be. Jake and I are very close, of course. Good friends first and lovers second. He's a lovely man, Noah, and I know you don't always think he is.'

Noah thought about offering a disagreement to this but couldn't find it in himself to do so.

'But we are also quite independent. If he wants to live there for a time then I will go over to visit and for long times I am sure, but I wouldn't stay there. My life is here.'

'But Flora, if he lived there for years?'

'He won't. He'd miss his parents too much.'

'And you, Flora!'

'Oh yes, and me, I suppose.'

Noah thought about pushing her more on what she was and was not telling him in a rare conversation of depth around Jake, but he thought better of it. After all, the thought of Flora being home alone in St Ives with monkey nuts away and away for some time was quite an intoxicating one and not one he wanted her to think that much about that she might change her mind.

A series of cars drove past and several tourists wandered by as St Ives life carried on all around them. How many people had been past this spot, how many had paused to take in the day, their troubles and burdens, hopes and aspirations carried by them, each and every one in their heart? In our world of never-ending happenings, how do we stop?

'So!' declared Flora, keen to get them back on track of talking about the painting, 'Let's set about writing down potential names for our mysterious painting. You scribe.'

'Of course,' replied Noah, wine finished and coffee freshly arrived.

'Now then, if this painting is famous it will be easy to find.'

'What do you mean by famous?' asked Noah, a little surprised by the suggestion having not really thought of it like that.

'Well, think it through, OK? Your grandfather keeps this painting in total privacy, telling nobody. Nobody! Nobody? Add to this he was very wealthy and already has an art collection to die for so why hide it? He then gives it to you and asks one thing alone.'

'To keep it totally private.'

'Yes! Now does that suggest that this painting is a non-descript?'

'Not really,' replied a disconcerted Noah, alarm bells that he was constantly trying to allay now going off in his head. 'Maybe he painted it himself and that's the reason he wanted it kept private?' he offered without any conviction.

'Maybe it's stolen treasure!' said Flora far too loudly causing them both to look around to make sure no one was listening. Around them the other two outside tables were occupied. Four older people, all in their sixties, who Noah partly recognised as residents from the higher part of town, had replaced the couple who had laughed at Noah's lunch and were now sat happily making their way through their own very hearty lunch. Laughter and general hilarity filled the air around them as they talked through warm spring air, their faces reflecting the fine St Ives weather. Behind them sat a middle-aged man with his back to them wearing a dog-eared trilby and a perky cravat. He was reading a chunky newspaper and chain-smoking as he worked his way through copious amounts of strong black coffee while whistling and humming tunes of a general upbeat nature to himself, the St Ives day clearly having a positive effect on him.

'I think it's fair to say we are not surrounded by the worlds secret agents!' laughed Noah.

'Well I think', went on Flora, lowering her voice as she did so, the thought and fear of conspiracy having taken over them both, 'that we should still go back to your place.'

'And make love!' declared Noah eagerly, leaning back in his chair and laughing out loudly. 'How lovely. At last, young Flora, we make the breakthrough! This is great news. I really should ring my mother. Maybe the *Echo* too? The real question is who do we sell the rights to our wedding pictures to? *Hello* or *The Beano*? I think the former as the cash will help fund our new lavish lifestyle. This really is excellent news!'

Flora looked at Noah and simply smiled, waiting for him to finish.

'And get on the Internet and see what we can find, silly!'

'Sexual positions you mean! How enlightened. I like that in a woman!'

'Do you want me to kick you?'

'Not really, although the mark you left would be a perfect memento for me to show the courts.'

She gave him a half smile that told him now was the time to move on and her amusement tank was running dry.

'Right,' Noah responded, galvanised by the Flora stare, 'Well, yes, research is the next vital step. Great idea. However, my Internet connection is broken.'

'Still?'

'Yes, still.'

'You have called someone to come and get it fixed, haven't you?'

'Well, sort of,' replied Noah with absolutely no conviction in his voice.

'You mean you haven't, have you?'

'No, not as such.'

'As such?'

'At all… '

'How long is that now?'

'A week or so… '

'A month, at least.'

'Well, now you are just being technical. Although on the upside I'm clearly not addicted to Internet porn!'

Flora just shook her head while muttering something about magazines that Noah couldn't quite catch.

'OK,' she said, 'I have a photo of the painting on my phone. My place, then.'

'OK. Jake in?'

'No, he's in the shop all day.'

'Oh, shame. I was so hoping to discuss business matters with him. You see, I've been reading the *Financial Times*, as is my want, and it says that surf gear is on its way out due to there being a severe shortage of worldwide waves.'

Flora shot him a look of upset mixed with amusement. She couldn't help but laugh at Noah but she did wish he would stop going on about Jake. She knew he liked him really so the joke did on occasion wear a little thin.

'Come on then,' she said, not wanting to fall out with him.

They left their money for the bill on the table shouting their goodbyes to Jane who ran the café, and then started walking across St Ives. Down along Back Road West and around the corner onto the opening out to the magnificent sweep of Porthmeor Beach that greeted them, as it normally did, with a blast of wind. Walking up towards the Tate they saw a very busy Sylvia who was just serving a couple on the terrace of the café. They shouted their greetings to one another as they walked by.

'Looks like you picked a good day to be off!' said Noah.

'Great day for the café though. So wonderful when it gets busy, so buzzy and alive. Chatter becomes the music.'

'And you love that don't you?' said Noah.

'I do. I know people think that somehow you should want more, but why?'

Noah smiled. He adored the simplicity of Flora. She gave so much and in return wanted so little.

'I love being here,' replied Flora pointing out to the ocean before them. They were standing by the wall just past the café and under the gaze of the imperious Tate. The sun hit their backs and warmed them against the still cool westerly wind that touched their bodies. If you were going to find a breeze in St Ives you would normally find it here, which was why you would find the surfers here too. Flora stretched out her arms as the breeze ran through her hair and lifted it from her face. Noah watched her and thought if she had ever been more beautiful he could not remember it. He longed to take her in his arms and hold her so tight, to whisper in her ears that he loved her and that he would protect her for all time. Not that she needed protecting. In truth he knew she would protect him, if he had her, and he didn't.

She turned to him and saw he had been looking at her and assumed he was wondering why she had chosen her life.

'You see, Noah, I have never wanted to fill my mind with anything other than this. You know our friends who have gone on to "be something" and they come back here and look at me as though I have failed when I know I have succeeded. I have only ever wanted to be at one with the ocean and myself and every day I get to do that. It's my life and from it I draw huge inspiration and I feel alive. No more, no less. It's enough to feel alive, isn't it?'

'Yes it is,' replied Noah, simply, 'yes it is.'

'Come on then, trendsetter, let's go and do some digging.'

'OK,' said Noah, stealing one last look out to sea and then turning to follow. Up the steps by the cemetery and down Barnoon Hill before cutting over the park with its beautiful piece of Barbara Hepworth sculpture that sat through time and watched over the seaside town. Then up through the bustle of the main artery road that came into the town and then still climbing up some more and the challenge of the steps before finally making their way to Jake's very flash penthouse apartment on Talland Road.

As they walked up the steps and Flora opened the door to reveal an apartment bathed in stunning light and views that stretched across the bay over to Godrevy and beyond, Noah made his usual collection of huffing noises as he sort to underline to Flora this was not right for her and she, in turn, ignored his usual mutterings and got on with the wonderful task of putting on fresh coffee.

'Go and sit on the terrace!' she called out from the kitchen, 'The air and view will take away your grumpiness,' she added helpfully.

Noah stepped out of the pull-back doors that glided almost as smoothly as Jake, and he sat himself down on a steamer chair that was bleached by Cornish sun. He knew he should not go on about Jake so much and he counselled himself to give it a rest and be more pleasant about the man. He knew this was what Flora wanted. More settled in his mind with these thoughts decided, he looked out across Porthminster beach, families enjoying the warm April sun, and over to the harbour where the sea was in and the fishing boats bobbed up and down on the soft currents. Across the bay the ever-watchful eye of Godrevy lighthouse nodded back to Noah, and the world, all at once, seemed to be at peace. Seagulls sang overhead, happy to be gliding on mellow sunny currents as they danced through the air. A smile flickered across his face as he thought of nothing in particular. He let his head fall back on to the cushion that awaited him and within moments a velvet carpet had arrived and taken him into a luxurious sleep.

'You OK?' asked Flora, an hour having passed since Noah had sat down. She had been watching him from the doors for a few minutes now, afraid to wake him up with dark news from the beauty sleep he was lost in.

'Yea,' replied a happy Noah slowly waking up and stretching out as he did so, 'I'm great. A luxury to sleep like this. I could get used to it!'

'Good. Come on then, I've got something to show you.'

Noah noted the serious tone of her voice.

'Is it good news?' he asked hopefully.

Flora just nodded for him to follow her, aware that his life was about to change forever.

'What have you been looking at?' asked Noah, following Flora through the whitewashed lounge and through into the study. The computer screen had shut down and needed to be restarted with a password, which Flora was about to type in, but she stopped.

'Noah, sit down.'

Noah looked at her, her tone unsettling him, and then sat down on the chair by the side of the desk, Flora being sat at the desk in front of the computer.

'This is all pretty weird,' she said, wondering how to choose her words.

'Right?' replied Noah, trying to ensure there was no hint of concern in his voice and failing miserably. Realising his shortcoming he asked the inevitable follow up.

'Why, what have you found?'

'Well, I started by messing around really, you know just playing with names like the ones we were making up.'

'And they worked!?'

'Of course not. How on earth was *Boy With Funny Cloak On* ever going to work?'

Noah nodded, but did not manage a smile. The seriousness in Flora's voice was far too disconcerting for that.

Flora continued, 'So, I thought to myself if this painting is famous and missing, that is not in a recognised gallery, then maybe missing pictures from famous artists might just find it.'

Flora waited for Noah to ask a question. None arrived. Noah's mouth was all of a sudden extremely dry and he was waiting for whatever was set to follow. He felt light-headed and extremely unnerved. He simply nodded his head for her to go on.

'So I typed in missing paintings of Monet, and nothing. Then Cézanne, and nothing. Gauguin, and again, nothing. Several other painters I tried and I kept drawing blanks.'

'Blimey, how long was I asleep for?'

'I wish you were still asleep.' At this she turned to him and took his hand and kissed it. Under normal circumstances Noah would have been delighted with this turn of events. Instead he felt dread.

'So then I typed in Raphael.' As she spoke Flora turned to her desktop and typed in the password to reveal Joshua's birthday gift, 'And there it was, top of the list. *Portrait of a Young Man* painted by a certain Raphael of Urbino and painted in 1514!'

Noah leaned forward to gaze in wonder at what was definitely the picture that was sitting in his house.

'Raphael, you say? 1514? And it's lost?' he asked in amazement.

'No Noah, it's stolen.'

'Stolen!'

'Yes, stolen.'

'By Grandad?' he asked, incredulity in his voice.

'No, well not initially anyway. How he got it I have no idea!'

Noah heard the comment about Joshua but didn't bite. How could he?

'It was stolen by the Nazis in the Second World War.'

'The Nazis?' Noah's voice was broken in two as he repeated the unthinkable.

'Yes, from the Poles. It had been in one of their precious galleries but they had hidden their most treasured possessions and sadly the Germans found this and other pieces and confiscated them.'

'Stole them, you mean?'

'Yes. Stole them. They stole so much, Noah. The Nazis that is, the imperious party stealing works from whoever they conquered in a way of saying they were the nation of art.'

'Of thieves more like.'

'Of victors, Noah. History has a sad way of repeating this nasty trait. Just go to the National History Museum.'

'And what did the Germans do with the Raphael?'

Flora took a deep breath. This was not good and Noah knew it.

'Hans Frank took them.'

'I know that name. Why do I know that name?'

'You don't want to know.'

Noah sensed what was coming and his head dropped, tears touching his eyes, his brain doing somersaults trying to work out how on earth this had anything to do with his dear and precious and cute and cuddly and deceased grandad.

'He headed up, that is ran, the Poland occupation for the Nazis and oversaw mass persecution' Flora spoke quickly to move on from this fact as quickly as she could, 'but in 1945 Frank fled from the approaching armies with the painting and two others, one by Rembrandt and one by Da Vinci. When he was eventually arrested in Berlin months later by the Allies both these two paintings were found in his hidden crates. The Raphael was not.'

'But this painting that we have could be a copy, couldn't it?'

'Yes, of course,' declared Flora with as much enthusiasm as she could muster.

'But, if it was, why hide it?' said a more and more defeated Noah. He had answered his own question.

And there it was. A great painting, an important piece of history, lying propped against a St Ives wall having travelled through time on an incredible journey. Many people had touched it, taken control of its destiny, only to find it leave them as they left the earth themselves.

'This gallery that it had been at,' asked Noah wanting some more facts, 'you say that it is in Poland?'

Flora pulled up the facts and struggled to read out the name of the museum.

'It was, and still is, the C-zar-tory-ski Museum in Krakow,' she said, breaking the word up to try and pronounce it. 'The painting was bought by Prince Adam Czartoryski in 1798 and added to the collection there. Sadly it appears this was an obvious target for the Nazis.'

'Of course it was. Bastards.'

'And the museum has been trying to get the Raphael back ever since but all information trails have run dry.'

'Right. We may have some information for them then,' said Noah with absolute clarity in his voice.

'Well, yes we may, but there are a thousand and one things to consider.'

'What things, Flora? I mean this painting should be there. It's theirs, not ours.'

'Well, assuming it is genuine, and this is still a big huge "if" Noah, you have to think what returning it could do.'

'Do?'

'To the reputation of the man you adore, Noah.'

The thought hit Noah hard like a sucker punch straight between the eyes. To let this information out could destroy his Grandad's fine reputation and goodness knew what it would do to Natalya.

'How the hell did he get hold of this?' asked Noah, his voice shaking as he did so.

'Well Noah, it was the war, right? Joshua was there in a ranking position. He must have just been in the right place at the right time.'

Noah raised his eyebrows at that.

'Yes I know,' added Flora, 'the wrong place then. Either way, he brought it home and he kept it secret all this time and now he has given it to you.'

'Why the hell did he give it to me and not my Gran or my Mum?' he grumbled.

They let that thought rest in the air between them.

'Maybe', suggested Flora, 'he knew you would do something about this.'

'How?'

'I don't know but somehow, in some way, make sense of this for him.'

'But he told me not to tell anyone!'

'I know, I know. I can't make sense of it. It's just that you and he were so close and so we should not be surprised that he left with you his greatest secret.'

'Right. His greatest secret. This is fairly grim, isn't it?'

Flora nodded her head.

'It is,' she said softly.

The quiet of the room hung in the air.

'I didn't say it was going to be easy, Noah, you having to

deal with this. Joshua knew that too. He was a good man.'

'Clearly not that good.'

'We all make mistakes.'

'Yes. True. But we don't all steal highly valuable, probably now incredibly so, paintings from a nation that was ripped apart by terror and humiliation, do we?'

Flora stood and walked around to the back of Noah and placed her arms around him and simply held him. There was much to think about. History had just walked unannounced into St Ives.

Outside the trees bent into the stiff wind that was falling across the seaside town. These trees were now permanently bowed down into the regal winds that came, used to the power that thrust through their branches. Noah now fixed his eyes on these trees that he could see on the hillside, the very shape they now held adding to the enormous weight that now sat on his twisted shoulders.

'Just leave things be for now, Noah. Let's just let the depth of what we have found out take its place. We'll work something out, Noah, seriously, we will!' she said with force as she tried to get Noah's gaze back.

'It's going to be OK, all right Noah? Noah!'

Noah reluctantly nodded, rose to his feet and kissed Flora on her cheek.

'Thank you. I'm going to take a walk.'

'Shall I come?'

'No, no! I need some time.'

'Of course, I will maybe do some more research,' she said rising and walking with him to the door.

'Yea, sure, thank you,' managed an extremely weary Noah.

'Call me later, yes? Tonight would be nice?'

'I will.'

A quick embrace and with that he was gone.

Chapter 6

Confusion

Tess sat outside the beach café at Porthgwidden beach in the early Cornish evening, the sun with its dance for the day complete having finally dipped behind the island, yet the air still warm enough to be pleasant and to sit outside in. She sat with a large glass of her favourite Pinot Grigio and played with the wine as she moved her glass backwards and forwards watching the grape juice slide up each side and gently make its way back down. She loved to do this, finding the motion and journey of the wine to be almost hypnotic, and it had the effect of calming her. Then, after a while, she started looking through the glass and at how the light was catching the colour of the wine as she looked on and out towards the beautiful bay, its seas playing with the evening sun, and then further to the strength of Godrevy lighthouse.

All the time her mind was working overtime on her dinner partner for the evening, Mikhail Portichenko. He was due to meet her at eight o'clock and Tess had arrived an hour early to clear her mind and try and get her head in gear. It had been two weeks now since Mikhail had arrived and while he was supposed to be returning to Russia in a fortnight he had indicated to Natalya that this timescale was eminently flexible. Apparently he was on something of an extended break from work. He didn't quite call it a sabbatical, but he did say he could take his time. Tess didn't know what to think but Natalya was absolutely cock-a-hoop.

'Isn't that great, marvellous and fantastic news!' she had cooed to her daughter when calling in unannounced to Tess's studio one day with home-baked cakes and wine. Natalya would do this often, never calling ahead to see if it was convenient, assuming the rights of a mother to do what she felt was best. Tess had on occasions tried to tell her mother that calling out of the blue when her daughter was in the middle of work was not always helpful, though much appreciated of course. Natalya would have none of it. 'I am your mother, Tess, and I know what is best and therefore, my dear girl, I shall see you when I want.' And that was it. The dominant and exulted position of mother outranked all other points of view, even that of the normally extremely strong-willed and prevailing daughter.

Tess had smiled awkwardly at the news of her cousin's extended stay, not knowing if it was good news or not. In truth she had warmed to Mikhail. Hugely in fact and, for Tess, worryingly so. He had transpired to be extremely funny, very intelligent, well-read and sweetly attentive. The fact that he was also rather attractive didn't get past her either, much as she had tried to ignore these latter charms. She had found herself recently, without realising what she was doing, staring at the back of his neck from a doorway as he was delivering an amusing diatribe on the state of Russian football to his aunt. His dark hair, greying in places, fell into a point at the back of his neck, a neck that was tanned slightly and was lean and there to be kissed by some lucky woman. Natalya had thankfully not seen her daughter lost in these thoughts and Tess had caught herself within moments and left the room to actually slap her own hand by way of self-discipline. Such thoughts were clearly deluded, unhelpful and absolutely not going to happen, after all Mikhail was her cousin so this sort of thing was unacceptable on an it-all-seemed-very-weird front. Secondly, he was not her type. Tess normally went for men who she found very attractive but ones that she knew she could not get on with for too long. Further, these men needed to be ones that she could dominate. This control was her safety net and the main reason she would never settle down with one man. She'd tried it, several times in fact, and every time they just got in the way. Being an artist meant that having a long-term partner was of no use to anyone. Finally, she had reasoned, a lengthy relationship based in Russia and Cornwall was clearly never going to work. Sadly this last reason made the potential for a relationship with Mikhail quite appealing too. She scolded herself again and had tried to let that thought pass too. It hadn't.

Sitting here in the now cooling evening of a late May day, the light now starting to fade to grey, Tess tried to think of why she had agreed to dinner. He had asked her formally in front of Natalya which was both annoying and sweet. Natalya was overjoyed and immediately charged her daughter to agree to the request. Tess couldn't help but think they had discussed this beforehand and the knowing looks between them didn't dissuade her of this.

'I have nothing to wear,' offered a desperate Tess.

Her mother had returned a don't-be-silly look while Mikhail had just winked at her.

'Oh, OK then,' she had agreed after looking at both faces who were now looking at her lovingly and longingly, 'On the proviso you don't do your loud singing thing in public. It is both embarrassing and an attention-seeking disorder that you really should see someone about!'

They had all laughed at this. Mikhail had already become something of a talking point in St Ives where he was known as the singing Russian due to his want for regularly bursting into song fuelled even more after too many vodkas in the late night drinking sessions at The Sloop. The locals were an inviting bunch and Mikhail was wonderful company.

'Agreed,' Mikhail and Natalya had said together, then looked at each other and laughed uncontrollably like happy schoolchildren. Tess watched them and smiled. Their affection for one another was infectious and sweet, and to see her mother laughing so easily was pure joy to her. Since Mikhail had arrived, Natalya had become noticeably younger. She seemed to have regained her fitness and her vigour and there was no mistaking that the Russian nephew was having a wondrous effect on his grieving aunt. For this alone Tess was prepared to chance a dinner for two.

So now, days later, as she sat on the terrace, pulling her thick, long black Aran cardigan tight around her St Ives-tanned bare arms, she thought of the way Mikhail's face lit up and his cheeks rose high when he laughed, which he did often.

She knew so little of him, but what she did know she had decided she would make a choice to try and like. Indeed at times she had found herself doing more than just liking him and at that thought she found herself blushing. So Mikhail had been accepted by Tess, and that alone was quite a step in such a short space of time. It was an unusual and brave step for this most untrusting of women and Tess had decided to just roll with it.

'*Dobriy vecher!*'

Tess heard the clear tones of her Russian companion for the night and turned to see him arrive, all bluster and smiles, and coming upon her to give his customary welcome of three kisses followed by a huge bear hug.

'And good evening to you!' she replied, her breath having been squeezed in typical Mikhail fashion from her. As he sat down at her side she poured him a glass of wine from the now half-drunk bottle.

'It is a pleasant evening, is it not?' Mikhail declared, a huge grin in place, happiness literally dripping off him as he looked around the view set before him and cast his arm out to the view in wondrous and theatrical style.

'Yes, it is,' replied Tess, 'A beautiful evening and this is the perfect spot to enjoy it.'

'Indeed so Tess. I have travelled the world and this is as beautiful as anywhere.'

Tess looked at him with a more suspicious look than she had intended.

'What?' Mikhail declared in a mock wounded voice.

'That's the sort of thing I would have said. I think you are just humouring me.'

Mikhail took Tess's hand, kissed it in an easy manner and then, still holding her hand, he looked straight into her eyes causing an electric bolt of a hot sensation to shoot through her body.

'I would never say what I did not feel to you, Tess. Know that. This place is magical. I know it and of course you know it better than anyone!'

He stroked the top of her hand with his thumb, his fingers underneath and feeling gently into the palm, every sweet sensation of movement not lost on Tess. Then, with her senses suitably heightened, he gently let go and launched into a story of his day.

Tess smiled and listened to a story of her cousin wandering along a coast walk through to Lelant where he had joined an unsuspecting family from Scotland.

'Those crosses of accents must have been fun,' she laughed and laughed even more as her Russian dinner companion did several Scottish impressions.

'Yes, dear Tess, conversation was at times difficult but the human heart prevailed!'

Mikhail explained that the family had consisted of the parents, a wise old grandfather who looked ninety yet walked like he was forty years younger, four children ranging from three to eighteen and a dog that could have been anywhere in that age group too! He had met them in Carbis Bay on the beach and played football with them scoring, he said with great pride, several exceptional goals. They had in turn invited him to continue the walk with them and so he had been learning this Scottish accent on the way.

Tess listened and smiled through this descriptive and entertaining tale of a day that could have been normal for many, but for Mikhail had the wipe of stardust all over it. She had met many men over her life but none had enthralled her as this Russian was doing. He was a master storyteller, a man who seemed to love the magic of the moments, and she asked him before she could stop the question if all Russians were the same.

'The same? As what?'

'As you.'

'As me?' he asked mischievously. Tess gave him a generous smile that told him she would not be looking to massage his ego any further.

'Well, yes and no. We laugh very well. We enjoy sorrow very much. We embrace it all with Russian vigour of a need to swallow each and every morsel. It feeds our souls, yes? We take to silence when we need to like a well-worn friend. We tell tales that can last a lifetime, each time adding a new picture into the story to add to its grandeur. We hope for tomorrow because that luxury is all we can truly hope for. We live in yesterday because there our hopes and dreams were born or even died, the difference matters not to us Russians because a dream is a dream whether or not it comes to reality. We look for light in the darkness, always happily assuming we will never, ever find it but knowing that it is there to be seen if we look hard enough and we Russians know how to look for light better than any other nation for we have known such depths of dark. Are we all, each Russian, the same? Well, our characters differ. I am a little, as you say, eccentric, but yes, in storytelling, in life, I hope so, each one my brother and my sister, each one my flesh and blood.'

Tess listened, mesmerised, enchanted.

'Let me propose a toast!' declared Mikhail, keen to celebrate his mini speech.

'A toast?'

'To my fellow Russians and to you, dear Tess, a light amongst many lights!'

Tess inwardly glowed at the words, so kind and so happily received. She was enjoying this. They drank to their toast and Mikhail immediately asked for the wine list.

'Would you like to choose?' he asked her, his manners impeccable.

'No, you, please. I chose the first bottle of wine.'

'Then I shall choose a delightful red! Let's see. Ah! A Pinot Noir. From Burgundy too! Well, that's the decision made!'

They made their way into the café and took their seat by the window, its stunning view resting on the now plain to see flashing light of Godrevy Lighthouse, an ever-present glow in the face of darkness.

Over dinner they talked of childhood, of budding dreams, of hopes and desires, and of the flower all these things had grown into. They covered the territory of their pasts easily.

'We are very fortunate are we not?' said Mikhail, easing the red wine down as though he was drinking orange cordial. Tess had purposely slowed down, the early white wine on an empty stomach having taken its toll. Besides, she had learnt early on that you were never going to out-drink Mikhail Portichenko upon whom the effect of drink seemed only to add to his good humour.

'I mean I have all I need and you have all you need and we are happy, yes?'

'Apart from the things we can't control Mikhail, yes.'

'Ah yes. Apart from those things. God rest his soul. To Joshua Spearing. A fine man!' Mikhail declared loudly, raising his glass formally to the night sky from their warm window seat within the café. Tess joined the toast, aware of people stealing a glance, again, at the loud Russian. Pierre, who ran the café, gave her a cheeky smile and she let her right eyebrow acknowledge it.

'And do you have all you need?' she asked, regretting the question as she did so.

'You mean love, don't you?' he replied instantly. It was uncanny how he could seemingly read her mind with ease and Tess felt rather vulnerable with him, yet not uncomfortably so.

'Well, yes, in part, I guess I do.'

'Well, what about you?'

Tess smiled widely at this. She had asked him a question he had instantly avoided!

'Ha! Got you!'

'Got me?' he asked, a broad smile highlighting his question. 'OK,' he said, 'you got me! Well done. What about me, you asked. Well, you know already I am divorced of three years now and I have two children. Both, you know, are now grown up and they are now at university in St Petersburg. They are happy, very opinionated, very strong-willed and very much like you!'

Tess kicked him under the table and he acted out pain as though he had been shot by a sniper.

'Like you I think you mean?'

'Possibly,' he grinned. 'What I did not yet tell you and I tell you now, fair maiden, is I was married once before. It lasted ten days.'

'Married twice? Well, well, well. And the first one for a huge ten days? Impressive stuff. Do you mind if I ask why ten days?'

'Not at all, I will speak to you of anything. It was ten long and tortuous days, each one, I tell you, akin to a year in real life. We were like a hot furnace in lovemaking and all we did was badly burn one another. When we first met, well, within a few hours we were back at her place and screwing like there

88

was no tomorrow.' Mikhail paused here and said, 'Please excuse my language, Tess.'

'Don't be silly,' she rebuked him, 'please go on.'

'OK. Within a month we married. It was only a month because you have to wait that long in Russia to make it official. No one knew. My father would have killed me. Possibly really killed me. Her father, who was Chief of City Police, would most definitely have killed me. The thought and the desire of the marriage we craved kept us from exploding. After we got married we spontaneously combusted and I have the physical scars still I can show you. The mental ones I cannot. I was not prepared for that level of depth that she asked of me. She was, indeed she is, a remarkable woman, but God, she is driven like a strong wind. What is that French wind?'

'The Mistral?'

'Yes. That's it. She is like that. She blew into my life, lifted the very latches from my door, and then blew through me and left me broken.'

As Mikhail talked, Tess was aware of how incredibly serious he was, the depth of emotional scarring spilling out before her.

'She actually physically hurt you?' she asked, not being able to stop the question as it blurted out in confusion.

Mikhail waited, his face dropped to the table.

'Yes, though she did not mean to.'

Silence sat before them for the first time in the night, Tess regretting asking too much. Mikhail looked up, his eyes moist and his stare into Tess's eyes so deep.

'I lie. She did mean to. She is a driven woman. It is her undoing. She wants what she wants and sees no reason why her fire should not explode with hurt of any kind. It is who she is. I don't even know why I try and protect her by saying she did not mean to when clearly she did. She would hit me with a club she kept to protect herself and it hurt. I was tempted to retaliate, really I was, but I could not. It was too much, way too much. I talk of this never but you, Tess, have opened my heart.'

Tess had listened to this and was suddenly aware of her mouth being wide open in the shock of it all.

'And do you see her, now I mean, ever?'

'Oh yes. Absolutely. She is a politician in St Petersburg. Very well known. Very attractive and all over the news and billboards. I cannot escape her. It makes it all very surreal.'

'And you talk?'

Mikhail, who had just taken a mouthful of wine, spat it all back out.

'Talk? To her? Never. We never talk other than when in public we have no choice. We have been introduced often at many events where our paths cross and we are civil. We hate the sight of one another.'

Tess was amazed. Her easy-going cousin, who charmed everyone he met, had a secret that mixed with passion and hate. What other dark secrets were there?

'And your family knows of this marriage?'

'No one knows. Only you now. Just Tess.'

'And the witnesses at the wedding!'

Mikhail paused.

'Oh yes. Them, of course, assuming they still live.'

'She had them shot?' asked Tess, partly out of mischief.

'We chose the oldest people we could,' replied a suddenly weary Mikhail.

Silence returned, the heaviness of depth of memory sitting over them like a heavy blanket, Tess wondering whether to ask more about the ten-day marriage, the last chilling lines about the witnesses, or to move on to safer ground. Mikhail thankfully took control.

'Tess! Enough of me. I have some sorrow. I would not be a true Russian if I did not have sorrow! It was all in the past and I am now here, in this beautiful place with you, beautiful Tess!'

Tess smiled wide. He had the incredible habit of making her feel wonderful about herself.

'Thank you, Mikhail. You are too kind.'

'I am honest.'

'Yes. Well, beauty is what the beholder sees.'

'Ah! I like that. And what do you see?'

Tess blushed slightly.

'I see a kind and warm cousin who it seems is a wonderful man.'

'It seems?'

'Well, I don't know you well enough, Mikhail, to give you

a guarantee, but I am happy to believe the best of you so, yes, let me change that. Who is a wonderful man!'

'Ah yes. I like that,' laughed Mikhail, 'and you find me beautiful too, yes?'

Now it was Tess's turn to laugh.

'I can't comment on that, Mikhail. It is a lady's prerogative.'

'Prerogative?'

'My right as a lady to decline to answer!'

'I see. Well, this is as you say, fair enough. I shall simply have to make my own presumptions.'

'And they are?'

'I cannot say. A gentleman's prerogative.'

It was way past twelve and they were the last to leave the café having spent the final hour with Pierre talking about living in Paris. Apparently Mikhail had once lived there for a year building links between The Hermitage and The Louvre. He had an apartment on the Left Bank and it was an area Pierre knew well. Tess was fascinated to hear the two men talk, occasionally lapsing into French leaving Tess with nothing to do other than follow their words and be amazed by the linguistic skills of Mikhail who apparently, and not surprisingly anymore given the wonders of this man, spoke several languages fluently.

'And this was how long ago?' she asked.

'Oh, ten years.'

'And you all went?'

'The family?'

Tess nodded.

'Oh no. Yana would never have agreed to that!'

'Right.'

Mikhail heard the surprise in her voice.

'We had two children, heavily involved in school. Yana loves her home. I came back as often as I could and she came to visit and brought the children too. We had some good times and I felt I made the best of a difficult situation.'

'Yes, yes Mikhail. You don't need to explain yourself to me. I shouldn't have asked.'

'Just curious?'

Tess narrowed her eyes and let the two men continue to speak of the glories of Paris. Why she had even asked those personal questions was beyond her. Yes, she was curious, very and extremely curious. She had learnt so much more about the man, Mikhail, tonight and yet now, even now, she heard a whole new chapter being opened up before her.

As they later walked along the back streets of Downalong, the oldest part of St Ives and the night now firmly around them, Mikhail placed his jumper around the shoulders of Tess.

'Thank you.'

'You're welcome. I have enjoyed this night, very much.'

'I'm glad,' said Tess, looking into his face and liking it very much. 'We should do it again.'

'We should? Yes, we should! How marvellous! "*The lady cares for me!*"' He sang in a deep rich baritone voice that echoed off the old walls that surrounded them. 'Tomorrow?' he asked, a cheeky grin accompanying the question.

'Soon enough, Mikhail. I shall consult my diary.'

'Well, when you do, I shall accommodate mine to fit yours,' he laughed, a rich intoxicating noise that made Tess smile widely.

They arrived at the back gate to Tess's house. She leaned forward and kissed him quickly, yet softly on his lips, and then turned and left Mikhail Portichenko swooning with happiness. A perfectly divine evening.

Chapter 7

Decision Time

Noah sat on the edge of Zennor Head and did what he had come for; he gave his mind over to thought. Joshua had introduced a young Noah, five years old and ready to take on the world that he knew at that point, to this exact spot many years before. Their walk that day from St Ives had been hard for them both, Joshua with old legs that were willing yet ached enormously and Noah with young legs that were willing yet not used to long walks, but both were very happy to be in one another's company which gave them energy enough when mixed with stops off at a shop and a café for energy pick-ups along the way. The long walk had passed with grandfather telling grandson about stories from the area, of shipwrecks, of stormy nights and of buried treasure. Noah had listened intently, as he always would to Joshua, and the little boy, always a chatterbox and storyteller in his own right, had in turn told his grandfather stories of his own. He told his grandfather of his school where he was well and truly into the swing of things, of his funny and kind teacher, the scary and severe looking headmistress who Joshua managed to hear about and keep a straight face as she was a good friend, of playtime battles, of his love of football and all things Spurs, and of the many things he and his best friend Flora were doing at home. This last list went on for a very long time. It was a walk that over the years they would repeat often until Joshua's legs could no longer manage it, and when they got to that stage they would drive around the bay instead and take a small turn around the headland, reliving past walks and making new memories.

Noah smiled widely at the memory of Joshua. He always did but here, on this spot, he felt his grandad with him like nowhere else. He took his left hand and patted the ground beside him. 'Hello,' he whispered cheerily, quietly, a wave of euphoria sweeping through his hair and making the hairs on the back of his neck stand up.

The views across and out to sea were all-encompassing and spectacular. Zennor Head offered on a clear day, such as this day, outstanding views along the coast of the spectacular tip of south-west Cornwall and the craggy weather-beaten cliffs as they fell into the hungry sea. Here you really felt as though you were coming to the end of the country and the currents, visibly gathering in force and might as they met right there before your very eyes, headed inexorably towards the power of Longships and Land's End. The sea at this point was now very strong and dangerous, as though it was trying to suck the land into its very self. There was a true sense of something magical here the mix of all before you intoxicating the mind.

Being here was a tonic to Noah and one he much needed. The unbelievable shock of the Raphael had thrown him into a period of real upset. His grandad had left no clue, no letter or note, as to why such a treasure, a stolen one at that, had been passed down into his possession. Rather, Joshua had just spoken the words that he was to keep the gift he was passing on to Noah as a secret, an absolute and utter secret. Why? Still this one word burning itself time and time again across his brain. And then there was the huge ask of Noah actually being able to keep the gift as a secret and he had been simply unable to do so. For his grandad's memory he had wanted to keep his promise but the secret had seemed a strange request when he had initially uncovered what he thought to be a simple and old painting. And so he had seen no harm in telling Flora and in that act alone he had clearly broken his promise and in so doing had opened up a Pandora's box. Now, knowing the real reason for this having to be an absolute secret, he was faced with what he should do about telling his mother. Up to this point he had faithfully told no one else though Tess was clearly the obvious next person to tell.

'How can I possibly share this with her?' he considered

94

heavily, the breeze lifting his hair back from his face. How do you tell a proud and loving daughter that the father she adored was a major art thief, news that if it became public would strip the acclaimed and lauded Joshua Spearing of all the dignity he ever had, while he, the once powerful and esteemed man, lay in his grave powerless to protect his reputation. If this news ever broke, his grandad would be on the front page of every newspaper across the world and Tess and Natalya would be hounded by the press as the Spearing house of cards came falling down around them. That was something he could not do but he was sure there was something he could do. It was just the huge matter of working out what that was.

It was late in the afternoon of a mid-May day, a day that had seen four seasons and was now happily leaning towards the summer as the sun finally broke through the clouds hitting Noah with warmth that caused him to toss his head back, his hair falling away from his face, and to close his eyes and let the tension drip out of the back of his neck. A kinder breeze than the one that had buffeted his earlier walk now bathed his face with a benevolent cheer, and for a moment, a precious cleft in time, Noah was lost in the beauty of his surroundings.

His walks to Zennor were not always ones that he now took on his own. Flora loved walking and the two of them would often get out and about across the rugged Cornish landscape and explore. Sadly Flora was currently exploring Rome with her boyfriend, Jake, and the sudden piercing memory of this broke Noah from his sweet haven of solitude. Why had she, his precious Flora, chosen to live with a man who while being admittedly strikingly attractive, friendly and very wealthy at such a young age, did not have the desire to go walking like young Noah did? He smiled at that. He had found Jake's Achilles heel! How could she stay, his lovely Flora, with a man who did not appreciate the beauty of the outdoor life? This was his lifeline. He would use it over a cliff-top picnic on her return from Rome. 'Yes he can give you the world,' he would declare to her, 'but he won't walk it with you and what good is that?'

Noah checked his watch. He was meeting Uncle Mikhail for a quick pint at the Badger Inn at Lelant before the Russian went to meet his mother for dinner, and he would need to be heading back soon if he was going to be on time. His uncle had extended his trip to Cornwall, fabulous news that had made his grandma cry with happiness for several more weeks. The very thought of his uncle made Noah actually laugh out loud causing two elderly passing walkers to look at him in a bemused fashion. Noah gave them a purposeful vigorous wave causing them to walk even more energetically away from him. Yes, Mikhail was a truly wonderful man who had taken to life in St Ives like the proverbial duck to water. Had he really only been with them a month? It seemed like he had been part of their lives for considerably longer. The famous Sloop Inn was alive with him most nights as he intoxicated locals and tourists with his stories of the old country, Mother Russia! The fishermen and artists who would encamp in The Sloop would in turn captivate Mikhail with the mysteries of St Ives and the secrets of the seas. The fishermen were of particular fascination to Mikhail and the coxswain of the lifeboat, Robert Thelwain, hooked Mikhail with his stories of huge and frightening waters that tossed those at peril high in the ocean. The Russian would sit, captivated by every word, taking huge intakes of breath as his heart pumped quickly, his very body alive with the stories as though actually reliving the moments. It was a joy just to watch him almost ride the waves as he listened to the words of tales from the deep. The lifeboat crew would make the ordinary extraordinary, delighted in turn to see this new friend swoon to their tales. Such stories would often, as the night turned to the glorious early hours and the glasses were charged with whisky and vodka, lead to moments of great solemn silence when heroes would be remembered.

Mikhail pledged himself to help at sea, yet when he told them he could not swim but would do his best to learn, the pub erupted in riotous laughter. Together the new friends embraced one another as they sang old Cornish and Russian songs that they taught to each other over raucous drinking nights that went deep into the early hours. Noah would sometimes stay but invariably, drinking and exceptionally scary sea-time tales not being his strong suit, would escape out into the harbour and climb to his house leaving the songs of The Sloop to fill the night air behind him. The very town was awash with the joys of this lively Russian.

Noah had also seen a glint in his uncle's eye whenever they talked about Tess. He asked his mother about this and the thought was immediately dismissed as being preposterous and silly. Maybe it was, maybe it wasn't, but he wouldn't mind at all if they got together. His mother from as long as he could remember had told her Noah that she was a free spirit and had no intention, absolutely none at all, of ever settling down with anyone. Almost his first memory was of Tess saying to him, "It's me and you, kiddo, always just me and you", and it had been and they were very, very close, but Noah had never minded any boyfriend his mother had met, not hoping for a father but just wanting his mother to be happy. It had always been Tess as far as Noah could see that would, after a period of time, pull away to be on her own. Always she would sit her Noah down and tell him why she had moved on. "He was too serious", "he was just too laid back", "he was too old", "he was too young", and on it would go. Noah would just look at her, his open blue eyes able to believe anything she ever told him, and listen. Listening to his mother was always a pleasure, not the words that she spoke, but rather the warmth and tone which reached his ears and bathed his open soul.

Maybe Mikhail could break the spell and catch his mother. That would be good, he thought.

His thoughts inevitably returned to the *Portrait of a Young Man* by the great Raphael of Urbino. What a story, he thought miserably, this great piece of stolen art was here in St Ives. They had been able to establish that it had been missing since being stolen by the Nazis in the Second World War from the renowned Czartoryski Museum in Krakow, Poland. Noah had googled the piece from his phone as soon as he had left Flora's in the forlorn hope that firstly she had got it wrong, and she hadn't, and then that maybe there were just a few small articles hidden away in some corner of the Internet on the subject. Instead he found that there were pages and pages of stories attached to it. His wounded heart had sunk even more as the truth of the reality led him to know that this really was a huge thing.

And so this painting that remained firmly hidden in his

house and probably added value to the day, its current value no doubt an amount that he could never even imagine, continued to dominate his every thought. It was an unreal, dreamlike, fantastic sequence of events that had catapulted the young Noah Spearing from St Ives, English teacher and part-time aspiring poet, to newly set up co-conspirator in an art theft that, all these years on, still lay to the outside world unsolved. Noah had read on the Web of people who gave their lives, committed their very meaning of being, to find such a painting and right the wrongs of the Nazi war machine. There was, therefore, equally the hard fact that there would be many unscrupulous hunters who would come and take such a painting with force and violence and young Noah would be inconsequential. Yes, Noah knew that what his grandad had done was place himself and his family in absolute danger. Did he ever really consider the depths of that, where this secret could have taken them all, would now take them all? He must have done, thought Noah, but he could not level this with how this would have made his grandad feel. How did he deal with this and why, really why, did he place this burden now with his beloved grandson?

And there it came, there, on Zennor Head, as summer seemed to literally arrive around Noah, a sudden and absolute clarity of thought. There was only one thing to do; possibly the reason, the very reason that Joshua had entrusted his Noah to the task. Noah saw, almost as though the thought had been rocketed into his brain, that he had to return the painting to its rightful place. He would take it, in person, to the Czartoryski Museum. His thought processes now went into overdrive as he saw that this was the only option open to him and there was clearly no other choice to be made. To entrust anyone else could allow the secret to be released and this could and must not ever happen. Therefore using anything that could link this painting back to Joshua, to Cornwall, was out of the question. No, this needed doing by Noah's hands alone and he saw this with absolute, crystal clear, pure definition.

Piece upon piece his mind began to build the house of recovery. He would deliver the painting back to the museum by private appointment with the administrator and literally hand it over. Of course he would need to disguise himself and protect his identity but this would be easy enough with enough planning. A back-story would be needed for the appointment and this would need more thought. A long discussion with Flora was also needed when she returned. He knew she would immediately tell him this was not a good plan, that the dangers outweighed easily any conceivable positives, but Noah had already set his face like flint. He was doing this. Besides, the timing was simply too good to be ignored, his long summer vacation rushing up towards him and a trip to Europe was perfectly sensible for an English teacher wishing to examine the poets of the Continent. It was the perfect back-story, the easy cloak and besides he had no other plans. Yes, this would be an exciting trip. A smile lit up his face. The Raphael would be returned and the memory of his grandfather protected forever.

A little later, after Noah had spent time pondering his new summer vacation and managing somehow to not share the news with Mikhail, his mother was pondering whether or not to let the Russian plunder the depths of her heart, or if not her heart, at least her body.

'Tess, you are a grown woman. He is a grown man. You like each other a lot. You've already told me many, many times you like the look of him. I mean, Tess, for goodness' sake, the man's a dreamboat!'

'Sylvy, I know! But apart from all that, what's he got going for him?'

They both smiled.

'Well,' began Sylvia, 'there are undeniable good looks, the fine humour, the great character. There is the not inconsiderate point of the immense wealth and the fact that he can seemingly take time off at will because Daddy has provided cash and that cash could be whisking you around the world!'

'I don't want the cash and I certainly don't want whisking around the world. I've got my home, my town, and that is all I need.'

'Apart from a good shag?'

Tess tutted loudly and Sylvia laughed with a glorious dirty laugh quite loudly. They were sitting under a wall-heater outside The Sloop as the evening drew in on a pleasant end to what had been a less than pleasant day that had started with freezing cold winds and now was redeeming itself with a warm breeze that offered hope for the morrow.

Tess knew that Mikhail Portichenko had been a kind gentleman throughout the times they had been alone. He had never overstepped the mark, but he had made it clear if Tess were willing, he would happily do so. Tess had thumped him hard on his arm when he had voiced his thoughts, an extremely cheeky look accompanying the words, and since then Mikhail had kept any thoughts of having a relationship to himself. This had not stopped both Natalya and Noah asking Tess if there was anything going on between the two of them, and despite strenuous denials, both had encouraged Tess to take things further. It was, if Tess was being totally honest, probably the fact that everyone else was so keen that was the main thing putting her off. The truth was that she thought about him often. He accompanied her thoughts; most of the day when she saw him she found herself randomly playing with her hair and forgetting herself; as though she was a young lady. She would daydream about him and he had even entered her dreams and had done so sexually. These were undeniable truths of her mental fixation on the man and she knew that there was no doubt that she very much wanted Mikhail Portichenko.

'So you suggest what?' Tess asked her dear friend.

'That you give it all a go.'

'It?'

'You know, holding hands, kissing, playing with his willy!'

The two of them laughed like schoolgirls at that, causing several stares. They didn't care.

'So tonight,' went on Sylvia, 'during your meal, give him something to go on and see where it goes.'

Tess smiled. She was to eat a meal with Mikhail at the Porthgwidden Café to celebrate his being with them a month and Tess had already put on a slender white dress and underneath it some very nice underwear.

'OK baby, I will!' said Tess, leaning over to her friend and kissing her on the cheek and standing.

'Oh and Tess?' Sylvia said.

Tess turned.

'Yes?'

100

'Why such deliberation this time?'

'This time?' Tess asked, stepping back towards her friend and sitting back down.

'Yes, you know, this time, this man. Why is he causing you to ask questions you normally don't even think twice about?'

'Oh I don't know. Probably because he's Russian?' Tess replied without any conviction.

'You mean because he frightens you.'

Tess thought about denying the truth but just bit her lip.

'Yes.'

'Well, I read a great book, Tess, and… '

'Oh Sylvy, I've read, as you well know, enough self-help books to fill a bookshop!'

'I know. We both have! This though just hit a spot. Just hear me out honey,' Sylvia counselled her friend who was eager now to get going. 'It's called *Beyond Fear* and it talked a lot about moving past what you feel and you, my precious friend, often get to places with men and then pull away because you don't want to see it fail.'

'So?' stated Tess, pride in her voice.

'Well, this time you've reached a place with Mikhail before you've even started seeing him! This is a first for you, sweetie. It means you're more scared than normal.'

'Oh. I see. Right. I suppose,' Tess offered the words begrudgingly, each one having hit the spot and she knew to be right.

'And I'm just saying, please, this time, go with it. Roll with it. He has affected you like no one I've ever seen before, Tess. He's special to you.'

'Really Sylvy, he's just a man!' offered Tess with false firmness in her voice.

'Yes, but he's not is he?'

Again Tess started to deny what she knew to be true. Again she bit her lip and just nodded. Sylvia held her friend's hand.

'Just ride with this one, Tess. Please. For me.'

'For you?'

'Well, for you too. After all he's bound to be a quite extraordinary lay and I want to hear all about it!'

Two hours later with Tess and Mikhail on to their second bottle of wine, she gently placed her hand on to his across the table. He looked into her eyes and saw the glint that he had waited for since the moment he had met her had arrived. He was very happy.

'I feel like I know this place, this St Ives, so well,' he said, slowly, quietly. 'It is almost as though, in another life, I have been here, like there is something of me here.'

Tess smiled.

'You know, you are not the first Russian to be here.'

'Of course,' Mikhail responded, mildly upset to think that he was so pretentious to think so, although he was and he did. 'Though how my comrades would have found this place is a mystery to me.'

'They found it like everyone else.'

'Oh?'

'Circumstance and word of mouth. The two are like the symphony and the orchestra. Together they produce beauty. Have you heard of Naum Gabo?'

'The designer, yes?'

'And sculptor. He was Russian.'

'Indeed he was. From Bryansk.'

'Bryansk?'

'Yes. Western Russia. South of my beloved St Petersburg, but still western Russia so fine by me, though their football team is not a patch on my Zenit St Petersburg. A class apart you understand and they know it.'

Tess tutted at this. Men and football she just did not get. It made them sound so silly.

'Gabo was a class apart, Mikhail. Do you know his work?' she said, pulling him into line.

'Not really. A little perhaps.'

'It's OK,' teased Tess, 'you don't have to know everything!'

'I don't?' replied Mikhail, part of him clearly on show and clearly annoyed that he had shown a weakness.

'Well, Gabo lived here through the Second World War.'

Now Mikhail was taken aback. A famous Russian had led the way before him to this western tip of England.

'Here? In St Ives?'

'Yes. Here. He found solace and rest. He followed his good

102

friends Barbara Hepworth and Ben Nicholson, both established artists, here, escaping from the streets of London and the bombs that would come.'

'Ah yes, the dreadful war. And Gabo you say was here? Working here?'

'Yes.'

'But my mind is telling me he went to America.'

'Very good,' smiled Tess, 'but that was after the war. During the war he stayed here and he would have shared the same stories with the fishermen that you do in the same old Sloop.'

A huge grin filled Mikhail's face.

'This is marvellous news. I must know more about him. The forerunner to my arrival!'

Tess smiled. The huge self-confidence of this man would normally put her off instantly but with Mikhail it added to his charm.

'I like him,' she said, 'a lot actually. And I think he would have liked you.'

'Why?'

'He was a positive man. He was a Jew. He had seen much hatred in the world. He escaped Nazi Germany in the 1930s to flee to Paris and then London before eventually finding heaven here in St Ives. And yet through it all, and what awful things he must have seen, he was very positive, just like you.'

'Like me?'

'Yes, my Russian cousin. That's what I most admire in you. Gabo said, and I'm probably paraphrasing wildly here, that the creative mind was always positive, always assertive, had no room for doubt. That's you.'

They paused. Words of admiration causing moments of reflection.

Mikhail sat back in his chair, lost in thought, a smile stuck permanently on his lips. The Gabo news had just lifted him to a new plain of delight.

'This is a beautiful place, Tess,' he said, unable to hide his excitement of being out with Tess. He reached across the table and took her hand in his. She showed no resistance, rather squeezed his hand and held his gaze.

He went on, 'And I am still here despite only coming for a short time.'

'Yes, you are still here Mikhail.'

'And you, my love, are the reason.'

Tess studied him. He had been more serious tonight and somehow more sensual too as a result.

'"My love" is it now? We are moving on! And you call me your love just because I hold your hand?' asked an amused and turned-on Tess.

'Yes, my love, if you don't mind?'

'I might,' she said as his eyes continued to look deeply into hers making her feel giddy inside, 'but for now I like it.'

'And what else would you like?'

Those explosive words opened up a core of longing between them. Tess looked at him and saw eyes alight with passion. She knew exactly what else she wanted.

'I would like very much to get the bill, Mr Portichenko, and go down to the beach and look out to Godrevy and up to the stars as you kiss my neck. Then I shall lead you up to my house and let you kiss me anywhere you like. How does that sound?'

Mikhail was overcome with the stunning sensual summary of an evening he had dreamt about.

'It sounds perfect, my love.'

They paid the bill and walked down the slipway to the beach, both of them kicking off their footwear as they did so. Walking across the cool sand to the bottom end of the beach, the sea being out, they stopped by some rocks that hid them from the shore. The natural light of a bright moon and the full array of its orchestra of stars illuminated them. She turned into him and he, bending down, kissed her gently, she receiving the kiss and its electric current. His hands caressed her back and she reached up with her left hand to run her fingers through his hair that fell into his neck. Her right hand stroked his thigh and then, before she could stop herself, she was feeling for his erection causing him to moan as they fell on to the sand. It was moist under them but all feeling of cold just added to their excitement as the heat of sex overtook. Tess was undoing the belt of Mikhail's jeans as he was unbuttoning the buttons on the front of her dress, their hands warming quickly to the arts of passion, the need to feel one another deeply, burning bright under a warm St Ives May night.

Chapter 8

Planning

'So you are planning for an exciting European vacation eh?' asked Mikhail over a darkly-brewed rich coffee in Tess's kitchen. He had stayed overnight again, two weeks on from when he and Tess had first made love, sand clinging to them like conniving friends as they had laughed all the way back to her house up on Barnoon.

'Yes I am!' said Noah with an accompanying large grin, delighted his mother had finally seen sense with what had been staring them all in the face about her and the Russian. 'Europe awaits me!'

'Europe, watch out eh!' replied Mikhail with a twinkling eye. 'And are you as excited as you look?'

'Yes.' Noah thought of his mother and felt the need to add another truth. 'And a little nervous to be honest.'

'Ah yes. The old mix. Nerves will hold you back and excitement will send you forward. The latter will win, fear not, but the mix is important. It will keep you safe, but rely on excitement. That's the woman you want, my dear boy!' Mikhail declared and leaning forward to slap his young friend on his shoulder. The slap was too hard, something that all those in contact with Mikhail had learned to put up with. His hugs too were so breath-stripping that mental preparation was required. Tess had mentioned this to Mikhail on several occasions, telling him that his new British friends were simply not used to such over-exerted physical friendliness. "They would just prefer a chat," she had said. Mikhail had just laughed at this and kept muttering "a chat" and laughing for the whole morning.

'And why now?' the Russian asked.

'Now?' asked Noah.

'Yes, now! Why this sudden urgency to tread the European boards?'

Noah thought. The question was logical and his holiday did seem fanciful and therefore unusual.

'It just seems the perfect time. I mean, I have no other plans, and nothing holding me back, so I thought, why not?'

'Why not indeed, young Noah. Life is there to be lived! Squeeze the juice until there is no more juice to be had!' he declared while squeezing hard an imaginary huge orange in the thin air above the table.

'You're living proof of that Mikhail.'

Mikhail lifted his mug in appreciation of the compliment.

'Thank you my young friend. The compliment is happily received, though I know that I am lucky Noah. Money allows you to make choices.'

'Yes, but don't you need the spirit to make the right ones too?'

Mikhail liked that and he leaned over the table and gave Noah's hair a severe rub of affection. To some people this would have resulted in them needing to adjust their hair but not Noah whose hair was a constant tangled mess of blond wavy hair that seemed to fight with itself and leave his hairdresser an exasperated job. Luckily she was a very close friend with patience to spare and the fact that they spent more time talking about what they were into than over-concentrating on the complexities of Noah's messy mop helped.

'Yes you do!' Mikhail said, 'We can all buy art can we not, be it a Klimt, a Warhol or a Rothko, if you had the money of course, but can we all appreciate it? And what is art but life itself? Who is to say what constitutes art?' asked Mikhail as though addressing a crowded lecture hall, and not just the one student who sat before him enraptured.

'Here, here,' smiled Noah, banging the old coffee table with a thankful thud of appreciation. This had been something his grandad had been used to doing when he was enjoying something that was being said.

'Ah yes, young Noah. Who indeed? One man is content

with a landscape of sea, another needs a Renoir in their cityscape of grey.'

'Exactly Uncle, exactly! That's a brilliant quote, I must write it down. Did you just make it up?'

'Make it up?' asked Mikhail, genuinely perplexed by the question.

'Were the words your own?'

'My own?' thundered Mikhail, 'But of course! I am Mikhail Portichenko! I only deal in the original!'

'Of course!' replied a happy Noah. 'Well, give me the real deal any day of the week.'

'Ah yes, the real deal. And that is why you love your home, your Cornwall, your St Ives?'

'Yep. I've been away but it called me back.'

'Just like your mother!'

'Yes. Just like my mother.' Noah smiled widely at this. He did not see himself as the same as his mother at all, and yet in some things they were so obviously knitted together and when those likenesses were highlighted he liked that very much. It made him feel warm inside, safe too.

'So where will you go on your trip?' asked Mikhail.

'Oh, not sure yet. Still at the planning stage. Where would you suggest?'

Mikhail leaned back in his chair, considering the question with a serious face and rubbing his unshaven chin as he did so as though considering the most complex of questions.

'Well, this is my advice. I would be sure to not miss out on hidden gems while breathing in well-known ones too. How's that? There is nothing quite as grand as finding things for yourself. Go off the beaten track and see what you can find. Tourists and their easy-fodder tour guides don't know everything. How long are you going for?'

'Five weeks give or take.'

'Magnificent! Then you have time to see many things and I need to see all your plans before you go. You must give yourself time to breathe in a place, take in its very heart and soul. Imagine that each place you enter has centuries of history all still there, many that you simply cannot see but if you listen hard enough, you can hear. Listen there in a side street in La Rochelle to an ancient mariner gathering a crew, stand at the entrance to a great gallery in Paris and consider the young Pierre-Auguste Renoir walking in, unknown and afraid. Stand at the great docks of Cadiz and see the Spanish Armada leaving in all their pomp and ceremony, sit in a quiet corner away from the crowds in Rome's enormous Colosseum and hear the screams of the innocent.'

'I feel like I haven't done very much when you talk like this, Uncle.'

'Oh come on, Noah, you have ridden the waves so what else is there?'

'Clearly plenty,' laughed Noah.

'Well, what is your past experience of Europe?'

'Erm, very limited.'

'Tell me about it,' encouraged Mikhail with a smile.

'I will!' declared Noah, picking out another plain chocolate Hobnob. 'Mum and I went to Tuscany when I was little. Maybe six or seven? I remember it being very hot and we had a pool in the garden and there were lots of insects that kept biting her. I spent hours just fishing them out with a net. Loved it! We were next to a little village where we would walk in every morning hand in hand and go and buy fresh bread and fruit and mum would buy me a treat or two. The colours and smells of the place stayed with me, you know? I can almost close my eyes and see the sun coming down through the trees in the garden where we were and settling across the pool where I would jump in and out and I loved it!'

'You were clearly a water baby then?'

'Of course. In St Ives you can't really be anything else!'

'Tell me more about Tuscany, please,' said Mikhail with a happy smile.

'Well, Mum would sit at the café and write and draw.'

'Of course!'

'Yea, of course! I would spend hours in the park alternating my time between children who would come and go and the old men playing with throwing balls endlessly in the shade, well, *Bocce* as I know now of course! I remember the park was so brown, so opposite to what we have here, with so much Mediterranean sun to contend with and trees everywhere to hide from the sun. We went all over the place, all the towns and cities and villages. They included Florence which I just remember being so hot and busy and mum gripping my hand so tightly and giving me several lectures about never letting go. I can remember that grip, you know?' And he does. As he says the words Noah feels her grip on his hand. He feels no fear on that vice-like hold, rather he feels safe as he looks around the city, taking in its busy sights and sounds.

Mikhail watched this young man, aware that Noah has just ducked into his memory bank and he knew he was remembering a moment with Tess. At that moment too Mikhail felt emotion rise and his eyes automatically filled with tears as he sees such a love between son and mother. Do they really appreciate what they have, he wonders?

Noah then launched back into his memories of Italy and neither men notice that they had shared a moment of precious emotion.

'We went back with Grandad and Grandma a few years later and then Mum couldn't really get me to go again.'

'Go again?'

'Abroad.'

'Really? Why?'

'Surf of course. I spend all summer surfing. Well, I spend all year surfing, but summer, well, I have to be here. It's my life.'

'So you never went abroad again?'

'Well, yea, with school I went to Normandy to see the old battlefields of the war one year, and then skiing one year in Avoriaz which was just amazing and I would so like to do that again, but other than that, no.'

'And this summer then? Why are you going now?'

'It is different.'

'How?'

Noah sat back in one of the old kitchen chairs that he remembered from being a child. None of the chairs are in good shape as they were already ancient when Tess picked them up at an antique shop in Penzance when she bought the house. They are English-oak Chippendale chairs that are battered and bruised and typically Tess's choice.

'Grandad,' he says simply and that is enough.

'Ah yes. Of course. Stupid of me.'

Noah shook his head while Mikhail inwardly grimaced at his question. The boy had lost a man that for all time had been his world.

'Well, young Noah, I need to make you a list. A list of passions, of delights, of hidden gems! I shall start on it this very day!'

'Cool! We can have a planning night at The Sloop.'

'With vodka!' smiled Mikhail.

'With vodka!' laughed Noah, while making a mental note to not make that mistake again. The last time his uncle had got him drunk on the drink had seen him look yellow and feel terrible for days afterwards.

Tess walked into the kitchen and there was no denying the glow that came out of her as in her head she said, *'Ah my two boys'* but it came out as, 'Ah, Noah and Mikhail. Talking. How nice.'

'Let me make us some fresh coffee, my love,' said Mikhail, jumping to his feet with panache and pulling a seat away from the kitchen table for her to sit down at, bowing nobly as he did so. Tess duly took the seat, catching her son's eye and the two of them smiling together at the extravagant Russian. He in turn made a show for his small and intimate audience out of filling the kettle, rinsing out the cafetière, inhaling the fresh coffee and then emptying the boiled water into the pot. All of this was accompanied by a tune that he was whistling far too loudly that he had picked up that morning when fetching a paper.

Tess leaned over the old oak kitchen table, battered and bruised with a lifetime of tales, and took Noah's hand into her own.

'Love is it mother?' whispered Noah with a cheeky glint in his eye.

Tess just smiled. Maybe it was.

'He's very affectionate, aren't you Mikhail?' she said as he arrived at the table with her coffee and placed an arm around her.

'You are easy to love,' he said, the words resting between them all.

'She is!' said Noah quickly to break the spell. 'Well, I shall leave you two lovebirds alone. I'm off to see Flora. Monkey nuts is working today so she's all mine!'

'Monkey nuts?' asked Mikhail.

'He means Jake. Flora's delightful boyfriend and the reason my son is lovesick.'

'Ah, you want a taken girl, eh?'

'Well no, not really. I'm quite happy on my own,' replied Noah, far too quickly for his statement to actually be true.

'You want her, don't you?' pushed Mikhail with a certain voice.

'Wants a big word, Uncle.'

'But you do, don't you?'

'I, well, yes, sort of. Actually, and let's not talk about this again, yes I do. Period.'

'Period?' repeated Mikhail looking very confused.

'It also means there is nothing else to talk about,' laughed Noah while Mikhail just looked even more confused.

Noah continued, 'However, Monkey Nuts is pretty much everything I am not.'

'And yet he's the Renoir, young Noah, and you are the real deal.'

Noah laughed and Mikhail walked around the table to his young pupil and slapped him hard on the back in his affectionate Russian manner that left Noah coughing and Tess laughing hard. She could get used to this.

'Don't be late tonight, sweetheart!' called Tess as her son disappeared towards the back gate, stretching out his back as he did so. It was Natalya's birthday party and both Flora and Noah would be there. Noah gave her a thumb's up and a cheeky grin.

'And he really loves her?' asked Mikhail as Tess returned her eyes to him.

'Yes, he loves her. He always has.'

'And he has told her?'

'No.'

'No?!'

'No.'

'But he will?' asked Mikhail, incredulity written in his voice.

'I very much doubt it.'

'Ah, you English are impossible!' declared Mikhail. 'When will you realise you can't win a war if you don't face the issue head on?'

'There's the rub. We don't want a war!' replied Tess.

'My love,' Mikhail took her hand and smiled, 'you do. Your past is littered with wars and I don't just mean your country. If he does not tell her, he does not stand a chance.'

Tess waited, the words working their way through her brain and with her having no intention of letting them settle. She knew that her son's inability to step forward was probably linked to her own attitude towards relationships, an attitude that he had watched over his whole life and no doubt inherited. She also knew he should have done something about it and that she should have helped him and that for her Noah, with Flora, the clock was ticking, but this was life. Maybe they were both destined to not be with the ones they loved. She closed her eyes and let the words disappear.

Mikhail, aware that no response was coming, thought about a thousand things he should now say. He looked at Tess and her set jaw and simply managed, 'You and him are alike, yes?'

'Alike?' asked Tess, opening her eyes and looking at him.

'Yes. The answer may well be staring you in the face but you will not pursue it.'

'We won't?' replied Tess.

Again Mikhail thought through many things that he wanted to say but he could see such conversations could be awkward and all he wanted was his Tess and her laughing eyes back. He took her hand and stroked it softly. In silence they sat, the old grandfather clock ticking in the corner of the room and filling them with its steady, calming rhythm.

'So where are we going for our day out?' Flora said happily as she threw her surfboard into the back of Noah's old, battered blue Defender.

'We, my lovely Flora, are going to Sennen Cove,' replied Noah, as she climbed into the cabin and Noah turned on the engine, igniting his iPhone as it exploded with Jet singing *Are You Gonna Be My Girl*. He had of course lined up the song and took tremendous satisfaction in it as they drove up Higher Stennack and out of St Ives towards Zennor. It was the loveliest way around to Sennen Cove and they always drove this way, happy to take in the intoxicating coastal road with its amazing views that never failed to inspire. The windows were down inviting the smells and sounds of the sea and the heather to touch them. As they drove they talked quickly, hunger ravishing them for each other's news.

'So, I have some rather interesting things to tell you!' started Noah as they left St Ives behind them and drove into the country. Flora smiled. He would often start his sentences to her like he was starting a story, with huge emphasis on the word so.

'So! Do you?'

'I do indeed! It's been far too long since we've actually been able to talk properly, hasn't it?' said Noah, their diaries meaning time together had been at a premium since their huge discovery and this being the first time they could look forward to some lengthy uninterrupted talk around the Raphael without distraction. They had talked about things but only replaying what they had found. Now they would talk about what Noah had decided to do about it all and he was extremely keen to tell her his thoughts.

'Well, will you turn down the stereo so I can hear you?'

'Ah, right, yes. It is rather loud isn't it?'

'And obvious.'

'Obvious?' repeated Noah, not really wanting to be *that* obvious about wanting Flora.

'Yes. Jet. You play them all the time.'

'Ah. Jet. Of course, obvious, indeed. So I do. But they are jolly good are they not and they always make you happy.'

Flora nodded at that, a smile of absolute happiness written across her face.

'Is that better?' asked Noah, turning down the volume.

She nodded again. This time in a way-over-the-top manner that made Noah laugh. He was exceptionally happy too. He had her for the whole day. Jake was working and then off to a snazzy party in Newquay that was allegedly work related.

'Good! Well, are you ready for my news? Yes? Well, I'm going to Europe for the summer!'

Flora first reaction was one of mild panic.

'For the summer? You mean a few weeks?'

'No, I mean the summer, that is five weeks of it, i.e. the summer holidays.'

'Oh,' she replied, her voice low and startled. 'That's a long time then. Five weeks. Wow. I can't really imagine a summer without you here, I mean, St Ives without Noah?' she said, her words tumbling out with a mixture of upset and loss and confusion.

'Are you going to miss me, cute cheeks?' asked Noah innocently, concentrating on the winding roads before him and not for one minute thinking the answer would be such an emphatic yes.

'Yes!' replied Flora loudly, definitely, 'You can't go.'

'Can't?'

'Well, mustn't.'

'Mustn't?'

'Stop just repeating things!'

'Start making sense then,' said Noah, his tone changing to a lower place.

'Well, it's just that it's too long!' She wanted to say "and you cannot miss my wedding" but she had not yet told him about it and she knew now that was not the thing to say. Noah had never been kind about Jake and though she knew that mostly it was all in fun it just did not feel this was the right thing to start on.

'It's summer, that's all,' replied Noah, hoping for more from Flora and now seeking it. 'I'll be back as soon as you can say, well, say lots of things over and over again a lot of times. So, you are going to miss me?' Noah declared with a satisfied smile of mischief.

'Of course I'm going to miss you. Silly boy. We are virtually inseparable, you know.'

'Apart from when you are with monkey nuts!'

'Jake,' she reminded him, having, as she always did, to keep her boyfriend alive in their conversations as an actual person. 'His name is Jake, and yes, apart from then.'

'And when you are with your legion of girlfriends.'

'And then too, though you do turn up quite often even then I've noticed. Well, I say I've noticed, in fact everyone has noticed. They say we are as good as married,' she said and immediately regretted it knowing what she had to tell him and tell him today.

'We are indeed!' replied Noah happily, 'They're all quite correct in this assumption!'

'You are insufferable but you are not with me all the time,' went on Flora, in serious mode and speaking as though addressing her friends, 'I mean you're not with me when I am with Jake,' she paused, 'Actually you do turn up quite often even then, don't you!'

'Apart from the obvious!'

Flora hit his arm.

'He wouldn't thank you.'

'Oh, I don't know. I might inspire him.'

'He doesn't need inspiring, Noah, not when he's got me in front of him.'

Silence then descended over the two of them, Noah upset by the thought of Jake with Flora sexually, and Flora embarrassed by her joke. She was very self-conscious and her line was a surprise to her. Had she said it just to hurt him?

'So, why Europe?' she asked, hoping to move the conversation on from her and Jake.

Noah waited, still brooding over the Jake comment. Flora, knowing this, knew she needed to bring him around and get the thought of her and Jake out of Noah's mind.

'Pull over Noah, just there in the layby.'

They were at Higher Tregerthen, on their way round to Zennor. Here the landscape was open yet somehow also dark and brooding, its sensuality captivating the soul and causing many to just stop and breathe it in. This was most definitely one of the hidden jewels of the south-west of Cornwall. Noah pulled over as instructed and turned off his engine.

'Come on you,' Flora said, getting out of the car and leading Noah up the hill to where they would have a stunning view of the sea.

'Catch me, surf boy!' she cried, a start of ten yards giving her the edge. She was quick and very fit. Noah, fired up by the sight of his Flora in a short miniskirt and her thin, tanned legs running up and away from him, broke into a sprint and caught up with her just as they reached the summit, both falling to the floor and panting for breath as they did so. Noah lay on the ground, not as fit as Flora with cigarettes being his downfall, and now looking up at the sky for redemption as the pain in his lungs subsided. Flora rested on her arm beside him and looked down at him. Gently she leant forward and kissed his forehead with a soft kiss, leaning immediately back and looking at him.

'What was that for?' he asked, still wounded by the thought of Jake and her.

'You know why,' she replied easily, the words sitting before them as plain as day. They did not talk about how they really felt about one another because it was easier not to. Flora knew she was lucky to have Jake and she was happy, but, and this was the big proviso, if you took Noah out of her life would she be happy? Did Noah make her relationship with Jake work? She had never had to think about this before but with Noah now disappearing for the summer she was beginning to think about it now and she did not like it one bit.

'I will miss you over summer, Noah. It's a real shock. I'm just used to you being here and, well, I wanted you here...'

'Why?'

'Oh, you know.'

'No, I don't know,' replied Noah, intrigue now arriving in a traffic jam.

'All I am saying', started Flora, quickly and not ready to yet tell him her news, 'is that I hope you have a fabulous time.'

'Yea?'

'Yes. When do you go and why?'

Noah, the kiss and the unspoken words healing him, pulled himself up on one arm to face her.

'I go to return the Raphael.'

Flora looked at him, incredulous at what she had just heard. Noah saw the emotions flicker through her big, blue and grey eyes, eyes that carried a thousand of his emotions.

'You are joking!'

'Nope.'

'Look Noah, you don't even know it is the real deal.'

'It is.'

'But you don't know for sure!'

'I do.'

Flora looked hard at Noah.

'You are being very obstinate.'

'I'm being realistic.'

She sighed.

'Look,' he said, sitting up now and letting the sun kiss his

116

face, 'we both know we are talking about my Grandad here. It is the painting. If it isn't then I look silly and that is as bad as it gets. If it is the real deal then I have no choice really. I can't keep it. I mean I want to, well part of me wants to. It is a huge part of Grandad and he asked me to keep it but, when all is said and done, I can't. It belongs to the museum, to another country, not to me. It was stolen. A painting that has inspired greed for centuries now must be returned to its rightful place. I have no idea how Grandad got hold of it but he did and it's wrong and it should be back for the public to have.'

'OK. Hold on there. I agree with you, you know I do, and I'm pleased you wish to do this, but why not just return it in an easier way. I mean what about just taking it to the Polish Embassy in London?'

'Yea, I thought about that. Thing is, what if they track me down? Film me going in?'

'Well, what if they do?' countered Flora.

'Grandad. I can't expose him!'

'No. Of course not. Sorry. Well, why not post it?'

'The post could be tracked.'

'Post it from Exeter then?'

'But what if it gets lost?'

'Register it.'

'They will trace me.'

'Register it under a false name?'

'And they still trace me. I mean, Flora, this is big news. A painting worth who knows how much that has been lost for nearly seventy years suddenly shows up. They will want to track where that came from. Listen Flora, I've clearly thought about little else than this and I've considered all the angles and I think I have it sussed.'

Flora waited, her brain buzzing as she tried to weigh up what she was hearing.

'Listen Noah, I've done much more looking into this painting as I know you have and I don't like it one bit. You have to understand that this painting is tainted with many years of rich, evil men using it as a toy. I read that a Polish Foreign Minister only a few months ago was saying they knew that the painting was hidden in a European bank vault; they just couldn't pinpoint which one. My God, Noah, it's actually here!'

'I know,' said Noah softly.

'And I saw a clip from YouTube where some London historian was saying the painting is the most valuable piece of missing treasure from the Second World War that is still out there. He said the value would be in many, many millions. I mean, Noah, this is just way out of our league. You are playing with fire.'

'And Isabella Czartoryski said that the painted young man has "a beautiful face that seems to revive the soul" and he does and it is this purity both in him and my family name that I must protect.'

'Oh come on,' said Flora forcefully, anger in her voice, 'who made you a moral policeman, decision-maker in something so obviously dripping with things that could go wrong?'

Noah simply greeted this with silence. He had not been counting on Flora to counsel him so.

'Noah, Noah. I really am lost to this plan. I mean, you are going to a European country you know nothing about with a language you don't even speak and you are to undertake something that is almost bound to be extremely dangerous.'

'Dangerous? Oh come on, Flora.'

'Yes! You know the this-painting-has-inspired-greed speech you just gave me?'

'Yes. Well, we're not in Nazi Europe now you know.'

'How do you know!' shot back Flora.

'OK. I don't, I accept that,' said Noah quietly, 'but I do know while it sounds fanciful and foolish, well to me it just sounds right. Flora, you know that this painting has travelled across Europe to be eventually stolen by the Germans and then stolen by whoever, making its way to Grandad who probably was involved, no, let's stop skirting around this, was definitely involved. I have to make sure the painting now makes its way back to the actual museum in Krakow, I just have to. This has become something that I cannot shirk from Flora and you have to believe me that I have no other choice.'

'I don't, Noah, I don't have to agree with you at all. I think you are mad and I want to tell your mother!'

'And if you do I shall never speak to you again!' replied Noah angrily, forcefully, standing as he did so, their words now stuck in their heads and in the space between them. Eventually Noah, regretting his anger sat back down, Flora's face still set like stone as Noah took her hand, which she let him have, and softly said, 'Look, this would break my Mother and my Grandma. You know this, don't you?'

'I guess,' offered Flora with an uncertain voice.

'If you want to tell them then do it. I will, of course, always speak to you because to not do so would kill me,' said Noah and caused a small smile to escape from Flora's mouth.

'I won't tell,' she said, 'but I will worry with every minute I have, Noah, about you.' She turned to him now and her big tear-filled eyes took him in and told him she was genuinely afraid for him. 'You will promise to back out at any point won't you if this ever got out of hand?'

'Yes, of course. Listen I intend to deliver this in person to the director and tell him I have copies of everything so that they can't brush this under the carpet. The painting will then be back, where it belongs, and on show for all. This is our safety assured.'

'And how will you stay unknown?'

'I will be in disguise.'

'But they will trace you, Noah!'

'I have thought about this but I have to take the chance. I have researched the director, a man called Henryk Padowski, and he seems more than honourable. He is a local and educated man who has been there for years. Speaks fluent English of course, and looks really kind.'

'Looks really kind?' asked Flora, the resignation of knowing Noah was going through with this releasing in her the need to just support him.

'Yes. Well, you know, open face. He's forty, looks tanned and fit. Apparently keen on tennis. Greying hair but still looks the business. He has a family and lives in Krakow.'

'Blimey, you have done your research!'

'I didn't get where I am today... '

'English teacher in St Ives... '

'Without knowing my onions.'

'You do make me smile.'

'It's wind.'

Flora kicked him.

'Anyway, I believe he will be a confidante and understanding to my cause.'

Flora shook her head, confusion reigning.

'You can't know that, Noah. You can't go all that way on the hope that this man is as kind and understanding as he looks in photos.'

Noah said nothing, both of them knowing his mind was set.

'So you are really going to just walk right in there?'

'Yes, though as I said I am going in disguise.'

'Tell me about it,' laughed Flora.

'Well, I'm going to shave my hair off for a start when I leave St Ives and dye it dark.'

'Shave off your hair!' shouted Flora in anguish. She loved his scruffy hair. 'Noah! It's been messy and long and beautifully sun-kissed blonde as long as I can remember!' Flora said this with real emotion. She couldn't bear to think of him doing this.

'It will grow back. It's only hair!' said a surprised Noah.

Flora stroked his hair and Noah fell on to the ground in catlike mode, both of them laughing as he did so.

'You can't shave off your hair and dye it dark,' said Flora matter-of-factly.

'I can't?' he mumbled, knowing that if she didn't want him to, he wouldn't.

'No, you can't. Why not just wear a hat?'

'A hat? A hat! Brilliant! I could just wear a hat and keep my hair! Seriously Flora, I would never have thought of that.'

Noah wasn't being sarcastic. He often amazed himself how he managed to look past the blindingly obvious.

'I know. That's because you are a man and the most obvious things are lost on you.'

'You're not lost on me,' Noah said easily and quickly.

'True, but I'm not obvious.'

Flora now gave him a very long look full of concern and care and, if only they both knew, love.

'OK,' she said, 'but you must stay in touch with me at all times. This will ruin my summer!' she said.

'You could come with me?' replied Noah, hopefully. The thought had crossed his mind and he even thought the two of them would be a better diversion for anyone who showed any interest in him.

Flora's face dropped. She looked at Noah, full into his eyes, tears again filling hers as she did so. Noah returned her gaze, not sure what was happening but then his mind clicked in to what she was saying without speaking any words. He dropped his gaze to her left hand where there, on the wedding finger was an engagement ring.

'He asked me in Rome and I've just not had the right time to tell you. We will get married this summer.'

'Summer! Now? Whatever happened to the all-time classic twenty- year engagement, Flora?!'

Noah stood up. Flora did likewise.

There was a pause, both of them trying to find the right words to say about an obvious path for Jake and Flora that they had both been avoiding for far too long now. Noah spoke first.

'I'm pleased for you, for you both. I really am,' his words said without emotion and plainly, almost cruelly.

Flora placed her hand on his arm.

'I mean, it's not as if I didn't know this would happen,' he went on, 'and Jake is good for you. He offers you a tremendous future. He's sadly a generally wonderful guy.'

'He is. And so are you,' Flora replied, aware that this could affect their most precious friendship and so needing it not to.

'Yes, but I'm just plain, old Noah Spearing. You covered my credentials so clearly earlier, simple English teacher at St Ives Comprehensive with nothing to offer other than myself which is clearly not enough.'

Noah tried to offer his speech with a voice empty of bitterness. He did not succeed.

'Not enough for what?' asked Flora, wondering what Noah was actually saying.

'For anyone,' replied a very dejected Noah.

'Whoever gets you, Noah, will be the luckiest girl in the world,' aware as she said this that the thought of Noah with someone else was not one she would warm to and almost certain that another girl would not want the close friendship with Noah and her to continue.

Noah waited, hoping for his Flora to declare her love for

him over Jake, but knowing that this could not come. Jake was Mr Everything. At the side of him Noah just felt lacking. He always had. He had always known deep down that he could never be enough for his beautiful Flora. He turned to her.

'You know I really like you, Flora. I always have, but I could never truly satisfy you. I know this and you know this. We don't talk about it ever because it has been easier not to but now, well, now we must.'

Flora heard the words and did not know how to deal with them. Noah went on.

'I wander in my mind like a demented OAP and you're about the only one who loves me for it! I am genuinely pleased for you both.'

The day waited around them. Even the gulls seemed to stop mid-flight as the pain of an inevitable future bled into their minds, never to be pulled back, to be wiped out.

'It is wonderful news,' declared Noah with a sudden found strength to break the spell, 'as is the fact that I cannot attend said wedding as I will be abroad getting jiggy with some Polish surf girls!'

'Polish surf girls?'

That made them both laugh.

'Oh yea, they are hugely into surfing, seriously. Google it!'

Flora just laughed.

'Honestly! A place called Chalupy, I think.'

'Now you're just making names up!'

'I'm not! Well, maybe I am, but seriously there is good surf there, and I'm going to go and get in it and you and I, dear girl, need to get to Whitesand Bay and get into those waves. I'll beat you back to the car!'

They almost fell into the car as they ran down the hill and then, both putting aside the awkwardness they both felt because that was the easiest thing to do for both of them, they went to Sennen Cove, parking as they always did in the far car park past the huge lifeboat station and the fabulous chip shop they would often visit. They got changed at the back of the Defender, both so used to each other's bodies having grown up with one another. As Noah pulled off his old, torn Quicksilver T-shirt he revealed a toned and tanned torso that reflected hours of surfing in the water.

'Looking good, Mr Spearing!'

'Why, thank you, Miss Trembath. You are looking fairly hot yourself,' Noah offered with a huge smile on his face as Flora was at that point just pulling on her wetsuit and was in a rather compromising position bent over.

'Kindly avert your eyes, Mr Spearing.'

'I will do no such thing, Miss Trembath. My eyes are fully trained on your derrière.'

Five minutes later they had run along the promenade wall, down to the beach, into the sea and were swimming out on their trusted boards. Whitesand Bay was in all its glory, the sea already two thirds of its journey out and leaving a huge expanse of beach. The tourists would not arrive in force for another two months, though in truth this bay always had room compared to the busier beaches on the Atlantic coast. The breakers here could run for upwards of hundreds of yards on a good day and today was such a day. The two of them spent an hour of uninterrupted joy in the sea pausing at times past the swell to talk about the waves they were catching and the others that had caught them and tossed them high into the air for fun.

After drying off at the car, Noah offering to help Flora with her wetsuit and Flora offering to help throw Noah off the sea wall, the two of them got themselves a drink at The Old Success Inn and waited with their Guinness and glass of dry white on a bench in the sun by the car-park wall for their bowls of excellent thick, juicy pub chips to arrive. The sun was warming up. Maybe it would be a good summer. The road, the only road in and out of Sennen Cove, was quiet, and they looked across it to the sea and the sun in the west that was on its way down.

'Is your Grandma excited about tonight?'

It was the 28th of May and Natalya's birthday, her first since Joshua had died, was to be celebrated at Porth-la-Chy that night. Sylvia and Flora were doing all the cooking and they had been up since way too early getting it all ready. Noah, Tess, Mikhail and Natalya's dear friend, Enid, were all to be there.

'Of course. I think the added bonus of Mikhail keeps driving her forward.'

'Thank God he came.'

'Yes. I think without him the grief would have been far harder.'

'And not just for her.'

'No, indeed.'

The "Mikhail" effect on the family had been huge. His character was very uplifting but also the very fact that a new branch of the family had suddenly appeared with all the fabulous mystic of another country was in itself a wonderful diversion from their loss.

'He and Mum are getting rather close.'

Flora looked at him, a big smile on her face.

'Really? I can't believe Sylvia has not said.'

'She's sworn to secrecy. Only the two of us, and now you of course, know.'

'Not Natalya?'

'Well, not exactly. I mean, she knows all right. She was talking to me all about it in a roundabout coded way when I was round doing the gardens the other day. I just nodded and said I was sure she could be right. You know Grandma, she can read minds.'

'Yes, she can,' laughed Flora. 'She is one of life's beauties.'

The chips arrived and both tucked in with a surfer's hunger. Next to them, in the car park, was a stunning old Jaguar in dark blue, which Noah was drooling over.

'What is it?' asked Flora.

'A truly beautiful E-Type Jaguar Roadster.'

'Looks posh.'

'Indeed. Delectable, isn't it?'

'Well, as cars go, yes it is, and you know cars mean nothing to me.'

'Enzo Ferrari said "it was the most beautiful car ever made" and he's right. One day, eh?'

'When they release you from the Polish prison.'

'I shall return and buy such a car.'

'From the proceeds of your book *The Polish Prisoner*'

'Yes, that's right, and how my sweetheart waited for me, putting off her marriage to monkey nuts until she knew I was returned safely.'

'And sadly missing out on dear Jake as the forty-year wait

had been too much for him and he had given himself to another.'

'Leaving the door open for the heroic... '

'Yet now decrepit and arthritic, Noah Spearing. Sadly the freezing conditions in the Polish high-security prison doing for him.'

'Yet still alive and thankfully his manhood intact, returns to claim his bride and drive her in his new Jaguar.'

'Technically being driven by me as your knees have given way.'

'And drive her with his replaced knees paid for by the Polish High Commission in recognition of the miscarriage of justice from which they were paid enough euros to purchase the said car, to her long awaited honeymoon.'

'At Sennen Cove, where once again they surfed side by side on specially commissioned boards for old arthritic folk.'

'And they were happy ever after.'

'Amen.'

They picked up their glasses, Noah on his second pint of Guinness and Flora on her second Sauvignon Blanc, and they raised a toast to this happy, yet in some ways tragic story, of an epic passion and a flame that would never die.

'I'm going to miss you this summer, Noah Spearing.'

Noah held Flora's gaze.

'And I you, Miss Trembath.'

She wanted to say she needed him at the wedding, that without him the whole of the impending summer suddenly felt empty and devoid of fun. She wanted to say she felt happiness sweep through her body at the very thought of being with him, that when they were together she felt light and carefree.

She simply said, 'Come back to me safe, surf boy.'

'Oh Mikhail,' exclaimed Enid, after a flowing and highly expressive run of compliments about her dress, 'You really are the most perfect gentleman.'

'And if you weren't married, Enid, I would challenge that view!'

'Don't let that put you off, young man,' replied Enid, winking at Natalya as she did so, the two of them dissolving into raucous laughter that the Russian pulled out of them effortlessly and with glee.

Enid and Natalya had been close ever since they had met by chance at the harbour beach on a sunny summer day twenty-plus years earlier. Both of them were there with their only grandchild on a perfect, glowing St Ives moment where all seemed at peace and all seemed possible. Noah was playing in the sea, a water baby from birth, and Enid's grandson, Tim, had decided to seize the day and pulled his shorts down to wee freely in the sea. Noah, seeing this as a golden opportunity that he would be churlish to miss out on, followed suit, the two young boys shouting happily to one another as they did so. The grandmothers rushed to stop the show and amidst laughter hit it off immediately. Enid was a Cornish lady, having been brought up in St Just where she had met her husband, James. They had moved to St Ives when James had spotted a business opportunity and purchased an Estate Agency off an older man who was retiring after running the very trusted local business for many years. They had never looked back since and now a still highly energetic James, despite being sixty-nine, continued to run his highly profitable and much grown business and he had no intention whatsoever of retiring. He was president at the West Cornwall Golf Club where he was hosting a dinner that night but had assured Natalya that he would be round just as soon as he could to toast her and her birthday. They were all very close and Joshua was extremely missed by them all, their parties of four around the world now with a gap that could never be filled.

'I love your delicious dress too, Enid!' declared Natalya with great extravagance.

'Thank you, dear. I got it in Falmouth yesterday, at *Trudi's*.'

'Ah, *Trudi's*. Of course. It's been too long.'

'Well, she asked after you as you would expect and I assured her next time I go I will be taking you.'

'Well, we will see,' smiled Natalya, making progress all the time but not enough to yet go clothes shopping. 'Come over here and take a seat my lovely friend. Dinner is about to be served.'   •

The two of them took their seats at the large dining table, the room so elegantly lit with two huge dimmed chandeliers and numerous lit candelabras that reflected off mirrors and windows and gently bathed the party in a refined golden glow. Conversation flowed easily as the first course served by Sylvia and Flora of a pear and chicory salad with spiced pecans and a Roquefort dressing, was hungrily enjoyed by the small party that also included Tess and Noah. The little group of seven began their feast.

'This is delicious, Silvy!' declared Natalya.

'Yes it is and don't thank me, this is all Flora's doing!'

Flora smiled, a faint blush touching her cheeks as she did so. Tess looked at the girl, who she liked a lot, and wondered, as she often did, whether her Noah would ever tell her what he really thought.

'Well, Flora,' went on Natalya, 'you really have excelled yourself. You must come over on your day off next week and give me the recipe.'

Flora nodded happily.

'That would be lovely. Coffee time?'

'Yes, coffee and biscuit time as ever, my dear.'

Flora loved Natalya. The older lady had a way of making her feel loved and warm and safe. It was Natalya's gift.

'I suppose you have heard of Noah's European vacation?' Mikhail asked Flora, addressing her but using his loud, theatrical voice to address the table too.

'Yes. It all sounds very exciting. Europe is such a fabulous place. So much surfing to do!'

Tess immediately noticed the melancholy in the young girl's voice and noted it to mention to Noah later.

'Ah yes the surf! You two like that don't you!' declared Mikhail noticing nothing at all. 'Me, well, I can hardly even swim and sadly have all the balancing skills of a very drunken man, so I wouldn't be very good!'

'Have you tried it, Mikhail?' asked Natalya.

'I have indeed, Aunt. Young Noah took me out early on, convinced as he was that anyone could learn to surf and that I would be a great success. Sadly it was a disaster and even he had to accept defeat.'

'He was terrible,' laughed •Noah, 'just awful. I recommended he have lessons but he thought that a most amusing joke.'

'Because it was! I don't need lessons on anything. I either get it first time or I don't get it at all!'

'And you apply that to everything in your life?' asked Sylvia, with a mischievous glint in her eyes.

Mikhail, who was in full flow having had, as he often did, too much wine on an empty stomach answered without hesitation.

'Everything! Absolutely everything. It is the only way. It is the Russian way.'

'And this applies to matters of love too?' she asked, smiling as she did so and Tess, sat to Sylvia's left, immediately hit her best friend's leg under the table.

'Ah love. But of course. It is the best of ways to fall in love. I know when I meet someone what I feel at once!'

He stared longingly at Tess from across the table, who in turn gave him a hard stare, none of which was missed by the all-seeing Natalya who simply stored it all in her hard drive.

Enid, in an effort to save Tess's embarrassment, asked Flora,

'So will you be going too with Noah, Flora?'

It was an innocent question which Flora could not duck, though she was not sure how to deliver the news of her whereabouts to the audience around the table. Noah saved her.

'No Enid, she wanted to but she can't as she has some fabulous news of her own!' To his great credit he had delivered all these words with the utmost enthusiasm, in no way betraying the sadness he felt. 'Flora and Jake at last tie the knot while I'm away!'

'Oh lovely!' beamed Natalya.

'Absolutely fabulous!' joined in Enid, immediately thinking of another new dress and hat she would buy.

Tess stood, walked around the table passing her son purposely on the way and gently squeezing him on the shoulder as she did so, and went round to Flora who she kissed lovingly on the cheek. She had known Flora since she was a babe and in many ways Flora and Noah were like brother and sister. She had realised this may well stop them being a couple but had never tried to put her son off. Only he could do that. Now maybe he would move on, the spell of Flora finally broken by her marriage to Jake. This could be the making of him she thought hopefully, doubt though pulling at her and causing a sadness to rise.

'Congratulations, my sweetheart. He's a very, very lucky man. I hope he realises just how lucky.'

Flora smiled, embarrassed to be the centre of such attention and wanting the moment to pass as quickly as possible.

Mikhail rose, glass in hand, ever eager to declare a toast and even the unquenchable Russian aware of the discomfort Noah would be feeling.

'To Flora!'

The table joined him.

'To Flora!' they declared.

Much later as Noah walked down the hill with his mother, Mikhail having been told to stay with Natalya that night to allow Tess to walk alone with her son, they talked.

'So my boy, my darling boy, how are you?'

Noah knew the chat was coming and was happy to talk. He needed his mother's loving arm this night. It was a dark night with only a hint of a breeze but rather cool.

'Brilliant, stroke pretty crap to be honest. I've been better.'

Tess wrapped her arm into Noah's.

'We have to talk about it sweetheart.'

'Seriously, we don't.'

They walked a few silent paces.

'But we do,' she said softly, the truth of the words falling around them.

A few more paces, both aware of the noise of their steps and the night enveloped around them.

'And you love her still,' she said, the truth a matter of fact that fell out easily into the road.

'Aye.'

'And you want to be with her.'

'This is really helping, Mum. The sort of speech that would not have sent the men over the top in Flanders.'

They waited for a car to drive past them and Tess pulled her scarf around her neck for warmth.

'OK. Well, dear, are you sure you want her?' she asked as they approached the cemetery where Joshua now lay.

'Yes,' Noah replied hopelessly.

Tess swallowed hard. There was only one true course of action and she delivered it.

'Then you must tell her.'

'She knows, Mum,' said Noah, stopping to look at his mother who turned to hold his gaze. 'She knows! We do talk you know.'

Tess thought of how best to get these next few words out.

'I know you talk, my love, but I suspect you talk in riddles.'

'No, we don't,' he answered, way too quickly.

The sounds of the coastal night wrapped around them. They started to walk again.

'Well, maybe we do,' Noah conceded, 'but she knows.'

Tess knew her answer immediately but waited a few steps before she said softly, knowing her words needed to be calm to have any chance of getting through.

'So you've actually said to her, today, "Flora, before you do this you need to know I love you and I want to be with you for the rest of my life!"'

Noah laughed aloud at this.

'Of course not! How could I say that?'

'Because it's the truth, Noah. It is what you feel, and unless you say it, and you need to, you will never know how she would have responded. You will ask yourself this question for the rest of your life and its weight will hold you back for all of your time on this earth.'

'No, I won't ask this question, Mum! More like you will ask me the question for the rest of my life!'

Noah's voice was now a little sharp. He didn't need this. He was hurting enough and he had enough to deal with without this curve ball of a suicide mission for his feelings. They rounded the top of the hill and started their descent past the Tregony B&B and towards Tess's house. Tess tried again.

'Look sweetheart, I cannot tell you what to do. I never have and I am not going to start to do so now. Only you can do what you feel you should do because anything else will just be empty. I just feel she has a right to know.'

'She knows.'

Tess swallowed, keen to not overstep the mark at this critical conjuncture.

'I don't believe she does know, Noah.'

130

'How do you know, Mum? Have you become Mystic Tess?'

'Could be money in that!' she laughed, keen for the joy of it. 'Look, I just feel it's worth a shot. I am your mother and I am a woman. Just maybe Master Spearing, I know best here?'

'Look, let's just for a moment assume you are right, and she doesn't know truly how I feel.'

'Yes?' said Tess, seeing the light through the door that was beginning to open, the truth starting to creep out.

'Then if I tell her how I feel it could ruin everything and I can't take that chance. Our friendship relies on us being with others. We've always done this. If I just blurt out undying love then it will kill us as best friends and goodness knows what Jake will do to me.'

Tess, relieved to hear the honesty of the situation declared to the St Ives night sky just said, 'It's a choice you may feel you have to make, a chance worth taking.'

'It's not,' he said, quietly, almost inaudibly.

They had now reached the corner of Barnoon Hill.

'Come in with me. Don't go home tonight.'

'Mum, I'm twenty-four! I can look after myself. Don't worry about me, seriously, don't. You know I am not fine, but you know I was always going to have to face this so let's just not make a big thing about it.'

'You are twenty-five next week actually,' Tess said, smiling and wanting to ease her son out of his sadness.

'Indeed. A quarter of a century!'

'Which is why you need to stay in your old room tonight after I have made you some thick white toast plastered in golden syrup, with hot milk!'

Noah literally stood still at the offer.

'Golden syrup, you say?'

Tess nodded, a smile of love beaming.

'And hot milk with brown sugar?'

'Yes!' beamed Tess.

'Well, in that case, old room here I come.'

Ten minutes later the two of them were sitting around the kitchen table eating food that two hours earlier they could not have envisaged they would find room for after a delicious four-course meal. They had not mentioned Flora again. Enough had been said for now.

'Mum, can I ask you a question about Grandad?'

'Of course! We can always talk about Daddy.'

'Did he ever talk to you about the war?'

'Oh yes, lots of times! It was his favourite subject when I was a little girl, still so fresh in his mind of course. Mother used to give him a Paddington hard stare, but I think she really loved the stories as much as me. He talked to you too though didn't he, many times about the war and his stories no doubt blown up out of all proportion to entertain you even further?' Tess asked nonchalantly having no idea what Noah had been going through.

'Yes, oh yea. It's just that he said a few things, you know at the end that confused me a little.'

'Mmmm darling. What?' she asked, sipping a strong black coffee that would fuel her brain to start working as soon as she had put her son safely to bed. She was looking forward to getting into her work, ideas now beginning to build up at last, Mikhail for too long having been a distraction and this had annoyed her.

'Well, nothing big. You know, just stuff that I didn't know.'

Noah had not really thought through how to present this and now that he was here he was thinking on the hoof as how best to get the words out as he raised the subject. Thankfully the several coffees at grandma's mixed with the fresh night air had helped.

'He said', ventured Noah, 'that sometimes he would be given strange and unusual gifts.'

'Really?' said Tess, half interested but still concentrating equally on her delicious peanut- butter sandwich.

'You are listening aren't you, Mum?'

'Of course I am sweetie. Strange and unusual gifts you said.'

'Yes. Well, what would he mean by that?' asked Noah, throwing the bait out into the water.

'Prostitutes?'

'Mother!' declared Noah, always more shocked by his mother than she would ever be shocked by him.

'Well, I don't know. Who knows? Animals? Meals? Dreams?'

132

'Well, I got the feeling he was talking about something more literal than dreams. Something that he was given that made him feel uncomfortable.'

Tess now stopped eating and looked at him closely.

'What did he say he had been given?'

'Well, that's just it, Mother, he didn't. I thought you might know.'

Tess just looked confused. Clearly she was hiding nothing because evidently she didn't know anything.

'Look, I am sure if there is anything maybe Daddy was just preparing us for what we might find in his stuff after he had gone.'

'And has Grandma found anything?'

'Not that she's said to me. Mind you I doubt she's been through too much. She boxed a lot up and just put it in the loft letting time pass before she even thinks about it. She is using the out-of-sight-out-of-mind tactic. I suspect what she has hidden away won't see daylight until she's gone too and then we can have a good root around.'

'A happy and pleasant thought, mother!'

'Well, if you don't want to wait I'm sure Mama won't mind you looking sooner.'

Noah looked at his mother, now tucking into her third white crusty bread sandwich lathered in peanut butter. He loved her very much but was aware her mind was already on the work that she was now piling in calories to get her ready for. It was time for him to retire to bed and let her get on with it.

'You've been most helpful,' he said with a hint of sarcasm.

'I thank you,' she said, mouth full as she did so.

300 yards down the hill the painting by a certain Raphael sat safe in the loft of Noah Spearing's house. The great Raphael, who had known closely other artist greats such as Leonardo Da Vinci and Michelangelo, had never himself travelled to Cornwall, but now a small piece of him sat here, still, quiet. The portrait had been hidden for so long now, the extraordinary brushwork, clear and concise, the work of the great painter unseen and stolen from the adoring public gaze. Art historians and antiquity dealers the world over had a view

on just where one of the great stolen paintings of all time was now hiding. None would have placed it in the old harbour town of St Ives. However, had the young man in Raphael's masterpiece had ears that worked, then he would have heard the noise of breaking glass in the lounge downstairs as an intruder made their way into the house. It was done with great care so as not to alert any neighbours. The burglar was counting on no one being up in the neighbourhood at 3am and it was a fair assessment for no one was.

In the house the burglar came and went about the business they had come for. Each room in the house was meticulously searched, the intruder seeming to know that no one was at home. After an hour or so the house was once again quiet save for the fact that part of the window was missing in the lounge so naturally more of the night made its way into the house than was normal. The great painting, hidden still and untouched, rested once more.

In his old bed, the room unchanged from his sixth-form days with wall-to-wall posters of surf legends and bands, Noah slept soundly which was just as well because come the morning he would have a shock waiting for him that would shake him to the core.

Chapter 9

Someone's Watching

'Good morning darling, sleep well?' asked Tess, Noah gradually waking up to the sounds of his old room and the smell of fresh toast enticing him to come out of his sleep.

'Morning Mum,' managed Noah through tired eyes that were almost stuck together.

'Sleep well?' Tess asked again as she sat on the side of his bed and stroked his hair away from his eyes. Many children outgrow the touch of their parents, somehow finding that the tenderness of their childhood must be replaced by an adult strength of character that includes a "Do Not Touch" sign to their former doting parents. Not Noah. He had grown up in the loving clutches of his grandparents, their friends, his mother and various others, all of whom seemed to delight in ruffling up his hair and giving him the biggest squeeze they could. Uncle Mikhail was just the latest hugger in a long line of them.

'Aye,' he managed, his left eye opening wide now and turning to some fresh juice sitting on the breakfast tray on an old, battered bedside table.

Tess stood and walked over to the curtains, half opening them and then, in turn, slightly opening the sash window to let the sounds and air of the morning come flooding in.

'You slept at all?' asked Noah as he sat up and took the juice from its place on the tray to his mouth.

'Sleep? Pah!'

Noah laughed.

'I have something for you,' she said, disappearing from the room as she did so.

Noah, the day waking him up, drank his orange juice and waited in the sweet intoxication of being somewhere he loved. Tess returned within a minute and sat on the side of his bed holding to her chest a photo frame turned to her.

'Is it a picture of you?' Noah smiled, causing Tess to laugh.

'Not me, no, you cheeky boy, although it is someone rather close to us both... '

Noah did not need to ask any more questions as Tess handed him an old black and white photograph of several young men in military uniform. They were positioned in a group, seven of them in all. Snow was all around them and the men smiled happily at the camera, three stood at the back, two kneeling in the centre and then two sitting on the floor, both of whom were laughing heartily. This was no smile forced out for the camera shot; rather, this was a group of men clearly having the time of their lives. Joshua was one of the men at the front, Noah recognising him immediately as his mind connected a few old photos of his grandad and grandma in old photos of them at their house.

'He looks happy, doesn't he?' laughed Noah.

'Yes, he does,' replied Tess, happily. 'I thought about the photo after you had gone up the stairs to Bedfordshire. It's the only one I have of him from that time. Somewhere along the line your Grandad lost his old photos but I found this one and sneaked it out.'

'Lost?'

'Well, Mama has always detested the glorification, as she saw it, of the war Grandad fought in, she hates any sort of violence as you well know. On one of Grandad's trips away she gathered up any photos connected to the war and hid them all in the loft.'

'Really? Wow! That must have been upsetting for Grandad.'

'Yep. It caused quite a differing of opinions though Grandad got over it once he worked out she had simply hidden them and not burnt them as she suggested! She knew he sneaked up to the loft to visit them from time to time and he knew he better not talk about them. On the purge Grandma had missed this photo. I found it in one in an old drawer and felt sneaky taking it! To be honest it has been hidden in the corner of my studio so Mum wouldn't see it so I want you to have it where I am sure it will have pride of place!'

Noah thought about saying he couldn't possibly but then simply nodded, a huge grin on his face as he looked down at the photo of seven men in greatcoats, protected as much as they could against the weather and no doubt blissfully unaware of the grim fate that many of them would face.

'They look really young,' Noah said, the faces of the servicemen all seeming to hold his gaze.

'Yes, they do. There's no date on the back or any clue in case you were thinking of taking the frame apart. I would guess this is some sort of training for them or they are just out for a lark. There are no guns, look, or anything like that, just the military uniform to give away what they are involved in.'

'Yes,' said Noah softly, 'just the military uniform. My God, what would become of them?'

Two hours later and Noah's world was being upturned.

'And you are saying that nothing, absolutely nothing, has been taken are you?' asked PC Permain in a dull, solid voice that he kept purely for business.

'Yes I am. Nothing that I can see anyway.'

'And you say you don't have an alarm?'

'No, I didn't say that. I do have an alarm as you well know and hence the sensors you can see clearly in every room and the big red box over the front door,' replied a now extremely weary Noah.

He had arrived home just before lunch. He had an afternoon of household necessities he had to deal with and then he was to get freshened up and go out and meet his friends in the harbour-front bar of Hub to celebrate his birthday. Technically this wasn't until the following Tuesday but that was when he was back at school so Friday night made sense to all. It was funny he thought that school still dictated his going-out nights despite the fact that he was now an adult. The wary lot of a teacher.

As he had approached his house he had seen his cat, imaginatively named Jumpers, looking particularly sorry for herself. She had limped over to him and he saw she had a small cut in a paw. Thinking nothing of it other than telling her off for not taking more care and attention, and of course she understood every word, he had arrived at his front door and crunched some glass under his feet. Panic within him had immediately been set loose as he had run into the house shouting manically to his neighbour, John, at the top of his voice. John Devereaux, who lived next door, was a kind, elderly man who rarely missed a trick on the happenings around Victoria Road and Place. Clearly, last night he had.

Without waiting, Noah ran straight upstairs taking two steps in a stride and could see at once that the loft was firmly shut which he took as a good sign. A burglar would never have replaced the hatch back down would he? Even so Noah got his trusty stepladders from the pantry downstairs, climbed back up the stairs with them and then climbed the rungs of the ladder and was just about to turn his attention to the loft door when John arrived.

'Now then, laddie, what's the problem? You'll have all Johns in St Ives town coming around to you shouting at the top of your voice like that.' John was part mumbling and part shouting himself. 'Now then, where are you, Noah? Noah?'

Noah didn't want anyone to see him going anywhere near the loft so he took a large sigh and climbed back down the steps and moved the ladder away from the landing and went downstairs. He picked up Jumpers and showed his old friend the cut on his tabby's paw.

'What am I looking at?' asked John, his eyes clearly not what they were and in truth the cut was so small that it would have taken someone with very good eyesight to see it.

'The cut!' exclaimed Noah in a voice that suggested he was showing the old man the cat's leg literally hanging off. 'In Jumpers' foot. There, look!'

Jumpers for her part had moved on from the cut, her interest now taken up by the bowl of biscuits Noah had got out for her to distract her from her misfortune. If she could have said "put me down" she would have done. The look she gave them both did the job just the same.

'Ah yes! I see it now!' John cried, a voice of euphoria filling the room.

'Good,' replied a relieved Noah.

'I can, of course, see nothing,' added John, laughing, 'I was being sarcastic, trying to keep up with the humour of you young folk.'

'Right. I see. Well, the point is I've been burgled!'

'Really?' That perked the old man up. He was as surprised by the news of the burglary as he was that he didn't know anything about it. Nothing usually got past him.

'When?' the older man asked, upset and anger already beginning to fill his mind.

'Last night.'

'Really?'

'Yes, really.' Noah was wondering why he had called for John at all. 'Look, can you please phone the police while I have a look around.'

'The police?'

'Yes, you know. Funny hats. Not a nice uniform. Poor sense of humour. The cars make a *nah nah* noise.' In times of crisis Noah invariably turned to black humour. He found it comforting as it deflected from any truths he really should have been facing.

'I suppose they do,' mumbled John as he made his way out of the front door to his house making a *nah nah* noise low and under his breath.

Noah looked at Jumpers who was happily eating more biscuits than she had ever seen in her bowl. She looked fine. The cut must have been a small one and no blood could be seen on his slate-tiled floor. He would get her looked at as soon as he could. He now turned to leap three steps at a time, catching the top step as he did so and falling heavily into the landing skirting board.

'Ow,' he said aloud as he looked up to the loft just as John again appeared at the door.

'I say lad, there's glass out on your front porch!'

'Yes. Thank you, John. That would be the burglars!' shouted down Noah from the top of the stairs as he pulled himself up.

'Burglars! Indeed. Just dreadful. Shall I clean up the glass?' he asked, making his way to Noah's sink to get a dustpan and brush to do the job.

'No, John!' he shouted too loudly, 'The police will need to see all that. Evidence.'

'Ah yes. Of course. Good thinking. Perhaps I had better phone the police then.'

'Thank you. Much appreciated,' Noah managed through clenched teeth. His head was beginning to bang. At last though, alone, Noah turned, got the stepladder and got up into the loft. He immediately saw he was in the clear. He had drawn a faint line on the hatch where it rested against the wood in the ceiling. The mark was still perfectly lined and so with a steadying heartbeat he climbed up into the loft. The Raphael waited for him untouched and safe. He could have wept and probably would have done had he not heard footsteps in the house and the voice of Mary Devereaux shouting up.

'I've brought you some cake, dear. It'll help. Now then,' he could hear her saying, 'let's get that kettle on. Plenty of sugar. That's what you need, and cake, plenty of cake.'

Mary was clearly not concerned about tampering with evidence. Noah smiled to himself as he closed up the loft again. They were safe. Him and his grandad's great secret remained safe. Suddenly, the need to receive a sugar-rush arrived with force and he went downstairs to satisfy his need.

Within twenty minutes the police, that is PC Permain, who had cycled across town on his super sporty police pushbike all gleaming black and his pride and joy, had arrived and was taking notes.

'And the alarm didn't go off because?'

'Because it appears I didn't put it on? I thought I had. I'm sure I had actually. Maybe it's broken.'

'Broken? How?'

'How am I to know that?'

'And it was last tested when?'

'Tested?'

'Yes sir, tested.'

'Tim, please don't call me sir. We did go to school together and we are out together tonight so let's cut the crap shall we. Look, the bloody alarm didn't go off, because if it had John and the rest of the neighbourhood would have heard it.'

'No need for the language, sir!'

Noah gave PC Permain a stare of impatience.

'Sorry, Noah. Just following procedure. I know this is hard but we have to ask basic questions.'

'You always were adept at basic,' mumbled Noah, receiving back from the policeman his own look of frustration.

Noah nodded.

'OK. Sorry.'

'Maybe the burglar dealt with the alarm?' offered the officer.

They walked together outside and looked up at the alarm box which had clearly been tampered with.

'It would appear your burglar knew what he or they were doing.'

'Yes, it would. An intelligent type then.'

PC Permain stood for a moment and considered what was before him.

'So why would a professional burglar, and looking at that we can assume he was, target your house in the middle of a tight-packed and frankly crazy place to carry out a burglary, and then steal nothing? It makes absolutely no sense whatsoever. It would appear he has targeted you and you alone and yet he steals nothing. Noah, why?'

Sadly, Noah thought he might know the answer and was now asking himself why he had been so stupid as to call the police before he knew if the painting was safe and anything was stolen. "Less haste more speed" rang as a chastening call in his head.

'I have no idea. Just bad luck on my part?'

PC Permain looked at Noah and smiled.

'There's not something you are not telling me here, is there?'

'Like what?' asked Noah too quickly and with a hint of anger in his voice.

'Well, you must agree, this does seem strange.'

'What, that a burglar has struck?'

'No,' replied Tim patiently. 'That a professional burglar has struck here in half-term week when the place is pretty packed. They've taken a huge gamble to break into your house and steal absolutely nothing.'

'Maybe they were surprised?'

'What, by your menacing tiger-like cat? By a full moon? Come on, Noah!'

'Look, I don't know, Tim. I must have been lucky, that's all.

Something spooked them. I've been lucky. Everyone's a winner.'

PC Permain seemed to give in at this point. He had three reports waiting to be written up and then a few errands to run before getting home, getting ready, and getting out for a big night out on the town.

'OK. Well, it still seems odd. My inspector will say the same.'

'Listen Tim, I'm the bloody victim here, remember? I'm lucky. As you say, the town is busy so someone somewhere must have been moving around and made him leave. Why me? I have no idea. Maybe another wasn't so lucky and you won't find out until an out-of-towner comes in the summer and finds they have been burgled.'

'Yes, yes, of course. You're probably right. Listen, you have a thorough look around and let me know if you come across anything missing or anything strange. Anything, you hear me? We'll have scientific around later but I doubt they'll find anything.'

'Thanks.'

'And you're still on for tonight. Not too spooked?' asked Tim, with concern in his voice. He was hoping to entice a young lady from the birthday party back to his later.

'Yea, sure. Shit happens.'

'Yes it does, though thankfully not too often around here. OK, well, take it easy. You've had a shock. Plenty of sweet tea and cake.' Officer Permain smiled as he bit into another large piece that had just been given to him.

'Yes, well, no worries of a shortage there with Mrs D around. Thanks man. Appreciate it.'

PC Tim Permain patted his friend on the arm, finished off his cake by placing a huge last piece in his mouth, and then left Noah to his thoughts.

It took Noah four tiring hours to be truly happy that there was nothing missing. During that time Mrs Devereaux had brought in three cups of heavily sugared and very strong tea, huge cheese and pickle sandwiches for lunch, two more slices of cake, one a liberally spread home-made strawberry jam sponge and the other a winning coffee and walnut, and all the latest gossip that she knew, which in Mary's case was quite a lot. Despite trying his hardest not to take any of it in, Noah learnt all about Joy Simms' unexpected news of a grandchild given her daughter was fourteen, Horace Shoreham's mix up when he locked himself out of his car at Godrevy Point and only wearing a T-shirt, Shirley Wheaton going away to Cyprus despite her fear of flying and heat and being abroad generally, and then the continuing saga that was Jean Whitehead's on-going plumbing issues. The list was never ending yet strangely comforting as Noah tried his best to think through why he had been burgled, that is to say why someone had broken into his house yet taken nothing. The obvious answer had to be knowledge of the Raphael, yet no one knew about it apart from Flora so it couldn't be the obvious answer. He decided to go and clear his head on Porthmeor beach in the surf. He now had just under three hours until he was meeting up at Hub and in the sea he could free his mind and concentrate on nothing but flight and motion.

The air was now cool with a strong breeze hitting him as soon as he got to the Island Square and turned to go down Island Road towards Porthmeor Road and then, turning right at the newly designed Sail Lofts, he arrived at his hallowed ground, Porthmeor Beach. He loved this walk above any other, his bare and hardened feet feeling sand and grit crunch below him as he carried for this ride his old classic Rip Curl surfboard that he loved as much as anything else in his world. He had four boards in all, each meticulously kept waxed and ready, but choosing his old and favourite surfboard, now looking quite tired yet thankfully well looked after, was an easy choice after the day he had endured.

The relationship between him, his boards and the sea was very personal and would be hard to explain to anyone but a fellow serious surfer. To be able to be together for so long, play together, fight together and rest together forged bonds non-surfers would know nothing about and would struggle to understand. There was a zone a surfer could get into and if they did, it was pure magic. For Noah he had over the course of his lifetime known that zone on this beach more than anywhere else. It was, for him, truly home.

The night was now verging on quite cold and there were,

therefore, only a handful of amateur surfers out which would make things easier. He zipped himself up and as he did so spotted a few of his good surfing friends out at sea, which was four hours off reaching high tide. Running into the sea with his board under his right arm he jumped over a few initial waves and then dived onto his board, bobbing under each wave as they came to welcome him. The surf was good tonight and he knew immediately that he would have a good session. Within minutes he had caught his first wave, gliding on its underbelly as he weaved and bobbed his way along its smooth curve. The wind and swell combined with his ability gave him a ride of beauty. As he caught wave after wave he felt somehow cleaner, sharper, easier in his mind. Nothing seemed to matter in the water. There was no right or wrong. It just was what it was.

After forty-five minutes or so he got out past the waves and rested on his board for a while, looking back to the shore and in particular Porthmeor café where Sylvia would be orchestrating with her small and trusted team the performance for the night. There would be Flora, Jake's Flora, her beautiful smile lighting up the place as she danced on her stage. He loved to be out here and look back to her, his unspoken girl, on shore. How would he feel when she was married? Would he still be able to surf so easily here? Later she would come round to Hub and meet everyone who was still out. Unlike many girls who Noah knew, Flora would not go home and get dressed up, spending enormous amounts of time on how she looked doing her hair and her make-up, not that Noah would have minded particularly if she did but he knew she would not. Instead she would simply come as she was because she wanted to be there as soon as possible and she saw nothing to be gained by spending time on herself. 'I am what I am,' she would say to him. And she was. To Noah, Flora had a simple beauty, an inner peace that had always touched him.

A wave, a long way from shore and starting its journey inwards now lifted him and Noah took it as a sign that it was time to get ashore and get ready. As he rolled in he thought still more of Flora. She was now lost to him and there was nothing he could see that he could do about it. The surf had calmed him though, stilled his inner spirit. It would be what it would be.

He thought then of Jake and wondered, just wondered, if Flora had told him of the painting, under strict secrecy of course, and that Jake's greed had got the better of him. It was a ridiculous thought as Noah knew that, (*a*) Flora would not have told Jake and that (*b*) even if Jake had found the painting what the hell would he have done with it? He was hardly a professional art thief! He dismissed the thought and filed it under ridiculous though its little roots of doubt had already begun to dig down into the earth of his mind.

It was getting on for half past eight when he eventually made his way down the steps from Victoria Place and began to walk along the wharf through the busy night to Hub, his drinking venue for the night, which was waiting happily for him just round from the trusted lifeboat station. Noah was dressed simply with some old and battered white G Star trainers, the plastic falling off the back of them and the sides being scuffed and marked. He wore faded Diesel jeans, again an old pair that were too long in the leg and as a result the hem at the back was now totally gone. The jeans rested on his hips, his white pants standing out above them in a look that his mother thought was hilarious. A white shirt with the sleeves rolled up just above his elbows and with the two bottom buttons undone to reveal his tanned and surfer-toned stomach and then the three buttons undone at the top of his shirt revealing his long necklace of beads that Flora had got for him. She had bought them back as a gift from a trip to Thailand she had made with Jake the year before and Noah wore them often, most days in fact, his hand often caressing the beads without him even thinking about what he was doing. They comforted him.

It was always hard and pretty much impossible for him to walk across the wharf without bumping into several people he knew, a problem exacerbated by the fact that he was now a teacher in the small town too. Thankfully, many of the older pupils who were now into going out would make their way to Penzance or Newquay for an evening where they could enjoy clubs and a far greater choice of hostelries than those on

145

offer in St Ives. Still, he repaid many greetings with greetings back and only Summer Davy's mum managed to stop him long enough to engage him in talk around the English exam which she thought had been far too hard for her dear daughter.

'Summer will be just fine,' he had said, knowing that in fact he had rarely come across a pupil so away with the fairies and that getting her to a grade standard was proving quite tortuous.

Just past The Sloop and there was John Devereaux who was just leaving the Balancing Eel with a package of hot fish and chips and on seeing Noah his alert eyes lit up.

'Now then lad, you look fabulous, although I can see your pants. Are you losing weight lad?'

'It's the look, John,' Noah replied, a big grin meeting his dear old friend.

'Right. Got you. I will recreate it for Mary later. I'll tell her it was your lead that did it.'

'Brilliant. Go for it.'

'Are you ready for your big night out then?'

'Yea, John. Looking forward to it. Are you coming over?' asked Noah, genuine and hopeful his old friend would oblige. The Devereauxs were popular with all of his friends as whenever they went to Noah's house, cake and biscuits were on tap from next door.

'I would, young lad, but these old bones want a good sit down. It's been a hectic day and besides tonight I am on guard duties.'

'Oh don't worry, John. They've been and gone now and I doubt very much we shall see them again.'

'Aye, but better safe than sorry. I want you, lad, to not be out tonight worrying. I've got my eyes on your house good and proper. Mary's taking the back door and I'm taking the front.'

Noah laughed at that and would recount the statement several times throughout the night. The Devereauxs were priceless.

'That's brilliant, really brilliant and much appreciated.' Many years of knowing John meant Noah knew it was pointless arguing with him. The Devereauxs wanted to act as security guards and so they would do just that and, better than that, they would enjoy it too. Besides anything, it was comforting for Noah to know the house was being looked over while he was out. The break-in meant he knew he was in trouble and he needed any help he could get.

'You're welcome, laddie. A lovely young man like you and it's the least we could do. Now then stay out as long as you want. I am, as you know, a night owl.'

This made Noah laugh again as he knew full well that John Devereaux was normally tucked up in his bed by 9pm at the very latest and indeed had been clearly fast asleep when the burglar had struck the night before.

'Indeed. Thank you. Have a nice night and enjoy those fish and chips!'

'Will do lad, and don't worry about bringing a girly back.' John winked extravagantly at this. 'Mary and I will be discreet,' and with that he walked off at pace, leaving Noah with a broad smile and with a much lighter heart than the one he had been carrying before they had met.

A quick glance at his watch showed he was running rather late and therefore a quick detour to his mother's to see if she was OK was now out of the question. He had phoned her and told her of the break-in and she was mortified and wanted to see him. Maybe he would call in later. She would almost certainly be up as usual until gone 2am.

'Where have you been?' shouted Tim, who was on the steps of Hub looking decidedly chipper.

'Oh, you know, busy day and all. Small matter of a break-in.'

'Yes, I know, but you must forget all that now. Turns out there were several break-ins last night so I am sure you were just one of a run. Nothing you can do now, son, so come on and get pissed,' Tim said, putting his arm around his friend and leading him into the loud and happy music in Hub. One of their friends, Mark, who they had all called Digger since they were young, a reference to his amazing ability to dig the most enormous holes on the beaches, came over to Noah to give him a big hug. Digger was one of the regular house DJs and he would be mixing up many of Noah's favourite tunes for the night. Noah then made his way to the bar to be greeted by the bar staff who he knew very well indeed. The night promised to be much fun.

'Hi, birthday boy!' greeted Sarah, 'Usual?' she said, already getting his Guinness glass into position to receive the black stuff.

'Thanks, honey. Yes please. You good?'

'Yea. Good. Busy tonight which is especially good.'

'All here for me!'

'Yea, right! I'll let you think that! Anyway Digger's got some great tunes lined up.'

'Of course he has. Digger's always got some great tunes lined up.'

'Hey man!' It was Sam. His best friend and, after Flora and his mother, his closest confidant.

'Hey man!' Noah replied, turning to give him a bear hug as he did so.

'Bad shit about your house, dude!'

'Yea, I know, but it's all cool really. Nothing gone, just the alarm knackered and that was as old as the house!'

'Yea, right. I'll fit you a new one for free.'

'But you're a postman?'

'A small yet valid point, I grant you. But I know a man who can.'

'For free?'

'Not exactly but as near as dammit. Leave it with me.'

'And it will work?'

'Of course it will bloody work!'

'And this won't involve Sparks will it?'

'Of course it will. He is our electrician friend, Noah.'

'And a danger to himself.'

'Ah yes, but that just adds to the charm of the man.'

'The danger!'

'Yes, especially the danger!'

Guinness arrived and drinks all round for a large group who had all gathered towards the back of the room and in front of the DJ desk. There for Noah were Tim's potential new girlfriend Alison, Charlie and his funny hat, Sofia and her inseparable twin Macey, Georgia, Nasher, Grant and his girlfriend Josie, Trudie and her boyfriend Gunter, who had come to Cornwall on holiday, met Trudie, and never gone back home to Munich, and dear old Bernie. All had been a tight-knit unit at the sixth-form college with over half of them having been at St Ives Comprehensive and birthdays were almost a religious date in the diary for them all when they would all gather dutifully at Hub to celebrate each other's golden moment. Missing were Flora and Jasper who were both working in town and would arrive later, Jessica, who lived and worked in Sydney and had a fair excuse, Noodles, who was serving time for possession of drugs, Samantha, living in London and unable to get the time to come, and Dominic, who no one had a clue where he was or what he was doing, his family having moved to Scotland just as they all left college. The first toast as ever had been to Dominic, wherever he was.

'And now might I propose our second toast of the evening,' called out Sam and easily gaining the attention of the group of happy friends. 'It has been our honour to know, and indeed, love, and in Sofia and Alison's case, make looooove to, dear old Noah.'

Noah simply shook his head in embarrassment. Sofia called out, 'I was asleep,' and Alison, who still hoped for her time again with Noah reached over to her dear friend and stroked his arm. Sam went on.

'Of course, I too would very much like to have my way with him but he is a hard man to pin down. However, the West Master is strong and cunning and Mr Spearing, I will have my day in the saddle with you, dear boy, oh yes I will!' Everyone happily laughed along. Sam knew how to hold an audience. 'Anyhow, we are here to celebrate your birthday my dear best pal in the whole world. Twenty-five years old and you don't look a day over thirty! The pollution in the sea continues to erode your admitted good looks and dye your mad scientist hair, but you are still looking hot, hot, hot particularly with that fine chest on display. And so may I, on behalf of us all, raise a glass to you and wish you a very merry, happy, and sex-filled birthday!'

A loud cheer went up and Digger, on cue, took the turntables and released the sound of a "Cash Cash" Basement Jaxx remix into the air.

It was getting on for eleven when Flora finally arrived. Noah had been able to talk at length with all his friends and had enjoyed a really good night, the endless banter soothing his worries around the break-in. He and Sam had been plotting their weekend and the two of them were to have the whole of Sunday, that is the part of Sunday after they both woke up, on a coastal walk to Zennor and then a long session at the Tinners Arms which would involve an enormous dinner and several pints followed by a lift home. Noah loved Sam dearly. They had been friends since being little eleven-year-olds having met at St Ives Comprehensive, young, giggly boys who together ensured they never really grew up. Sam never left St Ives, living with his father, his mother having died the year previously up in Ayr in a beautiful old and large house that overlooked the ocean. Sam was intelligent and quick-witted but had never had any intention of filling his time with work. He lived to surf and spent every spare hour in the sea. He worked as a postman because it kept him fit as opposed to his diet which was dreadful, and the flexible hours worked brilliantly with his social life. He had enjoyed the company of many girlfriends and aimed to keep it that way. He had no ambition other than to remain close to his friends and never leave St Ives and these were ambitions he was immensely good at fulfilling. He was also well known for having the biggest mouth in St Ives, not because he gossiped out of malice, rather he couldn't help himself. It was his great weakness and meant Noah would never be able to tell him about the Raphael.

When Flora walked into Hub to be met be her friends, they all crowded around her wanting to see her ring and talk about Jake. Sam walked over to her and gave her a big hug and whispered in her ear, 'It's a huge mistake.'

She pulled back from him and smiled.

'Thank you for that, Sam. Your encouragement as ever is much appreciated.'

Sam over-egged a huge bow and simply said, 'He does love you,' and let his gaze lead them both to Noah who at this point was engrossed in conversation with Digger. He had seen Flora arrive and had decided not to join the run to view her ring.

'Of course Jake loves me!' she said loudly for the friends around them both and turning her back on Sam she talked of the ring and the wedding plans and Jake. As she did so she filed Sam's words so that she could revisit them later. She knew that Noah loved her and, indeed, she loved him dearly too. However, she had convinced herself that this was the love of deep friendship, not that of a deep passion that would be needed to light up a marriage, but rather as a best friend that she intended to keep. And yet, and yet. The truth was that she had, on occasion, thought of Noah that way and she had liked it. She had liked it a lot but he had his life and they had never crossed that line. Just once, after buying him the beads he wore so often and seeing them on his chest and thinking of stroking that chest, had she seriously weighed up asking Noah if she could ever be sexy for him, if she could ever fulfil the role of lover. It was an impossible question fraught with the most hideous of consequence of losing him and she had been unable to do so, wilting away from the danger of the subject, waiting instead for him to make a move that never came. Sam's words told her that there was something wrong here and she knew it, fear nagging at her soul, but the game was afoot and her Jake was wonderful and this evening was not about to be spoilt by her getting lost on silly daydreams.

Flora stole a glance over towards Noah and she saw Alison talking earnestly to him. Alison was a very attractive girl, voluptuous and gorgeous and every man's dream. She knew Noah and her had enjoyed more than a few nights together and looking at them now they would no doubt enjoy another night of passion tonight. No, Jake would do for her. He was very successful, knew what he wanted and was very kind to her. She was a lucky girl. Everyone told her so.

Hub was now buzzing and very busy and now Digger had free rein to play old school music and he did so causing the crowd to erupt and turning the place into a small club on the harbour front, moving up and down as a Faithless "Insomnia" mix seemed to play forever.

At some point later in the night Jake and a few friends had arrived and had taken residence by the door looking out to the May night sky. They had been drinking all night on a pub-to-pub trip across St Ives and normally immaculate Jake was somewhat worse for wear. Flora was dancing in the middle of the room with Sam and Sam, being Sam, was using his many moves on her, moves that were somewhat suggestive and certainly on the borderline of risqué. Not that any of that mattered to Flora and Sam who were simply dancing and enjoying themselves as they had done many times before. They had known each other pretty much all their lives and were very close friends. The Noah factor was huge for them both and on occasion it did cause a few issues with them both wanting "their" Noah and the other one having got there first. Sam knew what Noah thought of Flora, knew the love he felt for her and knew the passion he felt too. He also knew that Noah felt very plain at the side of Jake and had been resigned to losing his Flora for some time. It was just great, this night with them all celebrating Noah's birthday, that they could all come out and enjoy themselves.

Flora at this point was lost in the music and lost to the room. Nothing at this point mattered to her. Flora, though, invited attention. She was very slim, her body toned from surfing and the fact that living in St Ives meant walking up and down hills all day long. She was a dream to watch as she danced easy movements as the music washed over her.

The punch that sent Sam crashing over the floor and into the bar was therefore unexpected and as soon as it had been delivered, precisely and with real force, Jake left before being forcibly ejected, his posse of friends blocking the door and allowing him to walk off alone into the night air. He did so only after standing over the now heavily bleeding from his nose Sam to see if he wanted to get up and have some more. He didn't. The room was still dancing and only the small section around Sam had cleared to see what was happening. Jake, aware of the faces turning and of Flora not even acknowledging him and tending to Sam, had then turned and left.

Jake, confusion now overtaking him and shame arriving far too quickly at his absolute and utter stupidity, took the walk along the front, past the lifeboat station and along Pednolva Walk. The moon was out and its light cast a stunning glow across the sea. Its magic tried to reach out and soothe Jake who was still fighting his demons of anger, still very much drunk and suddenly extremely tired.

The evening's end had very much been out of character

for Jake who was in essence a very focussed young man. He had grown up seeing his father be immensely successful and been told he was expected to carry on the family tradition. There was never any doubt that he would do just that and every action as he morphed through life demonstrated this. At school he captained every team he was ever in, he won every race he took part in and he excelled in education in general. He left school with straight As and then went to sixth-form college and did the same. It was all a walk in the park for him. His life was simply that easy. He didn't bother with university because it would have been time lost to earn copious sums of money, which he immediately began to do. He now ran a chain of surf shops with his father and had his own brand of surf gear that went around the world. They had been offered obscene sums of money for the brand but would not sell for another five years at least. They had a plan and as ever would stick to it. Jake was a man with clear goals and only he would decide when to sell.

Despite the out-of-character punch to Sam, a punch he was now deeply regretting knowing that he could never take it back and the impact it would have had on his Flora, he was not an unkind man. He was generous, very generous to those that were close to him, friends and work colleagues alike and he was already calculating what this would cost him to win round all those he had just alienated.

He thought of Flora, sweet Flora, in whom he saw a beautiful girl who gave him balance in his life, something that he knew and fully appreciated that he needed to even out his life and keep him from being a parody of himself. And yet Jake did have a dark side, a blackness that descended upon him when he could not get his own way. In the main he kept this in check, a skill his father had taught him, telling him from being a young boy that he was a chip off the old block. He was. And yet when drink dulled his senses he could find himself lose control and that had just happened in the most violent and, he knew, pathetic way. He liked Sam. Everyone liked Sam, but in that moment his brain was telling him that Sam was humiliating him, making him look inadequate, and therefore he, Jake, had no choice. No, when the dark mists arrived, Jake's brain told him that he ran this town, he was St Ives' shining son and everyone needed to know that. He, Jake, was the one who stood out and who, with his father, owned so many of the properties in and around the area. People respected Jake, bowed down to him almost. Why should he just stand there while this inadequate man, this man who couldn't even get a proper job, danced so suggestively around his beautiful Flora?

As he walked up Skidden Hill, the devil and the angel dancing on his shoulders and shouting at one another, Jake was aware of steps behind him, steps that he ignored for a while and then thought he had better just check in case that idiot of a postman, Sam, had come back for another punch. Jake knew no fear. He was a beautiful specimen of a man. Tall, incredibly toned and very muscular. He turned and to his surprise saw Noah.

'Noah?' he asked, softly, confused.

Noah simply walked up to Jake and hit him hard in the mouth causing a tooth to be immediately dislodged and blood to begin to flow. Noah simply turned and, in no particular hurry, started to walk back down the hill. Jake was initially surprised and stood in a sense of shock. He had known Noah for many years and never known him throw a punch ever.

It took Jake fifteen long seconds to scramble his brain and make sense of what had just happened, and then eight long strides to catch up with Noah and grab him by the shoulder, throwing him around as he did so and sending an almighty punch into his stomach. Noah, who had half expected and, indeed, hoped Jake would simply walk away, was not prepared for the punch at all. He had never fought anyone and did not understand the concept of it. The punch he had delivered to Jake was partly for hitting his best friend Sam, and partly for marrying the love of his life, Flora, and partly because he had endured a shitty day during which he had entertained a fleeting thought that just maybe Jake had been involved.

The initial punch to Noah literally lifted him off the ground. It was that hard. As he fell, a kick followed into the side of his ribs, searing pain filling Noah's body which was a worry as Noah had always assumed that alcohol would numb the effects of pain should you ever be unfortunate enough to meet any. Sadly this theory was worryingly falling apart. He rolled into a tight ball, trying as he did so to fall into a position where he could get his feet behind him and get into a sprint. Sadly Jake now stamped hard on his ankle causing any thoughts of escape to turn to hopes of mercy. He thought of looking up to appeal to Jake on this front but knew a punch would follow so he held his position of a tight rolled-up and now battered ball.

'Any time you want to walk away, you bastard, feel free,' Noah managed to call out against his better judgement and expecting another blow to come in response. He actually ached that much that he didn't understand how he could actually stand up ever again.

Jake waited above him, panting with exertion and anger but stopping himself taking further retribution. He liked Noah and he appreciated that Noah would have been appalled to see his dear friend, Sam, punched like that. Further, Jake knew that if Flora knew what had just happened he would take the trouble he was already in to a new stratosphere of enormous trouble and he did not want that.

'Have you finished?' asked Noah nervously from the safety of his foetus position.

'Yes, you little fuckwit. What the hell did you do that for?'

Noah peered through his arms to see Jake had indeed stepped back. He stretched out, pain all over his body.

'You know why. You hit Sam!'

'I know. I was there. He was being out of order though.'

'He was just being Sam,' Noah muttered and began to pull himself up, Jake stepping forward as he did so to help him stand.

'Yes, I know. I'm sorry.'

'Well, yes, you should be. You know he's harmless.'

'Well, to Flora maybe.'

'Exactly. That's my point. I mean, bloody hell Jake, we're talking about Flora here.'

'Yes, I know. Look, I've said sorry. Are you OK?'

Noah laughed and then regretted it as his ribs seared out with pain.

'No. You?'

'Well, you have, remarkably, dislodged a tooth which I am amazed by.'

'What, that I punched you or that I actually hit you quite hard.'

'Both.'

'Me too! I was just so angry.'

'OK. Fair enough. I understand. I'll come back with you and apologise. I just… '

'Lost it?'

'Yea. I have drunk far too much. I can't believe how stupid I've been,' he said, meaning every word. Jake stretched out his hand and Noah leaned forward to shake it. He knew Jake was not a bad guy and he also knew Sam could try anyone's patience. His best friend was a loveable rogue and as a result he was now being looked after by very attractive women in Hub while Jake and Noah stood in a quiet back street in St Ives and fought over him. Noah knew this story would amuse Sam for years to come.

'No hard feelings?' asked Noah.

'No. None at all. You know that. OK?'

'Yes, OK. I'm sorry too,' Noah found himself saying and laughing as he did so despite the pain that then travelled across his chest.

'What's so funny?' asked Jake as they walked back down Skidden Hill together as though the best of friends.

'Oh, you know, this isn't exactly my normal sort of night, Jake, and it is supposed to be my birthday celebration.'

'Oh, yea. Sorry. Come on, I'll make it up to you.'

And with that Jake placed an arm around Noah and the two of them walked, or in Noah's case, limped, onwards.

'Oh, and Noah?'

Noah turned, knowing already what Jake was about to ask him.

'Can we please keep this from Flora. She wouldn't understand.'

'Yes, no worries, although there's that tooth issue.'

'I will tell her that happened earlier,' replied Jake easily.

'Brilliant. There is also the small yet huge matter of getting her to forgive you over hitting Sam.'

'Oh, that's easy,' replied Jake, 'I'll buy her something beautiful.'

'Bastard,' replied Noah, causing Jake to simply laugh.

Chapter 10

Planning the Trip

'*In the long run the pessimist may be proved right, but the optimist has a better time on the trip!*'

'Great quote,' laughed Noah as Flora put down *Lonely Planet* having just read a quote from an article to educate her soon-to-be-travelling-across-Europe-with-an-invaluable-painting friend.

'Well, I just thought it matched where you are. I mean, travelling to a country you have never been to before with a painting that is so valuable in your possession is, to be blunt, and you do need to be told this Noah, laughable. I've got to the stage where I actually can't think about it as it is just too scary.' As she said this, her eyes watered and Noah, noticing at once, sought to reassure her.

'Oh come on, Flora,' he said, putting his hand on hers across the table. They were sitting outside the Porthgwidden Café, an overcast yet warm mid-June Saturday morning, tucked away in a quiet corner and overlooking the sea and sparsely populated beach, the school-break tourists not yet released from their drudgeries. Flora was not at work until two that afternoon as she would then cover the evening shift, so they were having a long lunch that was to include talking through Noah's plans. 'I'm going to be just fine. It's me, Noah, nothing ever goes wrong. Usually, that is.'

Flora just looked at him.

'I mean, what could go wrong other than, at worst, the painting gets stolen?'

'You get hurt?' she said at once.

'Well, yes, technically I could get hurt but I can run very fast you know. You remember. 1997 100 meters sprint champion of our form class! High shorts showing far too much thigh. Little vest. Red. Nipple rash for days afterwards.'

'You can't outrun a bullet.' Flora said this matter-of-factly, obliviously ignoring his attempts to soften her up. She had not intended to share her deep fears with Noah about his trip but now she found she could not help herself.

'Bullets! I'm not going to a war zone, Flora.'

'You don't know what you are going to!'

'I,' Noah started but then ran out of any other words. He of course had no idea what he was going to, only the presumption of a situation that he had flowered up in his mind.

'And if they find out about you, Noah?'

'First bullets and now the ominous sounding "They!"'

'Oh come on, Noah, face what you will not face. Yes, "they". The same people who magically broke into your house when no one even "knows" about the painting.' Flora's voice was now tight and shrill.

'Now come on, seriously, let's calm down here. I thought we had successfully filed that under plain coincidence.' Noah actually believed this. Nothing had happened since and there was no other explanation. He was also, as he spoke, getting a little angry with Flora. He really did not need all these negative angles at this time.

'Tim said there were other burglaries that night!'

'Tim made that up to make you feel better on your big night out.'

'Oh... '

'And if they catch you, well, if they... '

At this it all got too much for Flora who began to actually sob. Noah, anger having fled at Flora's outpouring of woe, stood straightaway and walked around to her, knelt down by her chair and held her until her tears dissolved. She had laid her head on his shoulder and now she pulled her head up and, with her eyes a tear-smeared blue, she leaned forward and gently kissed his cheek.

'I'm sorry,' she said, simply. 'I want to just be your happy person, all thrilled about all that you are doing, and instead I'm being all I did not intend to be.'

'Don't be sorry, Flora. I know you are concerned. It's a big thing. I know that.'

She nodded.

'But I firmly believe I will be fine. I'm a fine kind of guy, am I not?' Flora looked at Noah with a look of mild panic and Noah offered instead, 'Look, seriously, honestly, if people really were after me why has nothing happened since the alleged burglary?'

Flora again nodded, feeling it better to let her neck say what she knew she could not agree with in her voice.

'There has been no other attempted break-in has there, no one has followed me or cornered me or done anything else to me? You see, I'm just a lucky kind of guy, yes? So I will be fine. A simple trip. Shall I tell you about it?'

'Yes,' she said, pulling herself up straight and using tissue to wipe her eyes and blow her nose. What Noah had said was all true and it did go some way to calming her. Noah stood and retook his seat. 'Yes please. I want to know all about your trip and I want a copy of your itinerary. I want to know where you are and when. I shall follow you with a pin!'

'OK. I like it. I assume you want a doll, too? Voodoo is so this year,' said Noah, pleased to see he had made Flora smile, 'and I shall get a copy for Jake too as I am sure he will want to know exactly where I am and I suspect he too will follow me with a pin. No, a nail! Hammered in at each stop.'

Flora gave Noah a sarcastic stare.

'He is very interested, actually. He thinks it's great that you are going away.'

That made them both laugh.

'No, seriously Noah, Jake likes you very much.'

'Well, what's not to like, eh?' asked Noah, a triumph of spirit as ever. The fight had never come out either and both men had kept their side of the bargain. Flora did not need to know.

'Well, there is the issue around the unkempt eyebrows!' Flora offered with a smile.

'Ah yes. Well, that's the surf for you.'

'And the messy hair.'

'Again surf related.'

'The fact that one arm is longer than the other.'

'Technically not true but to the human eye, I grant you, one arm does look slightly gangly. Again, m'lord, surf related.'

'And the spots!'

'Spots?'

'Well, you had one the other week!'

'I did not!'

'You did. It was quite large actually and Sam said it was your own warning system in the sea to ward off amateurs. It was under your unkempt, messy right eyebrow if I remember correctly.'

'Ah yes. That spot. I remember it more as a tiny blemish but yes, there was a visitor to my facial features. We are all but human, Flora, when all is said and done. That spot was my body's way of keeping me grounded.'

'Shame you can't remember it then.'

They were smiling together again, this happy banter, their way of telling made-up things to one another was totally unique to them. They didn't do this with other people. It was like their own language, their way of relaxing into an easy rhythm with one another.

'So tell me about your trip, surf boy,' Flora asked, feeling a little lighter now as she did so.

'OK! I will! I thought of doing this run-through to music but then I couldn't decide on the music but here is as perfect a place as anywhere to tell you so here goes!'

Noah, looking as animated as Flora thought she had ever seen him, began.

'So, the trip! I shall start from my front door! It is, my dear, the only way to start any worthwhile trip. It is also, of course, quite a front door. Any journey would be delighted to make its start from such a door. A grand, fine door, a door that has seen many people come and go. Ah yes, that really is quite a door and from it, well, there the distance to Poland is only a mere few miles away! A trifle, if you will.'

Flora was laughing, of course, and Noah was in his element with Flora as his favourite audience.

'First thing I am doing is going to Tom's in London.'

'Tom? Isn't he the big rugby type from uni?'

'That's the one. Great guy. Fine forward. Good to have in a tug of war. It will be marvellous to catch up with him, spend

160

the night for gratis hence saving valuable pennies, and help him out by showing him a few of my own rugby moves!'

'Running away?'

'Ah yes! The old favourite! Run away! Don't look back, just run like the wind! It has never failed me yet, although it has confused a few of my coaches over the years and had me sadly dropped for a few games by that nasty Mr Evans you may remember?'

'Eeyore Evans, of course I can!'

'Yes, miserable git. Then, my little, excitable cherub, I go through the Channel Tunnel, onions around my neck and garlic round my ankles, through to our fine neighbours overseas. I turn left, remembering as I do so that I am now driving on the wrong side of the road, understanding that it is always important to follow these quaint little quirks of the Europeans, and go up past Bruges and over into Germany. Are you still following me?'

'I am,' replied Flora, who was inwardly assured to see such confidence to the trip coming out from Noah.

'Good. Right, well, here I shall hum loudly and perhaps break into Bavarian drinking songs at regular intervals. After singing myself hoarse I shall drop into Germany's fifth largest city, and as you well know, their fine financial centre, Frankfurt, for a night.'

Flora raised her eyebrows at this in an oh-haven't-you-been-doing-your-research way.

'Impressed, eh? Ah yes, those long lonely nights under a burning candle have not been wasted, young Flora. No sir! I have been doing my homework. No nook, no cranny and no granny have been left unturned in my quest. I can tell you for example, and for no fee whatsoever, that Frankfurt is a city famous for its fabulous skyscrapers and here I will find a fabulous little hotel in the city centre and a gaggle of German dancing girls to take me through the city's high spots, and I don't just mean the high-rise offices!'

'Boom, boom!'

'Quite! Then, lotion applied, aloe vera with a hint of jasmine, to soothe the rigours of the night, my nether regions helped in the car by a soft cushion that I have already packed, I go on through Germany and past the great cities of Leipzig and Dresden. Then, waving goodbye to my German friends in a vibrant and slightly camp manner, some of them now friends for life, literally imprinted on me forever, I leave Deutschland!'

Flora was giggling and Noah smiled widely.

'Can I record you laughing?' he asked, the question coming out as easily as day follows night.

'If you like.'

'I will, then.'

He produced his iPhone and set it to record and waited.

Flora looked at the phone and said, 'I can't just laugh.'

Noah waited.

'Noah, I am not going to laugh for order. I am not a performing circus animal that can just perform on the spot!'

He waited. She laughed. He picked up his phone and turned off the recorder and then he looked at her and just smiled.

'I have your voice too,' he said softly, a triumphant grin on his face.

'Come on, then,' she said quickly, aware that emotion would take her back to her fear and wanting instead to stay on the joys of Noah's monologue performance. 'On with the trip. I've not got all day!'

'OK! Exciting, isn't it? Well, then I arrive in the destination I am headed for, the rather splendid and much undervalued, Poland. Here, my dear floppy-eared girl, one ear I am bound to say is slightly larger than the other, I drop down into my destiny, Krakow. What a splendid sounding city, isn't it?'

'Yes, it is. Sounds almost like it is a jewel.'

'To the Poles it is. There I shall spend two nights in the rather splendid Sheraton Hotel, a huge hotel that I can hide in and just get the lay of the land.'

'Hide in?'

'Yea, you know, hold up. Like a secret spy!'

'Matt Damon!' pronounced Flora in the low monotone voice they used when doing impressions of the actor.

'Indeed so. "Matt Damon",' he repeated, them both laughing as he spoke the name with an increased over-the-top depth. 'Not sure which of the Bourne films to liken this trip to but will probably plump for the yet unreleased *Bourne – the easy trip with no issues*.'

'Catchy. Box-office smash. Let's hope nobody comes to watch it. Noah, are you really just fine with all this?'

'This?'

'Yes, the small matter of an incredibly expensive stolen painting, and you carrying it in secret across Europe and delivering it into the hands of people you have never met. I mean, come on, it's incredible.'

'Ah, "it". I see. Well, yea, I am. I mean, it is slightly nerve-wracking stroke scary, but it's also a buzz. I am intending to be very careful and cool and, crucially, I feel I am doing something good and, and this is perhaps the most important point of all, I've not watched all those Bourne movies over the years for nothing, you know.'

'I bet you have watched them again though, haven't you?'

Noah smiled, caught in the lights.

'Possibly. Research is key.'

Flora looked at him, her soft Noah. Not a bit of anger or malice in him. She would miss him so much. She was frightened for him, really frightened, but thrilled to see him so excited. It was time to close the conversation around Poland, her worry beginning to build back up and her not wanting Noah to see this.

'And then where do you go?'

'Ah yes! Then the real holiday begins! It is important in any top-secret gig that you have a pleasure to focus in on. I mean, every Bond movie finishes with James, and I can call him James, relaxing in some extraordinary venue with a bikini-clad beauty and my trip should be no different. Yes, I shall do my duty but focus on my reward!'

'Which is?'

'Well, as you know, at the conclusion of my mission I shall go north to the Baltic Sea and the most fabulous Chalupy to surf!'

Flora laughed.

'We both know that place does not exist!'

'It does! Really! You've not looked into this surf Mecca since I told you about it?' he asked in mock-exaggerated tones.

'That would have been silly as it doesn't exist!'

'Well, your loss, my dear girl. Some fab pictures you could have been looking at and I, cute cheeks, will be looking at the real thing! I can't believe you've not researched it. It is outstanding! I've told you! I am going there to surf and shall send you a few pictures to prove how awesome it is! I shall spend a few days there and then go up to Lithuania to catch the ferry across to Sweden.'

'Sweden! Wow. I've always wanted to go there. They say the light is fantastic and *Lonely Planet* features Scandinavia all the time.'

Noah resisted somehow the urge to tell her to meet him there, knowing by then she would be married to Jake.

'It looks great, outstanding in fact. I shall tour the country going up the east coast and down the west. Then drop into Denmark and then Holland and eventually get back here to… '

'To me!'

'To Mrs White.'

'It will still be me!'

'Yes, but who will I be?'

'A man with several stories to tell and some that you will never be able to tell. Will you tell Tess about the picture?'

Noah took a sip of his nearly finished drink, a thick fresh smoothie now reduced to chunks of chilled ice.

'Yes. When I'm back. She will worry too much and would no doubt attempt to dissuade me if I laid it all out before her now, I mean, can you imagine the pitch? Besides, once it is back in its rightful place, well, it will feel far away and hopefully it will not impact on her love for her father.'

'It hasn't impacted on yours, has it?'

Noah waited, weighing up his response.

'Well, no, a little perhaps. I mean, I don't know what happened, you know? I wasn't there. The man I knew, I know, is beautiful. He is my Grandad and I love him with everything, and all my memories, my times in my head with him, tell me he was a man of the most intoxicating beauty but now, well now there is a change. A man who had no dent on his character now carries a smudge and one of the darkest variety and I just hope, no I believe, he was just foolish and misguided, young and greedy. I absolutely do not believe this has anything to do with the Nazis and their kind. I think he just saw an opportunity and took it. How? Who knows? Who will ever know?'

Flora stretched over the table and stroked his hand.

'And he left you to put it right, Noah.'

'Yes. Yes, I believe that now. I think he did just that. And I will, I will put it right.'

And they sat there, the day resting its head on the brow of a Cornish breeze. Noah went to get more drinks and Flora sat and looked out to the sea and to Godrevy. She wondered what she would do without her Noah and she saw only a blank canvas of nothingness and so she immediately then thought of Jake and all the good times they had lined up to balance her mind. Then she came back to it all happening without Noah and her insides began to tremble a little. She again countered this fear with her happiness with her marriage things and anything else that she could get to fill her mind, and she got angry with this game of mind tennis that kept interrupting her life. And then she did what she always did, rather than think and focus and come to a conclusion, she picked out her phone and busied her mind with her friends. Soon enough Noah reappeared with drinks and she was able to again ignore the gapingly obvious needs of her heart. At night, her tossing and turning and disturbed sleep would not leave her alone and her mind would be forced to face the demons of her soul, but for now her mind was rescued.

Chapter 11

Leaving

'So, you are going.' It was a statement of fact from Tess, rather than a question. She had sensed a change in Mikhail a few weeks earlier and knew deep down that he was trying to work out the words and the time to tell her he must leave. Now, the middle of July having raced ahead of them, she told him what he could not say. He looked at her, his deep dark eyes suggesting he was about to deny it, but no words would dare to come out and do so. After a few seconds of silence when the clock in the kitchen had never ticked so loudly, he simply nodded.

Tess looked away from him, disconsolate and angry. She felt an immediate disgust, for him, for her. She turned to the kitchen table and went on folding some clothes that she had just got in from the washing line. The clothes would not be ironed. She had long since stopped the practice as a waste of time.

'Well, Mikhail, we both knew this could not last forever,' her back to him now and with no emotion in her voice, 'but no one can say we've not had a great time and I'm not blaming you in any way. No one took advantage of anyone here. We're both consenting adults. It's been great. Let's say no more on the matter.'

She felt the inevitable hand reach out and touch her on her shoulder and then the big Russian lean into her neck to breathe her in, something that she had only ever experienced before with him, the absolute and total way that he seemed to take through his nostrils the very core of her and this hugely emotive sensation was about to be lost. It was an intense experience that always moved her and it was like, to Mikhail, that nothing else mattered but the smell of her, and to Tess it was extraordinarily uplifting and sexual. She tried to ignore him and carried on talking about their future apart, letting the anger she felt remain strong and her wanting it to take over her emotions, but his hands were now stroking her arms, her neck, her head and her breasts, and soon she gave in, turning to him, and taking him in her arms, leading him to her bedroom at the front of the house that overlooked St Ives harbour from the impressive vantage point of Barnoon.

Afterwards, as she lay on his lap, caught between the desire to fly and that to stay, Mikhail propped up on pillows and smoking his Café Crèmes, they talked.

'If I could stay any longer I would, Tess, but I am needed back home. I mean, no one can stay away from work indefinitely, you know this! Imagine if you stayed away from here for too long. You have told me often you have to return here. I too, Tess, have these responsibilities. I would stay longer if I could but I've pushed the boundaries too far already. You don't know how far, you really don't. I have kept all this from you. It was best this way that you did not know the pressure I have been under. For sure I will be back, if you'll have me, my love, as soon as I can and you, my Tess, you must come to me whenever you like. It would be my biggest honour, my biggest thrill, to have you with me in St Petersburg, a place I have already taken you around in your head, yes? I would show you so much and give you private tours in the galleries. Tess, I have told you my Hermitage, well, it is amazing, magnificent. I can show you private pieces there that will stay with you all your life, pieces that can never go on show.'

She listened, stroking the inside of his strong thighs rhythmically, her fingers reaching up to his resting cock as she softly ran up and down every inch of him. As she did what she had done so often she wondered now with sorrow what she would do without him. She had grown very fond of him, this Russian, perhaps even loved him, though she had not told him so. The thought of building something with him, the power of it, was strong and despite her misgivings her mind

167

had run away with the thought of what it would be like to be with this man for a very long time indeed. Now, as he talked, she let herself imagine her trip to Russia to meet him and spend time with him, after all seeing her mother's homeland; experiencing the sights and sounds of her upbringing was an intoxicating thought and she knew Natalya would approve. Artistically, too, it would be an amazing journey and it would give her so much material to work with for years. At the same time, though, she was confused, as she ever was, her inner self-feeling drawn to do what she always did when a relationship reached a crossroad and she felt no choice but to cut herself off, protect the deep core of her and not think of him anymore. Her heart played all these thoughts through but her voice could only play one.

'Don't worry, Mikhail. I'll be fine. You go.'

'Oh Tess. Don't be so cold. I want you. Say you will come to me.'

She heard the love in his voice and it moved her. She propped herself up on her elbow and looked at him.

'I'm sorry, Mikhail. I know I am being difficult and you know why. Look, you go back, as you must and I do know you must. I'm not that stupid! Let us let the dust settle and see where it leaves us.' With these words Mikhail could not have known she was in fact offering a lifeline to the relationship that even surprised herself.

'Let the dust settle?' he asked, confused by the saying. His free hand was stroking her long, sun bleached hair, in the smooth strokes he knew she loved.

'Yes. It means let time pass so that we can see what we have after all.'

Mikhail let the joy of this giving of ground wash over the room. Then he let his humour talk.

'Ah yes. Another strange English saying; like "Look what the Cat has brought in," or "It never rains but when it pours". You English really are eccentric.'

He laughed, his deep husky laugh that always made her smile. It did so again.

'Yes, we are rather mad. Do you mind?'

'Mind? No, I love it. It is, as you say, quintessentially English. I have something to tell you.'

168

His voice had changed to deeply serious and so Tess let herself fall on to her back, her large breasts freely on show. With Mikhail he had so lavished her with love and filled her with confidence that she had felt at one with him almost at once. With some lovers Tess was very aware of her body and of the faults she thought she had. None of this had seemed to matter with Mikhail. She hid nothing. She let him see all of her and was at total ease with him.

Mikhail shifted his position too, sitting up very straight and looking seriously into Tess's upturned eyes.

'You know I love you. I tell you all the time. I think the world of you, Tess. I did not come to England for this. It has been a total surprise for me. I think you could echo these words for yourself too. I have been as you would say, caught short, and I do not know what to do.'

Tess smiled and nodded, not sure where he was going with all this but willing to let him do the talking.

'I just know that I think of you when I wake up, I think of you throughout my day and I think of you when I go to sleep. In short you have become my main thought pretty much since you picked me up at the airport, not knowing whether to like or loathe me.'

Tess thought about disagreeing with him here, but knowing this was true she kept her counsel and simply gave him a knowing smile.

'So, I go back to Russia with a heavy heart but go back I must and, as you say, we can let the dust settle, but I want you to know, to truly know, I leave in inner turmoil for I would, if I could, take this further now.'

He waited, wanting his Tess to speak, but she did not.

'You understand what I am saying?' he asked, deep emotion in his breaking voice, 'I would take this further now, I would.'

He was silent then, wondering if he had overstepped the mark and waiting for Tess to speak, wondering if at last she would declare her love for him, or if not her love, some greater vocalisation of her positive feelings for him at least. Outside the open bedroom windows the seagulls were in full cry. It was the beginning of the tourist season and the summer had been good so far causing the town to be busy and the tills to sing with a cheerful tune. The bustling streets were wonderful news for the ever active and vigilant seagulls who swept down on the unsuspecting visitor to take away their pasty or their ice cream with greed and relish. This life, all this life, was in full swing outside on the streets of St Ives but here, in the bedroom of Barnoon Terrace, all was still.

After a while Tess said only, 'It's OK.'

And then she got out of bed and walked through to her en-suite to shower leaving Mikhail confused and upset. Was he just a conquest to Tess or did he mean more than that? He had told her he loved her many times and she had never returned this other than to say he meant a lot to her. Perhaps she had been very hurt in the past and would always struggle to be too open? Perhaps he was not right for her and, though he knew she liked him, he was ever only going to be a passing fancy. He lit another cigar and tried to concentrate on the smoke it produced, rising high into the air of the bedroom, then catching the breeze as it disappeared through an open window into the eternal St Ives sky.

A couple of miles north and Noah sat with Flora at Godrevy Point.

'So, nearly there, Noah. You are going on your great adventure. I'm so excited for you.'

Noah sat at her side, the two of them on the rocks and looking out to the lighthouse in its entire close-up glory. It was a place they had come to often, a vantage point where you could view the beautiful and exuberant St Ives, but do so from a very quiet and private place.

'Good! It is exciting. I think I shall write a book called *Noah's Extraordinary Big and Scary Adventure*.

'Catchy.'

'I know. You will buy a copy, won't you?'

'I think I will. Maybe wait until the price has dropped. I will put it on my shelf in pride of place, a book written by the highly impressive young man, Noah Spearing, who travelled Europe and went to place names he made up!'

'Hazaar!'

They laughed and toasted imaginary champagne flutes.

'Mum's said I can take her trusted Golf so breaking down

in my Defender is no longer a problem! The Golf and I will deliver the important package!'

'No last minute changes, then?'

'Well, I wondered whether to take the back-up Nazi costume or not, but other than that... '

Flora chose to ignore that.

'And you're still sure?'

'Yep. No choice so no decision to make.'

'There's always a choice, Noah.'

The words sat between them with Noah having a thousand things he wanted to say but felt unable to do so.

'And you, dear Flora. You have an important date,' he said, looking into the distance and letting the words come. 'When I come back from Europe you will be married.'

She nodded.

'No last minute changes?'

She shook her head and gave him a forced smile.

'And you are still sure?' he asked mischievously as he now turned towards her, a big grin on his face to soften the depth of the question. 'Remember, Flora, in your own words, there is always a choice.'

They now looked at each other, Flora wondering if Noah was going to say any more, and Noah just grinning. Time waited for either to speak and truth tumble out like sand in an upturned hourglass.

'I'm only messing with you, Flora,' he said as silent seconds turned into what seemed like aching hours, aware he was making Flora feel uncomfortable and knowing that was unfair. 'Don't look so worried. You will have a wonderful day and honeymoon in, now where was it? I know it began with a P. Penzance?'

'Peru. As you well know.'

'That's it, Peru. Rhymes with poo. I just hope you find out about his big secret before you tie the knot.'

'Which is?' she asked against her better judgement.

Noah looked at her, her brown wavy hair tinted with flecks of gold by the sun flowing in the breeze, her big blue-grey eyes sparkling as light bounced off the sea towards them. She wore a tight white t-shirt with a dark blue soft, wool cardigan, ripped and tight faded-blue jeans and a pair of flip-flops covered in beads. To Noah she looked like the most beautiful thing he had ever seen.

'That he is…, no I can't say it.'

'Noah!'

'Well, it's not for me to say is it, being an interested party and all?'

'What do you mean, an interested party and all?'

'Well, we all know that if you left him at the alter young Noah here would be willing to take you on.'

'Take me on?' she asked, hitting his arm as she did so, 'Cheeky boy!'

'Well, you are a challenge, Miss Trembath, with your feisty centre. You're like a chilli-flavoured soft-centred caramel nut case! Everybody knows this!'

She jumped on him knocking him to the ground and then sat astride him and punched him on the chest. Noah rolled her over and they lay, side by side, panting. He leaned forward and kissed her, just a quick kiss on her lips, but he had kissed her. She looked at him, a fire having been ignited in her, a valley of desire suddenly filling inside her, the months now of building deep confusion reaching out to the doubts of this man who had just kissed her lips. Noah, who felt the same thing, sat up. He knew this was too close for comfort and would lead to his own humiliation. Words were needed and quickly.

'The point is, Jake is perfect and he will be fabulous for you.'

Flora, still lying on the floor and hearing these words, felt her excitement leave as quickly as it had come. A deep heaviness came in its place. She sat up and looked at Noah, his hair a mess as always, his blue eyes looking sad.

'We will always be dear friends, Noah, more than you will ever know,' she said, reaching out and stroking his face as she did so.

'Yes, we will,' he said, looking at her as tears filled his eyes causing him to look away, 'but it will never be the same.'

He stood and walked back to the car, Flora following him in a procession of woe.

Much later that night, with a bottle of red wine half-drunk to make him feel even more morose, Noah sat at his dining room table with a pen in his hand and paper in front of him. His mother's words that Flora had a right to know how he really felt were ringing in his head, and in fact had been ever since she had said them to him. He took another mouthful of wine and walked over to hisiPod, picking out "Trailer Park" to keep him company. He then returned to his writing position, his place to make his peace, and he wrote out his heart.

Dear Flora,

I don't think I will ever give you this letter but mother said I should so I thought I should at least write it! You see, despite me skirting around the issue and generally being a joker to impress you and hide the obvious, underneath it all there is more, so much more. It is the unspoken truth between us, easier to let our past be our future than complicate matters. But, as you stand at the point of marriage to a wonderful man who loves you and thinks he deserves you, I find myself in such a place of sadness.

You see, dear Flora, I love you. I have always loved you. And I don't mean in the "we are dear friends" love, although that we are, but in the sense that I want to have you and hold you and kiss you and take you and make you squirm with delight and kiss you again and make you scream in excitement. I WANT YOU, FLORA!!!!!

Why have I not said this to you, not made this clear? Rejection? Probably. Not wanting to change the beauty we have, not willing to risk losing it for declaring my love for you? Definitely. You just seem so happy in how we are and Jake, well, he is pretty fab. You know if I was a woman and all that I'd have him. Oh yes I would!

But he's not me, Flora, not at all me. Is that why you've chosen him?

We would be so good wouldn't we? Earlier today, when I kissed you, I swear we exchanged actual electricity between us. I know you felt it too. I could tell. And then tears filled my eyes when I told you to concentrate on Jake. Did you see them? Of course you did. Another thing easier left unspoken.

And so I won't give this letter to you because if we really felt these things we would have done something about it... wouldn't we? Or would we? Anyway. It would be wrong. You have chosen Jake now and I know I have let you do this. I am not blaming you, my sweet. I am blaming us both. We have let the ease of our surroundings sneak up on us and make our options for us rather than speak, well I speak for me here Flora, speak the truth of what I actually feel deep in my heart. Now, my mistake too late to rectify, I must give you the space you both deserve.

Anyway, it feels good to at last write the truth that is thus: I love Flora, I love Flora, I love Flora!!!!!!!!!

Do you know how often I have walked by Porthmeor Café and seen you and my heart has literally skipped a beat? How many times I have seen you with Jake and seen you laugh and wanted that laugh to be at my side, not his? How I have looked at photos of you in your apartment and I have longed for these photos to be in my house, your smile looking out at me? Do you know, my sweet, precious and beautiful Flora, how I would hold you, and make you feel warm and wanted? Do you know how I would love you, Flora? God, I would love you. Oh Flora. My sweet Flora. I would love you so that the stars in the heavens would watch in wonder. I would. I really would.

See that wet patch just above on the letter – these are my tears falling like sorrowful rain on the page as I write. Sweet Flora. Lost to me now, but in my heart always my love.

Your Noah.

Xxx

Noah sealed the letter and wrote 'To Cute Cheeks' on the front of the envelope, placing the sealed treasure in his bureau, a gift from Joshua given some years earlier.

'Every man should have a bureau,' he had declared as he stood at the door to Noah's house as it had been delivered. It was an old piece, clearly an antique, in an exotic, flame mahogany. Joshua had told him that it was over 200 years old at least.

'Older than me!' he had said and they had laughed at that.

Noah placed the letter in the far corner in a clear section. He closed the bureau door and locked it, placing the key under the table in a fold of the wood behind the front right leg. He noticed he now felt calm and he stood and watched himself for a little while. He had told Flora he loved her and what she meant to him, not to her face of course, but nonetheless his true thoughts were out. It felt like he had done something really positive for his own well-being, something good, something wonderful, and while Flora would never know, the truth was at least out of his head and committed to paper. He would phone his mother and tell her he had at least done this, swearing her to secrecy because he knew he would never, could never, give Flora the letter.

Chapter 12

The Bright Lights

Mikhail left two weeks before Noah. Since talking to Tess about his need to return to his home and his job Tess had pulled away from him. She did it instinctively, knowing that she had already given up too much of herself and seeing another man come into her life and then, when he was ready to do so, leave her. Mikhail was visibly heartbroken, walking around with his shoulders fallen and his tunes suddenly mournful and lost. He tried desperately to get under her protective layers that had now closed ranks as though stuck together with superglue but it didn't matter what he said or did, and he did say and try everything he could think of including enlisting Tess's family and friends to help, she would have none of it. Eventually, he took her silence as her right and concentrated solely on his original venture, that of making Natalya happy. On the morning that he left it was Sylvia who took him to the airport, Tess going down with a non-existent cold the night before.

'You meant the world to her,' Sylvia told him in the car.

'I know,' replied Mikhail miserably. 'I will come back for her.'

'Will you?'

Mikhail paused, rain lashing against the car as they drove north to the airport. He had loved being in Cornwall, a place initially so foreign to him and to his life and yet a place that had taken his soul and made him look at things in a different light. And yet there was no getting away from the fact that he had pressing business to attend to and that he had done nothing much of any note towards his work and projects at home since taking his leave from St Petersburg months before. It was time for action and he no longer had the time to hide.

'I hope so,' was all he could manage and as he said it he felt incredibly disconsolate and empty, disloyal and unkind.

Later, her cargo safely delivered to the airport and flown, Sylvia tried to talk to Tess about things but she knew it was hopeless to do so. She had seen the signs that now sat before her with her best friend many times before. Tess had a focussed look about her, which meant she would now work and work until her body could take no more. It would be a huge project of some sort, a theme that she would latch herself on to with total concentration and she would major on it and hone it until she felt she got somewhere near to her perfection, pulling out of herself so many new pieces, some of which would be thrown away and the remainder would form her new work to be placed in the public arena.

'Are we talking about this?' Sylvia asked, urgently almost, needing to either know there was a glimmer of interest in the subject or needing them both to get on with their lives.

Tess, magazines and postcards and photos strewn across her kitchen table managed, 'About what?'

There was no need to say any more on the subject.

'OK. Fair enough. Just take care, honey. You know where I am.'

Tess, a constant threat of indignation wanting to erupt and fall all over the wrong person, managed to lift her attention from her table and go over to her friend and give her a warm hug.

'I will be fine. Don't worry. You go and be creative in the kitchen and let me do the same here.'

Sylvia, grateful for the unexpected calmness of her friend, accepted her at her merit and left with a mental note to come back soon.

Tess, alone at last to her work, began the process of choosing the memories she was to pull together into a piece. As an artist her work was now quite well known. She exhibited predominantly in *Beachside*, the gallery in old St Ives overlooking the island. It had taken to her many years before and the owner, Jenny Dunster, was a similar age to Tess and the two were now really good friends. Jenny also acted as Tess's unofficial agent. For Jenny these creative periods that Tess had were superb for the gallery and her magnificent Tess. She had clients around the country and indeed, some internationally, who were on the mailing list specifically for work from Tess Spearing. A new exhibition was always heavily pre sold before it opened and prices were going up. Tess had early on always kept herself involved in pricing, needing to make her work still affordable, wanting to be seen to be in the middle of the dirty subject of worth. She had long since lost this battle finding that the market set what she could not control and also that money vexed her so, worked her up, that she was far better off not knowing anything at all. Instead, she would give pieces away every now and again to people she came across and did so with a feeling that she was being a naughty schoolgirl. It was a feeling she loved and an action that she knew would have horrified Jenny.

A new exhibition would have at least twenty pieces and this meant that at least twenty more would be discarded. This was, therefore, an enormous burden on Tess and her work methods were unconventional meaning she would work non-stop without thought for her own upkeep. Eventually she would grind to an artistic, emotional and physical halt and at that point Sylvia and Noah would rescue her and bring her back to life. It would be a process that would take a month or so and then, and only then, a more talkative and open Tess would arise, one who realised she needed to share her issues with people as well as her art. Then she would have her grief.

Noah enjoyed a much brighter send-off on a pleasant Sunday morning in St Ives. He got his car into the Island Square, no small feat given the tiny space and the number of people walking round these ever-popular backstreets of the old island, and parked managing to keep his mother's car from catching any of the tightly packed-together walls. Within fifteen minutes he had filled his car boot with several bags including his large, old, battered brown leather suitcase that had been Joshua's. Further, his luggage was made up of two surf boards and lots of Noah "gear"; his walking boots and a separate bag filled the back seats of the car and there, hidden underneath in the footwell in a long brown thick cardboard tube, lay the resting and now rolled-up Raphael. There it would lie in secret on yet another journey but with this one different. Here, its journey was home, its voice silent to the outside world for only a short while longer.

Waiting to wave him off were Sam who was somewhat and amusingly tearful, Tess, Sylvia, Natalya, Enid, Flora and John and Mary Devereaux. Given Noah was only going for what he had now decided would be four weeks he thought the turn-out was outstanding and very funny and he told them so. Mary and Enid had both baked cakes, which they gave him in tins adorned with pictures of St Ives just in case he needed reminding of what the old town looked like. Tess gave him a small camera and whispered in his ear.

'Take pictures on here for me, darling. Ones that you think might inspire me.'

Flora gave him a book, all wrapped up in beautiful cream paper with a huge blue bow around it.

'Thank you! Is it some slippers?' he asked, and added an over-the-top knowing wink to make her laugh.

'It's about our special friend. Open it later.'

He leaned forward and kissed her cheek, her favourite Tom Ford perfume resting on her neck. He breathed in deeply, intending to remember that smell for the next four weeks, in fact probably for his whole lifetime.

'You have a nice wedding and feel free to change your mind at the altar!' he laughed, saying it loud enough for the rest to hear and to smile accordingly. Flora just nodded and stepped back silently to hide in the crowd as they all waved madly. Noah backed out his car carefully into a crowded tourist-filled square and hooting his horn three times pulled off. He drove along Back Road West, his arm out of the window, waving royally, around the corner to the breathtaking and ocean-revealing panoramic view of Porthmeor Beach. 'Back soon!' he shouted to the sea as he drove past it and up past the Tate and then up further still around the back of the fabulous view across the harbour and then, at last, pulling up still more along Trelyon Avenue and away from his safe and beautiful St Ives on his unknown trip to save his grandad's reputation.

By the time he was driving up the A30, cars streaming the other way with tourists desperate to find the sun and escape the rat race, Noah was feeling a little jubilant. His sadness about Flora had not left him, but the adventure he was now on had filled his mind and here, now off and running at last after all this planning, and away from St Ives, Flora and the pain of her loss would hopefully fade just a little. He let his left hand drop into the back of the car to feel for the tube holding the Raphael. He had considered hiding the painting in the car but decided against it as if, on the off chance, he was pulled over and the car searched, the painting would look far less suspicious simply there in the car than hidden carefully in some secret place.

Noah drove straight through to London, well, Walton-on-Thames, to stay with an old university friend, Tom. They had roomed together in a house in Bath after their first year in halls and had the best of times. Tom had studied geography for no other reason than he was good at it. He got his degree more to please his parents than anything and then went on to do what he really wanted to do, make money. He had just completed his fourth year in the illustrious ranks of the City's stockbrokers, or as Noah called them, bank robbers, and at the age of twenty-five lived in a £750,000 house in leafy Walton-on-Thames, a brand new silver Audi R8 V10 meeting Tess's old and battered VW Golf as Noah pulled on to Tom's drive late in the afternoon. They had not met since Tom had paid a quick weekend visit to St Ives to surf the previous summer and Tom came bounding out of his door with all his usual energy to give Noah a huge bear hug.

'It is so good to see you!' he said, standing back and looking Noah up and down. 'You look great, well, I say great; you look like a beach bum, but a fine one!'

'Thank you, Tom! I'll take that as a compliment,' laughed Noah, so pleased to see his old friend after the journey. They had some good history between them, so many good times, many house parties and giggles in Bath, such laughter and freedom when real life seemed so far away. There was no getting away from the fact that those golden, almost hallucinogenic days were fabulous but behind them. It was good then to get back together and have the bright light of memories light up their conversations as these two old friends now met again and embraced afresh on a warm summer's afternoon in the London suburbs of the rich.

Tom, a strong-looking and well-built man who had starred in the university rugby team and now played number 8 in the pack of Esher Rugby Football Club had aged and Noah took great delight in telling him so.

'Must be the stress of the job, Noah, unlike you of course having half the year off on holiday, and the days you do work nipping down to the beach to surf as soon as the bell goes. No wonder the school is in special measures again, you lazy sod!'

'Oh, you have been doing your homework!' laughed Noah.

'What I don't know,' nodded Tom. 'Are we carrying all of this in?' he asked, looking at Noah's well-packed car.

'Oh no, I will just get a bit out, you know, family gold and all,' said Noah, climbing in and out of the car and getting the bits he wanted hidden in the house and leaving purposely the painting to last.

Tom carried the luggage that had been handed over and returned to say, 'You know some of us have to work really hard! It was the same on the rugby pitch, eh? You hiding out on the wing leaving the real work to us boys in the middle!'

Noah laughed again at this. He had loved rugby at university and had played for the first team on the wing, his speed being his greatest asset as opposed to his handling skills. Unlike Tom, he had not played rugby since his university days despite St Ives RUFC keen to get him involved in the new set up.

'I was always available for a pass, Tom, if only you ignorant forwards would have been bothered to pass it.'

'You would have only dropped it,' laughed Tom, causing Noah to just nod and laugh too.

'You're clearly doing very well, though!' Noah said, the painting now in his hand as he locked the car and motioned towards the drive which was shouting out loud and proud the success of the young stockbroker.

'If you are referring to my fine trappings, dear boy, then yes I am! I earn ridiculous sums of money and you should give it a go.'

'You are joking.'

Tom looked at Noah.

'Yes, of course I am joking. You wouldn't last five minutes, no offence meant.'

'None taken,' replied Noah, knowing that Tom was absolutely right. They were now looking around the Audi, a car built to impress and it was doing its job on Noah.

'I suspect our cleaning staff earn more than you do,' offered Tom with a huge grin.

'Yes, I suspect you are right. But are they happy?'

'There you have me!'

'Now then,' said Noah stepping back from the car, 'That really is a dream.'

'You should see the Porsche, in fact we will go out in it later.'

'Porsche? You have a Porsche as well?'

'Yep! Vintage 911 in the garage.'

'Cool! Colour?'

'Red.'

'Of course, what else, although you know what they say about men who have a red Porsche...?'

Tom, refusing to take the bait, helped pick up the rest of Noah's gear and they began to ferry it into the house.

'You're sure there is nothing valuable left in the car, Noah? We have had a lot of car thefts.'

'Really?' asked Noah, needing to get his brain back into gear and the realities of city life.

'Can't be too careful,' he had said in a mature voice that had made Noah laugh.

'You are in the bedroom on the back.' Tom nodded towards the stairs and walked towards the kitchen at the back of the house.

'Crime, eh?' tutted Noah, who was about to recount the low crime rates in St Ives as opposed to the metropolis when he thought about his own confusing burglary. 'OK, I will get my boards and that should just about do it.'

By the time Noah joined Tom in the kitchen he had just about emptied his car into his room for the night. As the kettle worked its way into a state with the promise of a brew to come, Tom let Noah begin to savour the evening he had lined up for them both.

'Tonight, young Noah, I have a treat for you! One of the girls from the firm lives just down by the river and she's having a party and we are invited! They're going to love you.'

'They are?' asked Noah, a cheeky grin across his face.

'They are. Your cheeky little smile. Your delightful tan. Your scrummy little body.'

'A little homoerotic, Tom?'

'Of course! I am a rugby player!'

'That you are!'

The party was in full swing by the time the two old university friends arrived. Tom seemed to know everyone with bear hugs and kisses being handed out to each and all, and Noah followed dutifully in his wake nodding his head, smiling in a demented way and despite being introduced on each occasion he would fail to remember anyone! The music was very loud in the house as the revellers spilled out on to the huge garden that fell away to the mighty old dame, the River Thames.

'I'm going to catch up with a few colleagues, Noah, just thirty minutes or so. Will you be OK? You can come with me if you like but you will be very bored. Discussions will be around finance and my boss will be there and he will almost certainly try to recruit you and then realise you are not for us at which point he will ignore you.'

'That's a nice world you've got going on there, my friend!' replied Noah, not at all insulted and with absolutely zero interest in joining Tom.

'I know! Good, isn't it? The cruelness keeps us sharp. Anyway, necessity will be dealt with as quick as I can in, as requested, the games room.'

'Enjoy man!' shouted Noah over the sound of the music that was blasting out Maximo Park on the terrace where they stood. 'You go and enjoy yourself and I will get in there and dance,' said Noah, looking towards the house and being enticed by the music.

'Ah, the old Spearing magic dance moves, eh?'

'Yep. Why not? Come and impress the ladies with your Tom turns soon.'

'Ah yes! Well, with that thought now safely deposited, I'll be back as quick as I can. The Master will return!'

And with that Tom left and Noah for a moment was lost in thought. It was amazing that at university each and every one of them was on a similar level. Sure you were from different backgrounds and class, but there, at university, you were all tasked with doing the same thing, passing your degree, and even the wealthy kids were rarely rolling in cash. There was so little to actually differentiate you; have you stand out in a lecture room with each student labelled in their clothes but these clothes so interchangeable with only the label inside adding the actual price tag. Course results were crucially no respecter of a person's privileged position and the poorest kids could come out with the best degree. Getting on to an actual degree course was a more debatable matter but as Noah thought about it, it seemed to him that once on a course, it was one of life's great levellers.

Now this had all changed and here, in the actual working world, the difference between the choices the student had made, between the classes that caused choices to be more obvious, well, here the contrast between one life and another was herculean. Look at Tom, in the middle of all his chosen life, money almost literally dripping off the people that surrounded him, their wealth and in many cases their class so clear to the naked eye. How incredibly different to all that was Noah's life, his simple life really, teaching in St Ives, a place where only a few families could boast wealth on anything like this scale. Would he want that? Would Noah want much more than he had, an opportunity to climb the scales of the City? He laughed aloud at this. London alone would exhaust him and as for being in the City, well, he knew he would be eaten alive by these get-rich-quick types that would devour him and spit him out as soon as they realised there was no fat to chew on. That was exactly what Tom was saying when he had described his boss meeting Noah.

Noah smiled, looked at the dance floor that had taken over a once large lounge and was now full of sweaty bodies, and he put down his bottle of beer and jumped right in. There was a place he could feel absolutely at home, a safety zone that broke down all the thinking into a beat that bodies could get lost in. He did just that.

By 2am the two happy friends got out of the taxi, the Porsche having been left over for the night in the light of the moon by the river, and they staggered up the drive. Both were a little drunk, but very much on a high after dancing like the old days when they had enjoyed a legendary reputation for holding a dance floor. The night would no doubt keep Tom's work colleagues talking about his dancing, and his extremely cute friend, for a long time. As Tom got to the front door and began to put his key into the lock he realised it was already slightly ajar. He did a double take and looked back to Noah who was merrily swinging his head from side to side as he whistled "Sex on Fire".

'It's already open,' he whispered to Noah who looked back at him and smiled.

'You daft lad. Not locking your own door. Mind you, it is Walton-on-Thames. Very secure, I am sure, with you highbrow types.'

'Someone has broken in,' he whispered in serious tones to Noah who immediately felt a slight panic begin to rise within him as his merry spirit was sliced away by a bevy of words.

Tom pushed the door open gingerly and was about to turn on the hall light when he heard a noise upstairs. It was a bang and for a moment the sound registered before he realised it was a window being hastily opened.

'You stay there and guard this door. If anyone comes downstairs hit them with this.' A startled Noah received the gothic-looking candlestick holder handed to him from on top of the drawers in the hallway as his alcoholic state quickly left him and the cold fear of the endangered Raphael hit him. He started to whisper to Tom only to see him run to the back of the house just as a thud seemed to land there. He could then clearly hear a fight develop and Noah fought with his orders to stay put, the need to run upstairs and check on the Raphael, and the probably more desperate need to go and help his friend. The grunts from the back garden persuaded him to go and help Tom.

He ran for the back door shouting repeatedly, 'You bastard!' as loud as he could only to see a darkly-dressed figure disappearing over the back fence just as he arrived. Tom sat on the floor, a huge grin showing him to be very happy indeed.

'That was fun. Not had a good fight like that for ages, apart from weekly on the field of play of course, but that doesn't really count,' he laughed.

Noah looked around the ground, his eyes adjusting to the dark of the garden.

'Did he have anything?'

'He pulled a knife.'

'A knife!' said Noah, huge shock making him feel the acute danger of what could have been.

'Yep. A professional-looking bastard of a knife that he was just about to lunge at me with when your angry warrior-cry tones came floating out of the house.'

'Well, I thought I'd better sound mean.'

'With a shout of, "You bastard?"'

'Yea,' said Noah, 'it was all I could think of.'

Tom stood up, laughing heartily as though what had just happened was quite normal, and patted his friend on the back.

'Well, it worked!' he said, a huge grin of satisfaction beaming at his friend, 'Because he ran off at great speed which, given he had a knife, I was happy about.'

'And you're fine?'

'I'm cool. On top of a great night I have this story to add! I'm going to be the office man of the moment for some time, dear boy, and it is all thanks to you!'

Noah smiled, keen to get out the next question with as little emphasis as possible.

'And did he have anything with him?' he said carefully, slowly.

'Eh?'

'Had he stolen anything?'

'Yea, there was a cardboard tube in his hand.'

Noah's heart sank.

'But he dropped that when he had to deal with me. It's over there and it's not mine. What is it?'

Noah stepped quickly over to the edge of the garden where the tube had fallen.

'Just a moment, Tom,' he said as he ran into the kitchen. Turning on the light, he saw immediately that the tape had already begun to be ripped off, the tape that safely secured the lid, and yet, mercifully, the tape had not been removed suggesting the thief had been disturbed just in time. Noah

186

ripped the tape now and carefully pulled out the contents. The Raphael had not been touched. Tom arrived.

'What the fuck is it, Noah?' he asked good-naturedly, clearly delighted by the aggravation. 'Is it a priceless Monet?'

Noah laughed.

'Sort of. Not something big and famous, of course, but a rather important family heirloom,' he replied as easily as he could and now carefully wrapping the canvas in its protective paper and placing it back into the tube. 'Have you got some tape?'

'Sure. Top drawer over there.'

'Thanks.'

'Right,' said Tom, going over to open a bottle of whisky. 'Want one?'

'Oh yes.'

'I guess I won't call the police then.'

Noah looked at him.

'Well, you must, Tom. Whoever it was broke into your house. Who knows what they took?'

'He took nothing, Noah. We both know that. The big, strong fellow came for your family heirloom but he hadn't counted on us coming home early and in a taxi. Further, he had not counted on encountering the great and mighty Esher number 8 and his friend with a scary cry that would put the fear of God in any man on earth. No sir. He will be looking at the bruises I gave him for some time to come. Marvellous stuff. Tom Fossdin, who once again rose to the action cry and was again triumphant. Mind you, I have to say he was huge, big chap. Very strong too. Yes, it was your fine warrior cry that did it, "YOU BASTARD!!!!!".'

They laughed at that and together triumphantly declared, "You Bastard!", the luxury of fear receding as relief took over their overly-worked adrenaline-filled bodies.

A calm descended as Tom put on the kettle and Noah took the picture back upstairs. Returning he implored Tom to call the police.

'No, no need. He was here for you, Noah, and I don't think you want them looking into that painting do you?'

'I guess not,' was all Noah could manage as he thought through what on earth he could say next.

187

Silence arrived as guilt sat heavily on Noah's shoulders and Tom, realising his friend's discomfort said, 'Come on Noah, you know you can trust me. We've been through a lot together haven't we? You know I don't give a fuck about anything much but sadly I have always had a soft spot for my you, my dear friend, and as regards tonight, well, you know I've had much fun, although I have to say that last bit was something of a surprise. Come on, let's go sit down and talk.'

The two of them retired to the lounge with a huge cafetière of strong fresh coffee , Tom holding a bag of frozen peas to the swelling that was now coming out on his eye. Noah looked at him with sorrow.

'Oh, don't worry man. How often have you seen me doing this after rugby games? Water off a duck's back and all that.'

'But this is all my fault,' said a mournful Noah.

'Technically yes, I will grant you that, but don't be ridiculous and please don't worry on my account. Why spoil the habit of a lifetime of friendship, eh? All that matters is that you and I are cool.'

'I know, but a knife, he had a knife!'

'Yes, so he did. It's not good my friend, not good at all! You are targeted and that makes me very unhappy. So, this is about what exactly?'

'I can't talk about it, Tom,' replied Noah, quickly.

'I understand,' replied Tom, easily and without pressure, 'but tell me something because I can't let you leave here without me having some hope that I am actually going to see you again!'

Noah nodded.

'I have something.'

'The painting?'

Noah nodded again.

'How?'

'Oh Tom, really, I shouldn't...' Noah said, desperate to share yet knowing he must not.

'OK, but seriously I need to know you are going to be OK. Just tell me why are you carrying it around with you if it means that much to someone who is serious enough to hurt you to get it back? I mean you can see that would bother me, can't you?'

Noah thought of his answer and then simply said, 'It's probably best we don't talk about it but I can tell you this is nothing to do with me as such. The painting has come into my possession and I just have to get it back.'

'Back?'

'Away from me, from my family.'

Tom sat, listening, wondering how best to help a clearly distressed and in danger Noah. Noah continued.

'You see, I was given it by someone and it was not that person's to give. I, oh Tom, I can't say anymore. You can see how serious it is and if I tell you then you will know and who knows what might happen.'

Tom held his hand up.

'Yea, you know best but this is extremely dangerous so you better be very sure you know what you are doing and that you can do it quickly and safely.'

'Well, tonight suggests I cannot do the latter but I do believe this will all be over within a few days and I can get on with my life because once I return that picture, there will be no reason for whoever to come after me.'

'Seriously?' asked Tom, a firm gravitas to his voice.

'Yes. And honestly, when I do this you will see the story in the news and you will know and, I hope, know why it is best I say no more for now.'

'Noah, I am suitably intrigued and assuaged as to your assurances. Do you want me to help you?'

'Help me?' asked Noah.

'Yep, take a few days off and come with you?'

'God no, Tom!'

'Well, thank you very much!' offered Tom in mock indignation.

'I mean, I am very, very grateful, but I am travelling very light and a man alone to draw as little attention to myself as possible so it's better I do this on my own.'

'Sure?' asked Tom one more time.

'Yes, sure.'

'OK. Well, listen, your safety is now your prime concern, and this is my advice; as a starting point you must think about who knew you were coming here?'

'Just my mum and girlfriend.'

'Girlfriend?'

'Well, not girlfriend. A friend, who is a girl. Flora. You remember her?'

'Ah! Flora. Mmmmmm, yes of course, now there's a nice thought to pierce a nightmare of woe. Well, it definitely wasn't her unless she's being doing a shit-load of working out!'

They laughed at that.

'Which means this is beyond serious, Noah. You are clearly being followed by someone who knows much more about this than you thought was possible. Are you sure you cannot give up on the reason as to why you are carrying that tube up there around with you?' asked Tom, while adjusting the frozen peas around his ever-swelling face.

'No. If I fail, my family name will be destroyed and I've said too much but this is why I must do this.'

Tom paused, weighing up his words.

'OK. Well, you need to think about what you are doing as I would suggest it is not safe with you.'

'I'm returning it, Tom.'

'Returning it where?'

'It's a long story and I don't intend to tell it, but I am simply taking something that could be seen to some as valuable to its right place. No one knows what I am doing.'

'No one?'

Noah thought about Flora.

'No one.'

'Well, you now know you are very wrong there, Noah. Someone does know.'

'But that's impossible,' started Noah, the hopeless truth hitting him hard and causing his words to tail off.

Tom, partly out of the deferential need to let his friend think, and partly out of a sudden urge to pee, left the room. He returned moments later to find Noah unmoved. Pouring them fresh coffee he began to deliver his hastily thought plans to get his friend out of his poor situation.

'Listen man, I can see I am not about to change your mind here and this clearly matters so we will make this OK, right?'

Noah smiled slightly, a glimmer of hope touching his dream again. Tom, now in his stride, began to give his direction.

'The first thing to note is that your car is marked. They followed you here, didn't they?'

'I guess,' managed Noah.

'So from now on you're going to take my car.'

'The Audi?' asked an amazed Noah.

'Yep! Why not? It will suit a man like you, high-flying leader of education, down to the ground!'

'But I'm going abroad and the insurance and…'

'Abroad, you say? Well, this really is getting intriguing!'

Noah rolled his eyes at his friend. Tom continued.

'It's all fine. So what are your plans?'

'I catch the Eurostar at Folkestone mid-afternoon,' said Noah, quickly.

'So we can go round to see my broker in the morning and get it all sorted.'

'But the train? My car is all pre-booked.'

'I'll get my PA to ring in the morning and sort out. She's a genius and can achieve anything, and I do mean anything.'

'That was your PA last night, Gemma, yea?'

'Aye! Nice girl, eh?'

'But beyond drunk?'

'Indeed. But tomorrow morning, i.e. in a few short hours, she will be bright-eyed and bushy-tailed. As will I. That's the City for you and I have no idea how we do it but we do. We burn the candle at both ends until it can't burn anymore and yet still we manage to keep the country moving along.'

'We are indebted.'

Tom afforded Noah a short bow of his head.

'But the expense, Tom, I mean, come on.'

'It's no worries. It's only money, Noah, and I have, as I believe we have established, shed loads of that. Are you short of cash?'

'No! No, not at all, but the car is very valuable and…'

'And it is insured. It's all good. I shall give you my gold card too, for fuel.'

'You'll do no such thing!'

'Shut up, daft lad, and enjoy it. The car is my treat and after tonight you need to listen to me. OK?'

'But, I, well, I can't. There are so many "what ifs?" running through my mind and…'

'Bloody hell, Noah, you're taking it. It will keep you safe from psycho hard men and trust me if you'd met him on your own you'd have been squashed, no question.'

'I know, though you have clearly discounted the possibility that I have been taking fight lessons,' laughed Noah.

'Yea, right. Now then, give me a moment to think. You go and get some toast on. When you come back I will have completed my cunning and foolproof plan. This is my gift.'

'Really?' asked Noah, rising to go to the kitchen. Tom nodded enthusiastically.

Toast duly toasted and buttered, Noah's sodden with copious amounts of Golden Syrup that made Tom just shake his head, Esher's number 8 shared his plan.

'OK. Here goes. Tomorrow morning we get sorted with trains and brokers and shit. Then, I take you for a lovely breakfast by the river. Your train's when from Folkestone, exactly?'

'Half past two.'

'Fabulous. Well, having given you a delightful breakfast we will come back here and fill up the Golf.'

'The Golf?' asked Noah, confused.

'Yes, the Golf. Bear with me. Then we will make a big thing of waving goodbye etc.'

'Can we hug?'

'Oh yea. Big hugs and everything.'

'Tongues?'

'Probably not,' grimaced Tom.

'Fair enough,' laughed Noah.

'And then I will wave you off as you drive to a huge new multi-storey in town, right to the top floor in fact.'

'The top floor?'

'Indeed so. And I'll be there waiting for you in the Audi. We will do a swap of your luggage and you are away.'

Noah looked at Tom closely.

'You're being serious, right?'

'Of course. And one more thing, your phone.'

Noah looked at his phone. He had just had it upgraded to a new one that took fabulous pictures.

'You need to leave that with me as well.'

192

'My phone? There are no rude pictures on it. It's new! I've not had time.'

'No rude pictures? In that case! No, seriously, if these guys are professionals they will be tracking your phone.'

'Tracking my phone? Come on, Tom. Aren't you getting rather carried away?'

'Man with knife?' offered Tom.

'Yes, I guess,' returned Noah.

'So, better safe than sorry?'

Noah thought of many answers but none made better sense than better safe than sorry.

'But I need a phone.'

'Yes, you do, which is why we will call in at the supermarket and get you a new one.'

'Can we get bananas too?'

'Yes, we can. And maybe a balaclava for you, eh?'

They laughed, partly out of the joke and partly out of adrenaline still flowing from the night's unbelievable activities.

'Have you done this before?' asked Noah.

'What?'

'Well, all this cloak and dagger stuff. It's like you are an expert.'

'No,' Tom laughed, 'but I'd like to. It's fun. I do however have some inside knowledge.'

'You do?'

'Yea. Look over there.'

Noah looked to where Tom was pointing, only to see several shelves full of DVDs.

'Look closer, second row.'

Noah did so and smiled as he saw the complete set of DVDs on the TV series, *Spooks*.

'Ah, secret service, eh?'

Tom held out his hand.

'Settled?'

Noah thought for a moment and then took his friend's hand.

'Settled!'

Chapter 13

Alone

'Out the house and turn left!'

The words of his grandfather rang through Noah's brain as he drove out of Calais towards whatever faced him. Joshua had been a man who loved to deliver one-liners that had meant something to him and repeat them over again and again. As a result the sayings had imprinted themselves on young Noah's brain so that he found often when he was doing things his grandad's phrases would come to mind. This particular one simply related to the fact that when you walked out of Porth-la-Chy, Joshua's house, you had to turn left to leave the drive and go on your journey. Right would have taken you over the cliff. "Out the house and turn left" was a mantra for Joshua that basically meant it was the start of the journey and got you on your way. Noah was warmed by the arrival of his grandad's words this afternoon as the vulnerability of being on his own following the aggression of the night before bore down deeply on him.

The short hours available to him for sleep to visit had not been kind with rest being an elusive lover as his mind had worked through, over and over again, just who was after the painting and how on earth they knew. The steady realisation that it had only been Joshua's life that had kept these people away was the only conclusion that he could get to. Why else would this all now be out in the open in some mad, free-for-all game when for years the painting had remained a secret treasure? And so the mystery of his assailant began to take a more solid form as Noah reasoned that whoever was now very much in play to get the picture had stayed away until his grandad had died. Was this out of some kind of respect for Joshua and now they were coming to get what they thought was theirs or was it out of fear, fear of the UK authorities and how they would protect one of their own? Whatever the truth, it was clear that "they" knew that Joshua had the painting and that as soon as he had died it had become open house to go and collect it. So many questions sprung from this with the main ones being who was it or who were they, and then did these mystery bandits know what Noah knew as to the origin of this painting? Noah decided that given the violence and underhand nature of their search to date, the brazen break-in in Cornwall and now the break-in with violence at Tom's, and the answer was almost certainly, and very worryingly, yes.

Hours of middle-of-the-night thinking had stretched into an endless chasm of not actually knowing anything other than conjecture as Noah tried to work through how someone else knew his secret. Did this go back to his grandad actually confiding in a friend he thought he could trust, an old and trusted confidant, maybe, that he opened up to one late night after an evening of too much alcohol? If it was, then Joshua had a lifetime of friends as possibilities and, therefore, this thought process was for a needle in an infinite stack of possible choices.

The simplest solution was the hardest to swallow. The people now after Noah could well be connected to whenever the painting actually came into Joshua Spearing's possession and then this related to the obvious missing pieces of the jigsaw – when was this and how had it happened? Questions had pounded through the distressed Noah's brain, the very weight of them causing his very head to feel heavy, the night's revelry and then violence, refusing to equal a sum of incredible tiredness and then sleep.

Wrapped around all his thoughts was the constant cloak of darkness that was the very difficult-to-swallow big final question. How did the people chasing Noah now know that he, this now extremely vulnerable and very much alone Noah, had the painting? It had taken Noah less than three nanoseconds to connect last night's attempted robbery with the break-in at his home in St Ives. It was clear he had been tracked now for some time and at last, in Tom's house, they had found what they were looking for only to be thwarted by a big muscle-bound man who met force with greater force. Sadly, in a one-to-one fighting situation, Noah knew he would not be so lucky. Watchfulness was his only ally, mixed with luck, good fortune and a happy fate! Noah smiled to himself and repeated his mantra.

'Out the house and turn left!'

Being in a beautiful new top-of-the-range Audi sports car helped ease his mood and his mind wandered thankfully to matters away from being the subject of an international arts theft. Flora, as ever, visited him in his mind's eye. The secret love-letter, written at last, had allowed him to place down his thoughts and set his true feelings for her straight. This would have to be enough and time would tell if there would ever be any more for them. Maybe when they were old, time having washed through the cycles of life, and the two of them sitting huddled outside The Sloop Inn around a warming dram or two, he would produce the letter. That made him smile.

High above him in the weather-streaked late afternoon sky, the sun began to step back and the threat of a storm began to dust its colours across the heavens in readiness to once again take over its canvas. The world went on. It always did.

Noah thought of his mother. She visited his thoughts often, normally with a smile and a hug for him that made him feel warm and happy. He had often considered his close relationship with his mother and their easy life together. His love for her was an easy gift to give, her ability to love him from the beginning, unconditionally, totally, meant he would never feel alone. It was true that often Tess would be caught up in her own life, time simply not there to be at her son's side, but he easily forgave this failing because he knew she was, save for him, alone. His life had taught him that whatever the gap between them, it would only be a matter of time before the two of them would simply spin back together and be.

He had needed Tess as much as any other time in his life around his decisions over Flora. These last decisions in particular had been so very difficult but, as ever, his mother had respected his view and supported him. As for the painting, and his not sharing anything of the knowledge of it with Tess, well, he felt bad about that. Right now, lonely and fearful, he wanted nothing more than to have his mother by his side. Equally he knew where that would have gone. Her initial fears and upset would have been almost instantaneously replaced by her cutting through all the honour that she would have seen clouding her son's judgement and alerting the authorities. Tess held no truck with what people thought of her or anyone; in fact she despised others who held such vanity in the need to have others' approval. Noah could hear her saying even now as he drove through the green clutches of the French countryside, 'If people wanted to judge Grandad then let them do it!'

Life was so simple to Tess. Her ease with which she saw black and white gave her son great comfort but, on this occasion, pause to let her see the quarry.

No. Noah was assured he was doing the right thing. He knew it was madness, what he was doing, but it was a noble lunacy that deserved to be right. And so he continued with his quest, his foot firmly placed on the Audi accelerator, as he now drove at speed to take the painting back to Poland. As for the posse-touched-with-violence in possible pursuit he could do nothing than hope he outran and outsmarted them and, in turn, hope his mother would never learn just how stupid he had been.

Before he had left his phone with Tom he had sent two text messages, one to Tess and the other to Flora.

To Tess, he said, *'Hi Mum, trust you are busy doing nothing as usual! No doubt you have shut up shop at the house so do please look after yourself. Can't use my phone after today as broken but fear not I am getting a temporary one. Will ring you at the weekend. If you need me I will be staying at The Sheraton under the name Charles Devere – don't ask but it made me smile! Love you! Noah X'*

He knew the text would slightly worry Tess, after all she was his mother and mothers were supposed to worry, but he hoped his bright, cheery tone would keep her cool. He also knew that she was caught up in a project and that normally meant she had little headspace to worry and a high probability that it would be several days before she even got to the text.

As for Flora, he simply said, *'Hey. Phone cropped so last text for now. Saturday – enjoy. Poland here I come! X'*

Trying to be cool and nonchalant had never been easy for Noah but this text needed to do the trick. Sadly, within the few seconds after sending the text and him about to turn off the phone, Flora texted back with, '*But I need you XXX.*'

'Bugger,' thought Noah, stuck between texting and calling and turning off his phone. He did the latter, paused, and then turned it back on.

'Time to go!' shouted Tom from downstairs.

'Coming, big lad!' Noah responded and sent back a simple row of kisses and then, with a heavy heart, turned off his phone, his last communication with Flora feeling like a betrayal. What other choice did he have?

Much later in the day and here he was, driving across the north-eastern tip of France and quickly entering Belgium, a country he had never visited before. He hadn't known what to expect of this country knowing virtually nothing about it and found it to be truly beautiful, full of delightful canals, dykes and extraordinary tree rows that he knew his mother would spend days photographing. He pulled over and took some shots himself as instructed by Tess on the camera she had given him. As he did so the late evening sun began to disappear and send out elaborate Rubens shadows chasing across the tapestry of fields that lay majestically before him.

'Take time,' he told himself as his heart began to rise again, partly out of his mind suddenly taking him back to last night and partly out of exhaustion washing over him as the beauty before him risked being lost on him. He waited, allowing his focus to rest on the portfolio of the sights before him, chopping out each one with the camera and concentrating on focus. It helped and like a ship finding harbour he felt some calm return.

Back in the car the journey continued, and Noah, downing several chocolate bars and drinking coke, cut across the bottom of Holland as he dropped into Germany to complete the second leg of his journey. As he drove he played his music, track after track reviving a mixture of release, memories and the trick of filling his mind with an alternative to the many other things that wanted to take over. Listening to a mixture of The Beatles, Blur, The Clash, Tori Amos, The Bluetones, Bloc Party, Fairport Convention, Midlake, Pharrell Williams and the rest were a good antidote to the cacophony of fears that were lined up to knock on his door and present their wares. The night was now drawing in and the darkness took the joy of the journey away, any treasures to be viewed now being hidden by the brush of the evening curtain falling down.

Frankfurt would be his home for the night. He had not booked a hotel for fear of anyone tracking him so driving into a modern-looking Frankfurt he found a small hotel just off the pretty and tree-lined *Bockenheimer Anlage*. He dropped off his bags using his surprisingly effective school-learnt German, and having already decided that the painting should stay with him at all times, headed into the centre with the Raphael over his shoulder, safely rolled in its tape-protected case.

By 11pm he was sitting just back from the River Main enjoying a tuna, black olives and anchovy pizza and taking in the view of the stunning St Bartholomew's Cathedral, a building that hid the immense devastation it had suffered during a bomb-laden war. As he ate, Noah took in the people and the surroundings of the square around him, taking joy in a city not looking at him, his invisibility a relief. The scene before him appeared very vibrant, summer blessing them all with a warm evening to be sitting out in and many were out late to enjoy it. Before him a young man played guitar and was accompanied by a beautiful young lady whose long, messy hair took Noah immediately to thoughts of Flora. Looking high into the sky above him he sent her wishes of love and happiness and then ordered another beer to help him relax and take his thoughts further away from her. He was here, he told himself, to carry out the job of protecting his grandad and being morose about Flora was not going to help him. Life would go on without him there. Indeed he had called his mother earlier from a call box only to get her answerphone which was never switched on. Knowing she would be working, he had called Sylvia instead and asked her to pass on his love.

By 11.45pm the square showed a few signs of people beginning to gradually slip away and Noah, quite tired now with the adrenalin having all but left him, the beer and heavy food having taken effect and the previous days all catching up with him, left his table and headed back for his hotel. Using the hotel map for help with directions he headed north along *Hasengasse* and then turned down a side street only to, within metres, become aware of someone behind him. The night was much quieter now, but there were still plenty of people and traffic around and Noah calmed himself by turning his music up in his iPod and telling himself not to be so paranoid. Teenage Fanclub were working their way melodically and perfectly through *Grand Prix* and their rhythm entering his ears for a moment hooked him back in to his own world.

A cashpoint caught his attention so he slowed, allowing the person behind to overtake, but as Noah withdrew his bank card the person behind him had also stopped to light a cigarette. Time slowed down to a slow-motion pace as Noah waited for some cash to leave the teller machine. As the euros arrived, Noah slowly, nervously, slipped the money into his wallet and looked back to the figure now smoking and, apparently, waiting. The figure was tall and dressed darkly in jeans, a hoodie drawn up over the head and well-worn trainers giving nothing away. Noah was painfully aware now of cold sweat on his brow and genuine fear making his heart pound inside him, a banging beat that actually seemed to hurt. A decision needed to be made and Noah, bracing himself for trouble, started to walk away from the teller and westwards along the street, casting a look over his shoulder as he did so. The figure had not moved though it seemed to be looking his way. Noah, pace now quickening, continued to make his way along *Töngesgasse* and towards the rebuilt and pretty Liebfrauenkirche as he again checked behind to see the figure which worryingly had now started to walk his way. His heart, now thumping and all tiredness having left him, was telling him to run and he did so, quickly, towards the square and the safety of numbers. Here, people continued to enjoy the warm summer night and here, surrounded by too many people for there to be too much fear, Noah turned to await his foe, feeling this was as good a place to make a stand as any. Within moments his hooded friend arrived in the square and walked up towards Noah who was stealing himself to face the inevitable. Then, at 20 feet away, the young man revealed himself, pushing his hood back to reveal a kind and happy face as he turned to embrace a lovely young girl who had been waiting for him by a fountain in the square.

Noah, feeling suitably stupid and wonderfully relieved at the same time, made his way out of the square, hailed a taxi and made his way back to his hotel where sleep would come soon and dreams would relive the chase that never was.

By 10am the next morning he was in his car and leaving Frankfurt. His sleep had mercifully arrived very quickly and surprisingly he had slept until the room service arrived with his breakfast. A certain peace had awoken with him and a full day of no actual incidents began to assuage him that he was in the clear and he could now just concentrate on getting the job done. The city gave way to German countryside and he was pleased to be away from his stop-off and again be on his journey. It would be a long day of driving but by the end of it he would be in Krakow and he could begin to weigh up his plans in the actual place that would decide his family's future. As he drove on and on he now feverishly replayed his scheme over and over again, the flight to delivery of the famous painting back to the Czartoryski. The plan had seemed remarkably simple when he had made it. He was to stay at The Sheraton which, for better or worse, had been pre-booked for some time, check out the lie of the land around the museum, and then deliver the painting into the hands of the director, Henryk Padowski. Noah had already had an appointment set up with him, the story being that Noah was doing a research piece on the Czartoryski for *The Observer* newspaper under the charming alias of Charles Devere PhD. A friend from university, another rugby player who worked at the paper, had kindly set up the meeting by email with the director's PA. It had all been surprisingly easy with the power of an English newspaper unlocking the door to Mr Padowski very easily.

The journey from St Ives to Poland had all gone very well indeed and apart from the obvious hiccup in London with some unknown hit man with a knife ready to inflict pain and violence, a minor blip in a blue sky smiled Noah to himself darkly, nothing else had happened. There had been no hit in the square in Frankfurt by a young couple in love with one another, no break-in to the rather delightful Audi car overnight. Presumably Tom's brilliant plan with the change of car had worked and Noah, on an open road with absolutely no cars behind him, felt suddenly rather elated, a rush of happiness flooding into his bloodstream. He was better, too, for his full night's sleep and he now, for the first time since London, began to truly relax into the journey, his entire music library continuing to work its way through tune after tune and filling the car on shuffle.

It was ten o'clock in the evening when Noah finally checked into his room at The Sheraton in Krakow, already booked and prepaid, and wonderfully and somewhat poetically, Noah thought, in the name of this imaginary Charles Devere, art historian. Noah smiled to himself as he entered his room, resplendent in his new role, and walked straight over to the menu by the bed and ordered room service, pausing as he did so in the mirror and chatting to Charles about the journey in a two-way conversation that made him laugh. Noah had fully intended to go into the city and relax in the Old Town which looked so impressive in the articles he had seen, but a mixture of his tiredness from a long day at the wheel and the fact that the city had greeted him with an almighty storm, helped him decide a good night's sleep was the best policy.

By eleven o'clock he was feeling exceptionally sleepy, a destroyed cheese sandwich and two bottles of beer emptied. He went over to his bag and, picking out his well-worn journal, he saw the package from Flora resting there. He had purposely waited to open it, wanting the exploits of the delivery to be out of the way and, in truth, the wedding that would be happening in three days now, to be out of the way too. Still, his hand wavered over the book and then, without thinking about it, he had picked it out of his bag and returned to the bed.

He looked at the package, weighing it in his hands as he did so. It was clearly a book and quite a weighty one too. He smiled as he saw how she had wrapped it. Typical Flora. Beautiful thick cream paper, a lovely rich and luxurious blue bow, and yet it was all pulled together with Sellotape too long and the paper not in line and cut roughly. He loved her for that, for her ability to be her and not hide it. Did she even know she did this, that her very imperfections made her to him, Noah, perfect? He had been determined to wait for this moment but now, curiosity and the need to be closer to the girl he had lost taking over, he could not resist.

'Well, Flora,' he said to the package, 'here goes.'

He gently pulled back paper to reveal the anticipated book, no surprise there, but when he turned it over to reveal the title a smile lit up his face. *Raphael!*, it declared in large letters, and then underneath, *From Urbino to Rome*. The preface told him it was written by the National Gallery primarily to accompany the first ever major exhibition of paintings and drawings by the master in Britain from October 2004 through to January of the following year. No one knew that one painting that was not featured in the exhibition was hiding just a few hundred miles west and had been for some time. His stomach lurched at that. He turned the page and found Flora's handwriting greeting him. Her writing was small and simple and, like her wrapping of presents, slightly messy and yet unique. He smiled at the letters before even reading them and ran the fingers of his right hand over them.

'My Flora,' he whispered several times while reading her note.

'To Noah. The great traveller! Here is a book about your new friend. In many ways you are quite alike and here's why:
1. You both have very fancy names
2. You both look quite dapper, yet not dashing. For the record I much prefer dapper
3. You are both artists, Raphael with his paintings and you with your beautiful words
4. You both have flowing locks
5. You are both surf boys
OK, I may have made the last one up but you never know! I love you, Noah Spearing, and I am thinking of you and sending you a big kiss on your quest. This little gift will give you something to remember your journey and the very special reason you have gone on it. Keep safe and come back to me soon. Surfing without you is just not the same.
Your Flora,
    XX'

After reading the note nine times Noah decided he really should stop trying to read her undying love into it. Clearly she loved him very much, but also it was plain to see that this adorable girl was, in only a mere few days, about to get married to that big guy with the extremely hard punch. Still, he took great comfort from her words and putting down the book he allowed sleep to take him with a huge smile on his face. Three simple words played over and over again in his head. 'She loves me, she loves me, she loves me, she loves me...,' and with those fine words he went shadow-boxing into his dreams.

Chapter 14

The Letter

With Mikhail having left her in St Ives and Noah about to do so, Tess had set about painting a series that she had thought about for some time. The way she worked was to allow ideas to germinate over a period of time, usually for several mind-chewing months and then, when she was ready and it was time for release, they just spilled out like water from a tap that would not turn off. This was the time to seize the moment with glee and she did so, willingly giving over her mind, her body, her very soul, to this process that would use and abuse her.

She had been working hard now in her studio, which took up the whole of the back of her house on the first floor, for several weeks and the project was showing its usual mixture of pieces coming together and others causing her tremendous stress and upset. She had done this, worked like this, for several years and though and she knew her patterns and had learnt to relax into them more as she had got older, the process still gave her the mixed bag of unrelenting artistic release laced through with the streaks of acute anxiety.

Tess loved working in her studio. It was her place to be lost to the world and to be in the middle of all she knew so well. When she had found this house, her precious haven of a home, and made this space into her studio, she had felt at last that she had truly found herself. Here she would turn off her phone, which in truth was no hardship as she rarely had it on, unplug her house phone, lock her back gate and hide away for as long as she wanted to, often only eventually disturbed by the need to buy materials of food, or by Noah and Sylvia climbing over the back wall to find out if she was actually alive. They would normally leave her for a week or so before going to such extremes.

Tess's work had suffered in recent months with Mikhail not only taking up her actual time, but also taking up almost all of her precious thinking time. Where her mind was often an open sky where ideas could float and develop and she would allow ideas to germinate and play, it had become, with Mikhail in her life, blocked to these easy free-flowing thoughts. Her mind had instead become bogged down, ideas not flowing anywhere particularly and her artistic flow blocked by a sudden thick sea mist that stunted all artistic rhythm. Few drawings therefore had been made, little had inspired her photography and few words had been written in her many notebooks that she always kept on the go. Instead she had been lost to the love of a man, a man who had left her as they all did and now, mercifully, her creative star was again rising and the mist that had clouded her confused mind was at last disappearing.

With renewed energy and excitement, therefore, Tess started laying on thick brush strokes on her canvases, layering one statement down after another with a myriad number of different shades of blues as she sort to replay the depth of the colour of the ocean. How she loved her life with oils, the smell, the texture, the dimensions of work that she could produce. It made her happy, her focus not being off-put by peripheral matters that clawed at her mind. Of course this period of working would not last, and she knew this from experience and had learnt to flow with her own tides, working so hard when she was released to do so, trying to not get too frustrated when for one reason or another her energies would at last fade as tiredness would, as inevitably as night and day, arrive.

During the start of this new project, Tess had been forced to leave her studio a little more often than she would normally have done so to see her son, her precious Noah, and talk through his plans of his grand tour! She didn't really know why he had planned such an escape on his own other than the obvious need for him to hide from the oncoming loss of his Flora. Tess liked Flora a lot. She did not know why the two of them could not talk openly about how they felt, just lay it all out and see where it got them, though she did understand clearly that this too could end in fear, hurt and betrayal and she wanted to keep them both from these disaster zones entering their lives. Somehow, though, as she looked at them both, so often lost in their easy friendship, she did not see the same risks in them at least sharing their truths with one another. It hurt her to see them make a possible mistake that would be so hard to ever rectify. At the same time she wondered if Noah too was destined to live his life on his own, like her, find his own way and be free to roam the earth like a star parades around the breadth of the sky. It had suited her so why not her son also? These fleeting thoughts that connected her own psyche to her son were ones that she did not major in on too often finding the actual energy it sapped from her too much to carry. It would be what it would be and that was enough. Any thoughts of greater depth took her places she did want to be, these reflections inevitably leading to her own inability to form a single lasting relationship and the effect on the mind of her son. It hurt so much to think that her actions, her own inability to find her companion for any length of time, would permanently make a bed for her own son. It was a depressing notion and one that she saw as unhelpful, refusing to entertain the thoughts other than to recognise the possibility.

When Noah at last left St Ives for his trip, the now released Tess felt a tremendous surge of energy and for two solid days without sleep and with a mountain of crisps, chocolate, red wine and tea, she worked. On the third day she awoke, aching profusely across her whole body as she found her eyes trying to open from a deep sleep that had seen her lying by accident against the corner of an old, battered sofa stuck in the middle of her room. She felt a banging in her head and then realised that in fact the banging was coming from her back door down at the bottom of the house. Mumbling various obscenities under her breath, she pulled herself up and looked in a mirror on the wall, only to wish she had not bothered. The uncomfortable sleep had not been kind to her. She thought twice and then twice more about whether to bother to go down to her door, but with Noah away and knowing the knocking would almost certainly be her dear friend, Sylvia, she made her way, begrudgingly, down to her back door.

'I'm coming, I'm coming!' she called as cheerfully as she could muster under a cloud of a headache that was just making itself known with a constant pounding drum roll.

She pulled back the lock on the top of the door and twisted the key to unveil a rather flustered-looking Sylvia standing in bright sunshine at her back door.

'Well, don't you look bloody marvellous!' she declared.

'Do I indeed?' replied Tess, with as serious a voice as she could muster. 'And you are here because?'

Sylvia offered the question a slight scowl.

'Well, partly because it's been three days since I last saw you and partly because Noah called to ask how you were and seeing as I did not know I lied, obviously, and thought it best to come and tell you he had tried to call you. He knows you are in one of your deep artistic experiences, but he was also concerned knowing that "you know who" had also gone and…'

'Yes, yes, yes, OK. You win. What day is it?'

'It's Tuesday Tess! What day is it, indeed!'

'Tuesday. Right. Tuesday. Well, there's no need to go on and on is there? It really is not helping my "artistic experience" or my headache. Your silent apology accepted, therefore, for your unnecessary interruption and things are actually going quite well here as it happens. Thank you for not asking. Let me apologise to you and anyone else I have offended for doing my work. As for Noah and his tour of a lifetime, well, that was his choice, not mine. No need to worry about me, as ever. Apart from the crap food, far too much wine and lack of anything like you would call actual sleep, I am just dandy. Finally, as for that bastard of a Russian, well, he's gone hasn't he and so he is clearly now, as you very well know, an irrelevance to me. OK? Now, rant over. Could I offer you some tea?'

Sylvia smiled. She had learnt over many years to ride with the punches her friend delivered. Tess could be fiery and say things she may or may not have really thought with the same depth with which they would be delivered. She could cut with words quite harsh, and yet the next day have moved on from them as though nothing of any hurtful level had been said and leaving them still stuck in the recipient's head. She said it was her artistic temperament and Sylvia told her it was just her bad attitude. However you looked at it, it was Tess.

'Tea would be lovely Tess,' Sylvia replied lightly, 'What a lovely thought indeed,' she added, walking in and over to the kitchen table and handing over some fresh croissants before sitting down. The kitchen door was now wide open and the sounds of a beautiful St Ives morning were making their way into the room.

'How's it really going then?' Sylvia asked.

'My painting?'

'Yes.'

'I told you! It's going very well.'

'I thought you were being "humorous".'

'Well, think again, baby. I am making progress. Well, that is, I think I am making progress. I'm just throwing it all on, getting it all out.'

'I do hope so,' Sylvia replied, pulling as she did so a little sarcastic smirk from Tess.

Tess, kettle boiled, poured the tea, putting plenty of milk and three sugars into hers and a touch of milk and no sugar into her friend's. Sitting down at the table she leaned forward and took her friend's hand.

'I'm a crap friend at times, aren't I?'

'Yes.'

'But I'm also a brilliant friend, aren't I?'

'Yes.'

'So two and two...'

'Equals five.'

'Radiohead.'

'Correct.'

A moment of silence rested as they sipped their drinks and Sylvia watched the amusing sight of watching Tess hungrily devour two croissants.

'Thom Yorke came into the café yesterday. He'd been to the Tate.'

'He did not?' replied an amazed Tess, her eyes suddenly breaking wide open.

'No, he didn't,' laughed Sylvia. 'But I made you slightly regret your cutting off from the world, didn't I? Can you

208

imagine? I mean, I don't go into fame and all that crap, after all I know you and you are famous.'

'In Latvia.'

'Indeed, but if Thom Yorke came into the café I would seriously scream.'

'Wouldn't be very nice would it? Screaming. Punters wouldn't like it! Still, it would be understandable. Please forgive me, Sylvy, for being me.'

'Don't be silly. If I didn't accept you I would have dumped you a long time ago! I do know that you are high on crap food and wine and no doubt hardly sleeping at all. Looking at you would you say that's a fair assessment?'

'Perhaps so,' smiled Tess, 'you could be a detective!'

'I shall send Flora over with some good food.'

'Oh, that would be nice. Aren't you the sweetie?'

'Yes I am.'

'And dear Flora, how is she? I mean, it's the big day on Saturday!'

'A little morose actually. Prematch nerves, I suspect. I think Noah's going has upset her more than she's letting on.'

'Really?'

'Yes. Really. We both know they've been like best friends for so long. She needed him here.'

'He couldn't face it,' replied Tess quickly, defensively.

'I know,' replied Sylvia softly, 'I know.'

Tess saw a thought flash across her brain and a moment of recognition hit her.

'Can you ask her to pop by after work?'

'Tonight?'

'Yes. Please. Allows me to get a full day in and do a few errands. I better get a visit in to see Mother too.'

'OK. It will be about ten then.'

'Yea. Ten's great. I can see Flora and then get cracking!' replied a gleeful Tess.

'It's hilarious, isn't it? 10pm is like morning for you when you are working.'

'Indeed. The proverbial night owl. Hoot, hoot!'

'And you, dear Tess, how are you?'

Tess felt a moment of anger rise as she heard the question behind the question.

'Sylvy, I am not working this hard to have my mind caught up in once again thinking about him! Can we do this another time please?'

Sylvia nodded. A pause filled the air, the noise of it rising like a backwards vacuum of sound.

'Well done for not scolding me, Tess!' Sylvia said, breaking the spell.

Tess smiled. Her friend knew her too well!

'And yes,' Sylvia said, 'we can talk about what we are not talking about whenever you want to talk about it when you are done here. I miss you so get done soon and let's have a few days away together.'

'I'd like that.'

'I would, too. Maybe Bath, one of our nice hotels, time in the beauty spa, and looking at you, my God, you're going to need it!'

'How rude!' laughed Tess 'Though you are of course quite right and I would love that very much indeed. Last time we were there we picked up a rather special young man did we not?'

'Well, you did. I of course was out of the restaurant for just a few moments speaking to Craig and letting him know we were fine when in I came and there he was.'

'Rather a dish.'

'Yes and pretty good on the dance floor!'

'And the bedroom!' replied a now fully awake Tess, the memories of a past glory exhilarating through her brain. 'Mmmm!'

They laughed. They had done much together, been friends forever and seen each other go through life and all its turns. Sylvia had married in her early twenties to the man of her life, Craig Baker, her sixth-form sweetheart, a man who Tess very much approved of, and eight miscarriages she knew of and twenty-five years later they were still very much in love. Flora had started working with Sylvia, a family friend and neighbour, as soon as she had turned fourteen and the importance of the young girl to the older woman was clear and unspoken.

Sylvia stood and Tess joined her. The two ladies hugged. Sylvia turned to go and then, just as she got to the gate, she turned back.

'And one more thing.'

'Yes?'

'Please, please get me a key cut for this back gate so that I don't have to keep climbing over that bloody wall. My back thinks I'm having a laugh and tourists think it is peculiar behaviour!'

'It is peculiar behaviour', laughed Tess, 'and no, you can't have a key. You know that nobody has one so that no one can get in. That is the point! Break this rule and I will have you all in and out and that, dear girl, would never do.'

It was close on 10.30pm by the time Flora actually made it to Tess's house. It had been a long and busy day with the fine weather making the café packed all night as the holiday crowd and locals crammed in to see the sun setting in fabulous form with glorious reds and oranges filling the sky as it showed off to the west-facing beach-front café.

Calling in, therefore, with food provisions for Tess was a big ask as Flora was exceptionally tired and still faced a mountain of tasks that needed dealing with in preparation for her marriage at the weekend, but it was Tess, dear Tess, and Flora was pleased to have the connection of her missing Noah. As she arrived Flora was thankful to find the back gate unlocked as trying to raise Tess from the front door was a helpless task if she was up in her studio. The front door was always locked and was not blessed with a bell and you could knock as hard as you liked but the front door simply sat on the front of a porch that, in turn, was protected by a thick wooden door that refused to let any sound through. If Tess was locked away working you could only have any possible hope of raising her by knocking on the back door that was directly under her studio. The problem was that invariably if Tess was working she would make sure the back gate was securely locked meaning anyone who wanted to get to her would need to demonstrate their resolve by climbing the back wall. Thankfully the gate, this beautiful night, was unlocked and the last-ditch climb was rendered unnecessary.

Flora liked Tess a lot finding her to be a very strong-minded lady who had always been there for her and talked to her at great length over many years, never once treating her as anything other than an equal. Flora did struggle, along with others, with the moods Tess would have, ever-changeable dependant on where she was in her head. She had known Tess, though, since being a little girl and this gave Flora the advantage over new people to Tess of recognising what mood she was in before entering into conversation. On this night, a warm July evening, Flora entered the back gate to find Tess sitting on the back doorstep with a cigarette between her fingers and a welcoming smile on her face. Flora breathed a sigh of relief, the Tess she wanted to find was the one that was waiting for her, and a big smile filled her face as Tess patted the step to her side and motioned for Flora to come and join her.

'How's work been?' she asked Flora as she sat down beside her and she placed her arm around her back and pulled her in for a hug.

'Hectic,' replied Flora, feeling the weight of her mind begin to slip back as she sat down on the huge stone step that Tess had bought from a local quarry many years before and rooted it at the back of her house.

'And how are you?'

'Busy and flustered.'

'Ah, of course you are. It's a big thing this marriage stuff with so much to do. That's why I never did it!'

Flora laughed. The subject of Tess and her relationships was one she and Noah had discussed many times. If only Tess knew how many times and what they had discussed!

'It's just that, well, I feel there's so much still to do and it should be easier, shouldn't it? Is that silly?'

'No sweetheart,' replied Tess, turning to Flora and gently stroking her arm. 'Of course not. God knows, you see how flustered I can get. You are an angel in comparison.'

'I am not! You should see me when I shout at Jake.'

'Cigarette?'

'No, thank you,' she smiled, Tess knowing she never smoked and yet always still asking her if she wanted one and had done since she was a teenager.

'Wine?'

'Better not.'

'Coffee?'

'Your beautiful fresh coffee or instant?'

'My beautiful fresh coffee!' smiled Tess, rising to fetch some, the aroma reaching out into the backyard that was so full of pots of plants and fruit and vegetables that threw summer smells into the air. Flora threw her head back, her hair falling down behind her as she gazed upwards through the streetlights at the night sky. As she did so she wondered where all her time had gone, why this still moment was almost a memory to her and so far from her norm that it hurt.

'There you are,' said Tess, handing over a white porcelain mug of steaming black coffee to Flora, 'just as you like it.'

'Thank you; blissful!'

'You're welcome.'

Flora took a sip of the coffee, feeling calmed as she did so. Since being a little girl she had loved the sensation of the adult called Tess treating her as an equal, talking to her and knowing that her opinion really mattered.

'You know, Tess, you've always been very kind to me and, well, I just wanted to say thank you.'

Tess gave Flora a quizzical look.

'Oh, you know, sitting here, a moment's peace, I almost want to curl up with you here and hide until it's all over.'

'Well, you can,' replied Tess, knowing what was coming next, what she had planned through her day and was now about to deliver.

'I wish I could! I just wanted to say that to you, that's all.'

Tess leaned over and gave Flora a kiss on her cheek.

'Well, thank you. That is much appreciated. I know I can be a moody cow too and don't try to deny it,' Tess added in quickly, seeing Flora open her mouth to protest against what they both knew to be true.

'You are a special girl, young Flora.'

'I am not!'

'Yes, you are. Probably more so because you don't realise it. I knew it the moment I met you. You do not carry the weight of the world's expectations, present oncoming marriage train excepted. You have a free spirit and you float. Honestly, I really believe you do. Keep that sweetheart, it is a gift. Life will come, is coming, and it will try and take this off you, to nullify the true essence of who you are. Don't let this happen. You hear me?'

'Some people think I waste away.'

'Why?'

'Because I don't look to, as they see it, move forward.'

'Forward?'

'You know, work in some great task, or be working towards some amazing feat.'

'And do you want to?'

'If by task or feat they mean recognition, then of course not. You know this!'

'I do, sweetheart, I do and that is your gift. Never fear what others say, Flora. More often than not they lash out with their views from the depths of their own inadequacies. I should know because that's what I normally do! People just speak from their own journeys, honey. They do not see that you travel with your source intact and that, sweet girl, is why you are happy and many people are not.'

'I am happy. At least most of the time.'

'And now?'

Flora took a deep breath. It was easy to talk to Tess when she was in such an open place in her head and Flora wanted to talk.

'I feel a little sad, Tess, truth be known.'

'Why?'

'Well, I think you know why.'

'Noah.'

'Yes. Noah. I'm just so confused by it all. I wish he was here, here for me now. It just feels wrong without him here.'

Tess waited, time waited for Flora to find her truth.

'I mean, he just makes me feel good and the thought of him being away when I am about to marry Jake is just all plain silly. I feel stressed when if he were here he would calm me down and laugh with me and everything would be better. He claims his phone has broken.'

'Yes, he sent me that text too.'

Flora shot Tess a quick look back.

'But it isn't, is it?'

'It might be, sweetie. I mean, we are talking about Noah here and his record on anything techy is not great, is it?'

'Yea, might be then,' said Flora finding a slight smile as she did so.

Tess waited, weighing up her words.

'So you miss him?' Tess asked, the words teasing out some more words to stumble quickly and easily from the young girl's mouth.

'Yes, truly, madly, totally.'

'And don't you think that's interesting?' Tess asked, her voice as level as she could keep it.

'Interesting?' asked Flora, a mild panic forming inside her as she thought of Noah, her Noah and her need for him right now.

'I want to ask you something,' Tess asked, exhilaration rising as she did so.

'Yes?'

'If you knew a secret, something that could change a person's life were they to know this secret, would you share it with them?'

'I don't know. I guess if it was a good thing, at least if I thought it was a good thing and really important, then I would.'

'And if you weren't sure?'

'I'd probably ask a special person like you to help me!'

'Yes! Good answer. Well Flora, I have that decision to make now and I want to ask you what I should do.'

'Right,' replied Flora, lost in where the conversation had suddenly lurched from Noah to some quest Tess was on. 'Can you tell me more?'

'I can!,' smiled Tess. 'The thing is I have something that I think is so important that it would be wrong to not share it and I feel, therefore, I must.'

'Then you must,' replied Flora, 'I am sure you have thought it all through and if it is that important then what choice do you have?'

'That's right,' replied a satisfied though now quite nervous Tess, 'What choice do I have? In that case, Flora, I want to give you something.'

'Me?'

'Yes you.'

'OK,' Flora replied, confusion on her voice.

'It's not from me, it's from someone else who isn't here right now.'

Flora held Tess's gaze, not knowing what was coming next and feeling the conversation being strangely linked to the Joshua birthday-gift surprise.

215

'You see Noah wrote you a letter.'

'I haven't had it!' Flora replied quickly.

'No. He never gave it you. He hid it in his old bureau and made the mistake of telling me he had done just that.'

'Right?' said Flora, her heart now thumping at her ribcage banging so hard as though it was actually trying to get out. She watched, in seeming slow motion, as Tess pulled out a white envelope from the side of the step. This moment had clearly been thought through.

'And it's here, Flora, sealed, unopened.'

Tess handed the letter to Flora, the young girl's hand trembling as she accepted it.

'And what does it say, this letter?'

'Ah, that's not for me to tell you, Flora. Not that I know exactly, of course. I haven't read it, but I have a good idea.'

'Right. And that idea is?'

Tess smiled.

'It's your letter. Read it. If you want Noah to never know you read it just give it back to me. He writes like me and I will happily forge the writing of your name on the front of the envelope and place it back where I found it two hours ago. He will never know you read it.'

'But Tess, if he wanted me to read it he would have given it to me, wouldn't he?' Flora's words fell out in staccato steps, her nerves on edge.

'Would he?'

Flora, without even realising it, had naturally grasped the letter and was holding it close to her breast. There was no way on earth that she was not going to read the letter.

'Can I read it now, here?'

'Of course you can. I'll leave you in peace. I'll be in the studio.'

Tess rose, knowing that she would not be going to the studio to do any work. She did not know if what she had just done was right or wrong or if Noah would, if he ever found out, be so angry with her that they could actually fall out. She knew only that she had acted on impulse yet but for the sake of a thousand reasons; she knew she had known no other choice.

Chapter 15

Henryk Awaits

A bright and inexplicably hopeful Krakow Wednesday morning greeted him, sun smiling at him cheerfully as he pulled his head up from the pillow, his face now turned to the window to catch the rays as they rested on armies of floating dust in his room, the blinds letting in this stream having not been fully drawn from the previous night. Noah stretched out letting out an exclamation of relief and then lent over to retrieve his phone and was relieved to see it was still early morning. He touched his book and was about to open it again to read Flora's note when he stopped himself. Work needed to be done and now was not the time for sentimentality to take over.

He got up, stretched, and showered, and as he did so thought streamed through his mind of the day ahead. The visit, the towering moment of truth with the man who would hold the key to his future, a Mr Henryk Padowski, was arranged for 11am. The director was expecting an art historian from London doing a journalistic piece on the museum and he would be getting a huge surprise instead. How he would take the news, what immediate impact it would have upon him, well, Noah had no way of knowing. All he could do, and had done, was replay again and again how the conversation would run, how he would bring up the real reason for his visit, and hope that Henryk would be both reasoned and understanding. Ultimately, though, he knew that it would be what it would be and that it was impossible to plan for an exact here. What was clear to him was the line he needed to deliver early and precisely, that he had the painting, that all was recorded to ensure the gallery was kept honest, and that he, Noah Spearing, was not under any circumstances to be unveiled. These were his terms and all Mr Padowski had to do was agree to them. It was a simple plan with the truth of fragility written all over it.

Noah had decided to leave the painting in the train station baggage collection. It was a huge gamble but a calculated risk. He felt to take it with him was simply an unacceptable option as Henryk may simply call security and that, if he had the painting with him, would be the end of that. He had considered hiding the painting in his room but again, should he be arrested, this would be the first place they would look. The second place they would look would be his car and so this had ruled out the Audi as a hiding place. No, the train station by way of elimination made sense so that was to be his first journey of the day.

Noah had decided against having breakfast in the restaurant, its huge open spaces and tall ceilings being far too much on show for him. A low profile was required so a pleasant continental breakfast had been delivered to his room and quickly consumed. As he left the hotel, leaving behind him its ultra-modern furnishings, reflections everywhere caused by the huge windows that played with the light, he stepped into welcome fresh air and looked up to the sky. It was the natural thing to do for someone born and brought up by the coast. What was the weather bringing today? The sky was now threatening, that was for sure. No rain now, but rain would most definitely arrive, and heavy at that. How often, thought Noah as he crossed the road and began to make his way across town, had he looked up at the Cornish sky to assess what was coming? It was amazing that as a local he knew, could accurately predict virtually normally without fail, the day ahead from how the morning sky looked. People would never believe that, but Noah smiled. He knew it to be true. A feeling of nostalgia swept over him as he thought to a dark, brooding, menacing sky that would signal a storm back home. This sky, the Krakow sky, was different, more obviously grey. At home the dark clouds intermingled with the sun and created a dark blue grey all of their own making. It was a colour he had grown to recognise and love and it was one he would have welcomed to see now.

It was a good walk across a buzzing and beautiful Krakow to get to the train station and it would have been easier to get a taxi but Noah had figured it would clear his head and allow him to get his focus right. Besides, once the painting was safely hidden, it was a relatively short walk back to the Czartoryski and this was good; deposit the painting into yet another "safe" place and then go right ahead and do the deed leaving him no time to procrastinate. His life would then be well, his grandad's memory restored, and Noah could at last get back on the way to things being normal.

Noah, or Charles Devere as he was now, wore a dark navy lightly pinstriped suit, something he would never do in "normal" life. He had purchased it from the Sue Ryder charity shop on Tregenna Place, paying £30 for a £300 suit. It fit, which was a pleasant surprise, and after it had been dry-cleaned it had mostly lost that fusty smell with just a stale hint to happily remind him of his clothing's fine origin. He also wore as suggested by Flora a hat, a trilby to be precise, and this, in a masterstroke of late-night thinking, was one of his grandfather's old favourites. It was a little on the tight side, having to cope with Noah's plethora of hair, but it was a discomfort worth having for two reasons. Firstly, it was Joshua's and gave Noah a sense of injection of the bravery of that man, bravery he most definitely needed at this time; and secondly, it would not blow off in the wind and, given he didn't intend to take it off at all, this was perfect. Finally, Noah wore black-rimmed spectacles. They were actually a pair of fashion accessories he had picked up several years earlier for club wear but here, on the streets of Krakow, he looked quite the debonair businessman about town.

As he walked across a city as foreign to him as the earth upon which he strode, he was hugely impressed by the beauty of the city, the Old Town in particular glowing with fabulous architecture, Gothic, Renaissance and Baroque all standing out and screaming for attention. Looking down at him from every angle as he walked on his mission of mercy were a myriad of church spires that followed him now as he walked over the pretty, cobbled streets, ugly gargoyles spitting their venom, demanding that Noah keep his evil secret well away from them.

He skirted the *Rynek Glowny* with its huge 10-acre square, the largest in any of Europe's medieval cities, with its sixteenth-century Renaissance Cloth Hall and the splendid fourteenth-century Gothic Basilica of the Virgin Mary, and even with all that was on his mind he was able to admire what he saw, underlining, he reasoned, that this was a good day. It was a beyond-striking square, the main one in Krakow and the regular meeting place for many of its inhabitants and tourists alike. It was huge and magnificent and reminded Noah of some of the great squares he had seen on his travels across Europe.

'Fabulous,' he muttered under his breath, pausing to take a few shots with his eyes, just as his mother would do. Noah did look around with his mother's insatiable attitude to take in where she was, a hunger within him to take in what was before his viewpoint. At first glance at the people before him Krakow presented itself to him as a city like pretty much every other city, people going about their business with varying degrees of haste or lethargy. The streets teemed with those who had and those who were desperate to have and this universal truth hit home as Noah reckoned on what city in the world does not have these extremes. There was an energy before Noah's eyes here, though, an undeniable vibe that seemed to rest on the many young people he saw. Noah had read that this was a university city, a well-read place, and this all matched openness, an ease that seemed to float in the air. This historic part of the city that he was now well and truly in the centre of was simply stunning and its people, almost perhaps in recognition of the ground they proudly walked on, seemed to walk just that little bit taller, with more pride and purpose, a sense of time and place in their every step. If places actually have their own soul then this place spoke to Noah of elegance and an easy self-assurance, not a brashness that most cities courted in order to scream out their value to you. No, here, in the centre of Krakow, Noah felt a peace and this calmed him immensely on this most stellar of mornings as he made his way to deliver this city's lost treasure.

He walked up to the Czartorykski, the area mercilessly

almost free of traffic, as it was across the whole of the Old Town apart from access and the one tram line towards the south of the Old Town, and he had his first view of the reason he had come here. The museum was more impressive in the flesh than the pictures he had seen, its beautiful façade promising treasures within, and Noah waited for a while at the side of a street café, a tree shading him from the sun to take in the place he had only looked at tirelessly on the internet.

'Coffee?' asked a voice and Noah turned, startled by another voice directed at him and saw a waiter who had assumed Noah was going to drink.

Noah thought of just shaking his head but then said, 'Yes, please,' and took a seat and then mumbled as he realised not only had the waiter assumed he was English but that also Noah had responded in English. Still it felt good to just sit down and take a few moments to look across the road to the Czartoryski and wait awhile. The coffee arrived within moments, thick, black aromatic coffee and Noah, who had already noticed the city was teeming with a copious amount of coffee shops, took a sip and smiled at the glorious taste that met his lips. As he sat there he gathered his energies for what lay ahead. Sticking to the plan was his main goal and the fact that he was already off plan made him wince a little. Still what harm could a little coffee do? The boost to his system was welcome and somehow it felt comforting to be sitting so close to the reason he had come across Europe. Flora had spoken of danger and yet here, on pretty Jana Street at the top of the Old Town, Noah felt fine, nervous yes, but also fine. The golden glow of the walls of the museum was really beautiful and uplifting and Noah allowed his eyes to drift over the lines and the texture. After a few minutes Noah realised in part he was putting off the inevitable and so he finished his coffee and rose, waving to the waiter and then regretting the action knowing that he would be more easily remembered now should it ever come to that. Realising he was hopelessly unsuitable for covert operations he half grimaced as he walked away to the station.

He felt a whole range of emotions gnawing at him now, many of which had come to the fore when he had unwrapped his present from Flora the night before. With much effort he fought against them, pushing them down into the safe in his memory where he kept them hidden just as he had for the majority of the trip. It was the only way; hide the painting, deliver the news, make a delivery and move on with the rest of his life.

He was walking quickly now, his pace having speeded up as he headed east towards the train station. At one point he caught a reflection of himself, the man he saw being so not as he normally looked that he found himself laugh out loud, the moment arriving easily and calming him as it did so. Soon he was arriving at the legendary *Krakow Glowny*, a lively station that Noah had thankfully researched and knew exactly where to take his package, which he did without fuss. How strange that within a few moments he handed over what had dominated his life for months now, one moment in his hands and the next being taken away from him. The strangeness of the moment immediately prompted a lightness of his load and a guilt of leaving it alone, without him. He had handed over the heavily wrapped package with no questions of any gravitas, mercilessly, asked. He paid the fee, was given his reclaim ticket and that was that. Maybe this was a sign of just how simply this whole thing could go? Why not, he reminded himself cheerily as he turned to leave. There had been no visit of darkness on his plans since London and another night had passed without incident. He quickly left the station, focus firmly in the ascendency, and walked back to the Czartoryski and his waiting meeting.

Arriving at the museum he walked through opening doors and into the clearly aged building and walked without hesitation straight to reception and informed them of his arrival for his meeting with the director. He was shown to a waiting seat where he sat and tried to fend off a thousand thoughts that wanted to be answered, humming "Pie Jesu" nervously, as he awaited his fate. Mercifully within only a few minutes he was met by a delightful young man who greeted him in perfect English and announced himself as Henryk's PA.

'Delighted to meet you, Mr Devere. Follow me please.'

Pleasant chat ensued as they walked back and through to Henryk.

'Good journey, sir?'

'Yes indeed, splendid really,' replied Noah in a painfully clipped Queen's English accent that suddenly came from nowhere. It made the Cornishman grimace and he decided immediately to soften that immensely when he met the director.

'Good, very good. And your stay?'

'The Sheraton', answered Noah quickly before realising the immediate error, 'was my first choice,' he quickly added, 'but how expensive!'

The young man laughed.

'Ah yes, business class only there I think.'

'So I'm here in the Old Town in a cheap little place which is quite lovely,' beamed Noah while wondering what name he could make up if asked anymore about this dreamt-up hotel. Happily within moments Noah was shown through a door and into the director's waiting room where he was shown to a comfortable seat and given a sweet steaming tea in a brightly-coloured and beautiful china teacup. His nerves remained but they had steadied from the walk through the museum and the long corridor that had brought him here, at last, to Henryk. Now was the moment and there was nothing more he could do, except, perhaps, run! He smiled at that.

'What will buzz will bee,' he whispered under his breath, another of Joshua's sayings, as the door opened and out stepped the man who would decide his destiny, a man who up until now he had only seen in photographs.

'Charles,' Henryk declared loudly, looking exactly like his photos and reaching out both hands to grasp Noah's as he rose from his chair, almost dropping his teacup as he did so. 'Pleasure to meet you, absolute pleasure. We don't get many visitors from London so it's always a joy, particularly someone so interested in art and history which is what we are all about here at the Czartoryski,' declared Henryk in perfect English, charm and kindness flowing out of him and lowering Noah's nerves.

'The pleasure is all mine, sir,' replied Noah, jovially, warming immediately to the director as Henryk showed him into a very modern office. As they walked through to the room Noah realised he had modified his own accent into something sounding far more reasonable with the pompous edge having happily disappeared.

'Please,' said Henryk pointing to two white leather sofas in the corner of the room that sat around a huge black marble fireplace that was very grand and no doubt very old too.

'Impressive office, Mr Padowski.'

'Oh please, no formalities, you must call me Henryk.'

'Yes, sure, Henryk it is, and please do call me Charles,' they both then laughed, 'In fact you already did!'

The door opened, causing Noah to jump a little, and in walked Henryk's PA with fresh tea and an assortment of pastries and biscuits.

'Oh, that's very kind,' said Noah. Henryk waved this away in an it's-the-least-we-can-do fashion.

'So, good trip?'

'Yes, flew in last night,' started Noah, the first lie easily out.

'And staying anywhere nice?'

'Yes, a pleasant place around the corner. I was just laughing with your man that I had looked at The Sheraton but it was far too expensive!'

'Ah yes, indeed. A safe choice for visitors with cash but faceless really. You did the right thing staying here in the heart of things. Good man, Charles!'

'Indeed. Thank you. I intend to come back. It's a beautiful city that you have here!' said Noah easily.

'It is, it is, Charles. Wonderful. If you wouldn't mind the imposition let me make a note to drop you some suggestions for a future visit,' said Henryk, immediately adding a note on his iPad.

'Thank you, that really is too kind,' replied a happy Noah, revelling in the nice man that sat before him.

'So, how can we help you, Charles? I understand from London that you want to ask me specifically about the history of the Czartoryski?'

'I do,' replied Noah, eyeing up a chocolate biscuit and wondering whether it wasn't just easier to go along with the story rather than get into the small matter of the Raphael.

'Please,' said Henryk, spotting the young man's gaze and lifting up the plate of biscuits to the waiting hand of the Englishman.

'So, where shall we start?' said Henryk.

'Well, the area that really interests us is around the Second World War.'

'Ah yes, of course! You English will never get over that, will you? All your questions seem linked to that war. Your final glory, yes?'

'I guess, though not mine of course. It seems a different life, a different world to mine.'

'Indeed. Me too. My parents were very young then, let me see, probably not even ten, and yet somehow, the whole size of the war, the way it encapsulated the world, was something that was bound to stay in our psyche forever. Europe will be forever scarred from those wounds I think. Blood, as they say, runs deep, does it not?'

'Yes. And, I guess, the pure ideologies that opposed one another?' offered Noah.

'Indeed. This is the true depth of that conflict.'

'And your museum was in the middle of it.'

'That it was. A dreadfully difficult time in our history, a history that stretches back... '

'Over 200 years!'

'Ah yes, of course. You are the research expert. You know all these things, anyway. That's what Google is for, yes?'

'Yes', laughed Noah, 'that's exactly what Google is for. What on earth did we do before it?'

Henryk laughed loudly at this, leaning forward and pouring them both tea.

'Sugar?' he asked Noah.

'Yes please. Two.'

'Ah, sweet tooth, like my wife. Me, I just have a drop of milk.'

'Probably as it should be.'

'It is funny about the Internet because when I was a student, majoring of course in art history...'

'Yes, I read you did that in Paris.'

'I did. Well done, Charles. It's not an exam but you are doing well! Anyway I did much research in the famous treasures of art throughout the great halls of Paris, that finest of cities, and do you know, I did all of it by book; all of it! Often I would be carrying those huge, large reference books from one part of the floor to the other, my arms aching from the sheer weight of them, my shoulders shot through with pain!'

'Yes. I love those old books actually. There is something very warming about them don't you think?'

'There is and I always thought I would never be converted to modern technology, swearing allegiance to the old ways, but I have been, of course, and love the ease of access of knowledge.'

'Though you have kept your books,' said Noah looking around the room to the impressively filled bookshelves.

'Ah yes. I couldn't be without them to be frank. They are like an extension of me and I do look at them often. As good as my computer is it cannot beat the open page, the smell of the book, the dust that greets you!'

They both laughed at that.

'So Charles, you could have got, and will have got, all the background you needed on the Czartoryski Museum online, so why are you here?'

'Well, to visit.'

'Of course.'

'The way it actually looks, the smells, the sense of history first hand. You know, get a feel of the place.'

'And you must! I will take you round, of course, but thereafter you must go where you like. It really is a gem of a building with its treasure trove of antiquities.'

'And, of course, I am here to meet you.'

'Me?'

'Yes, indeed. You have been here for many years now.'

'I have, making me an antiquity, eh?' Henryk laughed.

'And, therefore, you know the history of the place better than any book.'

'That I do. That's the historian in you.'

'I guess it is,' replied Noah, feeling like he was filling more and more the role of reporter and moving further away from the lost Raphael conversation he had come to have.

'So, shall we start the grand tour?' asked Henryk, surprising Noah by jumping up out of his seat with a real spring in his step and clearly excited about showing the man from *The Observer* around the place. Noah crumbled.

'Yes, indeed!' he replied, with a surprising amount of

enthusiasm, part of him undoubtedly pleased to be able to put off the inevitable.

As they walked towards the door of the office, Henryk already beginning to talk about the museum, Noah managed an inward smile telling himself as he did so that this way he could get to know the director better and in doing so ensure that he was the right man to share the news of the Raphael with and that when he did so, Henryk would most definitely believe him and be supportive. Yes, Noah told himself, this time could be relationship building which would only make the handing over of the Raphael an even safer exchange.

The fact that Noah was oblivious to removing his hat on entering the office of the director, and was now to be caught on every camera around the museum, had eluded him. His future as an international spy had got off to an unfortunate start.

Five hours later, after an extensive tour and a delightful lunch with Henryk, Noah left the museum with an invitation to dinner that night at the Padowski's and the heavy realisation as he did so that he had not only made sure his cover would be blown with his face now on every camera throughout the museum, but that his plan that had involved a quick in-and-out visit at the museum was in total and utter tatters. He had fallen under the happy spell of a wonderful man, Henryk, who he considered from the moment he had met him as lovely, and, as was ever the case with Noah, had allowed the happy circumstance of time to become irrelevant. No news about the Raphael had been shared, its dirty secret still buried under the earth of time. At one point an opportune time had arrived, the war talked about and the German occupation and cruelty raised, but with Noah having the words in his mouth to ask specifically about the stolen paintings, the words refused to develop into a noise.

Henryk had walked Noah to the door and shook his hand warmly saying, 'I've really enjoyed that, Charles. Such a pleasure taking an enthusiast around our rooms. We shall look forward to welcoming you to our home this evening!'

Noah had smiled broadly and set off with the initial glow of Henryk's warm words slowly dissipating as thoughts of failure crept over his mind.

On leaving the museum he walked north to the *Planty*, the

strip of parkland that circled the Old Town, and then followed it in a clockwise route south making his way back to The Sheraton. The sun had mercifully arrived and a walk of shame was lifted by the touch of the sun as the people around him filled their day. It was a very pretty park, full of a collection of differing gardens adorned by fountains and monuments and as Noah's eye was pulled in this and that direction he convinced himself that the building of a relationship with Henryk was, on balance, the best of things. What harm could it do, he considered. A kiss of hope on his cheeks. He made his way back to the hotel where it nestled happily on the banks of the Wisla River. Retiring to his room and away from the crowds of business types and wealthier travellers in the busy public areas in the hotel, Noah ordered a sandwich and then to take his mind off the night and the inevitable need to talk to Henryk about the painting, he turned on the TV and began a favourite pastime playing on the room's PlayStation on FIFA. His heart, sadly, wasn't in it and form, inevitably linked to mindset, dipped.

Stretching he made his way to his bedside and picked up Flora's gift only to then quickly place it down knowing that emotionally it was too heavy for him now. He then picked up one of his novels that he had brought with him, a new Tom Sharpe novel, and thankfully had a few laughs as the minutes turned into an hour and then it was time to go. He so wanted to get changed but felt that his casual gear was simply too casual to have him pass as any sort of serious art researcher, and so he stayed in the same old, drab clothes he had worn all day and he made his way to front of the hotel and caught a taxi. The drive up to Henryk's apartment in the leafy and highly exclusive area of *Bronowice* took about 20 minutes as they negotiated the traffic out of the city as it meandered regally and slowly through the roads of inertia and then finally opened out into the quieter havens of the rich.

It was half-past seven, with the grand dame of dusk getting ready for her arrival, as Noah began to walk up the fine steps of the apartments that housed the Padowski residence. Noah came armed with a beautiful white bouquet of flowers and a very expensive French red wine to the front of the rather beautiful looking and mightily impressive entrance door which, before he had chance to get to the ancient gold-ridden looking bell knob, swung open and a delightful young girl of maybe six or seven with long dark curls, skipped down the remaining steps left between Noah and the door, and grasped his hand.

'Hello, Charles,' she said in perfect English, 'A pleasure to meet you. Daddy sent me down to get you.'

'Did he indeed?' replied Noah, as she grasped his hand and led him up the last few steps and through into a grand entrance foyer with a fine-looking chandelier that filled the entrance.

'We are on the ground floor because we get the garden!'

'Of course, I love gardens!' he answered, truthfully. Growing up with his grandma had left him no option but to adore anything that incorporated plants and space for nature.

'That's good,' declared the little girl happily and in a tone of a well-done-you, 'I can show you around my garden if you like. You would like that, wouldn't you!'

'Sure. I'd like that very much,' laughed Noah happily. 'What's your name little lady?'

'Anna,' replied the little girl, extremely happy to have been called a little lady.

'Well, Anna, your English is perfect.'

'Of course it is, silly,' she said as they reached the open door that opened into another grand inner hallway for Apartment number 2. There, waiting for him, was Henryk and in his arms a little one asleep.

'Welcome to our home,' announced Henryk, 'ah, and you've brought gifts. No need, really no need, but a delight all the same.'

'Not at all, it was the least I could do,' replied a happy Noah, thrilled to see the most excellent Henryk again.

'Well, thank you. I trust the welcoming party was to your liking,' he added, nodding towards the hallway for Noah to follow him in.

'She's fantastic, I mean, her English, well, it's perfect!'

'Indeed. That's because her mother is English! A little detail I may have forgotten to tell you! I thought about that earlier when I was on my way home. Quite funny really.'

Noah managed an awkward smile while inside his heart

dropped to well below his ankles. He had naively been hoping for an easy evening of niceties with an audience that spoke no English save his host and that would lead to a private conversation with Henryk and the real reason for him being there. Clearly his research had not been that good after all and now an evening of talking of England and inventing more lies awaited. It was another setback of potential woe and disaster that was forming at the back of an orderly queue of similar mistakes.

They had walked past a hallway of exquisite photographs and paintings and arrived into a huge kitchen-dining area at the back of the house that opened onto a veranda that in turn fell away towards a large and extremely pretty garden. This was Krakow top grade real estate and this apartment, despite the housing crashes, was still worth a lot of money.

'And here she is, the reason you got your interview,' declared Henryk proudly.

Catherine Padowski, her long dark hair imaging exactly that of her daughter's, stepped up to Noah and kissed him on both cheeks, taking off him the flowers and wine as she did so.

'Hello Charles, such a pleasure. Thank you so much for these flowers, they are divine! We don't get many visitors from England and I was so keen to make sure that we didn't miss out on a connection from the mother ship.'

'Right,' was all he could muster, wondering what on earth she meant by mother ship and looking helplessly at Catherine and then back to Henryk.

Henryk laughed and explained.

'You see, I never have visitors unless I have to. Not really my thing. Normally I leave it to PR but in this case...'

'In this case,' took over Catherine, while leading them onto the covered veranda to sit down on some lovely comfortable chairs that made the most of the garden view, 'he made the mistake of mentioning your colleague's email and I told him he had to see you and bring you home for dinner.'

'Right, well, that's just my luck,' replied a now hapless Noah.

'Yes it is, young man, and I hope Henryk obliged you with a full tour of the beautiful museum?' asked Catherine happily;

oblivious it appeared to the young man's extreme discomfort.

'He did. He was brilliant. I had a great day to be honest, Mrs Padowski,' replied the crestfallen Noah, determined as he did so to appear engaged and upbeat.

'Oh Catherine, please.'

'Sorry, yes, erm, Catherine, it was so useful. I mean, you can only learn so much from researching on the Web and books. Face to face with history adds so much, don't you think?'

Noah's brain was now working on super-fast broadband. Catherine was English, which meant what exactly? Did it matter? Of course not! Just relax he told himself over and over in his head, everything would be just fine.

'Now, drinks anyone?' asked Catherine.

'I'll just put Sofia down,' replied Henryk, allowing Catherine to kiss her cheek as he went past.

'Anna,' Catherine called to her daughter who was at the bottom of the garden tying something or other together, 'time for bed!'

'But Mamma,' she replied as she ran up the lawn towards them, 'Charles said he'd love to look at my garden!'

Catherine looked at Noah, apologies in her eyes.

'Do you mind? It is her pride and joy.'

'Mind? No, of course not. I'd love to!' he said, bouncing out of his chair and delighted to get some space away from the adults to think. At the door his tour guide for the garden awaited, a huge smile on her face and her hand held out.

'Thanks, Charles. Wine or beer to start?'

'Wine would be lovely thank you. Whatever you have.'

Noah and Anna walked down the lawn, swinging their held hands as they did so.

'You have funny hair,' she said, without any hint of humour in her voice.

'Well, thank you,' replied Noah, smiling in return, 'and you have lovely hair.'

'Like Mamma's.'

'Yes indeed, like Mamma's. So, this is your garden?'

'It is!' she said proudly as they arrived at her bit of the garden that included her flowers and her vegetable plot. 'I'm growing lots of things. Daddy says it's good to grow things as it helps the environment.'

'It does. Daddy is very clever.'

She nodded proudly at that.

'Do you have a garden?' she asked expectantly.

'No, but…'

'So you don't you want to help the environment?' Anna said quickly and with much disapproval.

'Yes, I do!' laughed Noah, 'I don't have the space for a garden. My grandma has a garden and I spend a lot of time there. I love it very much. I hope one day I can have a garden like yours.'

That answer pleased little Anna a lot and she promptly began to explain in detail what had been in her garden, what was now in her garden and what would be coming. Noah, entranced by the little girl, offered much encouragement and shared some ideas from his own gardening background that Anna lapped up, apart from when he suggested using fluttering flags tied to sticks to wade off uninvited guests from the sky, to which the young girl replied, 'Oh, don't be silly, Noah. Don't you know who my Daddy is? The birds would never be so naughty!'

'Come on, you two!' called Henryk's voice, interrupting the children thought Noah as the two of them walked hand in hand back to Noah's fate.

'Can I stay up a little longer, Daddy?' asked Anna as they arrived to her waiting parents.

'No, sweetheart, it's far too late already. Have you enjoyed meeting Charles?'

'Yes,' she said, walking right up to him and kissing him on his cheek. 'He's lovely, though he does have funny hair and some funny ideas about the garden,' she said, a smile on her face as she left with her parting quip filling the air to be met by the sound of laughter.

'She's lovely,' said Noah to her clearly proud parents and then, eager to gain the initiative said, 'So, Catherine, how long have you been here?'

'Krakow?'

'I guess.'

Catherine looked at Henryk who was sitting back in his chair, relaxed, with a glass of Sauvignon Blanc in his hand.

'Twelve years?'

'Yes, it will be', Henryk agreed, 'at Christmas at least.'

'Christmas?' asked Noah.

'When we got married,' added Catherine.

'Ah, right. So you met?'

'Here,' she replied, 'at the museum.'

'And no, she hadn't come to interview me,' said Henryk, a big smile as he did so. 'She was touring.'

'With my boyfriend, in fact,' Catherine added.

'And I happened to be going out for lunch', took over Henryk, 'when I saw them trying to make sense of our cafeteria signage. In those days it was not too foreigner friendly really and, to be honest, not much of a café either! I went over to help and ended up having lunch with them.'

And much more, thought Noah.

'And much more,' said Catherine.

'Wow! And that was?'

'Oh, about fifteen, sixteen years ago. It was summer too,' said Catherine, reliving the memories as she did so. 'I went home, couldn't get this one out of my mind and then... '

'And then', continued Henryk, 'she wrote to me and I arranged what I told her was a pre-arranged trip to London and the rest, as they say, is history!'

'And so you came here to live. I can see why. Krakow is a beautiful city.'

'It is,' replied Catherine, 'and Poland is beautiful too. It's poor of course, in so many things, yet rich in so many others. In many ways it is the opposite of England.'

'And do you miss it?'

'England?'

'Yes.'

'Well, not really. I mean, I do go back all the time. I'm sure Henryk has told you what I do?'

'No darling,' interjected Henryk, 'I actually forgot to tell him anything at all, we were having such fun!'

'Oh Henryk! How you run an internationally famous art museum continues to amaze me!'

'And me too,' laughed Henryk.

'Well, what do you do?' asked Noah, trying to keep his voice lifted and not betray the nerves he felt creeping in upon him.

'I'm a journalist like you,' she replied proudly, immediately sending Noah's head into a downward spiral.

'I like to think of myself as a pure historian,' he muttered.

'Of course you do. Feels less dirty doesn't it?' she laughed. 'And yet here you are doing a piece for a newspaper! Well, as I said, I'm a journalist, though freelance now, of course, with two little ones to look after as well, but I do a lot of work for *The Observer*, given that's where I worked. No wonder you looked a bit blank earlier when I mentioned the mother ship!'

'I'm afraid blank is my favoured look,' said Noah, hoping to lift his suddenly sinking head and heart with a little bit of much needed mirth.

'Do you mind if I use the bathroom?' he asked, needing to buy himself some valuable thinking time.

'Of course, make yourself at home,' said Catherine. 'It's the first door on the left as you came in through the hallway. I'll get dinner out while Henryk checks in on Anna and we can all meet here in a few minutes.'

Noah walked down the corridor and straight to the entrance door to the apartment, reaching it and placing his hand on the handle to leave and forget his plan altogether. Thoughts raced around his head and fear drove them on, yet one thing stood out in his mind, that of his grandad and putting the past right.

He heard Joshua's voice say, 'Easy does it, tiger boy!'

Another something that would stay with Noah forever. 'Yes, easy does it,' he thought. He stepped back and turned back to find the toilet door only to find himself stepping into the broom cupboard as he did so.

'Wrong room, stupid,' he laughed to himself, stepping out, closing the door gently, and then finding the cloakroom. He washed his face with crisp, cold water and then, looking at himself in the mirror said simply, 'Out of the house and turn left.' It was the only mantra he had now and he would use it to keep going. Sure, this was a huge risk and with Catherine being a journalist it just got bigger, but he saw no choice. He had chosen to trust Henryk and nothing in the day he had spent with him had caused him anything to dissuade this view. He liked the man, and indeed now his family too. Henryk could help, no, he would help him. Resolve returned he left the cloakroom and went back to waiting dinner and whatever else the evening would have in store.

'So, you worked at *The Observer*?' declared Noah, thinking it best to dive in at the deep end with Catherine, rather than just wait for the inevitable net to come and catch him out.

'Yes. After the LSE I went straight there.'

'And your area is art?' asked Noah, his heart almost waiting to see if it was worth beating.

'No!' she laughed, Henryk too. 'I know very little about art, even after all these years living with Henryk. We've always said that would have killed us. You know, two artists together. My view has always been that opposites attract!'

'Right!' replied a relieved Noah, his heart now happily anticipating skipping. They were eating a spicy vegetable pasta dish at the kitchen table and as they did so a suddenly more relaxed Noah felt he could enjoy it. The French doors were wide open, the night now creeping in as the candles began to take over the light.

'And you work in?' he asked Catherine.

'Finance, and as you can imagine I've had a lot of work to do over the last few years. My area is European fiscal studies and my contacts are, in the main, within the European Community so I spend a lot of time in most of the major European cities, particularly Zurich, The Hague, Berlin, you know, the usual.'

'Now come on,' laughed Henryk, 'try and look interested!' Catherine hit her husband's arm.

'I know I can't make the business world interesting for you arty types but without us you wouldn't sell your work.'

'Sadly true, my love,' smiled Henryk, 'it is the ancient balance between artistic credibility and the need to live.'

'I read a piece on that recently,' offered Noah, who actually had, though he couldn't remember where.

'Recently?' asked Henryk.

'Yes,' replied Noah.

'That would have been your research on me, Charles. I did a piece for *The Sunday Times* last year on exactly the balance,' said Henryk.

'Right. I'm sure you're right then,' said Noah, hoping he had not just made a fool of himself in some way. 'I've read so much.'

'That's good!' declared Henryk, 'Though I doubt there was too much there on me. I prefer a low profile.'

'No, there wasn't,' replied Noah, feeling like a pry now and not wanting to come across as one. Henryk sensed his discomfort.

'Hey Charles, don't feel bad about research. I think you're new to this, yes?'

'I am,' replied Noah happily, delighted to make his credentials as raw as possible. The less connected they felt he was, the less they would ask him about things he would need to make up.

'Without thorough research you cannot do your job,' said Catherine. 'Full and absolute knowledge means you can operate in the field with integrity and in interview this is what catches the interviewee out. They are always like rabbits in headlamps when you know the truth, and when you don't? Well, then they smell your ineptitude and place your balls in a blender.'

'How delightful,' laughed Henryk and yet Noah knew the conversation had just shifted. He didn't want to steal a glance at Catherine but he did and she was looking straight at him, straight through him, in fact. A pause in proceedings followed where they ate and drank in quiet.

'Do you…' Henryk began to say before being cut off by his wife.

'So Charles, why are you actually here?'

Noah looked at her, then to Henryk who had heard the change in tone in his wife's voice and was now looking at Noah. Noah was calculating his response but Catherine's open and kind eyes were demanding a truthful response. He wanted to lie but could only say, 'What do you mean?'

'Well, Charles, I did a little research myself.'

'Darling!' declared Henryk, protestation in his voice.

'Oh, come on sweetie, it's my job to look after you, too!'

'And?' asked Noah, walking into the net willingly.

'And your friend at *The Observer* confirmed you are simply a friend and asked for the favour to be able to see Henryk.'

'I did,' replied Noah honestly.

'And I wondered whether to call the whole thing off and tell you, Henryk, what I had found out, but I didn't.'

'Because?' asked a confused Henryk.

'Because you rarely do interviews and because I just sensed there was more to this than meets the eye. I was excited', she continued, turning her full glare towards a now wilting Noah, 'because Charles Devere doesn't actually exist, does he?'

'He may do,' replied Noah, a faint sense of amusement in his reply.

'Well he may,' smiled Catherine, 'but it's Noah Spearing who sits before us.'

'Noah Spearing?' said Henryk with surprise but not, noted a sinking through the floor Noah, anger. Noah's mouth had literally dropped open at the mention of his actual name and he felt an immediate cold sweat break out. His face said "how on earth" and she answered.

'Because unlike you two head-in-the-clouds types, I am a reporter and I know what to ask and of whom. Your friend did not give you away, or so he thought. He said you had studied together and I asked him what course. I was charming and playing with him and he told me. He also told me you played rugby together for the university team.'

Idiot, thought Noah, though seeing Catherine Padowski in action left him under no illusion that most people would wilt under her cross-examination skills.

'So I checked the course and there was no Charles, so… '

Catherine looked at both men who were waiting for the next part of the story and both quite obviously impressed. Henryk also looked intrigued and strangely, Noah noted, not at all uncomfortable. Why on earth was he not looking upset and wondering if they had let a lunatic into their house? Noah just sat and looked as he felt, perplexed and worried.

'I checked Bath university paper cuttings and there was Sam Troughton and there, my dear Noah, was you. And how did I know it was you? Well, I had asked Sam to confirm your CV for me, to include a photograph, of course, so that the museum could have this on record and he sent a fabulous piece of made up work on you, Noah. You should be proud of him really.'

'I should?'

'Yes. The picture, of course, confirmed who you really were and then it was just a case of working backwards to your grandfather.'

Noah, who had already felt disorientated, now felt sick. Catherine poured him some water.

'But why not tell me?' Henryk was asking happily, Noah waiting to see a burst of anger that seemed to not even be on the tracks.

'You know why, dear,' she said.

'Well, of course I probably wouldn't have allowed the meeting!' replied a smiling Henryk to the obvious.

'But he's Joshua Spearing's grandson,' she simply said, causing Henryk to drop his fork and look at Noah with searching eyes.

'Really?' he asked of Noah, with kindness in his voice. Noah just nodded, trying to gather how the hell they even knew who his grandfather was, causing Catherine to deliver the answer to the unasked question that hung in the air.

'Joshua was one of our dearest benefactors, Noah. You didn't know?' she asked, seeing the young man grow very pale before her questions. Noah simply shook his head. 'You must miss him dreadfully. He was a lovely man. Over the past ten years he has privately donated hundreds of thousands of pounds, without which many of the recent improvements you saw today would not have been possible, but surely you knew something of this?' she asked, doubt in her voice as she saw the young man before her now looking quite ill.

Noah simply rose from the table, managed to utter, 'excuse me', and ran to the cloakroom to be very sick indeed. It took him nearly ten minutes to gather himself and return to the Padowskis who had retreated to the lounge where the dimmed lights accompanied by more candles and a blessedly warm room offered some comfort to the young Cornishman.

'Coffee?' asked Catherine. Noah nodded, sitting across from the Padowskis in a deep and extremely comfortable rich blue sofa and waiting for his senses to return.

'So, you really didn't know about Joshua and us, did you?' asked Catherine, placing Noah's coffee on a small table in front of him.

'No,' he answered softly.

'And yet you came,' stated Henryk, intrigued by the turns of the night.

'Yes,' offered Noah, 'I had to.'

238

'Had to?' asked Henryk.

'Yes. I have something of yours,' Noah replied, now holding his black coffee and sipping from it, welcoming its strength.

'Something of mine?' asked Henryk incredulously.

'No. Of the Czartoryski's,' said Noah.

The room waited while Noah drank his coffee and then, having finished it, asked for more.

'You see,' Noah said, coffee replenished and in urgent need of a pick-up. He sat there drained of all energy, his shoulders slumped and shooting pains suddenly arching across them. There was at last an urgent need to just be free of the truth, the need to pour out his vintage story before them. 'I have something you must have back but', and with this he looked at them both, 'I needed to know I could trust you first.'

Henryk and Catherine looked at one another. Catherine walked over to Noah's side and sat beside him, her hand on his shoulder.

'You can,' she said softly and Noah nodded, 'but just because I say you can, how can you know you can believe us?'

'Because', replied Noah, silent tears now falling down his cheeks, 'I have no choice.'

'Oh, but you do, Noah,' she said, using his actual name to help calm him, the caring mother in her reaching to this lost boy.

'You see, Grandad had found something,' Noah said, keeping his head down as he delivered the sweetened truth, 'and he asked me on his deathbed to get it back to where it belonged.'

'Something?' asked Henryk.

'Yes,' said Noah, now looking up at them both, 'I have the missing Raphael.'

Silence now greeted the scene, such silence that you cannot hear it because of the deafening noise of rushing blood in the head. Henryk, who was already sitting up, now pulled himself into a bolt upright pose on the edge of his sofa. Catherine just looked at Noah, astonished.

'The missing Raphael, Noah? Do you know what you are saying?' Henryk asked, in a voice filled with alarm rather than joy.

'I do,' Noah replied in a simple voice, his energy strangely

239

returning as his version of the truth was beginning to spill out.

'I can't tell you how Grandad got this because I don't know. All I know is that he had fought hard to get what was rightfully the Czartoryski's all along.'

Noah had been put on the spot with the news of his grandfather being involved with the museum all along, but this had played into his hands for the storyline that he now made up as he went along. It was simple. He could deny all knowledge and just use Joshua's good name, a name that was clearly held in the highest regard together with his grandad's clear connection with the Czartoryski for his advantage now.

'Well, well, well,' Catherine was saying, 'Joshua Spearing delivers what many through the decades have been unable to do so. He rights a wrong committed against the Polish people. His name will be honoured by Poland, Noah.'

'Oh no!' said Noah quickly, 'This cannot happen. Grandad was clear. No publicity. I don't know how he got this but he did not want it linked to him in any way.'

Catherine looked to Henryk who simply smiled.

'Wily old devil,' he said, shaking his head now and beginning to laugh, 'Wily old devil! Of course, he's right, who in their right mind would want that picture and its history linked to them. Still, he found it, eh? Incredible! Truly! I would say I didn't know he had it in him but somehow this is all quite to form. I mean, when I met him… '

'You met him?' asked an awestruck Noah, the very mention of another knowing his grandad making his presence more real in the room with them.

'Oh yes, several times. Only the once here and that was ten years ago. He was holidaying and had asked, just as you did, to see me. He did it under his real name though.'

They all smiled at that.

'And why?' asked Noah, his head again beginning to spin as he wondered if what was to come would need to change his story again.

'To tell me he wanted to support the museum. He told me he had read much about the Czartoryski and that through his love of the arts, a love matched by his wife too, who must have been a real beauty in her younger days I might add… '

'He had a photo of Grandma?'

'No, he actually had Grandma with him! She was so wonderful! Is she well?'

'Erm, yes. Very much so,' said Noah, now past the amazed stage in what he was hearing and moving to the I-must-be-dreaming stage. Joshua and Natalya both had been to the Czartoryski before him! 'He had an immense passion for art, a shared love with my Grandma. You should see their collection. It is, I am told, priceless, but more to the point a collection that they have loved. They always said that was the point, to truly love the work you invested in. The Czartoryski must have meant a lot to them.'

'Yes,' Catherine said, 'it clearly did. And now you bring us news of our collection's greatest treasure. I presume it is at home, somewhere nice and safe?'

Noah thought about answering truthfully, but simply said, 'No, it is near here. In the city, at least.'

Henryk just shook his head and uttered, 'Wow. What! Really?'

'So how do you propose we get the Raphael back to the museum without Joshua's name being involved?' asked Catherine, now sat back in the sofa but remaining at Noah's side.

'So you will keep his name hidden?' asked Noah, relief in his voice.

Catherine looked at her husband.

'After what he did for the museum,' began Hernryk, 'and the man he was Noah, the true man he was. Of course, if we can have a way that works and this was his wish then nothing would give us greater pleasure. How were you looking to pull this off, Noah?' Henryk asked, keen to learn the next steps.

'Well, apart from making a real mess of it, I was hoping to do it by simply returning it to you, in magnificent disguise, of course. I was going to tell you I had pictures of it so that you would have to release the news that you had it back, and then I would disappear as quickly as I came. You would no doubt need to authenticate it and the Raphael, returned, would once again live here,' replied Noah, with a true account of what he had planned. 'As for how we keep Grandad out of it I have no idea, I mean, given I did not know about the small matter of him actually being here before me and all this happening! I was just concentrating on being here, meeting you and getting out.'

241

'So let's keep it that simple,' laughed Henryk. 'Well, we will claim it arrived in a simple cylinder and we will use one we have, we get many hundreds sent in each month with various posters and things, and we will go from there.'

'But the police?' asked Catherine.

'Will be delighted to have the Raphael back and the evidence will be truly compromised because we will simply say the packaging, in all the excitement, was thrown away. It will then be a matter of going through the waste where they will not find anything that links to you and ultimately we, the Polish people, have got what we all want! Raphael's portrait of a happy and fabulous looking young man, painted in 1514 and purchased by our very own Prince Adam Jerzy Czartoryski in 1798, stolen during the Second World War by a Nazi nation intent on destroying the very culture of each country it occupied, and at last returned and on display here, in our precious city of Krakow. To that, my dear, precious Catherine and you, my new best friend Noah, I raise a glass,' and he did that, encouraging the others to raise freshly-charged glasses which he now filled, 'to Joshua Spearing, a true friend of the Czartoryski.'

They stood, toasted their glasses, and all declared in unison:

'To Joshua!'

Chapter 16

A Shadow Appears

Noah awoke with the same thought he normally found to accompany the start of his days, that of Flora. It was now Thursday and in two days' time she would be woefully married. He dwelt in his mind's eye on her face for a little while too long, and then leaned over to the side of the bed to get his mobile and look at her photo only to then remember that he didn't have his mobile with him due to Tom's over-the-top security measures. He cursed the memory of it as while it had procured him a fabulous car to drive it had lost him his contact with home and more to the point this morning, his glimpse of the girl he was about to lose forever. He looked at the time on his watch and was amazed to say it read eleven in the morning. He had always had this ridiculous ability to sleep no matter what stress was going around his body. He jumped out of bed, slipped the TV on for company and then went to use the toilet and shower.

It had been a late night with Noah leaving Henryk and Catherine at 1.30am. The taxi had been nice and quick taking him down several short cuts that only a local would know, before dropping him directly outside the hotel. Within half an hour he was asleep, exhausted from the day but also satisfied that Joshua's name would be protected and that his task was almost now done and feeling as close to his grandad as he had felt, safe in the knowledge that Joshua had walked these very streets before him. Discussions around how best to carry out the task of getting the painting into the museum had been weighed carefully but they had eventually agreed that Noah would drop off the invaluable missing treasure at the museum that very lunchtime so he now had to get a move on to stay on schedule. With the painting at last safely back in the hands of the illustrious gallery and its identity checked and confirmed Henryk would then call a meeting of the trustees of the Czartoryski with the amazing news of the mysterious arrival of the stolen Raphael in the post. A meeting with the world's press would then be lined up for the following day. This last important piece of the jigsaw was there to satisfy Noah that nothing could stop the news that the Raphael had, at last, returned.

Despite Noah's mind inevitably returning to Flora as he had awoke, he now found himself singing in the shower. He laughed as he did so knowing he was singing marvellously out of tune and the wrong words, but as he sang he felt an undeniable sense of relief and happiness. He resolved to text his mother as soon as he was out of the shower to ask her to consider meeting him in Krakow. He felt that she would love the place, its history, its beauty, its undeniable hold of history and the very thought of getting normality back into his life and his mother back at his side made him very happy. Within a few minutes the text was sent, Noah exclaiming he was in a superb room, 318, under his delightful pseudonym, with a view and a mini-bar and the need to have his mother with him if she could bear to part from her work. It was time to share the burden and let her mother make of it what she would.

Then Noah, happy with the effect he knew his text would have on his mother, sat on his bed, still damp from the shower and with the hotel-supplied dressing gown wrapped around him to dry him out. Now, text delivered, he pondered what exactly to say to Tess about the Raphael. He had asked her in the text to consider coming out for a few days before he headed out of the city. He was half thinking of telling her the full story and then, if the Padowskis would be so kind, introducing her to them. It would be a wonderful gift, people that had known Joshua sharing their story, their warm thoughts, of him to her, a new door opening to both Noah and his mother and a fresh insight into their beloved Joshua. Yes, that would all do very nicely.

Noah glanced at the TV. It was 11.30am now and the news

244

headlines were just running. He had ordered room service, a continental breakfast, and was now feeling the hunger calls from his stomach. However, all this was forgotten as many pictures of Henryk Padowski and then one of Catherine suddenly began to fill his TV screen. He had no idea what was being said but there were pictures of police cars outside their block, the very apartment that he had been at just a few hours previously. Now, in place of a quiet neighbourhood there were many lights flashing into the night sky, and an ambulance heading off with, it would appear, a casualty on board. The reporter was talking into the screen, a high-pitched voice of utter seriousness and concern. Something dreadful had clearly happened and Noah felt the panic rise, the same panic that had dogged him since the attack in London returning to haunt him again. A knock on the door hit him like a left hook but mercifully he heard a lady's voice shout room service and he went to let the woman in, not for his breakfast, which would now not be touched, but rather for her to tell him what the TV reporter was saying.

'Can you speak English,' he asked her.

'Yes,' she replied in a perfectly tanged southern-American accent, 'I am from Tennessee!'

'Right,' replied Noah, managing a weak smile and trying to keep the wild sense of fear that was taking over his body from coming out and scaring her, 'You're here on tour?' he managed.

'Yes I am, sir. I am here for three months. I am taking a year out from my studies of European Art and this seemed the perfect base. Beautiful isn't it?'

'Yes it is. I'm just visiting,' replied Noah limply, aware that surely the feelings of terror he was now feeling would be betrayed through his eyes.

'Great. You see, my Dad works for Sheraton and had all the contacts. I could give you a tour, if you like, of the city,' the girl said, clearly eager to get into a long conversation with this handsome young Englishman.

'Right. Yea, well, I'm only here for a few days with friends who live here', at this he stole a glance at the TV screen, 'but thanks for the offer.'

'Well, you know where I am. I'm Candice by the way,' she said, offering her hand.

'Noah,' he replied, shaking her hand. 'Right, well, thanks for breakfast. Do you speak Polish?'

'Why yes, of course!' she replied happily.

'Great. Well, would you mind just telling me about this story,' he asked pointing to the screen as the reporter continued to talk about the scene that had unfolded behind her, 'What has happened?'

'Ah yes, sir, this story is all over the news. It's the Padowskis; quite a well-known local couple in the city. He runs the Czartoryski, the fabulous art gallery in the Old City. You've heard of it?'

'Yes, I have,' managed Noah.

'Well, they were attacked last night in their own home.'

'Attacked?' said Noah, with panic clearly showing in his voice, causing the young American to look closely at him.

'Yes, shocking isn't it? Mr Padowski, they are saying, is severely wounded and unconscious. Probably won't come round at all, they are saying. Mrs Padowski protected the children. It's so awful, isn't it? It's all over the news, sir. Dreadful, truly dreadful. This sort of thing simply doesn't happen here in Krakow. Sir, sir! Are you all right sir?'

Noah was just staring at the screen. The girl's words had entered his head and he had sat back on the bed, all colour having drained from his face.

'Sir. Shall I call a doctor? You look very ill,' Candice said some fear now in her voice as she saw the young man looking decidedly poorly. She had already had one guest have a heart attack in front of her and she did not want to see another one fall ill.

Noah caught himself.

'No. I'm fine, really I am,' he said, 'it's just that I was at the museum yesterday. It was wonderful, you know?'

Candice relaxed, safe in the natural fear of a fellow traveller in a foreign city.

'Yes,' she said, 'these things really shake you up, don't they, particularly with us being so far away from home.'

'Yes, they do,' said Noah, calmer now as the realisation of what was happening began to close around him. Adrenaline was kicking in and self-preservation meant he had to act quickly.

'Thanks for bringing up breakfast,' he said, rising from the bed and showing Candice to the door.

'Maybe see you around?' she asked as she left.

'Maybe so,' replied Noah, managing a smile for her as he then mercifully closed the door and fell against it. Sorrow began to swell up inside him like a rising tide and he fought hard to keep the noise of his hurt quiet as his body shook with fear and tears fell in abundance as his insides wretched. Violence had followed Noah from London and had found Henryk and Catherine. Henryk was now dreadfully wounded and they, whoever they were, would now know that Noah had the Raphael with him here in Krakow. He had not told the Padowskis where the Raphael was but he knew the inevitable roll of the dice would come hurtling towards him and that it was only a matter of time before they would have him and all would come tumbling down. Noah scolded himself. Who on earth did he think he was? How had he really thought this painting would not have dreadful consequences, how stupid could he have been? It was stolen in shocking circumstances and violence would always continue to follow it with Noah now firmly in the path it was travelling on.

Maybe, he considered, his mind in overdrive, he too had been followed last night? Maybe the fact that he had come straight back to the hotel with a taxi driver who fancied himself as a Formula One driver had saved him? Maybe, indeed almost certainly, they were now waiting for him outside. He stood, catching himself on a wardrobe door as dizziness threatened to send him back to the ground. Feeling like this, how the hell was he going to do anything? *Come on Noah*, he called to himself as he forced his brain to click in. He walked over to the window and pulled his curtain back. His room overlooked the streets below where Krakow was in full swing under a pleasant summer sky and he scanned the scene below him. Noah had no idea what he was looking for and there were literally hundreds of people out there and many just waiting for something or other. No doubt, though, one of them was waiting for him.

What to do? He had gone to bed last night with salvation and the rest of his Raphael-free life in his grasp. Now this had been ripped away from him and everything was lost. His thoughts raced but kept returning to the one thing he knew he had to keep safe, Joshua's memory and, therefore, the picture. He went into the bathroom and, holding on to the sink with both hands, spoke to himself in the mirror.

'You are here now, Noah, you hear me, here now. This is happening and you are here to do the right thing. Yes? Yes!'

Noah was speaking with assertion, drilling into his brain what he knew to be true. He could not do anything by hiding as the net was closing and he would be caught and it would all be over. No, action was the only way forward to save this grim self-made disaster of a situation that now slapped him around the face.

'For Grandad,' he said, still holding his own stare in the mirror, 'for Grandad! Get the picture and get out. OK! Get the picture and get the fuck out. Come on!'

The mention of Joshua caused him to grow two inches. His name gave him the strength he now needed. His focus once again falling into play, he dressed quickly in his normal clothes, old and ripped and faded Diesel jeans, his battered, aged Etnies white trainers, bright red socks, a stripy blue and white T-shirt and a faded grey rugby top from Superdry. These were his clothes, his skin. Again, this encouraged him. Then he thought about how to hide his face. He picked up his blue stripy Diesel beanie hat and his dark black Animal wrap-around sunglasses. These would have to be disguise enough.

He checked he had his wallet with the baggage ticket and with that safely in his front trouser pocket he made to leave his room, only remembering just as the door was shutting that his mobile phone was on his bed. He walked back into his room, picked it up, and then left at last, looking carefully up and down the corridor before walking down towards the lift. The door to his room closed softly and automatically behind him as he walked to the lift, pressing the button to call it to him. Seeing a very comfortable chair by the back wall he sat down and waited, placing the phone down at his side as he used both hands to knead some tension away from his temples. He then picked out of his pocket his wallet, lifted out the reclaim ticket for the painting and took off his right trainer. He placed the ticket under the lining of the trainer and put the shoe back on.

'Am I going mad?' he whispered to himself as he replaced

his wallet in his pocket. The lift beeped its arrival and Noah made his way into it leaving his phone on the chair where a text awaited. It said simply:

The stranger awakes! I would love to come, my sweetheart. Have done a quick check online and I can get a flight and be with you Saturday morning. Will come to the hotel. I love you SO MUCH 'Charles'! Take care. Mum X.

Noah caught the lift to the basement and the garage where he walked past all the cars, glancing quickly as he did so towards the Audi where he noted that it appeared totally untouched. Onwards and out into the Krakow late morning, pausing at no time to look right or left for his inevitable assailants. He reasoned if he was being followed there was very little he could do about it. These people were clearly used to violence and doing what they needed to do to get what they wanted. It was a miracle, he reasoned, that he was even still in one piece so the best thing he could do was stay close to his continued freedom and just keep rolling the dice.

As he walked north towards the station, he thought back to his two days in Krakow and how they had unfolded, trying desperately as he did so to look for some clue as to the madness that was following him. Clearly whoever was after the painting had not known where he was staying and that had given him some initial time. In this instance the Audi had most definitely helped him in getting him here in one piece, a thought for which he thanked Tom in his mind. His assailants must have decided he would make his way to the Czartoryski, but why? How did they know? Anyway, he had been seen going into the museum, he assumed, without the painting and left, too, without it. Had they followed him back to the hotel then? He was on foot and they could have got to him easily. But could they? He had walked down busy streets in broad daylight and had then gone back to the hotel. Maybe they had just decided to wait, to see what happened next. And then, of course, he had gone to Henryk and Catherine's, there and back in a taxi possibly making following him the more tricky target, a quick moving taxi taking him back to a highbrow hotel? They had obviously decided the Padowskis in their own home without hotel security and CCTV were the easier option and had struck with such shocking force that Henryk was probably in a coma and Catherine, no doubt, petrified.

Noah needed a plan but in this environment of fear he could not see past getting his hands on the Raphael and escaping and yet, as he walked and the fresh air and adrenalin mixed together, he began to reason that maybe this was not the best way forward. It was now lunchtime and he suddenly felt very tired and hungry. He was once again at the *Rynek Glowny*, Krakow's great medieval market square, as big a square as Noah had ever seen in his travels. With the fair weather blessing the city again today, the square was awash with people meeting, talking, laughing and eating. Noah felt a slight calm rest over him as he knew here, now, he was safe. Perhaps a short break and some food were needed, time to think, refuel, in the middle of a storm.

He stopped at a café, with its twenty or so tables in the square in the midday sunshine, sitting purposely in full view on an outside table. He ordered coffee, still water with ice and two plain croissants. Within minutes the feast had arrived and he hungrily demolished the patisseries and ordered some more.

'Do you mind if I join you?'

Noah looked up to see a tall man in a black leather jacket, black shirt and jeans. His initial reaction was panic but the man's face was open and not threatening.

'Do I have a choice?' was all Noah could manage.

'You always have a choice, Mr Devere.'

Mr Devere! Interesting immediately that this man did not know who Noah really was.

'Right, *prosze*,' responded Noah meekly, pointing to the chair opposite him and wondering where this was going.

'Inspector Fabian Milosz,' informed the policeman as he sat down heavily across from Noah. He was about forty years old and in good shape but eyes betrayed his extreme tiredness. As though guessing what Noah was thinking he said, 'It's been a long night, Mr Devere. Do you know why?'

Noah thought it was best to play dumb, realising that him sat there eating food as fast as he could get it down him hardly showed a man in remorse for what had happened to his friends. Noah just shook his head.

'Last night you visited the Padowskis.'

'I did,' replied Noah, knowing as he did so that mercifully Catherine had not blown his cover.

'And you left around eleven?' said Inspector Milosz, waiting for Noah to correct him.

'It was closer to 1.30am,' said Noah.

'Ah yes,' smiled Milosz, as though Noah had just passed his first test, and then after thumbing through his notebook he said, 'You left at half past one. The taxi took you straight to The Sheraton, did it not?'

'Yes,' replied Noah, 'what's all this about?' he asked in a firm voice.

Milosz tried to place the words he was about to deliver in the right order.

'The Padowskis were attacked after you left.'

'What?' exclaimed Noah, 'Attacked? By who?'

Milosz waited, sizing up the young man before him and deciding there and then that he was of no threat.

'We don't know.'

'What happened?'

'Two men at three in the morning. They were through the back door. It was all very quick and efficient and a thoroughly professional job.'

'And are they all right?' Noah asked, his eyes wide open as he did so.

Milosz shook his head.

'Well, the press are reporting that Mr Padowski has life-threatening injuries. This isn't true, thankfully. We thought it best to let them run with the story. He is very badly beaten though, nastily so actually, and in hospital where I suspect he will stay for some time.'

'My God. And Catherine?' having no problem finding raw emotion to flow through his words.

'Physically, fine. Mentally, who knows? The daughters are fine, thank God. Slept through the whole thing. Of course, if they had not had a panic button directly into us, Mr Padowski being an important person and in charge of very expensive items in our precious Czartoryski, and had Catherine not been able to press it, then who knows.' Milosz let that thought drift between them.

'Were they robbers?' asked Noah, feeling he should ask the question.

'Not that we can ascertain. It seems it was personal. Mrs Padowski asked us to make sure you were safe so of course I had you followed.'

'Followed?' asked Noah, unsure where this was going.

'Of course. I needed to know you were not a suspect and where you went could have led to a reason for you to have been involved. However, coming here for coffee and croissants hardly smacks of a hardened criminal, Mr Devere, though walking out through the garage was an interesting one.'

'I needed to check the car was OK,' Noah replied quickly.

'Well, it is a nice car,' replied Milosz with a smile. 'Paid well?'

'Rich parents.'

'Ah yes, the blessings of a charmed English life, yes?'

'Yes, that's about the size of it,' replied Noah with an awkward smile. Inside he breathed a sigh of relief. Joshua was looking over him. If he had continued to the station then this could have all been over, the Raphael in police hands and Joshua's name in the papers around the world.

'But I have to tell you', continued Milosz, 'that we do not know why the Padowskis were targeted and that you may very well be in danger too.'

'Me?' asked Noah, not needing to add fear in his voice as it was there already in abundance.

'Yes. Did you see anything, anything at all last night that made you in any way suspicious?'

'Suspicious?'

'Yes. Something out of the ordinary when you arrived or when you left?'

Noah thought back but could not bring anything of use to mind other than the shouting out truth that this was because of the Raphael. He felt awful. He was the cause of this violence. Joshua had been right. This thing should have been kept secret.

'No, I can't,' Noah said, utter helplessness in his voice.

'So, you can see I have a problem here.'

'You do?' asked Noah, his mind all over the place, part pleased that his friends were not as hurt as he had thought, part terrified at what was coming next and part simply and totally confused and lost.

'Yes, I do,' replied a softly spoken Milosz. 'A violent crime and none of you appears to know why. You were at the Padowskis' discussing the museum, right?'

'Yes.'

'And what were you talking about?'

WHAT WERE YOU TALKING ABOUT!!!!! The words pinballed around his brain.

'Oh, you know.'

Milosz simply waited, the silence between them causing Noah to feel like his brain was on show.

'The museum, its history, where it goes next,' offered Noah none too convincingly.

'And you stayed rather late, did you not?'

'We get on very well,' replied Noah, meekly.

'Clearly. And you spoke all night about the museum?'

'Well, no. Mrs Padowski has links with the paper I am doing the story for.'

'And that would be?' asked the police inspector who had been making notes throughout and was now poised to write this down too.

'*The Observer.*'

'Indeed so,' Milosz said, 'Mrs Padowski said as much. Freelance, she said.'

'Yes. Freelance,' replied Noah, aware that if the police checked this out they would probably find out the same information that Catherine Padowski had.

'OK, don't worry,' said the inspector, leaning over the table and patting Noah on the arm, 'All your details check out with what I already knew and Mrs Padowski speaks very highly of you. I am simply here to make sure you are fine and to see what you knew,' said Milosz, seeing a visibly shaken young man sitting before him. He stood now and said. 'Here's my card. Keep in touch with anything you think about. Anything at all, OK? I need these people caught and fast. I did not like what I found last night and I will not have this violence in my city. How long are you here for?'

'Oh, just a few more days.'

'Good. Call me before you leave?'

'Yes, of course. And can I see Henryk?'

'Well, that's up to them, of course, but I see no harm in you contacting them. You are clearly good friends.'

253

'Thank you,' replied Noah, some sort of calm settling over him.

'And you take care,' said Milosz.

'Yes, sure,' replied Noah, rising and offering his hand. The two men shook hands warmly and with that Milosz left and disappeared as quickly as he had arrived.

Noah sat back down in his chair, actual relief now hitting him again as Henryk's injuries became clear. It was clearly bad but not as bad as he had feared. Catherine had kept his name out of the story and for that he would be eternally grateful. If there had been any lingering doubts of trust of Henryk and Catherine, they were now well and truly dealt with. Noah wandered over to a newspaper kiosk and bought a pen and a small pack of envelopes and paper. He returned to the café table, ordered more coffee, and wrote a short note

Dear Henryk and Catherine, I cannot for the life of me fathom what evil was behind the attack on you last night. It shames me to say I too was attacked on my last night in England but I had thought the danger was gone. I was mistaken and brought violence to your house for which I will never be able to forgive myself. I have no idea who they are but I do know they are after the painting that we all hold dear. Please rest assured that the painting is safe and away from these people. I will make sure this stays the same until you are able to take it off me and at last return what rightfully belongs to the Czartoryski. I cannot change the dread of last night, but I am glad, so very glad, that you will once again be able to look in the eyes of a long lost Czartoryski friend.

Please forgive my stupidity.
With much love and affection always,
Charles XXX

Noah sealed the letter and wrote the address on the front of the envelope, an address he had been given by Henryk only the day before. He walked back to the kiosk, bought a stamp, and then posted the letter.

Suddenly thinking about his mother he reached into his pocket to see if she had replied to his earlier text. No phone was there. He tried every other pocket he had and then retried. No phone.

'Bugger,' he muttered. Remembering the last place he had seen it was when he left his room, he decided to go back to the hotel and see if it was there and also reasoning that this would give him further valuable thinking time as to his next move. He reasoned that going back to the station at this point having just met the police was probably not the smartest move and so the eternal walk back to the hallowed painting would have to wait.

He walked back then along the route he had just followed which seemed to have succeeded at keeping him out of trouble, and walked out of the Old Town into the busy traffic flow of a Krakow afternoon in full flow. A thought passed fleetingly through his brain that just maybe the attack on the Padowskis was a total coincidence, just maybe there was a slight chance that the Raphael was safe. He paused at the lights, looking up and down the busy roads and then turned left to walk down *Grodzka* towards his temporary home. Traffic whipped past him, busy people all unaware of the drama that was playing out in the young man who walked purposely and anonymously down the road.

Turning right he left the busier roads behind and began to walk down a much quieter backstreet drawing breath as he did so, relieved to have some quiet return to his thumping head. Crossing the road, he turned to check it was clear. A dark van out of seemingly nowhere suddenly screeched to a halt behind him, the door at the side sliding open as it did so. Two large men dressed in dark clothing jumped out of the van and got hold of Noah who had just turned to run away but miserably was cut down. They picked him up in a vice-like grip and literally threw him like trash into a skip, with much force, into the back of the van, jumping back in with him and shouting in some foreign language to the driver who promptly drove off at high speed.

Noah, who was already feeling very dazed from his head cracking against the inside of the van into which he had been thrown, made to get up only to be hit extremely hard by one of the thickset men, knocking him out instantly.

'Welcome back at last, Mr Noah Spearing,' said a deep voice with a heavy accent.

Noah began to open his eyes and was immediately aware of several things. Firstly, he was in a dark room and tied extremely tightly to a heavy chair. In front of him was a table with a light on it that was placed to shine directly into his eyes. The effect was dazzling and painful to a head that was already throbbing with immense pain from the blows it had received. Noah felt his whole body crying out with hurt. He lifted his head and, slanting his eyes against the bright light that was burning into his temples, he managed, 'Who are you?'

'Ah yes, the eternal question. You will not know this, Mr Spearing. You will simply give us what we want to know and we can all get on with our lives.'

'I will?'

'You will, and that is the last time you will ask an unprompted question. I alone am asking the questions here and you will simply shut the fuck up unless you have an answer for me. Understood?'

Noah, fearful beyond anything he could remember in his entire life, simply nodded. His "interrogator" was coming into focus before him. He was a tall, athletic-looking man, with a fine bone structure and no expression in his face whatsoever other than the desire to get on with the business sitting before him. The room waited.

'So, firstly, the good news. Thanks to our benefactor you will not be killed. Normally we torture those unfortunate souls we work on and then kill them anyway after we have what we want. In your case you will not be killed, at least not on purpose, and assuming, of course, you tell us what we need to know. However, if your body gives way under interrogation, then so be it. Occupational hazard I am afraid.' The man nodded to a presence at the back of the room.

'Who's that?' asked Noah, quickly.

Bang! A fist thudded into his chest at such force that Noah felt at least a couple of ribs break immediately and had the feeling that he could not breath. Several moments passed as he choked and coughed and cried.

'You're a stupid little fuck, aren't you?' said the man, 'I was clear, wasn't I? You are not to speak unless spoken to. I am sure we are now clear on this point, are we not?'

Noah managed to nod, even that small movement sending immense pain around his body.

'Right, let's get to it. The exciting bit. Interrogation! Much maligned in your arrogant western press but without it, Mr

Spearing, where would we be? I am delighted to tell you I learnt all my trade in places you will never know exist and that my talents have brought me much work around the globe. I do not fail, you see, and therefore my reputation is, as you say, legendary. With you, a young boy not used to this sort of thing, we should wrap this up all quite quickly. OK?'

At this the door at the back of the room was opened, a small shaft of light entering the room and then, with the figure that had been at the back of the room exiting, the light was gone.

'So, I have been asked to first of all let you have some time to consider your fate, Mr Spearing, rather than just jumping in to straightforward violence which is my normal trademark which I was allowed to let loose on that city trader type friend of yours in leafy London.'

Noah, his spirit already as low as it had ever been in his life, now felt his world tumble into an abyss of dizzying darkness.

'Tom, lovely and now sadly departed, Tom, told me of course what you had told him, though cleverly, I might add, you had not told him too much, had you? Shame really as if you had told him more he would have told me more and perhaps we would not be here now. You see, they always tell, Noah, in the end. You will learn that. He's history now, of course, and that's your fault. I hope that makes you feel good about yourself.'

The room paused, the horror and reality of unrestrained violence painting itself across the walls of this dark cell.

'And then your latest confidant, last night. Rather sad I was so rudely interrupted while working over your new best friend, a Mr Padowski. He cried too. Terrified he was. Wet himself almost instantly. Just like you, in fact. Laughable.'

Noah was crying non-stop now. He saw no way out and simply sat in terror, all thoughts of redemption now lost. The room seemed to reek of his own urine that he had been unable to control as it flowed out of him. Desperation was now his only friend.

'So, I am going to have my dinner. I do like to take on a few pounds before working them off, if you get my drift, and you do get my drift don't you, Mr Spearing?'

The man had leaned in close to Noah's face to deliver this last sentence. Noah smelt the man's fresh aftershave and clean clothes. He smelt and looked expensive.

'So, sit back and enjoy the prospect of violence, well, as much as you can, which isn't much is it? Still, there we have it, you, tied to a heavy wooden chair that is screwed into the wooden floor, and me taking a short break before coming back to seriously, if you so choose as you do still have a choice, hurt you, and I will hurt you. You are going nowhere until I say so and that, my dear Englishman, is up to you. The question I will ask you when I return is a simple one. You have the painting. My master wants it. Give it to us or else. And would you like to know what the "or else" will entail before I leave for my afternoon sustenance?'

Noah looked up at the man, his neck muscles feeling unable to carry the weight, tears wet on his cheeks and his eyes pleading for mercy.

'You do! Marvellous,' said the man, 'well, I will start with your fingers, breaking each one individually. That normally gets us off and running. The problem is, you know, the fingers can be healed, though they are never the same. I believe you are a surfer, Mr Spearing?'

Noah's head jumped at that. They knew exactly who he was. Inside all that was he began to shut down. Hope was gone.

'So, we need to strike where you fear the most, Mr Spearing, so after the fingers it will be the knee caps I'm afraid. If it goes that far then I will be truly sorry for you because you will never be surfing again after I've done with you. So, please, just let us get this over with the moment I return. OK? Fine. See you shortly, say a couple of hours? Super.'

The man left, turning the light out on the table as he did so and leaving Noah in total and utter darkness.

The moments passed, Noah in and out of consciousness and trying to work out what to do next. He knew his protection of his grandfather's name against these men was clearly useless. Somehow or other they knew the whole story, or at least most of it. However, Noah also knew that to tell them the whole truth about where the painting was and who knew about it could once again put the Padowskis at risk and how could he do that? He was terrified and had no idea how he could endure any more pain whatsoever and so, in his helpless and lost state, he waited because he had nothing else in his power to do.

As thoughts came and then the blank canvas of his end returned, Noah tried to get his mind to concentrate on goodness and for some reason his brain kept bringing him back to his writing. He had to try and stay alive in his mind or else he would have no chance. What was that line, he thought, trying to remember a poem, something he had been working on at home and which could lift him. A line called to him from deep in his brain and he reached out for it.

Her wings lay broken, yet her spirit stayed true,
her wonders stripped that they might get to you.

Noah, wishing another line had come to him, found himself just repeating this section from the heart of a lengthy piece he was working on around the death of the Greek goddess Nike in an historic and mythical battle. How he needed the winged goddess of victory now and yet in his poem he had imagined her final demise, the very death of the immortal ancients. The mighty Zeus, fighting hard, had sensed the tragedy and turned around and had seen her cut down, his very angel of life-affirming glory thrown to the battle-torn ground. How his heart had been broken at that point, the very driving force of eternity brought down to earth.

Gloom now spread through Noah and the darkness called him home. He was lost to the world and his fate would soon arrive, the only words he could replay stuck on this tale of woe.

Sometime later, and Noah had a sense that it was much later, the man returned, throwing the door open and turning on the table light. Behind him another figure had also arrived, maybe the same as before.

'Good evening or morning! Could be either. You haven't got a clue, have you?'

Noah, suddenly very alert and at a heightened state of anxiety, shook his head. He felt incredible thirst and the man, seemingly sensing this asked if he wanted a drink. Noah nodded and the man produced a bottle of water and began to let him drink. At first Noah simply gagged, but slowly he began to get some water into his swollen throat. It hurt to drink but the water was welcome.

'So, Mr Spearing, you have had plenty of time to think. It is in fact Friday afternoon, a nice day outside as it happens, and you probably want to live to see late Friday night, yes?'

Again Noah nodded his head.

'So tell me, where is the painting?'

Noah thought it interesting that the man simply referred to the Raphael as the painting. Maybe he didn't know the true identity of the painting. Maybe these guys didn't know everything after all.

Noah hesitated and the man, looking straight at Noah's eyes, produced a claw-hammer, seeing the effect of terror it produced in his prey's eyes.

'An effective weapon, the claw-hammer. In many ways a somewhat barbaric piece that has always in some form or other been used since ancient times in warfare around our fair globe. Imagine this on the fields of some of the great battles of the Middle Ages. I tell you this hammer, commonplace now in every DIY store in the world, would have been worth a fortune then. They would have marvelled at its shape, its weight and its effectiveness. This one', the man continued, eyeing up the hammer and weighing it in his hand as he did so as though he was fingering an expensive watch, 'is a beautiful piece. I'm sure you will appreciate its work very much indeed.'

The last words were left hanging in the air as the door opened and now a third man entered the room and walked behind Noah, untying his right arm and forcing his hand into a flattish position on the old wooden table in front of him. Noah made to shout an objection but something deep inside held it back as the man with the hammer let it crash down on his little finger and shatter it. Noah felt the pain like no other pain and yet with all his might kept his scream of pain inside his head.

The room waited, only the noise of Noah whimpering as quietly as he could, audible in the air.

Then, and without warning, a second crash of the hammer and the second finger was smashed open. Again, Noah found strength he did not know he had to keep the scream that wanted to tear open the room, inside his head. He felt incredibly faint all of a sudden and passed out only to wake in what seemed like moments later with water soaking his face and upper body, extremely cold water that had been thrown over him.

'So?' asked the man, tossing the hammer between his hands in a steady and easy rhythm. 'Where is it?'

Noah looked up and found himself spitting at the man without realising what he was doing. The fist that hit him full in the face was hard and caused immediate damage, blood flowing out of his cracked lip and opening up his upper gums that gave way to more rushes of blood. The man stepped back to the figure at the back of the room and hushed voices could be heard, the torturer's voice sounding irritated.

He came back to Noah.

'We break,' he said simply and sullenly, the three men leaving at the same time and this time leaving the light full on Noah's face allowing him to look at the blood all around him. It was surreal. Noah's mind settled on a scene from *Reservoir Dogs* right here with Noah in the middle of it, a mad Mr Blonde prepared to do his worst and almost definitely would do just that, and Noah faced with nothing more than the hapless fate that met the tortured policeman in the film.

Noah once again suddenly alert, began to think through his options. He knew he could not hold out much longer. He was in utter and complete agony. Where the strength had come from to last through what he had already endured was amazing to him. Maybe he had some of his grandfather's bravery in him after all. Noah thought of Joshua and his mother. He felt their care, their love, and there, in that dark, cold threatening room, Noah whispered out his love for them. He thought of Flora and all the excitement that would be there at home on this, her last day, before the wedding. That life now seemed a million miles away to the prisoner, Noah.

'Flora,' he said softly through painful lips, 'I will forever love you.'

He looked at his hand, now crudely tied back to the chair arm. His two battered and broken fingers covered in blood and shockingly out of shape. What would happen next was the question filling his head. He knew he would give way and so he then asked what he could do. He had to give them something to make them stop, at least buy him some time.

Maybe the police would realise he was missing. Maybe the hotel would have reported he had not returned. He knew he was clutching at straws but that was all he had.

The pain, unbearable, stung into him, but the light, bright and as burning as ever, stopped him finding sleep. Instead he could do nothing but wait and work through the intense hurt that was underlining everything and try and think of a line to keep him from further violence. He decided buying time was all he had and so he would tell them lies to try and buy more. It was all he had, apart from the truth.

Sometime later, it seemed like hours but could have been any amount of time, the door re-opened and in walked the third man, the one who had held his hand down for his fingers to be broken and then retied the damaged goods back to the chair as the torturer had been getting instructions.

'Hello,' he said, pulling up a seat and lighting a cigarette. 'How are you feeling?'

Noah just looked, a blank expression being all he could muster. The man was smaller than the man with the hammer and not so clean-cut, more thug-like and yet with a face that betrayed more emotion and more life.

'Cat got your tongue?' the man cruelly asked. 'Listen, you can talk to me. I am not the interrogator. I am his hired henchman and the man who might just be able to keep you from having all those pretty, tanned fingers broken. The pain gets worse you know, not easier. This is not like the films where some fabulous saviour will arrive in the nick of time while you have been bravely, stoically, putting up with the pain of torture offering little smart comments along the way. I mean, fair play to you Englishman, you have managed to spit at Alexis and not scream through several very terrifying moments, but these, my poor boy, are but the starter, the entrée! Each nasty piece of pain will be like filing sandpaper over an open wound that just gets deeper and deeper until you can stand no more. That is your breaking point and that is when you crumble. Time is all you have and yours is almost through your hourglass.'

Noah just listened, his eyes searching out some humanity on the man before him and finding none at all. The man went on.

'To be fair the stench of your piss is enough to show you

are a poor, disheartened bastard. I think I can discern that your bowels have broken too. Very nice. Some shit smells far worse and I can tell you I have smelt enough in my time. No, I am sure your girlfriend would be impressed.'

Noah's eyes came alive to that insult.

'Or would that be boyfriend? Never quite know with you Englishmen, particularly those of you with money. I think on balance,' the man said, leaning in and stroking Noah's bloodied right cheek, 'that you prefer boys. I'm right, aren't I? Nice car by the way. I might just have that for myself if the boss says I can. Anyway, smoke?' he said, offering Noah the packet. Noah shook his head, a moment of brightness hitting him as he realised this man knew nothing of Flora.

'Water, then?'

Noah nodded and managed, 'Yes please.'

'He speaks!' the man declared, 'And with a please, too. How lovely. How very English of you. Here I am with men intent on leaving you with scars for the rest of your life, and yet you can still say please to me. This is why I like you English, so, how do you say, delightful! I fear, though, that this is why Alexis hates you. He's never been keen on the English, never quite forgiven your empire days. What good Serbian could, eh? Every time he sees you he thinks of your niceness and cowardice and your great betrayal.'

Noah, lost in this monologue, just listened, the depths of fear calling him downwards to Hades depths.

The man stepped forward causing Noah to flinch.

'Fear not,' he said, 'just untying your left hand. Pointless undoing the right one, eh?' he laughed. He sat back down and gave Noah a fresh water-bottle, which he took quickly to his mouth and duly gagged on. Then, water touching his throat, Noah tried again and slowly drank from the bottle.

The man watched him.

'Attractive guy like you, what the hell are you doing here in this mess?'

Noah shrugged.

'I mean, you could be home with your boy on the beach. Far west of England, isn't it?'

Noah, amazed at being told what he thought they could not know, just nodded.

'Don't know it myself,' he said, 'only London. Nice city. I believe you met the boss there recently!' he laughed.

Noah now knew then that whoever the figure at the back of the room had been was probably the same one who had attacked Tom in London. He also became fearful. This man now before him was telling him far too much and placing this with the fact that Noah had seen the faces of both interrogators meant almost certainly that he would have no chance getting out of this alive despite the earlier promise. His body almost relaxed in the simple truth of redemption lost, hope having now gone and only the end to wait for.

'London's nice,' Noah said, chancing his arm at conversation through cracked lips.

'Yes, it is,' replied the man, almost as though they were in natural conversation. 'Please, have more water,' he said, producing another bottle even though Noah had not finished the one he had.

'My name is Sergei by the way. Shame we couldn't have met under better circumstances but chance is the mother of all beginnings and so here we are, eh! Maybe another time?' he looked at Noah. 'Probably not, actually. Anyway, I'm not just here for idle chatter as you say. I am here for a reason and you know this.'

Noah knew that his window was limited to avoid much more pain.

'You see, the boss man has taken something of a liking to you and for some reason would prefer us not to keep hurting you. Nice to see, in my book. Normally the bosses, and I have seen my fair share of them over the years, just want information and for us to inflict as much damage as we care to. Alexis likes this method best, maximum damage. It is rather his trademark and he does so like death after a severe beating, and I do mean severe. Death leaves no loose ends you see.'

'And you?' asked Noah, nothing to lose by asking the question.

'I am just here to help, young Englishman. It pays well and I get to travel to great places. You people are nothing to me. Rather, you are my way to make my living.'

'Torture?'

'Work, Englishman, work. You make me laugh. As though

the English have not for many years built their empire on such things.'

'Empire?' asked Noah, a fresh wave of pain flowing through his hand and arm as he connected the conversation to a few minutes earlier and the talk of betrayal.

'You think you no longer have an empire?' asked Sergei, laughter in his voice. 'Oh, but you do. It is just no longer made of pure Englishmen, of course, but it is happily based in your country, the criminal home for the uber rich, and they, my hurting friend, are my employer nine times out of ten. The new Empire Englishman, the new style country gent made up of every nation of the world. Almost certainly a fortune built from money made illegally, washed through every foul-drained bank in the world and happily stored in those grand streets of London. What a foolish, clever contradiction of a country, my friend.'

'It's money that pays you,' managed Noah.

'Yes it is, my young damaged friend, yes it is! I am loyal and have been through much fire, torture like you can never imagine. I am to be trusted. That is why I am here.'

'I don't know what to say.'

'Well, you need to say something because otherwise Alexis will be released back into this room and you, my sad and fearful friend, will die.'

'But he said I wouldn't!' shot back Noah, fear again rising and rising as the endgame fell once again into the viewfinder.

'He did, didn't he!' laughed Sergei, 'I think that was for the benefit of our guest.'

'The man at the back?'

'Yes.'

'The boss?'

'Indeed yes. The boss. He knows what he needs and he knows it will take whatever it takes to get it, including your death. Your death warrant was signed the moment we were asked to be involved.'

They waited, Sergei seeing Noah's discomfort build and wanting it to do so.

'So, a simple question you now need to answer. Where is the painting?'

Noah took a chance.

'The Matisse is in my room.'

'Ah, but it isn't,' he said, not rising at all to the wrong artist being named. For some reason this opened a chink of light into Noah's mind.

'It isn't?' said Noah, surprised.

'First place the boss looked, of course. We had your room card, after all.'

Of course they did! His wallet, no doubt his phone now, everything apart from the reclaim ticket which continued to rest safely beneath his foot. Noah weighed up what to say next. The fact that the mention of Matisse had not been jumped on was beginning to raise a line of thought.

'I'm waiting,' said Sergei, impatience in his voice. Clearly this could not go on forever. No doubt Alexis was very hungrily waiting to get back in the room and inflict some more physical damage. Noah took a chance, reasoning that if the boss had not told them the artist that there may be some division he could build. He needed time to think so he needed to spread a lie to buy him more time.

'It is in the room,' Noah said.

'Ah, come on,' replied Sergei, a little anger beginning to find its way into his voice, 'we've been there. It isn't there. We are trained operatives. We don't just check under the bed.'

The door opened and two people walked in. Alexis walked forward and quickly arrived at Noah's side and struck him hard across the face causing a sting to reverberate across Noah's already aching jaw. Alexis laughed.

'I'm so pleased you have decided to give me this fun,' he said, rolling up his sleeves. 'I always enjoy torturing any Englishman. You are normally quite brave which means I get that little bit longer to work on you. Sergei, my friend, please hold the man steady. I have work to do.'

'But it is in the room!' shouted Noah, fear stretched through his croaking voice, his last chance for time now being played out.

Smash, as Alexis's right hand pummelled into Noah's chest again, causing immense pain to again echo around his body. Noah screamed. A further hit followed, this time to the side of his rib cage causing him to gag and cry out. Again another punch followed, again to the same spot. Wave after wave now came, Noah, a punch bag for the man to work on. Noah began to lose himself between the pain he was feeling and the hold he had begun to get on a plan. He was slipping away when the pummelling stopped.

'Well?' asked Alexis, short of breath after his exertions, Sergei standing back to survey Alexis's handiwork.

Noah considered his response. Was the truth his only option? No, he would try one last time.

'It's in my room, bastard. I'm not stupid. I'd hidden it.'

'Really?' asked Alexis smiling at the cheek of the young Englishman who had managed to insult him despite the pain he was feeling. 'Where?'

'And if I tell you?' chanced Noah, seeing the need to make this as convincing as he could manage.

'I won't kill you assuming, of course, that you are not lying.'

'But you will kill me anyway.'

A pause.

'I would like to, yes,' replied Alexis, 'but on this occasion, and I grant you a rare occasion, this will not happen if you tell us the truth. Now, for the final time before I batter you senseless, where is the fucking painting?'

Alexis had shouted with maximum aggression in his voice. Noah thought through the lie he was about to tell, knowing that with it he would have a few hours maximum to live before they came back to do their worst. His only hope was the police and with this he played his final card. He would lie about where the painting was but tell them the real artist to see if this caused them to internally combust with one another; his last chance saloon.

'There's a large modern picture on the wall, behind the desk,' Noah stammered out, his breathing heavily restricted by whatever damage had been done to his ribs. Alexis looked to the back of the room for confirmation.

'The Raphael is behind there. I stuck it on with tape.'

Alexis turned to the back of the room again to see what the response would be when dull thuds echoed through the dark room sending Alexis and then Sergei to the floor. The light too was shattered sending chards of glass over Noah's already heavily cut face. The man from the back of the room walked forward and Noah, now alert despite his beating, braced himself for death. The same thud of a silent gun tore into the bodies around him, the man clearly needing to make sure they were dead. Then silence as the man placed his gun down on the table.

'Do it!' shouted Noah, tears falling down his cheeks, 'Do it now!'

Instead he heard the ripping of tape being unwound and then torn before being placed across his mouth. Noah, totally petrified, waited. He had expected death but instead the man walked out of the room, closing the door softly behind him and leaving Noah in perfect silence.

Chapter 17

The Last Chance

Tess had no idea why Noah was not answering his phone, which had annoyingly just rung out every time she had called it. He had never been very good with his phone anyway, though she knew that compared to her, Noah was a saint for at least replying within a few days. Tess could often take weeks to reply to a text if, indeed, she replied at all.

She had caught the early EasyJet flight from Bristol having left St Ives at 2.30am and making the 6.30am flight easily, something she hated doing. Any saved time was always wasted time in Tess's eyes but on this occasion she knew she could not take a chance. She had been finishing off a painting and had spent the time waiting in the airport cursing every minute and thinking of the strokes she could have been applying instead to her work. Still she was thankful to be on her way to her boy, Noah, having felt a rising need to see him since seeing Flora on the Tuesday night and so the arrival of his text had been a real blessing. An uncomfortable feeling had sat with her and she couldn't shake it no matter how hard she had sought to immerse herself in other things. She put this feeling of disquiet down to her upset for Noah and his love for Flora and, as she often did when she thought of him, she just wanted to give him a big cuddle.

The Tuesday night handover of the letter had been difficult. She had left Flora alone to read the letter and gone to her studio to ostensibly work but in reality sit on the top step of the stairs and wait for magic to happen. She had envisaged in her hopeful thoughts tears of love and relief from Flora, a triumphant little cry and the young girl running into the house to find Tess and share her love for Noah. What actually happened was a few minutes of absolute silence passed and then the back gate could be heard opening and closing and that, much to Tess's immense sadness, was that. For a moment Tess had started to rush down the stairs to run after her but she had stopped herself by the back door. Time and knowledge would take care of eventuality. Wednesday had come and gone and then Thursday without a whisper from Flora, and then the welcome text had arrived from Noah. She took this as a sign that she was needed and, relieved, she had made her plans to cross to Poland.

On the Thursday night she had sent a text to Flora that said:

Flora. Hi. I am so sorry if giving you the letter upset you. It was a selfish thing for a mother to do. Noah had written the letter in confidence and I shall return our secret to where I found it. He will never know you saw it. This is your special week and you did not need that. I know Noah wishes you the best life, the happiest life and if he knew what I had done he would be mortified. So please, try and forgive me and put this from your mind. Noah will be fine. I'm going to see him, in fact, on Saturday so don't worry about a thing. He's staying at the swanky Sheraton, don't you know! Oh yes, that means I can't make the wedding but I will be thinking of you fondly. Sorry again! I hope you understand. You are so lovely, Flora, and I wish you the happiest of days. Tess Xx

The text back from Flora was instant:

Tess. Thank you for the text. It was lovely of you, the text and giving me the letter. I shall treasure it always. You cannot know how it has moved me and what it means to me. I just couldn't face talking about it. Sorry for running off like that and doing a disappearing act. I have not known how to talk to you about it and just could not thread a text together. Forgive me. Anyway, I am really glad you are going to Noah. He will be thrilled to see you and I don't like him being out there on his own, particularly with me not having a number to text him on. Give him my love, always. Flora X

Tess had read and reread the text several times reading meanings and subtexts into the letter and ending up with all sorts of levels of meanings. However, she could not get away from the fact that clearly Flora was marrying Jake on Saturday and that, ultimately, was that. Tess considered sending the mobile number to Flora that Noah had texted her on but decided against it. She had done enough damage already.

The very busy flight from Bristol had been kind to her in that bizarrely she had a spare seat next to her. She had closed her eyes, allowed sleep to arrive, and dreamt of sun and sky. She had awoken to the news that they would shortly be landing and within forty-five minutes she had found herself getting on to the *Balice Ekspres*, the direct train across and into the heart of Krakow at the *Krakow Glowny*. Eighteen minutes later and she was getting off the train and walking past the hallowed baggage collection towards the taxi rank, unaware of the irreplaceable art and cursed illegally procured family heirloom that was hiding metres away from her.

By 11.30am she had arrived at The Sheraton only to be told by reception that Mr Devere had not been seen for a couple of days and that would she mind waiting while they called the manager to come and see her. He did, all smiles and professional veneer that Tess wiped away immediately as she demanded news of her son that he simply did not have.

'And you say your name is Spearing?' asked a confused hotel manager, wishing he had not taken a double shift after all.

'Yes? Charles has his father's surname, you idiot,' replied a testy Tess, the change of name that her son had employed winding her up even more.

'Indeed so,' replied the manager trying to placate this loud lady in a busy hotel foyer, 'but I have no news of him and I would rather you not call me an idiot!'

'Yes, well, I would rather you did not act like one,' replied Tess in a classic fencer's riposte that made the manager turn a bright shade of 'let me hide' red. He tried to find words but was struggling to find any ground to reason with this mad woman standing before him.

'Then I shall wait in his room!' she declared, an easy request and one that the manager thought of denying until the bombastic English lady produced several items of identification, a picture of Noah and an AMEX Platinum card that her father had insisted she have and, while she hated its pomposity, she did rather enjoy the look on the manager's face as it unlocked his acceptance to get her a room card.

Tess waited for the room card with a mixture of fear and fatigue hitting her. She had taken a seat in the reception window that overlooked the front of the hotel. As the busy hotel went about its business, people passing by her with a myriad number of things to do, Tess found herself quietly exhausted and tears silently began to fall down her cheeks. It was through these tears that she saw the silhouette of a man arrive through the revolving doors and make his way to the lifts. A young lady simultaneously arrived at her side at the same time with her room card and Tess, without thinking, stood to follow the man and just got to the lift as the door closed. She stood, entranced, and watched the lift rise to the third floor. Noah's floor. Another lift stood free and she went into that one and pressed the button for the third floor, a few seconds passing like long minutes as it pulled its way effortlessly up through the building to complete its short journey. The doors opened and she stepped out, looking up and down the corridor but seeing no one.

Room 318, the text had said, was Noah's and that was where she headed arriving at the door quickly and finding it shut. She placed her ear up to the door and could hear movement from within and, without thinking twice, she knocked.

Noah was at this point about to pass out again. He had managed to loosen slightly the tape around his mouth by pushing his tongue out against it and it yielding eventually in the right corner due to a mixture of saliva and a fresh blood flow from his lips. However, the work had caused his mouth to feel extremely dry and now, tired out and emotionally drained, his body slumped. He faded in and out of consciousness, tiredness trying to lure him into the world of darkness and yet he kicking against it as he felt to accept this fate may see him never wake again. Noah actually felt like his body was gradually shutting down. The silence of this dungeon was in itself unsettling. Every move Noah made was magnified in the absolute quiet that surrounded him, each echo of nothingness reminding him of his desperate state. Suddenly, though, a noise, some distance away, caused him to become absolutely still and alert. His immediate thought was that his captor, having discovered his lie, had come back to continue to torture him. Fear arrived as this thought did and Noah, already hurting beyond any pain he could have ever imagined, felt fresh stinging tears fall down his cheeks.

Noah, his ears finely tuned in the darkness and now on high alert, listened intently and he realised quickly that the noise he could hear was different to what he would have expected at his returning captor. The new arrivals were moving in a sporadic fashion, a run of feet moving at pace and then stopping. Listening now as intently as he could, he could make out faint whispering and somehow the noise settled him as his logic cried out that this was not his tormentor but possibly, rather, his saviour. Someone was staking this place out and being careful with how they made their way through the godforsaken building.

Noah began to make as much noise as he could, rocking in his chair which only caused a faint rustle of clothes as he was tightly held down, and he forced out a murmuring under the tight tape across his face. It was all he could manage but he felt he had to muster all he could. The noise got closer and as it did so he could hear the opening of doors and a single word being used as they made their way closer to him. The word was *oczyszcać*.

Minutes passed and as each one did Noah felt more hopeful as the noises got closer, his adrenalin now running at full tilt as he prepared himself for his door to be opened and then, all of sudden, it happened. The door was locked and so it was suddenly and with force smashed open, the noise deafening to Noah's ears having been dealing with absolute silence for hours upon end. A torch lit up his face and several people crowded into the room, the polish language filling the air, words of focus and direction, not of anger. Suddenly a light switch was found and the room erupted with brightness causing Noah to tightly close his bruised and battered eyes against the glow.

'Mr. Devere I assume,' said a warm voice that Noah recognized, 'We have been looking for you for a few days now. Good to see you are alive, though somewhat, I think you English would say, the worse for wear.'

People were now by Noah's side, setting him free. Noah opened his eyes, slowly, and there in front of him with a big grin on his face was Inspector Fabian Milosz. The tape was pulled off his face quickly causing Noah to flinch with pain.

'Pardon,' said the medic, one of several who were now at his side.

Noah tried to speak but nothing would come. Instead he turned to one of the medics who had already got hold of some water, which he now gently helped Noah to try and drink.

Moments passed, Milosz issuing orders around him like an experienced orchestra conductor as more people arrived, including a stretcher for Noah. The room was clearly a crime scene, two bodies lying slain on the floor, and the police were extremely busy.

Noah, still at this point in the chair though, of course, mercifully untied, was slowly coming round as more water now rested in his mouth than falling out. He felt elation in the middle of immense pain, the former going some way to alleviate his agonies. Before him his angels busily worked, going about their jobs, him with his life now to lead.

'Safe now,' he muttered, 'safe now,' a small smile touching the corners of his mouth. Milosz returned to face him, a beaming smile on his own face.

'I do love it when we find what we are looking for.'

'How?' stammered Noah.

'Ah yes, how indeed. Well, we were following you, of course, only to have you taken from under our noises by the men in the van.' Milosz looked around the room at the two dead men.

'I assume these are the men?' he asked.

Noah nodded.

'The plot thickens, eh? From then on in it's simply been a matter of finding the van which one of our patrolmen did a few hours ago.'

'Followed me?' managed Noah. Milosz laughed.

'Of course we followed you. No one walks out of a hotel through the underground garage unless they have something to hide, Mr Devere.'

At this point Noah would have told the inspector anything had he but asked but thankfully he was not about to ask. Noah clearly needed urgent medical attention and Milosz simply said, 'You are indeed safe now and we need to get you to a hospital. We will have plenty of time to talk when you are up to it. The medics will take good care of you and I will let the Padowskis know you are safe. They have been very worried. I might keep the senseless beating out of the conversation for now.'

'Henryk?' asked Noah.

'He's OK. Home now, in fact, having discharged himself, though of course he looks like he went a good few rounds with a pro. Mind you, he looks far better than you do. Quite an interesting collection of beaten up victims we are amassing, eh?' Milosz winked at Noah now, the inspector clearly delighted to have Noah safe and getting closer to finding out why all this carnage had happened.

'Just one question before I let you go, yes?'

At this, one of the medics protested to the inspector who in turn held up his hand for just a moment of time.

'Who shot these men?'

'A man,' managed Noah, pain to even open his mouth.

'A single man?'

Noah nodded.

'Do you know who he was?'

Noah truthfully, and with pain racking through his body, shook his head and then said, 'They said he was the boss.'

'And he shot them? Just like that?'

Noah nodded.

The medic was now getting agitated with the inspector, who held up his hands and said, 'Sorry! Enough questions for now. Bad man kills bad men will do for now. Please, Mr Devere, rest. Your body needs help right now and these people will help it do just that. I will call at the hospital tomorrow and see you and we can chat then.'

The medics eased Noah out of the chair and helped him on to the waiting stretcher, each movement causing fresh waves of agony to echo around his body. Once on the stretcher Noah turned to the inspector and said, 'What day is it?'

'Saturday,' replied Milosz.

'Oh. And what time?'

'Lunchtime and, looking at you, I think you could probably do with a good meal.'

Noah's head cried out for his mother, his other girl now being lost to him.

Tess waited. The movement in the room had stopped and time stood still around her. Tess knocked again, this time far too loudly and accompanied the rhythmical beat with a shout of, 'I'm going nowhere so open the door whoever you are!'

Sure enough footsteps made their way to the door and whoever was inside was clearly eyeing her up through the keyhole. Tess could almost hear the person in Noah's room thinking, calculating.

'The door, please,' shouted Tess again, loudly, demanding.

Then, slowly, the door opened and Mikhail Portichenko, a warm smile on his face, stepped out and, looking past Tess, he scanned wildly up and down the corridor.

'Did anyone follow you?' he asked, clear fear in his voice as he did so.

'No!' stated Tess without anything but certainty in her own voice.

'Good, well, come inside,' Mikhail said, ushering her in to the room and adding, 'Noah is not here,' as he did so.

Tess walked into a room that was in a dreadful mess. Clearly it had been taken apart with someone looking for something, everything thrown around, a huge picture broken in half on the floor by her feet. Tess turned to Mikhail who had followed her into the room and he, his face full of the kindness that had so touched her so often at home, stepped forward and held her. Tess, ever on her guard, allowed herself to be hugged but gave nothing back; after all, this was the man who had left her to return to his own home having been yet another man to have come into her life and then left it. Further, he was now in her son's room and her son was not so she waited for an explanation to come.

Mikhail stepped back. She weighed him up. He looked extremely tired and dishevelled and not himself.

'Mikhail,' started Tess, upset and anger rising in her voice, 'Where the hell is he and what the hell are you doing here?'

Mikhail held up his hands in a calming motion.

'I have much to tell you Tess, but for now know that I believe your son is safe, but as I said, missing at present.'

276

'Missing? At present? You are talking in riddles!'

Mikhail waited, allowing the air to find him time to give a more suitable answer.

'He is in trouble.'

'Trouble? He's here on holiday, and with you it seems,' she added grumpily, assuming the only reason the Russian was here, was because her son, her precious Noah, had decided to spend some of his vacation with the man who had walked out on her.

'It is good to see you, my Tess, so good to see you.'

'Well, first of all, I'm not *your* Tess, and while under other circumstances it may have been good to see you, and I stress *may*, I need you to tell me right now exactly what is going on.'

'Yes, yes, of course my, erm, Tess, please, be seated.' He pointed over to the window and two comfortable chairs that were by the window overlooking the view of the majestic Wisla River, happily going about its business and unaware and uncaring of the drama unfolding. It had seen more than enough history to know it rarely affected its flow.

Tess sat, her back bolt upright, giving nothing to this man who sat before her. Mikhail sat across from her, waiting for some words to come from Tess, but finding none forthcoming he decided to step forward with his story.

'I've missed you, Tess, so missed you. I know you don't want to hear this but the nights have been so long and I have been counting the days to see you and yet it is this day, this sad day that you come back into my life.'

'Now Mikhail,' Tess addressed the Russian in a stern voice, holding his flickering eyes in her most definite gaze, 'enough of the missed-me lines for now please, as heartfelt as they may or may not be.'

'But my love, they are!' he proclaimed, his voice cut by Tess's hardness.

Tess held up her hand.

'Please, please, enough already. If you call me my love once more I will slap you.' Tess's voice was raised yet controlled. 'I want to hear about my son, my Noah. Where is he?'

At this Mikhail nodded and stood, walking around to the window at their side and gazed into the distance.

'I am afraid,' he said after a few moments had passed, 'and I don't thing I can dress this up any other way, that Noah is in danger.'

Tess waited; she had known something was amiss and now she could feel fear creep up through her body, which she immediately fought to hold it all in check. Fear would not help her at this time and she knew that. She needed to be alert more than she had ever been before and so concentration was key. Adrenalin began to take over and win the battle over fear and still she waited.

'What do you know about his trip to Krakow?' asked Mikhail, now having returned to his seat and looking directly at Tess.

'Part of his trip across Europe,' offered Tess.

'Well, yes,' replied Mikhail, 'but what specifically was he here for?'

'Europe?' asked Tess, confused.

'No, Krakow.'

Tess shook her head, not knowing what on earth Mikhail was getting at.

'What are you doing here?' Tess asked, cutting through the confusion and Mikhail's obvious discomfort. 'Did he ask you to meet him here, eh? All those stories you told him about the real Europe! I should be here on holiday with him, not you! I'm his mother. You're just some distant relative who decided to show up after my dear father died and then disappeared again. Fat use you were clearly!'

'I am Mikhail Portichenko and I love you and your Noah and yes, he asked me to spend some time with him on his holiday to show him bits he would not have visited and yes, Krakow was the perfect place to start.'

'Well, why didn't he tell me this?'

'About Krakow?'

'No, about you, you stupid man!' snapped back Tess, now clearly angry as well as annoyed.

Mikhail leaned forward and tried to take one of Tess's hands only for it to be pulled forcibly away from him.

'Now Tess, you know he adores you, and you were in England with your work and a wedding to attend to. He knew that and you know that. I, well, I am an easy get out for him.

You and I both know he is a little infatuated with me and as much as this annoys you, it is the truth!'

At this, Tess smiled. Yes, she did know that. Mikhail saw the smile. His first small victory.

He went on, 'So he rang me, out of the blue I might add with no invitation from me, and asked if I had some time. I had a few days and some business in Krakow I could attend to here, so I happily agreed. I mean, seeing Noah, what a delight for me. How could I resist?'

'How indeed,' replied Tess with sarcasm riddled through her voice. 'So you met him when?'

'Erm…'

'Erm?' shouted Tess, 'Erm? How difficult a question was that, Mikhail? What are you not telling me?'

Mikhail looked at Tess, a flash of fresh anger crossing his face that Tess saw immediately.

'Ah, getting some real emotion at last are we? Thank God,' she goaded.

'Look,' replied Mikhail, regaining his composure instantly, 'it's the awkwardness of the situation. You are being most rude by the way so now I will be most frank. I met up with him on Thursday morning, here in the lobby, and had a delightful day. I showed him many of Krakow's treasures, all of which he was delighted with, had a fabulous dinner and parted happily after much fun, late in the Krakow night. Then, yesterday morning I got a call from him. He was very agitated and said he needed me to meet him here as soon as I could. I came at once, of course, and as I arrived there was Noah being led out of the hotel by two policemen. Well, I…, Tess, are you all right?'

Tess had turned quite pale, the lack of sleep and the news she was hearing all catching up with her.

'Wait there,' said Mikhail rising and going to the fridge in the room to see what he could find. He rustled up water and chocolate and brought them back for her. 'Eat and drink, Tess. You will need the energy.'

Tess shook her head defiantly, determined not to take anything from the Russian.

'Please, Tess, please. I need you to be with me on this now. OK?'

Tess nodded and obediently drank the water and started

on the chocolate. Mikhail waited, a sombre Russian face waiting for Tess.

'Go on,' she said, 'I need to hear everything you know.'

'Well, I went to the police station and using a contact got to see him early afternoon. Do you know he's been using a false name?'

Tess nodded. She had no idea why Noah had adopted the name and it did not look good at the side of what she was now listening to. 'Charles Devere, indeed,' she muttered to herself, shaking her head in confusion.

'Well, it seems he borrowed a friend's car and sadly the car was carrying drugs.'

'Drugs? No. Not possible, absolutely not my Noah. This has never been his thing and is not possible.'

'I am afraid it was possible. They found speed.'

'They could find what the hell they want Mikhail but it has nothing to do with my Noah!'

'They don't know your Noah do they Tess? They don't know anything other than they found some drugs. This is, therefore, the danger he faces.'

'A friend's car,' Tess was mumbling, 'a friend's car. How stupid can you get?'

'Ah yes, a friend from London. Noah wouldn't give me his name. He is being protective.'

'I'll give him protective, Mikhail. Take me down there, now!'

Mikhail held up his hands.

'Steady Tess, steady, he is in custody and I have already offered to post bail. The judge will consider this but not until Monday. It will be fine and we will get him then. He is absolutely fine. My contacts have made sure of that. In fact when I saw him this morning he was in high spirits.'

Tess smiled, momentary relief washing through her.

'Oh, you saw him?'

'Yes, of course. You know this is a big day for him with Flora and all?'

'I know!' replied Tess in an I-know-everything-about-my-son-you-know voice to ensure the Russian knew his place.

Mikhail nodded.

'Yes, of course you know. Sorry. Well, in some ways he sees this as amusing.'

'Amusing?'

'You know, such a big thing to take his mind off what he cannot forget.'

'Yes,' replied Tess, almost agreeing, 'I can see that.'

They waited for a moment, Tess sipping her water and Mikhail looking out of the window, lost it seemed in thought. Tess realised what a friend Mikhail had been and felt upset for being too hard on him. It was never, she thought, easy to fall out with this Russian for too long. She leaned forward.

'I'm sorry, Mikhail. I am tired and confused. Thank you for being there for my son.'

'Please,' replied Mikhail, happily taking her hand, 'spending time with Noah is always my pleasure.'

Tess smiled.

'You have the most beautiful eyes,' said Mikhail, holding Tess in a gaze of lustful adoration. Tess momentarily forgot herself and enjoyed the look.

'Now steady on Russian! Tell me a few more answers then you can waste your breath some more on adoration. Why the change of car?'

Mikhail smiled widely at this. The defences were coming down at last!

'Apparently it's a fabulous car off a rich friend that Noah said was too tempting to turn down the offer to borrow for his trip.'

Tess, knowing the owner immediately, kept counsel. There would be time enough to deal with that young man and deal she would.

'And how were the drugs found?'

'Unlucky, really. There was a police dog team in the car park looking for something else and one of them picked up on the drugs. Apparently they got quite excited.'

'And drugs you say? Was there much there?'

'No m'learned Lord,' replied Mikhail, smiling now and enjoying the game, 'just more than enough for purely domestic use.'

'But not enough to suggest Noah was smuggling?'

'Bingo!' replied Mikhail, laughing as he did so. 'And the final piece?'

Tess looked around the room.

'They ripped the room apart hoping to find more?'

'Indeed.'

'And did they?' she asked, hesitancy causing the question to come out slowly.

'No. Of course not. He knew absolutely nothing about it.'

Tess let the news settle, her mind putting all she had heard into some semblance of order.

'So he will be OK?'

Mikhail, standing now and coming round to Tess to place his arm round her shoulder, said,

'Yes. Justice needs to take its time and be seen to be done, but I have it on absolute authority that all will be fine.'

'OK,' Tess replied, letting the Russian's arm stay rested around her shoulder, his breath now touching her hair as he waited behind her. She turned to him.

'So, let's go and see him.'

'Ah, I am afraid we cannot today. Polish laws state only one visiting hour per day and that was this morning. You will have to wait until tomorrow morning.'

'But he must know I am here!'

'He does know, Tess,' replied Mikhail, confidence growing in him now, 'that's why he sent me here.'

Tess smiled. It was all making sense now. Of course he knew as she had sent him several texts! She felt suddenly very tired.

'Do you mind if I rest awhile, Mikhail? I'm suddenly feeling very wasted.'

'No, of course not!' he replied, standing quickly and clearing the bed, trying to give the room a more tidy appearance in as quick a time as he could do so.

Tess went to the bathroom and returned with a bathrobe wrapped around her clothed shoulders.

'I'm cold,' she said as she made her way to the bed.

'It's the shock,' said Mikhail, making his way over to her as she lay down in the bed and pulled the covers over her. He leaned forward and gently kissed the top of her head.

'My pretty lady,' he whispered over and over again as Tess, smiling now, fell into a much-needed sleep.

It was early evening before Noah came round, the quiet room

slowly bubbling into focus as consciousness returned. As his eyes began the tortuous journey to work and accustom to the dim light that greeted him, a familiar voice in the corner of the room from somebody who had clearly been watching him greeted him.

'Mr Devere! A pleasure,' said Inspector Milosz, real joy in his voice. 'We never thought we lost you but you didn't look too good. Amazing what a bit of torture can do, isn't it?'

Milosz had arrived at his side to see Noah's worried eyes greet him.

'Don't worry, young man! I'm not here to interview you. I'm off duty to be honest. Just wanted to make sure you were OK really so I've been catching up on a bit of reading.'

Here, the inspector produced a paperback book almost as evidence.

'One of your chaps, Faulks, he's good. Captures some of the heart we Poles understand. Are you sure he's from your country?'

Noah managed a weak smile. He felt pain but it seemed somehow distant, as though he was sitting in another body observing his own. The drugs had numbed him and given him a false sense of how bad he would feel if they were not doing their job to comatose him.

'Am I OK?' Noah managed.

Milosz smiled, almost paternally. The inspector was a young man, in his early thirties. He had a baby himself and knew what it was to feel the pain of someone you loved. He felt close enough in age to understand what Noah felt, his fear, his desperation, his longing for friends and family that he knew Noah would be feeling very far away from right now. He also felt old enough to offer the injured Noah the maturity of support that he clearly needed right now.

'You are fine. That is if you accept the severely broken fingers, the broken ribs and the broken nose.'

Milosz paused.

'And the small matter of the missing teeth, the jaw thankfully not broken but as near as dammit, and the severe bruising across your body from a beating well done. Other than that, Mr Devere, you have a clean bill of health! The Olympic training may well be out for a few months, but all in good time, eh?'

283

Noah smiled.

'So I am OK?' he asked, doubt in his voice.

'Yes!' replied Milosz, 'You need to rest, of course, and you remain under observation to make sure there is nothing that has been missed, but yes, you are OK.'

'But my fingers,' muttered Noah, 'what they did...' his voice tailed off as tears came to his eyes.

'Will take time,' said the policeman, softly. 'Now you must sleep some more. Your body needs that more than anything right now. It is exhausted and in deep trauma. It craves rest. I shall leave you alone and come back and see you tomorrow. Maybe bring you some croissants, eh? My card is here Noah, OK? You can call me at any time, for anything. Right?'

Noah nodded, truly grateful for the policeman's time. Milosz stood and walked towards the door.

'We have an armed guard at your door so you need fear no one. No one is coming back to get you. All is fine. So rest, yes?'

Noah managed a weak smile as he felt the tide of sleep rising again. Sleep! Yes, that sounded a very good idea indeed.

As her son was falling to sleep, Tess was waking up. She did so with a start, initially wondering where she was and then, as her day unfolded and replayed in her mind, she sat up quickly looking for Mikhail. She called for him but there was no one there. Sitting up too quickly, the room tilted for a moment, and she waited for her head to settle. To the side of the bed she saw the telephone and without thinking twice, she picked it up and called down to reception.

'Good evening, Mr Devere,' the receptionist said automatically, 'How can I help you?'

Tess caught herself, wanting to immediately tell the receptionist her son was not Mr Devere at all, but realising this was not the time she simply said, 'It's his mother!'

'Ah yes. Mrs Devere. Good evening to you. How can I help?'

'Well, first of all my name is', Tess stopped herself. It was no point annoying the receptionist with her actual name. Devere was fine. 'Pronounced de-veer, not der-ver,' Tess added with as much authority as she could muster and feeling rather bad as she did so.

'Ah, right,' responded the bewildered receptionist, 'I am so sorry Mrs Devere,' she announced, immediately getting the pronunciation correct.

'And then second of all I want you to put me through to the main police station please.'

A pause.

'The police station? Is there a problem I can help with?'

'No, it's no problem, just silly me. I lost my watch today while sightseeing. Typical really. I'm always losing things, but this watch, well, it's very important to me. A gift from my mother.'

'Well, let me call for you,' offered the receptionist.

'No, thank you. The watch is very unique and I will need to explain it in detail.'

'Ah. I understand. Well, one question first. Do you speak Polish?'

'No,' replied Tess, wondering how she was ever going to get past this persistently helpful receptionist.

'OK. I shall call the police station for you then, make sure I have an English speaker for you, and then put you through. Would that be to your liking, Mrs Devere?'

'Right. Erm, yes, indeed. Thank you so much.'

'Good. Please replace the receiver and I shall call you back within a few moments and connect you.'

'Thank you,' said Tess, placing down the phone as instructed and simply waiting. As she did so she thought of Noah, of him alone in a dreadful police station, and tears filled her eyes. A few moments passed and the phone rang, making her jump as it did so.

'Mrs Devere?' asked the receptionist, 'I have the police for you. I have explained that you have lost something and they will help you now.'

'Thank you,' said Tess, feeling oddly annoyed at the efficiency of the receptionist: A click and then a new flurry of voices as she was connected to the activity of a police incoming-call desk.

'Hello?' Tess asked.

'Hello, Mrs Devere. How are you?'

'Erm, I am OK, sort of. At least I will be when you have helped me. How are you?' Tess managed, trying to keep her voice firm yet fair.

'I'm fine, thankyou madam. It's been a long day and I

finish at eight so ask me in an hour or so. My name is Officer Janski and I am here to help you. So, you've lost something I understand. Something precious, is it?'

'Yes, it is. Very precious. It's my son. And you have him.'

'Right,' replied Officer Janski, not expecting the response, 'Your son?'

'Yes, my son,' replied Tess, with nothing but full and absolute authority in her voice. 'And I am coming to see him now no matter what your silly visiting hours are. So, his name is Charles Devere and I want you to make arrangements for me to come and see him now.'

'OK, hold on there, Mrs Devere. I have no idea what you are talking about. You are saying we are holding your son within a police cell?'

'I am and you are.'

'OK. I see. Well, let me see what I can find out for you,' replied the officer, his tone changing as he realised he was simply dealing with a felon's mother.

Tess, immediately hearing the change of tone, took control.

'Now listen here, young man. You had better realise who you are talking to. I am the daughter of a British peer and knight of the realm and as such I am to be treated with nothing but respect. Do not, I repeat, do not treat me and my beautiful British son with anything but utter and total respect or you will regret it. Do you hear me?'

'Yes,' replied the officer begrudgingly. This lady may just be slightly important so a certain decorum would need to be followed. Tess went on.

'The boy you hold… '

'Boy?'

'Young man that is, should not be with you. I'm coming to get him. Do you understand?'

Officer Janski, tired after a long day, concluded it was simply better to humour the clearly deranged Englishwoman.

'Yes, I understand. Now before you come down to see us, Mrs Devere, and we shall ensure we have fresh tea waiting for you, I need to ascertain where your son is. Would that be acceptable to you?'

'Yes,' replied Tess tersely, 'and no need to be smart with me and please be quick about it.'

'Indeed,' replied the officer, rolling his eyes as he did so, 'I will place you on hold and there will be silence. Please simply wait. I won't be long. We really can't keep such an important visitor as you waiting can we?' he said, without any hint of sarcasm in his voice save for the words spoken.

Tess pressed the monitor button on the phone and stood to look in the mirror on the wall. She looked at herself and thought how very tired she looked.

'And old,' she said, seeing lines that appeared to continue to multiply quicker than the years that followed. Her hair looked greasy, her skin on her face dry.

'God, Tess, you need to do something to yourself.'

She pulled her T-shirt off and looked at herself once more. There she stood, jeans sitting on her hips, the unusual hours and life she led meant she fought away weight though tell-tale love handles were appearing and she hated them. She thought herself not unattractive still and she knew that men still turned to look at her and she liked that. In fact, she liked that too much and she despised that in herself. Her breasts seemed to still be growing, something she had witnessed and marvelled at in her mother, but they were now not the shape she had once loved and murmuring discord, Tess picked up a clean blouse and fastened it up quickly.

'Right then, Mrs Devere,' the voice rang out of the monitor. Tess rushed over to the receiver and picked it up.

'Yes?' she said, quickly.

'I'm afraid I have some bad news.'

Tess, slumped on to the bed and repeated the words she had just heard.

'Bad news?'

'Yes. Your son is not here.'

'Not there?'

'That's right,' replied Officer Janski, choosing his words carefully. 'He's at the hospital, the University Hospital. He's OK, so please don't worry, but he has had a rough ride.'

Tess was silent, thoughts rushing through her head. Why had Mikhail lied to her? Was he protecting her? Yes, of course he was. Mikhail was protecting her. He knew how she would react. The connection between Mikhail and the protection of her son was like an easy sum in her mind. It happened automatically and she didn't need to think twice about it. Clearly these drug people had attacked her Noah. She would get to Noah now and she would make it all all right.

'Mrs Devere, Mrs Devere?' called Officer Janski, concern in his voice. He had thought about not telling her anything but knew it would be impossible to stop her coming down to the police station anyway.

'Yes, I am here,' said Tess, quietly now. 'Thank you. I shall go to him.'

'Shall we send a car?' asked the officer, having already placed a call directly to Milosz who was in turn making his way to the hospital to meet the mother, amazed to hear that the young man's mother was actually in the city. How on earth had that happened?

'No. There won't be any need. I have my cousin here with me. He has been helping my son anyway. He will bring me. Thank you, officer. Sorry for being sharp with you, it's just that, well, he's my son.'

'Yes, I know. I have a son myself.'

'You do? Well, that's great. Treasure him.'

'I do.'

'Right, thank you. Goodnight, officer.'

'Goodnight, Mrs Devere. I am sure your son will be pleased to see you.'

Tess readied herself, busy for the moment that Mikhail would arrive back from wherever he had disappeared off to so that they could leave immediately on his return. Her mind kept trying to run away with itself with the news that Noah was in hospital, but she told herself that the officer had said Noah was fine and that kept her calm. She showered quickly, and then dressed in jeans and a striped blue sweatshirt. At the mirror she added make-up and worked through the injuries her son could have that would mean he was in hospital but fine. She focussed in on a broken leg for some reason and then began thinking about getting him home with a broken leg and how it would affect him. Surfing would be out of the question for months and she thought of him lying there in hospital, so sad as he thought about the waves he would not be catching. Now, where on earth was Mikhail?

Then, as if he knew she had been willing him back, the

door was being opened, and there he was, big smile on his face, arms opened wide to hug her and within moments she was in his arms, feeling safe and needing his love more than she cared to think about.

'I'm so pleased you're back, Mikhail,' Tess said, not moving from the embrace she was being held in, her head resting on the Russian's chest.

'Of course you are, my love,' he said, and as he did so she could see the smile on his face in her mind.

'And thank you for trying to protect me over Noah. It was typical of you and I fear I have been so very unkind to you.'

They stepped apart from each other, Mikhail stroking her arms and looking seriously into her face.

'You know, the hospital,' she said.

'Hospital?' repeated Mikhail, his voice very serious as he did so.

'Yes! I rang the police and they told me he was in hospital, but don't worry,' she said quickly, seeing Mikhail's expression drop, 'they said he's fine.'

'Right,' replied Mikhail, his face suddenly looking drained and empty, 'and what else did they say?'

'Well, nothing really. I said we would get down straightaway.'

'We?'

'Yes, you and I.'

'Right,' Mikhail replied, a long pause following and Tess, eager to get on, stepped forward, kissed him on his cheek and then went to her case to pick out a jumper just in case the Krakow night turned out to be cool later.

'So let's go, yes?' Tess said, having reached the door and turning to see the Russian walking quickly towards her.

'Mikhail?' she said, seeing an expression in his face she had never seen before.

'I'm sorry,' he said.

Chapter 18

Escape

Milosz walked into Noah's room just as he was tucking into his pudding.

'Hello!' Noah said, seeing the inspector arrive and feeling happy about it. He liked this man and not just because he had probably saved his life. 'Do you want some apple pie?'

'I don't,' he replied with a poker face that was giving nothing away as he pulled up a chair and sat at Noah's side. Noah continued eating.

'You do know it's ten o'clock and rather late to be having pudding, don't you?' Milosz said, smiling now. Noah shot him a grin back. It was good to be eating.

'What are you doing back?' Noah managed between another mouthful. It was extremely painful to be eating but the pain was numbed and the food was desperately needed, hunger having arrived all of a sudden.

'I needed to ask you something.'

'Right,' replied Noah hesitantly as he wondered what was coming next. Noah had tried, between waking fitfully and the pain, to work out a story that would work as to why he was targeted as well as the Padowskis but at this point he had come up with nothing that seemed to stack up. If this was the start of his formal interviewing then the game would be up.

'Now, tell me,' Milosz asked, 'is it possible your mother is here?'

Noah stopped eating.

'Erm, no! My mother, here?' he said as his memory played with him and he remembered the text and his missing phone and the rest fell into place. 'Actually, perhaps she is here. I sent her a text on Thursday just prior to my new friends kidnapping me. I've not thought about her actually coming because we never got into a conversation about it.'

'So you sent her a text. Right. What did you say?'

'To come and visit me, of course,' Noah replied, the simple pleasure of eating food releasing such happiness in him. 'Why? Is she here?' he asked and not expecting the reply that shot back.

'So it would appear. A Devere called the main station around an hour ago from your hotel room.'

'What?' said Noah, sitting up and feeling various pains rush through his body as he did so. 'Mother, she is here? And in my hotel room? How on earth did she manage that?' a mixture of delight that his mother was here flowed with fear that it was not Tess; after all, Milosz had used the new surname.

'Well, I assume they let her in. I mean, by all accounts from the officer who took her call, she is not the type of lady who takes no for an answer. It was fair to say she gave him a right going over and made it clear that she would be coming to see you and that you were related to a lord.'

Noah laughed. It was his mother, surely.

'No, she doesn't do "no" very well. I'm sorry about that.'

'Two pompous, all-knowing English troublemakers. That's all I need,' smiled Milosz, sitting back in his chair. 'Well, she said she was on her way here so I'm surprised she didn't beat me to your bedside. I mean, it's been a good hour and a half since she called. Apparently she has a man with her who would be bringing her.'

'Really?' said Noah, 'She said that?'

'Yes.'

'OK. Well, I've no idea who that might be.'

'No idea? Isn't that a little strange? I mean, she is your mother.'

'Thank you for that, Inspector, but with my mother she is a constant mystery! Maybe she decided to have a cheeky weekend here with a new lover?'

'Yes, maybe,' replied Milosz, pressing the screen on his mobile as he did so and calling the police station.

Noah sat forward and stepped out of bed making his way

less than quickly to the bathroom. He was however feeling remarkably bright given all he had been through. Apart from the obvious pain, the relief of his freedom and the knowledge that the painting remained safe now released nothing but good feelings around his body. Add to this the outstanding news that his mother had arrived, well, that really lifted him. She would be very shocked to see him in this state but after she got over it, well, all would be well. Noah looked at himself in the mirror and caught his smile looking back at himself. Then a vision flashed across his mind of Tom and desolation again washed through him. He shook his head, washed his face in the sink and returned to the room.

'Your mother's cousin. Who would that be?' asked Milosz as Noah sat next to him on the edge of his bed.

'My mother's cousin?

'Yes. That's what she said. Her cousin was with her and he would bring her over, so who is he?'

Noah spirits were lifted as he smiled broadly. A male and her mum's cousin. Surely it wasn't Mikhail, was it? As he thought it he knew it most probably was. There was no one else that he could think of that she was so close to, certainly no one else she would have come to Krakow with.

'Well, there is a cousin she is very close to. He lives in Russia but... '

'Russia?'

'Yes. St Petersburg.'

'How very civilised.'

'I mean, I had no idea, but we are talking about my mum here.'

'Right. His name?'

Noah was not sure what to do at this point. To share Mikhail's name would open up the reality of his own name and then the whole house of cards could collapse. However, surely the police would have Noah's real name by now? This was a pointless pretence.

'His name, Noah, please?' pressed the inspector.

'Mikhail Portichenko.'

Milosz nodded and wrote the name down.

'Well, assuming you are right they should be here by now. It has been too long.'

'Too long? What do you mean?'

'I mean, her son is lying injured in a hospital bed and a mother would have been here in no time.'

'Right. How far are we from The Sheraton?'

'We are just round from the *Glowny.*'

'Right. Not far then,' replied Noah, anxiety immediately laced through his voice.

'Well, unless they walked, which seems highly unlikely.'

'Yes, it does; let's go look,' said Noah, lifting himself off the bed only for the policeman to hold up a hand.

'Come on now, you are in no state to go anywhere. Don't worry, I will go now and check on your room at the hotel. I will make sure all is fine, which I am sure it will be. If they arrive in the meantime my officer will call me.'

'Right. Yes, well, please can you hurry and can you call me as soon as you are there?' Noah replied, nerves rising like steam from a boiling kettle as he did so. Was it Mikhail who was here? The dark shudder of a violent energy passed over him once more and he found himself beginning to get tense.

'Come on, Noah,' he told himself. It was obviously his mother from the description and the fact that he had asked her to come. Mikhail was an easy choice to ask to come and help and then finally, and importantly, there was an armed guard at his bedside to make sure he was safe.

'Come on, Noah,' he repeated, as Milosz disappeared and Noah decided a shower was probably a good thing. If Tess was due she would have 20,000 questions and Noah knew he would need to be as alert as he could be as this would take some explaining if he was to keep the Raphael out of the story. Noah walked over to his wardrobe and saw his loyal Etnies there. He picked them out and walked over to his bed and lifted the inner sole of the right one to see the baggage reclaim ticket happily still there. He placed the ticket back, hidden, in his trainer and put them down by the bed. Incredible luck, he realised, had kept him and the ticket safe throughout all these unbelievable last few days. Happiness touched his spirits again as he went through to the bathroom.

As he showered Officer Bublanski looked into the room of his young charge only to see he was not there. His much respected and superior officer had given him a quick pep talk before leaving as to the need to be extra vigilant and so the empty bed was a concern. Bublanski was in truth not really cut out to be an armed guard. He found it nerve-wracking and would have preferred to be sitting behind one of several warm and unthreatening desks he could think about back at the station. Even worse was working this late shift on his own in this sleepy hospital corridor where everyone seemed to have gone to sleep apart from him. He was a soft and kind man given to spending as much time with his family as he could. Four wonderful children and another on the way were the very apples of his eye together with his beautiful wife, Elana. At least here he could spend all his time thinking of them and this was, on balance, far preferable to paperwork, but this quiet hospital was giving him an uncomfortable chill he couldn't shake.

So with his heart racing he now stepped into the room where he heard the steady hum of the shower and, panic over, he turned to return to the safety of his seat only to find the butt of a revolver pointing menacingly straight into his head.

Bublanski was about to reason with this tall, well-built man, when the man put his finger up to his mouth. Bublanski nodded, reasoning compliance to be the best way forward at this stage. The assailant with the revolver now pointed towards the tall built-in wardrobe and Bublanski, sensing that he was about to be put in there, started to get very nervous. He hated small spaces and knew he would be extremely claustrophobic. Still, as he made his way over the room, the shower still singing away in the background and the young Englishman singing away with it, Bublanski realised it was better to feel uncomfortable in the wardrobe than be dead. It was a thought wasted because as he opened the door a shot was fired into his head, killing him instantly and ending a life so full that all within it would be left to feel empty and crushed.

Noah stepped out of the shower having worked his way successfully through "Local boy in a photograph" and as much as he was still in immense pain, pain that he knew was numbed by various painkillers so goodness knows what it would actually be like, he felt rather euphoric. His plan had not been uncovered, his friends, the Padowskis, were safe, his beloved mother was on her way and he could, once the painting was delivered, get on with his trip. The black cloud of Flora's happy day had played on his mind but somehow the knowledge that she would now be married had helped begin to place a lid on this box. It was what it was. Noah fastened his dressing gown around him and walked into his room only to see his dear Uncle Mikhail sitting before him on a chair by the wardrobe in the corner of the room, a huge grin on his face.

'Mikhail!' said Noah, 'I knew it was you!' so extremely delighted to see him. Mikhail got up and made his way over the room to embrace his young friend as gently as he could.

'Knew it was me?' asked Mikhail, as he held the wounded boy in his arms.

'Yes,' said Noah stepping back, 'the police. Mum had said she with her cousin.'

'Of course, of course,' laughed Mikhail, 'I was with her. You should have seen her demanding to see her precious son!'

'I know!' laughed Noah, clutching his broken ribs as he did so as several shots of pain wracked through his body.

Mikhail, seeing Noah grasp his body, helped him to the side of the bed saying, 'Dreadful business,' as he did so.

'Yea, I've looked better. You should have seen me when they found me!'

'You will tell me all about it and I will see justice is done.'

'Ah ha! My uncle to the rescue!'

'Now then, Noah, keep the noise down or else we will have the nursing staff in,' Mikhail said, holding his hand up for silence as he did so, his voice suddenly alert and serious.

'Armed guard more like,' replied Noah, looking towards the door as he did so.

'Ah, fear not, young man. Our uniformed friend has gone for a walk. It's amazing what a little Russian charm and a backhand of notes can achieve, eh!'

Mikhail laughed, his cheeky face screwing up in the way that cracked Noah up. He loved this man, his mother's cousin.

'Where's Mum? The police said she should have been here by now?'

At the mention of Tess, Mikhail's expression changed, a seriousness filling his face as he pointed towards the bed for Noah to sit down. Noah would not move.

'Where is she?' he demanded, standing up as he did so. Mikhail held up two calming hands.

'She's fine. Waiting for us nearby.'

'Waiting for us? Why?'

'I have things to tell you, Noah, amazing things, but for now we need to get out of here and quickly.'

'We do?'

'We do.'

'But the police, they rescued me. You should have seen me, Mikhail.'

'I know, I know, but listen to me, we have to get out if you want to keep the Raphael safe.'

The mention of the painting by name made the room spin around at once. Noah looked carefully into Mikhail's face which was giving nothing away other than concern.

'Listen very carefully to me, Noah, as this will need to be quick. Your Grandmother knew all about it, knew Joshua was gifting it to you and knew, or so she thought, that you would keep it hidden. It was not until Tess said that she was going to see you here in Krakow and miss the wedding that she felt worried enough to share the story.'

'With you?'

'Of course with me. She knows I know of these things and that I know of family.'

Noah nodded, a thousand thoughts now bouncing around his head. His Grandmother had known. Of course she had, she had accompanied Joshua on his visit to the Czartoryski after all. Noah once again marvelled at his own stupidity.

'So after she had called me and I had promised her not to worry, that I would come out here and look after the pair of you, I made some enquiries. You know I have a lot of contacts, Noah, and it did not take me long to find you were talking to Henryk Padowski. You thought he was a good man, yes?'

'Of course!' Noah replied with much passion.

'Well, he's not. He's an art mercenary with the Czartoryski as a wonderful cover.'

'No, surely not!' said Noah, who up to this point had

refused to sit down, and now sat down on the bed his world spinning again.

'Nice men are criminals too, you know. The police magically found you, did they not?' Mikhail asked, sarcasm in his voice.

'Yes,' murmured Noah, his head bowed and his heart broken by the wounds now being inflicted.

'Did you not think it was an incredible coincidence?'

'Not really, although now you mention it...' Noah rubbed his head trying vainly to rid himself of the now banging pain, 'but the Padowskis were set upon?'

Mikhail gave Noah a disbelieving look and Noah realised with a sinking feeling that he had been in the middle of a play with him playing the part of the fool.

'You are just totally out of your depth, Noah. What you have brought into this country was dynamite and there was only ever going to be one outcome with this. BOOM!' Mikhail said, banging his fists together as he did so. 'And so, thankfully, I got here and met with Tess at your hotel and... '

'You told her?'

'Of course I told her. Every last detail and the fact that she had stupidly parachuted herself straight into the middle of your mad stage set, Noah. Here are men with guns and violence. This police force is not like your own. Here in Eastern Europe we are all in and out of each other's pockets, Noah. There is no easy good guy bad guy role model. You have been, and I have to say this, Noah, extremely foolish and played every step of the way.'

Mikhail let that comment settle for a few moments and then went on.

'And yet we can make this right,' declared Mikhail, extreme confidence in his strong voice.

'We can?' replied Noah, looking up.

'I assume they have the painting?' Mikhail said, stating the words as a matter of fact.

'No!' replied Noah, some pride in his voice as he did so.

'No!' responded Mikhail, amazement in his voice. 'Well, that really is something. In that case we really do have a chance.'

'To do what?'

'To escape with all intact.'

'But, the police!'

'I have contacts, Noah. This corruption goes right to the top and so I cannot control the police, but my contacts are strong and I know we can escape if we get going now. Look, in this bag, I have brought some of your clean clothes for you. Get changed now. Time is critical.'

Noah looked at Mikhail, then at the bag.

'And mum?'

'Waits in the car for us outside. She knows what we must do. As soon as I told her everything her one concern was you getting out of the hospital and the police trap. She waits Noah, for us to put this right. Yes?'

'Right.'

Noah had doubts and many questions but he also had an overriding trust in his dear Mikhail and together with the pain and tiredness that swept over him like the waves of the ocean, it was an easy choice to take to trust Mikhail over all else he thought through. Decision made, Noah got dressed, pain now building as he pulled clothes over his damaged body.

'Place this cap on,' said Mikhail, handing over a blue NY Yankees hat to Noah and placing another on his head. 'Just to confuse the cameras! Now come on, the stairwell awaits us.'

'This is like a movie,' Noah whispered as they stepped out into the deserted corridor, handily placed at the end of the corridor and next to the exit.

'Yes it is but the pain is for real, right?' Mikhail grinned back.

They were at the exit door and Mikhail produced a security card which he swiped over the door lock and it flicked from red to green and they were away.

'How on earth?' asked Noah.

'Ways and means,' replied Mikhail, 'ways and means.'

They reached the top of the stairs and made their way down and out through the main doors and into the cool of the summer night, the air hitting Noah like cold water and making him feel as alert as he had felt since waking up in the hospital earlier in the day.

'Where's mum?' he asked, as they made their way into a car park and walked past the few cars that were there at that time of night.

'Over there in the far corner away from watching eyes,' replied Mikhail, walking purposely forward and urging his young charge onwards. Noah followed in a procession of pain and confusion, the pain from his ribs digging into him and through him. As he walked, trying to keep up, he peered into the darkness of the car park, lights all seeming to be out as the cars disappeared and the asphalt reigned supreme.

'Right!' said Mikhail, turning around as he did so and pointing towards the far corner of the deserted car park. Noah peered and as panic started to rise lights were dipped on and off several times from a car that had appeared hidden. Noah was suddenly filled with elation and relief as he ran, that is wobbled, with as much speed as he could muster towards the car. The driver's door opened and out stepped Tess, her arms wide open, tears flooding from her eyes and her voice simply saying, 'Noah, Noah, Noah.'

They embraced for several moments, each whispering their love for one another and Mikhail behind them waiting.

'Come here, you daft, stupid boy,' said Tess into her son's ear, smelling the very essence of him as she allowed tears of relief to fall down her cheeks.

'And you too!' she said looking up and calling Mikhail into the hug.

Mikhail joined the embrace and asked, 'What is daft?' causing them all to laugh. It was a welcome moment of hilarity in the darkness of their situation. Then, without needing to say anything, Mikhail stepped away and the three of them made their way into the car, Mikhail to the driver's seat and mother and son into the back. Tess looked closely at her son, the dark thankfully making his wounds not look as horrendous as Mikhail had prepared her for. In the dim light they simply looked very bad instead.

'What have they done to you, my sweetheart?' she said, cupping his cheeks in her hands, tears starting again to flow down her own.

'I'm OK, mum. It's only superficial.'

'Apart from the broken ribs, bones and the missing teeth, eh?' laughed Mikhail who was turned around to look at them both from the front. Noah looked at him. 'I read your charts.'

'Oh. Right. Well, it will all heal mum or be replaced. I

299

mean, I have had enough breaks over the years, haven't I?'

And he had. A mixture of surf and rugby made for a delicious recipe of potential injuries, many of which Noah had experienced. Tess relented.

'All right, sweetheart. Now is not the time for me to go all sentimental on you or give you the severe lecture you need on your utter and absolute stupidity in attempting whatever you were attempting on your own. I mean, carrying a piece of no doubt priceless art across Europe on your own! What were you thinking?'

'I'm sure you just said you were going to save the lecture, Tess,' offered Mikhail. Tess looked at him.

'Yes, so I did. I just want to know, Noah, what were you going to do with it?'

Noah looked at the two people he was now sharing a car with in a corner of a deserted car park in the dead of night in Krakow.

'Give it back, of course. It was never ours to have.'

'But you said it was a gift, Mikhail?' Tess said, looking at the Russian for confirmation.

'That's what your mother said,' he replied, his hand over his mouth as he did so.

'It was not,' said Noah, taking his mother's hand as he did so. 'That painting was stolen from the Czartoryski. I don't know how Grandad got it, but he did and he hid it and there can be no other reason for doing so other than he knew.'

Noah let the implications of that settle in. He had purposely omitted for his mother's sake who the actual thieves were.

'I just thought the best way to protect his reputation and to do the right thing was to return it.'

'And so Charles Devere was born!' declared Tess.

'So he was,' said Noah.

'Took quite a beating for his trouble,' added Mikhail, 'and risked his own stupid life!'

'To protect the memory and reputation of his grandad,' said Tess, proudly.

The company of three let the news work its way into their minds and then Noah asked the inevitable question.

'So, what do we do now?'

'Look,' said Mikhail, his face aglow now and full of action, 'your amazing and admirable intentions were never going to work. A painting of this value that has been hidden for so long will now remain hidden forever. It is worth so much money, Noah, that you and your family and your friends even would never need to work again and could live a life of absolute luxury.'

'I won't sell it!' said Noah forcibly.

'Listen to me,' replied Mikhail with force now in his own voice. 'This painting will see you lose your life. Can't you see that? I mean, after these last few days? The corrupt art historian, the corrupt police, the beatings, the murders, this painting is death.'

'How do you know about the murders?' asked Noah, the question coming out before he could stop it, his mother looking very pale at his side.

'The policeman at the hospital, of course,' replied Mikhail and went on without stopping. 'You do know they know exactly who you are, don't you?'

'How?' asked a confident Noah.

'Border control, stupid,' replied a now agitated Mikhail. Tess thought about interrupting but saw only sense in all her Russian cousin was saying plus she had doubted him far too much. Where would they be without him?

'Noah, it is time, as they say, to wake up and smell the coffee! I have friends who can help now. This is out of your hands. If we do this right the painting will be gone, Joshua's name will never surface and you will have a sizable sum of money that your grandad would have wanted you to have.'

'No,' declared an adamant Noah, 'the painting must go back to the museum. It belongs there. How can I add to what has already been done? It is wrong. I won't do it.' Noah was about to add that the Padowskis knew exactly who he was and that they knew Joshua but for some reason he kept this back. A voice in his head was telling him to see the light and in this glow he thought of the Padowskis. To him clarity of thought made it obvious that they were not part of this. It was an unbelievable option and one that he could not accept. He could not, would not, believe that they were rotten.

'Oh Noah, listen to yourself,' shouted Mikhail, his voice as angry as Tess had ever heard, 'you act like the policeman of the world. Typical English. You do not know how to negotiate to what is easy, rather, you must always do what is right and this road will only lead to frustration, anger, separation and death. How will you put this right, Noah? How?'

'Steady on, Mikhail,' butted in Tess, 'he's very tired and vulnerable right now.'

'Ha,' Mikhail laughed, snorted the word out, 'vulnerable? He has travelled across Europe to deliver this painting. He is stupid, yes! Out of his mind, yes, but vulnerable, no! Not your precious Noah. This young man is on a one-man crusade to put right the world! It is stupidity, Noah, and it is time to make up your mind. The only way you can get this painting back in that museum is to go public through the press. I suggest this is best done in London as I would not fancy your chances of doing it here in Krakow. Even if you manage to find someone honest enough to not deliver you immediately into the criminal underworld, the so-called experts will be brought, declare it fake, and you will have destroyed Joshua Spearing's reputation for nothing. At least in London you should have a better chance of getting the truth out but even then you wash Joshua's name through the world media. Is that what you want? Is it? Of course it isn't,' replied Mikhail to himself, 'Only I can make this go away now.'

Noah sat still, saying nothing, his face impassive, refusing to be drawn out by the overbearing Russian clearly desperate to impose his view. As he sat there listening hardly at all to the speech being laid out before him, Noah thought of Henryk and of the television stories around his beating. He thought of Catherine and how worried she would have been on the dreadful night when intruders entered the house. He thought of the Padowskis' daughters, and in particular of the beautiful little Anna, so prim and proper, showing him around the garden, her garden, her hand holding his so tight with absolute trust and friendship. A love like that, thought Noah, was only possible from a child. He realised then that these thoughts were where his heart was. These people had not tricked him. He could not believe it. He would not believe it. All of a sudden thoughts shot through his mind at a million miles an hour about Mikhail, how he had come into their lives, how he had disappeared and then magically reappeared here in his darkest moments, and the one factor in all of this? The Raphael.

'I mean,' carried on Mikhail, getting more and more flustered by the non response from Noah, 'you are not to blame. How were you to know? Eh? You did the right thing. For this you are to be commended. I can see I let my mouth run away with me calling you stupid. The old Russian mad man makes a mistake again, Noah. That's all. I am sorry.'

At this Mikhail glanced at Tess who gave him a warm smile back. Yes, softness, Mikhail reminded himself, was the better approach and the only way to truly win the hearts and minds of this deluded pair.

'It's just that the world, Noah, is full of evil people and you know what rules this world? It's money, pure and simple. Capital and this painting, well, these just sum our world up, don't they? You never had a chance.'

And still no response came. Mikhail saw Noah looking through him. He was clearly not listening. Tess would have to get involved here. He looked at her.

'Tess, please. He's not listening to me. You have to talk to him too. Get him on board now. It is probably only a matter of moments before the police arrive. We are all, right now, in immense danger and Noah is not helping!'

His big face lay all its charm and kindness and concern that it could on Tess and she, fully convinced of everything Mikhail had proposed other than the cash of which she would have none , lifted her son's good hand to her mouth and kissed it.

'I know this must be unbearable for you, Noah, I really do.'

Noah looked at Tess, his mind calculating what to do and using any of the time that they had left before this thing exploded to work out what to do next.

'My father', Tess went on, 'was a wonderful man. You know I adored him and I know that you adored him. If he could see us now he would laugh, then cry, then laugh some more. My word, I bet he got in some scrapes in his time and this painting, well, this painting is just incredible, but Noah,' and at this she looked in his eyes and saw his mind elsewhere yet his eyes still giving to her, 'we have no choice here. This thing is too big for us. We have to let Mikhail help, through whatever contacts he has. We have to get out of this and stay alive. We need to get that painting away and you and I away. I mean, look at you, battered, twisted and bruised. What would Flora say?'

The mention of her name caused Noah's eyes to wince with the pain of her loss and while Tess regretted the pain, she knew she had to use her name to spur him on to action.

'She would say,' Tess went on, 'that we have to act.'

'Did she know about this?' asked Mikhail, heightened intensity in his voice.

'Of course not,' shot back Noah, his first words spoken for several minutes. Tess and Mikhail, aware of this, waited.

Noah, decision made, said, 'Right. I agree. We have no choice. We have to act and Mikhail, you seem to know what we need to do and I have no plan at all now, so I am all yours.'

Noah looked at Mikhail who looked like he had just won millions on the Euro Lottery. He then turned to his mother who just looked scared. Noah leaned over to her and gave her a half hug, wincing as he did so.

Turning back to Mikhail he said, 'So what do we do now?'

'Retrieve the painting and head to a private airfield where we get out of here. I just need to make a few phone calls and all will be set up.'

'Right,' replied Noah, 'so we need to go now, yes?'

'We do,' said Mikhail, starting the car engine. 'Where to?'

'Well, we will have to wait,' replied Noah.

'Wait?' replied Mikhail, with frustration and anger clearly in his voice.

'Yes, Mikhail, wait,' replied Noah with new-found strength in his voice as he felt he was regaining the situation. 'The painting is at the *Glowny* and this will be closed now.'

'The train station?' Mikhail asked, incredulity written across the question.

'Yes, the train station.'

'But?'

'You'll see,' replied Noah, 'it was the only safe place I could think of.'

Mikhail grunted at that while picking up his phone and typing something in. It was now nearing past two in the morning and all was still around them save for the occasional roar of sirens as a procession of ambulances arrived no doubt with needy souls.

'Where is the painting in the station, Noah?' asked Mikhail, turning to the back of the car again and clearly forcing calmness into his voice and trying to make the question sound as nonchalant as possible.

'Why?'

A pause.

'Because the station opens at 5am and we can get it then unless you're about to tell me it is in storage!' Mikhail declared, information hitting him from his internet search.

Noah laughed. Tess looked at him. Noah laughed harder.

'Noah, what's so funny?' she asked, laughing a little herself now, the relief of seeing her son laughing hard. Mikhail just looked at him and waited.

'Well?' Mikhail asked eventually.

'You couldn't write it, could you?' replied Noah, laughter subsiding. 'Yes, it is in storage. What time does it open?'

'Seven,' replied Mikhail tersely.

'Storage?' asked Tess.

'Yep!' replied Noah proudly, 'Best place I could think of.'

'And the reclaim ticket?' asked Mikhail.

'Hidden at the station, of course,' lied Noah, knowing the actual ticket was burning through to his right foot.

'OK. Well, we will have to stay in the car and try and get a little sleep. We will drive to a backstreet and do this now,' he said, starting the car and taking the car away from the dark secret no doubt discovered now in the hospital. 'Tomorrow we must act quickly and get the painting.'

'And afterwards?' asked Noah.

'Afterwards?'

'Yes, the Raphael. What happens?'

'I will deal with it. You will get your money. It will be over.'

'OK,' replied Noah, 'though I don't want any money.'

'And nor do I,' added Tess, causing Mikhail to laugh coarsely.

'All in good time you two and I am sure you will change your mind. I can only imagine how thrilled Joshua would have been to hear of you both giving away your inheritance so freely.'

'Indeed,' said Noah, turning to his mother and leaning into her ear.

'Where's your phone, and whisper, Mum?'

'We left quickly and I must have left it in the room,' was all she could manage hopelessly. She would have bet good money on the phone being in her bag but when she had checked when Mikhail had gone into the hospital to get her boy, the phone was not there.

'OK. Don't show any alarm now, OK?' Noah waited. His mother did not flinch but her hand drew tight around his. He took that as she understood. 'Trust me, Mum, and just follow my lead. This is not right. I know what to do.'

Tess, who realised Mikhail was staring intently at the two of them through the car mirror said, 'And I love you too, sweetheart, so much. I am fine I really am. No need to worry about me! Mikhail will sort us out, won't you?'

'Of course I will!' he declared, 'And as soon as we park I will get some sleep and suggest you two do the same. You will need it.'

Noah, satisfied that Tess had given him the benefit of the doubt, sat back in his seat and waited. This would now play out and he only hoped the cavalry would arrive before he started getting his other hand and fingers broken.

At the hospital, Milosz was being grilled by his boss.

'You are a fucking imbecile, Milosz.'

'Sir?'

'Shut the fuck up. You had your man and left him here with one guard to keep him safe! I mean, for Christ's sake!'

'Yes, but sir, if I can just point out that the CCTV clearly shows the other man entering the room with the gun and... '

'I swear, you say one more word and I will cut your fucking legs off and I do mean that literally.'

Milosz decided silence was the way forward. The night was grim enough and he had little left at the moment to offer anyway.

'I mean, for fuck's sake, Milosz, Bublanski? He was a fine officer but a desk officer. You know this! He was not cut out to be guarding a dangerous criminal so what the hell did you send him here for?'

Milosz opened his mouth to try and explain that he had

not posted Bublanski, the station had, although he recognised he had asked for just the one guard and clearly this had been a mistake. These dangerous criminals should have faced more than a one-man welcome party at the hospital. What a mess. Further, Milosz knew that the young Mr Devere was not a dangerous criminal, rather, it just looked that way. His mouth opened yet no words came as he thought better of saying a single thing and promptly closed it again.

'So you can go and tell Elana he is dead and you can explain your fucking dog's dinner of a mess to her. Then you better find the little bastard and bring him to me. Do I make myself clear?'

Milosz looked at his boss, Chief Inspector Jankowski, his face very red, his eyes matching. It was indeed a very shocking situation and he was as amazed as anyone to find dear old Bublanski, a saint of a man and a highly loved and respected older officer who had fathered many of them in the force, now violently shot dead. He was one hundred per cent certain, though, that it was not in any way the work of Charles Devere. The young man was simply not capable of it. Milosz had seen him enough these last few days to build a character picture and he felt he knew him and this ability, this sense of a person, had rarely failed Milosz in all his years on the force. No, something else was happening here and he knew he had to work quickly to find out what that was. A huge piece of the jigsaw was out there and he had to find it. His first stop after going to break the news to Bublanski's wife would be to wake up the Padowskis. There, he was sure, lay the key.

'Well?' asked Jankowski, bile in his voice.

'You do, sir, of course, perfectly clear. This appalling situation will be dealt with.'

They waited for a while, the senior officer staring into his young officer's eyes. Jankowski knew Milosz to be his best and brightest officer yet here he had lost the plot. Hospital CCTV clearly showed the young man leaving the hospital with an older well-built man. They showed no sign of tension. Indeed, and most worryingly of all, they looked relaxed. In turn, Milosz knew he had made a serious error leaving Bublanski on his own and the officer had paid for that. Milosz had never felt as bad as he now felt, stood before his senior officer.

'Catch the men. They must pay. This is the only way to make up for this, Fabian, and you do have to make up for this, you hear me?'

'Yes sir,' replied Milosz, his mind already being caught up in the next moves. 'I won't let you down again, sir.'

Jankowski nodded. His anger assuaged with his overriding belief in Milosz, an officer he had personally recommended for several promotions, calming him at last. With that the senior officer left.

Tess had fought against sleep. She had heard Noah's words to not show any alarm and somehow this had soothed her. Mikhail was clearly not himself and this painting, whatever it was, was causing all sorts of problems. She knew only to trust her son and being sat in the back of the car with him, his head now resting on her breast as he slept overcome by exhaustion, his battered and bruised body in the right place now, she felt joy in the middle of the whirlpool. Then sleep came and Noah, half sleeping, not out of the lack of tiredness but because of the increasing pain that was now filling his body as the drugs wore off, smiled. His mother, his precious mother, had come to save him. His eyes felt the heaviness of another short burst of sleep falling upon him. He went towards it happily.

A flashback. He is in the sea. Porthmeor. Joshua is with him. His mother is on the shore taking pictures. The sun is out and it is warm but late. He knows this instinctively because there are not many others in the sea with them and he realises that this is their annual dip in the waves to celebrate his grandad's birthday. He does not know how old he is in this dream, but he feels very young and his grandad, in turn, feels much younger too, stronger, bigger.

'Grandad, another one, another one!' he shouts happily as another wave does indeed crash into them and they laugh and laugh, and it is his grandad now scooping him up into the air and shouting over the roar of the waves.

'You are King of the sea, my angel, King of the sea!'

And as Joshua says this a huge wave knocks them over and they rise again, both spluttering, sea coming out of their very noses as they look back to shore to see Tess waving and laughing back at them.

'I am the King of the sea,' laughs Noah, 'and you are King of the sea too, Grandad!' he shouts happily into the air.

'Yes,' shouts Joshua, pulling the boy towards him and kissing him in his neck as the sea mounts its assault around them, 'we are both Kings! You know that, don't you, both Kings, both Kings!!!'

'It's time.'

Noah heard the voice but could not connect it to his dream. He looked back at Joshua but he, Noah, was being pulled away from the dream.

'Grandad,' he said, his eyes still shut tight and his dream fading into nothing, 'Wait for me, Grandad, wait for me.'

Joshua looked and held out his arms but his face was now twisted and fear was filling his eyes and Noah immediately now opened his eyes to get away from the look of blind panic in his grandad's face only to now see a gun pointing at him from the front of the car. Noah felt immense panic immediately rise and instinctively sat up and turned to Tess, only to see her looking grim and terrified. He realised at the same time that they had driven to the train station and, clocking the time on the dashboard of the car, saw that his time has run out. It was 7am. Then, finally, the doors of the car were opened as one man got into the front passenger seat and another one got into the back next to Tess.

'It's over,' Mikhail said simply to them both. 'This mess, this dreadful mess that never ever needed to happen; well, it's over. These two men will keep your mother company as we go inside; insurance you understand.'

Mikhail said this without flinching at the silent tears of sorrow now rolling down Tess's cheeks. She shook her head as the truth of her lover's betrayal overwhelmed her. There is no greater pain he could have caused her than what was now happening and yet he seemed oblivious to it, his face set in stone at what he must do. The dagger had been inserted and was now just being twisted; pain upon pain for Tess.

'I won't do it,' said Noah instinctively, protectively looking towards his mother as the two of them held each other's hand tight. Noah, his senses now on overdrive, noticed as he said this several things all at once. Firstly, the two men who had joined them in the car looked blank. There was nothing to read in their eyes. It was clear that they were here to do a job and the simplicity of that was immediately chilling to Noah, telling him any odds he thought he had, had now just got significantly longer. Here were simply two more henchmen lined up to be used as Mikhail saw fit. Noah thought about saying what happened to the last two but knew it was pointless, knew he was totally out of his depth.

Secondly, he noticed that the station was already quite busy. There were plenty of people around meaning that Mikhail would still need to be careful and that this, just maybe, was not yet over.

Thirdly Noah saw that the weather was awful. Rain was lashing against the car meaning visibility from the car was extremely poor. A small point but one that might just help cause some confusion.

Noah then looked back at Tess and knew above all else that Mikhail now held the ace card. He knew Noah could do nothing to in any way endanger Tess. Noah, who was now looking fully into Mikhail's eyes, knew this too.

'Why?' asked Noah, condensation now filling the windows of the car.

Mikhail waited, considering his answer, his eyes now struggling to lift towards those of Tess who was staring at him intently.

'I never wanted this,' he stuttered, painfully aware of his men in the car with them yet still feeling the intense vulnerability of speaking to two people who he would now try and tell he genuinely cared for. Why is a question he had asked himself a thousand times and more because he, Mikhail, did feel such care and love for them. His life, though, has never been a simple one and this destiny, this dreadful turn in the road, was what he now must face with people who could have lightened his life, not added to its depth of darkness.

Twenty seconds or so passed in silence. Mikhail muttered something to the man next to him in the front of the car who in turn nodded to the man in the back and they stepped out.

Alone again, Mikhail looked at the two Spearings.

'I know you will never forgive me and I pray to God we can just get this over with as quickly as possible but you need to listen to what I am now going to say.'

'Listen?' shouted Tess, 'Fucking listen?' She leaned forward in the car far too quickly for Noah to stop her and promptly slapped Mikhail so hard that he actually yelped in pain. Noah grabbed hold of his mother and tried to pull her back just as Mikhail regained his balance and pushed her with such force that she was thrown violently backwards, landing on Noah's battered and bruised body and causing Tess to be winded.

'Enough!' shouted Mikhail, then whispers the same word again, 'Enough.'

Tess launched herself at Mikhail again, his words not halting her and her senses alive to fury as she realised it was him, Mikhail, who had tortured her son. Mikhail again pushed her, Tess being once again heavily thrown towards the back of the car whilst Mikhail screamed.

'Once more and this conversation, your last chance, is over. OK?'

Noah held his mother now. She was not crying anymore, rather defiantly staring out at the Russian who she had loved.

'I had no choice,' Mikhail said, shaking his head to the men who had stepped out of the car but were looking in to see if they were needed once more.

'Choice? Choice! You despicable man. You disgust me, you hear me, disgust me!'

The words hit Mikhail like the previous slap and he accepted them for he knew he had done the most heinous of things.

'Tess, I know. Noah,' he said, his eyes trying to hold a gaze but failing to do so, 'I am so, so sorry but you drove me to the depths.'

'You drove yourself there, you idiot,' said Tess, Noah keeping his words back and just trying to think while the war of words raged around him.

'Yes, Tess, I have been the worst of men and yet you will know of this painting and you will learn its sordid and torrid past. Its next journey is no less than it deserves.'

Tess allowed her eyes to wander to her son's. Noah, suddenly aware of his mother's glare felt he should offer an explanation but had no idea how to start. Mikhail took on the story instead.

'Your son, as you know, has the Raphael. It was Joshua's alone, he thought. Well, in fact, it was shared between him and my father. It just never made it back to Russia, that is until now.

The painting was, of course, stolen. Smell the coffee, Tess, your father was a criminal too! Do you want to expose that? Do you? I have simply come to take back what rightly belongs to my family. We've waited long enough. It is the right thing to do. I am doing what Joshua should have done many years ago. I am doing the right thing, the honourable thing. Again, I do not expect you to understand and I am very, very sorry for the pain I have caused you. I did not intend for all this complication. Money and betrayal, they go together like easy bedfellows and I am so sorry that we had to find out about my dirty part in all of this. I never wanted you to know. What we had, the three of us, was real. I mean this. I know you will never, ever believe it to be true, but I swear it. Please listen to me! Noah, I beg of you, just for one minute do what I say and you will be free. Do what I say and your mother and you will be safe and free and Joshua's fine memory protected. That is what you want, isn't it?'

Tess heard all the words and none of them made any sense. What did make sense was the incredible truth of his dreadful betrayal.

'You came into our lives, our grief-stricken lives, and you stole our hearts,' she was speaking with a low growl of a voice that Noah had never heard before and would never want to hear again, 'and you fucking talk about a painting and honour. What do you know of honour?'

'I know I fell in love with you,' Mikhail said, the words escaping before he could stop them, their power coming out and falling like bubbles between them all causing them to stop and wait as the magic of the words offered hope and then just burst before their very eyes.

'But my life was set on a course before I was even born. It is not free, like yours. I have not been honest with you both about that. I have duties you could never understand and ties with people and societies of the highest order in my homeland that mean selling that painting for those I work for is what I must do. Its value will be extraordinary and I think be the best part of $120 million dollars or more. This is not something we could ever hide from, Noah, hope we could just place a piece of history back and expect everything to be all right again! No, the sums are just too vast. They know you own half of it and they will accept me sharing some of this with you, taking

312

account, of course, of the years wasted in your country, your father's house.'

Tess now looked at Noah, her eyes asking for more as she tried to piece together what was truth and what was fiction.

Noah said simply, 'Yet Grandad gave it to me, at his last party. He told me not to open this package until he had died and then to tell no one about it. It was his gift to me.'

'From where?' said Tess.

'The war, I think,' replied Noah.

Tess's mouth was aghast at this.

'I think he gave it me Mum,' continued Noah, 'to do the right thing.'

'Yet it was not his gift to give, don't you see?' said Mikhail, his voice now soft and open.

Tess sat there, commuting what she had just heard and allowing the truth of this war bounty to hit her hard. She remembered Noah asking her only recently about stories from Joshua and the old days as the jigsaw fell into place and she felt an enormous responsibility for all that her son had endured, had carried on his own over the last few months. She felt anger at her father now too, and, as incredible as was the news she had just heard, she felt almost relief at this painting leaving them almost as soon as it had come into their lives.

'So you see,' Mikhail continued, 'Noah must give it back. There is no choice. None of us ever had a real choice except the one where I lost my heart to you, Tess. Now we must go. I have no more time. My eternal sorrow at the pain I have caused you both must be the cross I must now carry for the rest of my life. It was your beauty that almost persuaded me to look to give up my Russian life but you must trust me when I tell you they would never have let me go. They would have hunted me down and in so doing, hunted you two down too. It is better this way. Now come.'

Mikhail opened his door and as he did so the two men got back in.

'One word, Mikhail,' said Tess, causing him to stop and turn round, his eyes still soft and open.

'You will never be forgiven. You held my heart and now you have cut it up into tiny inconsequential pieces with a blunt knife. You are a disgrace to all that our family stands for, you hear me, you are an utter disgusting disgrace and I never, ever, want to hear from you again.'

Mikhail paused and then said, 'You have no idea what our family stands for. Don't worry, I won't darken your fantasy world again. You stay there in your bubble, Tess, and try to continue forgetting that there is a world outside of your precious door. It is the world that your dear father happily moved in and took what was not his to take. Noah, come on before I let my anger turn into rage.'

With that he was out of the car and Noah, seeing a gun being pointed at his mother from the man sitting next to her, opened his car door and with legs as though made out of concrete stepped heavily out to the Krakow morning, looking back at his mother as he did so.

'It'll be OK, Mum, I promise, I won't let you down.' Tears were rolling down his cheeks now. He felt hopeless.

'Don't worry, my little chick,' she said, using a name she had not used for him for many years but now doing so as she instinctively looked to him as his mother. 'Just give it to him. We can then get our livesback. Yes?'

Her eyes implored him to get it all over with as quickly as possible and so with all he could muster he replied, 'Yes. I will. I love you.'

'I love you, too.'

Mikhail pushed the door shut and the two of them walked with real purpose through a side entrance into the magnificent *Rynek Glowny* with Noah thinking through every angle he could, each line of thought with only one worthy ending, that of Raphael's *Portrait of a Young Man* returning to the Czartoryski Museum.

Across the city, Fabian Milosz sat in his car waiting for news, any news, to come through. He had never had a worse night in his life and now a mixture of fatigue, intense sadness and an increased risk of failure began to overtake his thoughts. He had left the hospital and gone straight to Officer Bublanski's house. The news had been received as bleakly as he had expected, the pregnant Elana Bublanski falling heavily with the sheer dreadfulness of it all, her children falling by her side and the cries of terror and disbelief still ringing in Milosz's ears hours later. He had promised to return later in the day, and he would. It was his duty.

As he had left the hospital after his dressing-down from his senior officer, Milosz had sprung into action. He had gone to see the Padowskis and they had offered nothing new. They looked terrified and extremely tired having been awoken in the middle of the night again. Nerves and fear were affecting everyone.

Every major road was blocked, cars were being searched, and every major travel point was being watched. And yet, here with the time now just past seven in the morning, it all seemed very hopeless. Time was everything and they may well have run out of it.

'Shit,' he muttered under his breath.

'Give it more time,' replied Tomasz, his right-hand man. They had served together for many years and they knew it was never over until it was well and truly finished.

'They've had time. Maybe I just misread the whole thing. Maybe Devere was involved. I mean, we are missing some huge part of this story, aren't we? Why has Devere left the hospital? What's he up to?'

'Come on, Fabian. Don't be ridiculous. You saw him. They tortured him and you trusted him. There's no way he left that hospital knowing that Bublanski had been shot.'

Silence as Milosz again tried hard to squeeze his brain and pull an answer, any answer, out into the mix.

'No, you are right. I believe it to be true but it just looks all so wrong, doesn't it? He, though, is not the problem here, I know it, just a poor unfortunate guy in the wrong story.'

'And have you ever been wrong before?'

'Not this wrong,' replied Milosz, feeling a sense of purpose, of hope, begin to rise in him again.

'So there you are. We wait.'

And then it happened.

'Milosz,' crackled his radio, 'Calling Inspector Milosz.'

Fabian sat up, adrenalin being pumped through his body as his whole demeanour became alive with the opportunity to act. This was their break, he knew it.

'Yes. Here. Who's that?'

'It's Malarz, sir, at the *Glowny*. You're not going to believe this but they just walked in.'

'They?' asked Milosz, as Tomasz turned on the engine and span the car into action. Their car was literally just five minutes away.

'Yes, Devere and the other one.'

'You're sure?'

'Well, same build. The big guy is still wearing his hat but Devere is plain to see.'

'And they seem together, friendly?' asked a confused inspector, the nagging fear of his Chief Inspector's voice pulling at his mind.

'Oh no, sir, not at all. The big one is holding something hidden in his coat and I would wager that it is a gun. The young one looks shocking.'

Milosz, a faint smile at the vindication of the young Englishman, continued to ask questions as the car now raced across the city.

'And what are they doing?' Milosz asked.

'They've just entered the toilets next to the reclaim.'

'The toilets?'

'Yep.'

'And they have not seen you?'

'No sir.'

'Sure?'

'Oh yes, positive.'

Milosz thought for a few moments, considered sending in his men now but considered that the toilet break was probably just a quick stop-off before they maybe finally led them to something that would actually connect the pieces.

'OK, sit tight. Keep your men back and don't let anyone else enter that toilet, OK?'

'Yes sir.'

'Just stay back for now and be ready. I will be with you in a few minutes. This is likely to be unpleasant so every precaution must be taken, do you copy?'

'Yes sir, I have that. We keep the toilet clear, we wait for you and we show extreme caution.'

As Noah walked into the cubicle to find the ticket he had pretended he had hidden he felt nothing but immense tiredness and pain. Mikhail had checked the toilets when they had entered

316

to find it mercifully empty while Noah went about using his final card to buy a little more time in the hope that help in the form of Milosz would arrive. It was all he had left. He climbed up to the old toilet cistern as slowly as was possible and pretended to make a real effort to find the ticket. After this he would walk out of the cubicle and tell the large and soon to be even angrier Russian that the ticket was gone. He thought of his mother and the deep, deep pain he felt for her hurt more than anything else.

'Come on!' shouted Mikhail, who had found and now placed a "closed for service" sign at the door of the toilets and was clearly not now set for waiting any longer.

Noah heard the voice of reckoning and slowly sauntered out of the cubicle.

'It's gone,' he said hopelessly.

Mikhail looked at him, anger rising.

'What do you mean it's gone?' he shouted.

'Maybe it's in another cubicle,' offered Noah, the thought releasing the hope of wasting more time, but Mikhail was having none of it.

'This is not a mistake you would make with your mother waiting in the car with two armed men. You are a fool, Noah.' As he said this he had stepped forward to face Noah who had instinctively cowered down, holding his arms over his head as he waited for the punch that would come.

'Stand up, you coward!' bellowed Mikhail, rage now pouring through his body, but Noah did nothing. He held his position and something in that caused Mikhail to step back.

A few moments passed and Noah opened an eye slightly to see the Russian had backed off and was beginning to use his mobile number. Fear gripped Noah as he heard Mikhail say simply, 'On my word, take a finger.'

'No!!!!' Noah shouted, throwing himself across the floor and clinging to Mikhail's legs.

Mikhail kicked him off.

'What do you mean, no?' he shouted, sending another kick for good measure into Noah's ribs.

Pain upon pain and Noah knew the game was up. He looked up from the toilet floor, his head going round and round, and he said simply, 'Please, don't harm my mother.'

Mikhail nodded. He put the phone back to his ear and said, 'Don't touch her. He has seen sense.'

Noah reached down to his trainer to take it off and retrieve the ticket but as he tried to fumble for the ticket he found that he could not get his fingers to function. He turned on to his back, the room now spinning and him painfully aware he was probably about to pass out.

'It's hidden under the lining of my trainer,' he whispered.

Mikhail knelt down and tore the lining back in the trainer to reveal the ticket at last.

'I am so sorry it came to this, Noah,' Mikhail said, genuine warmth in his voice now he had what he so desperately craved. Noah did not have the strength or words to reply.

Mikhail reached for his mobile phone again causing terror to fill Noah's eyes.

'It's OK,' said Mikhail immediately, 'I'm letting her go.'
Noah nodded.
Mikhail called the car.
'Do it,' he said.
Noah again looked in fear.

'It's fine,' said Mikhail, now resting his hand on the heavy breathing chest of the young man. 'They will leave her in the trunk of the car around the corner. She will be tied up and taped around her mouth but unharmed. I would never have harmed her, Noah, surely you know that?'

Noah looked at him, his look reminding the Russian of the call he had made to remove a finger and Mikhail seemed to read his mind.

'It was a trick, Noah! You fool. It was all I had left. Of course I didn't have men sitting ready to mutilate the one good thing I have ever known in my life. She almost saved me, you know Noah, almost.'

Mikhail reached into his pocket and produced some car keys, which he duly leant down and placed into Noah's side pocket.

'For the car and the release of Tess. Please tell her, above all, that I loved her. I am a foolish Russian. The damage was done long ago, long before I met you two. In fact, before any of us was even born our different destinies were mapped out. I could never change. I am truly sorry. History, well it made a pact. That it came to this is a cause of great sorrow. That is all I can say. Now I must go.'

He lifted Noah up carrying him back into the same cubicle Noah had pretended to get the ticket from. Here Mikhail efficiently and quickly tied Noah up and placed tape over his mouth only to see the young Englishman could not breath, his nose blocked with old and fresh blood, so he ripped off the tape causing Noah to wince with fresh pain.

Noah, his eyes pleading for answers, managed one last question,

'How did you know I had the Raphael?'

Mikhail smiled.

'Well, it was an educated guess. Your Grandmother would not even talk about the war so the thought of her knowing about the painting was simply never going to be the case. As for your Mother, well she's far too holy to be involved and so I was left with you, Joshua's fall guy.'

'Fall guy?' asked Noah.

'Yes. He knew you would look to put things right in a way he never had the courage to do. And he was right wasn't he! He just didn't count on me.'

Time waited, the words and their truth filling the void.

'OK, I have to go now,' said Mikhail breaking the spell. 'I will send you money Noah,' here Mikhail held the young man's gaze, 'and your life was never in danger… Never. I swear. God be with you.'

And before Noah could answer Mikhail had punched him hard and the lights had gone out.

Mikhail Portichenko strode purposely to the door of the toilets. A smile lit his face as the accomplishment of a lifetime's mission now sat before him. The return of the Raphael to his homeland was not the issue. Rather, the cash that would now be his was his crowning glory. It had been more than dreadful having to involve Noah and Tess, both of whom he had wept for, but what were feelings when put at the side of the state, family loyalty and capital. He was already set for life financially and being a wealthy man in St Petersburg was no mean feat, but the money from this would take him to another stratosphere of wealth, together with the share that would keep his masters more than happy. Oh yes, despite it all, today was a good day.

What happened next, all happened so fast. Mikhail stepped out of the toilet door into a busier station foyer, but was immediately aware that something was amiss. Within mini moments he realised there was no one near the door and he then saw the policemen, all situated far enough away to be away from physical danger, but close enough to be able to engage fire. Mikhail saw a plain-clothed policeman raise his hand and he called over to Mikhail in English.

'It's no use, Mikhail,' said Milosz, 'you clearly have no chance. Lie down flat on the floor with your legs and arms outstretched.'

Mikhail hesitated.

'Do it now or we will take you down.'

Mikhail needed no further incentive. He began to bend down then ripped out his automatic pistol from inside his coat only to be immediately cut down by snipers who had the situation covered and were in force within the terminal building.

People ran and screamed leaving the station quickly deserted save for the police and the target who now lay, unmoving, in a pool of seeping blood. Two officers ran forward to the fallen figure and one then gave a sweep of his hand across his throat signifying the death of the Russian.

Milosz, receiving the news, ran past the body into the toilet dreading what he might find and yet there he found in a crumpled heap the young and battered Charles Devere, his body a mangled mess, his face bruised and bloodied but mercifully he was still very much alive.

It was over.

A few yards away the Raphael sat. Resting. Waiting.

Chapter 19

Flora

She had read and reread Noah's "love letter" a thousand times, traced his words into her memory, adding his love into each single letter as it had made its way from his sweet, delectable hand onto the parched paper resting below his loving gaze. Her Noah, for that is what he had now become in her mind, now so far away and yet sitting easily in her very heart and holding it safe. How had she not seen this, not made the connection herself at some point over all the years they had spent in each other's pocket? Yet she had not.

Her future, waiting for her on the next day to come, now sat coldly before her. Jake, the man she was to call her husband after taking those weighty marriage vows, was out with his friends celebrating in the traditional way. In truth he had been doing just that, celebrating by getting extremely drunk, for what seemed like weeks now. A week away in Majorca with lots of his friends at his father's villa with money to this family no object, was followed by a stag-weekend of playing like little lords on a Scottish Estate. Now, his close Cornish posse around him, he was down at The Hub getting ready to commit to Flora, his Flora.

From a distance in her mind Flora had watched the revelries with increasing unease. She accepted that this was often the way for people to "celebrate" and that she knew the pressure was on Jake to deliver the best pre-wedding scenes he could, given his standing with his friends, but virtually all of it meant nothing to her and she felt tainted by it. Flora, for herself, had kept prenuptial celebrations very low-key with just a large dinner taking up the whole of the Café one night for female family and friends. Many had put pressure on her to do more, much more in fact, but she had on each occasion politely declined and told each one truthfully that she simply did not wish to make a fuss. It was not in her makeup and now, at this point, she was absolutely not going to become a social animal in the spotlight for the benefit of tradition.

Now, as the weight of her head closed in around her and the touch of the moment reminded her it was time, she reckoned on the simple fact that these last few weeks had seen an increasing depth of gap of character between her and Jake become all too apparent. She saw now that she had done what duty had told her mind she must do, not what her heart had cried out that she needed. It was, in truth, a flaw in her character, that she often did for others what she felt she must, at the exclusion of what her soul actually needed and now, at this point, the madness had to stop.

Earlier that afternoon, as she was leaving her and Jake's apartment, kissing him on the cheek and stepping towards the door to leave as Flora Trembath for the last time, he had been unable to let go of her arm, pulling her gently back towards him.

'What's wrong, Flora?' Jake had said, concern riddling his voice, his gatekeeper of doubt suddenly deserting him as the question he had been withholding for far too long, now came tumbling out.

'Oh, you know,' Flora had replied, whispered almost, 'prematch nerves, I guess.'

'Of course,' Jake had said, softly, warmly. He had stalled then, Flora looking to step away and he in two minds as to what to do next.

'Just come and sit down for a moment, will you?' he asked.

'Oh Jake, you know I would do but I have a thousand and one things to do and… '

'I know you do but please,' he said, his voice firm yet riddled with a need that now ached above all as he said, 'before you go from me, please just come and talk awhile. It seems we haven't done that for ages, doesn't it?'

Flora thought of saying, *with you away with the boys as normal*, but simply managed, 'No, we haven't, have we…'

322

He led her purposely to the window seat, one of her favourite spots in the apartment with its easy and expensive curved glass looking out on to a side balcony and a collection of plants in ancient pots that she had put together with her mother. Here, precious cuttings from home and from her father's plants, a vital memory of the man she missed dearly and, oh, what she would give to have had him with her through these last few, confusing days.

Jake knew he had neglected her and was upset with himself for allowing it to happen to the extent that it had. He was a kind man, though he would openly say he was self-centred and extremely focussed, yet he loved his Flora very deeply and would now tell her and remind her of that fact. He knew he had overdone the pre-wedding festivities but it had turned into a client opportunity and he just had to take it. He always "just" had to take it. The contract the business had got after the shooting weekend had just been amazing and would take them to another level of turnover. Of course, Flora had no idea that he had actually been shooting and he knew that, had she known, then she would have walked away there and then but why should he not do what all his wealthy friends did? He reasoned what she did not know would not hurt her and that in time she would see that it was necessary to feather the nest of corporate hospitality in whatever was necessary for the ultimate goal of success. Business was just so good at the moment, so easy. It was his time and as he told everyone, everyone apart from Flora of course, 'When it is your time you just have to keep grabbing it.'

'I'm sorry, baby,' he said as they both sat on the small window backless seat.

'Sorry?' asked Flora, her eyes upturned, red and watery, weariness of thought weighing heavily upon her.

'Yes sweetheart. We both know I have been rather unkind to you with my time of late, the wedding celebrations being abused by me and, once again, me out tonight.'

'That's OK,' Flora muttered, without any hint of truth in the statement.

'No, it's not,' Jake replied, easily, tenderly, 'I know it's not. I will make it up to you, Flo, I will.'

Seagulls sung and swooped in the air, their ever-happy

games playing out gracefully in the St Ives sky. It was an ancient dance of necessity and joy, of hope and strength and of epic proportions.

Jake continued.

'I want you to know that I truly love you, Flora.' He held her big eyes now and she held his. 'From the moment we got together, well, there was never anyone else. You are unique, you know that, don't you?'

'I am not,' she replied immediately, stubbornly.

'Yes you are,' he smiled, 'and you don't even see it. We both know I had not been short of girlfriends before you, Flora,' and he hadn't. The most beautiful girls flocked easily around Jake. He was an athletic man, his dark well-framed tone matched by family wealth meaning he was a catch of the best kind, 'but you were never interested in any of the things other girls saw were you?'

'Oh, I was,' flashed Flora, her interest in Jake's body being as keen as that of every other girl. Jake took the compliment and smiled again.

'Yes, well, I mean, our relationship is the one pure thing I have, do you know what I mean?'

And she did, she knew exactly what he meant. Flora liked Jake's family and friends very much, but their lives, their outlooks, were so very different to hers and she often questioned why Jake had chosen her. She was a fish out of his water and they both knew it, had known it for a long time, and the fear of this gap, this difference of her to his life, made her feel anxious and fearful for what could come. And yet she would be there, at a full-on party or a swanky dinner, and she would catch him looking at her, his defences down only for her, his love of what she gave him clear to her. Up to the letter from Noah, this had been enough to keep all her fears in check. Now the horses of her fears were in full gallop and she had no idea how to stop them.

'I worry about that, Jake, that you will tire of me, of how I am,' she said, the words coming out before she had a chance to stop them. 'We are on different tracks, baby, and you know this and I won't change!' she said with a force she had not intended.

Jake looked straight at Flora, knowing that something else was happening. He took her hand.

324

'To be honest, Flora, I think we both know the truth is the other way round. We cannot change who we are, not who we are deep in our heart, can we? You mean the world to me. You know this. My world, though, is so not Flora and I often feel I squeeze you into a box that you simply don't fit in, your light shining on me to keep me sane, to turn my impurity into purity, it's not the best promise of happiness, is it?'

Jake sat forward, emotion suddenly sweeping over him, a mixture of tiredness and facing reality making for a heady cocktail of unease. Flora watched him, only for a moment, then leaned forward and placed her arm around his now-drooped shoulders.

'It's OK, sweetie,' she said with care, 'it's OK.'

Jake, his shoulders now moving up and down, did something he had not done for as long as he could remember. He cried, really cried.

They had hugged then, stayed in each other's arms for some time, and then they had made love there by the window, quietly, easily, and Jake had cried again. Flora, finding herself there and yet somehow sitting above the whole thing, viewing it almost as an onlooker, just cared for him.

'It'll be OK, won't it?' he had asked, his eyes bloodshot as she had stood at the door once again to leave to stay with her mother, as had been arranged for months, on the night before her wedding.

'I don't know, Jake,' was all she could say with honesty, and then quickly leaning forward, she had kissed him on the cheek and left quickly without turning back.

Now much later, the half-moon resting high above her in the warm Cornish night sky, Flora sat in her mother's back garden on the same old battered bench that she could remember had been there all her life. Her mother, Jennie, had listened with tears and concern in her eyes to her daughter talk of her great confusion over the man she was about to marry. They had sat, as they always did, in the kitchen with a teapot and pack of McVitie's ginger nuts between them and their love to keep them safe.

'You must do what your heart tells you,' Jennie had said finally, after letting her daughter allow her words to come out in a torrent of truthful emotion and holding her daughter's hands and gaze as she did so. 'I can say no more to you than that, Flora. You know Dad would have told you the same.'

At the mention of her father, Flora, tears stinging her eyes again as they had done for so many days now, looked at her mother with doubt.

'Really? I'm not so sure, Mum. You know he would have talked of duty and the fact that this is the night before my wedding and why do I still have so many things running through my mind after all this time.'

Jennie smiled.

'Darling, I know what he would have said, I really do. I can even hear him saying it!'

'What Mum, what would he have said?' Flora asked, her heart pleading to hear her father's words.

'Well, he would have laughed first of all. He always said "these things are sent to try us", remember?'

Flora nodded. She did remember. She even heard his voice now saying it and it moved her as she did so.

'And he used to often say to me that big decisions always came with choices,' Jennie continued. 'John would have probably been the least surprised by Noah's letter, sweetheart, because he would have been the one most expecting it. Not that he would have known that Noah was sending it, of course, though you know what your Dad was like, he would have seen through what we all chose to not see.'

Flora smiled at that. Her dad had a way of knowing what was happening. They all missed that safety net.

'It's just that he was always the least surprised when something surprising happened, you know?' Jennie said, her eyes alive as she talked of the love of her life. 'He would have told you to follow your heart and he would have said that you could spend a lifetime to regret a moment. He would not have wanted you to do that now would he, Flora?'

Flora just shook her head, a faint smile pulling at the side of her lips.

'And now, my sweet, precious girl, something huge and surprising has indeed happened to you just as you are about to make the biggest commitment in your life and you know , deep down, that you must do what your heart tells you.'

326

'And what is that, Mum, seriously, tell me! What should I do?'

'Ah, sweetheart, I can't tell you that because I don't know! I know Jake is a lovely boy. He has a fine job and he will look after you in a most amazing way. Let's face it, Flora, up to teatime and you coming home all upset, I have spent the last few years assuming you two would be together forever! It's a big sea change for me to consider anything else.'

'I know, I know.'

Jennie thought about whether to share her thoughts about young Noah Spearing, a boy she had loved from the moment she had met him and one that she had assumed was lost to her daughter when he had left for university. She swallowed more tea and spoke.

'And yet Noah, well, he is Noah, isn't he? I remember seeing him with Tess for the first time, his wild hair all over the place, a shock of blond, and eyes to entice the very soul from the unbeliever. I, well, I shouldn't really say this, but I have always had the fondest regard for that young man. He has never stopped coming round to have tea with me you know, just because you moved out!'

'I know, Mum! You do know that you have told me this so often and always with some secret smile.'

Jennie nodded at that. She had always loved Noah, always seen the good aching through his pores. The thought of him in her daughter's life warmed her immensely but she was not about to tell her daughter that. It was unfair. Jake had been very lovely, too. He was opposite in most ways to Noah it was true, but both men had a wonderful charm about them that was wrapped around a clear love for her daughter and that, for Mrs Trembath, was enough.

'Well, there we are Flora, there we are. Listen,' Jennie said, standing now and walking behind her daughter and stroking her hair in a soft, easy fashion, something that she had done all of their lives, 'I'm going to go and take a little walk to the shops and back. I will get some milk or something else we don't need, maybe pop in on Mama for a while and see how she is getting on. I'll be back soon, don't you worry. You just get some thinking done. It will all be OK, you know.'

'Oh Mum!' Flora replied, turning around and holding

tightly to her mother's frame, 'how can it ever be all right when I am going to break someone's heart.'

'These things are sent to try us,' smiled Jennie Trembath, as she left her daughter to find her clarity.

And now, an hour later, Flora alone with her beating heart, she found herself making the decision that she knew she must. Slowly, tenderly, she placed her right hand over her left and her fingers touched her beautiful and ridiculously expensive engagement ring. Time stood still as she slid it off her wedding finger, its tight squeeze refusing to give up easily but eventually accepting the need to be removed and giving up the fight. She held it in front of her gaze, tenderly kissed it, and then placed it down in the china saucer of her now cold teacup.

She turned to her phone and picked it up, its easy weight in her hands yet it feeling right now heavy and foreign to her. She turned the phone and it angrily beeped at her as she discovered several missed calls from Jake showing like a slap across her face on its display page. She placed her finger on "Messages" and then picked Jake's name and began to type in the dialogue box:

I am so sorry Jake but I cannot do this. You know this breaks me to do this but we have to let each other go. You have your life to lead and I do not fit into it. We both know this to be true, though I know because of what I am doing now this will mean many times ahead of great sadness for us both. I love you, Jake. I will miss us so much, our fun, our times and our passion. But I have to make this decision. I am at home. Please come when you can, if you want to. I understand if you don't. Only Mum will be here and she will go out as soon as you arrive. I want to go and see your Mum, to tell her and to apologise. Dear, dear Jake. I am so sorry and I will be for the rest of my life. Flora XX.

Her finger hovered over the send key and then, angels urging her on, she knew she had no other choice and she pressed it. The deed was done and there was no turning back. She would now do her duty, allow her family and friends to make of it what they would, but she would not flee, not shrink from being there and talking of the why. She owed them all that and she would face that, as hard as it would be, and she knew it would be tortuous.

And then, after a few days, she would pack a bag and do what her heart had known deep down from before she was even born. She would go to Noah and there, wrapped in his arms, they would walk across the earth and keep each other safe.

Chapter 20

Portrait of a Young Man

It was a day when even the birds had decided it was best to be quiet. The sky was bereft of anything other than the poisonous smell of oncoming death. Doctor Hans Michael Frank, who had experienced the most pitiful of sleeps, had been up and about readying his escape since before sunrise, not that this day had any hope of actually seeing the sun. The advancing Russian army, intent on the most barbaric revenge they could inflict, had left the Führer no choice but to recall all his key generals to Berlin and Frank had been happy to receive this order. The oncoming wave of terror would leave every German killed in the most barbaric fashion possible and Frank had never considered that his final hours should be spent waiting for a deranged Bolshevik to take his life away from him.

This posting that had started out as pure bliss with so much sport to be had that he had been as high as a kite for months on end, had come to a gradual car crash with the continual news of the advancing allied troops and their bastard breakthroughs. Safety in bomb-blasted Berlin now seemed an eminently far better proposition to Frank than to have his throat cut slowly by a savage of a Russian. How the miserable so-called generals of the Master race had allowed themselves to be so outwitted by vastly inferior nations was a mystery and a great shame to him. He could see the Polish people once again growing in stature, their cowardly spines just stretching up that bit more as they realised the savage occupation was coming to an end. It was, to Frank, totally and utterly unforgiveable to let the Führer down like this, the glorious motherland tainted and possibly, no definitely, facing an improbable end. No, Frank was happy to be recalled at last to see what he could do back at home and now that his less than glorious leader called him back to Berlin, back into the fold at last, he would hopefully be given a job to do of the utmost importance to hold back the inevitable and save the nation. Frank reckoned on the fact that there was glory there, still the chance to make a name for himself that would go down in history and make up for time wasted as prison governor in this now godforsaken wasteland of Poland.

And yet these shards of joyous thoughts, these slight sunbeams of redemption, were continually perpetuated by the memory of the constant run of bad news that had made their way unannounced and unwelcome into his palatial Wawel Castle Headquarters for far too long now. He had been in Poland since the successful, no, glorious and historic, invasion in the autumn of 1939, and it had been a posting that had come at the most perfect of times. At that point he had annoyingly found himself more and more marginalised as the big guns had taken over the party and he had become a minister without portfolio. It had been a great insult and embarrassment for Frank and his family from Hitler himself as he, Frank, was one of the few who had been there at the Führer's side from the beginning where he had nobly served as Hitler's personal legal adviser. How dare the Führer forget the sacrifices he had made and yet how could you question the self-proclaimed God of the world? Those who did were not around for too long afterwards.

For many years Frank had, therefore, done the only thing he could do and that was keep his head down and work hard and prove his loyalty, and he did this with a vim and gusto that even a hardened critic could not fail to be impressed by. Such work had at last been recognised and repaid by the Führer, with a high-ranking appointment of great gravitas as the General Governor of the Occupied Polish Territories, a vital position to ensure Germany was protected from these territories and guarantee that all that could be milked from Poland would be and Frank took to the posting with relish.

It was a fine return to form for him and he, determined to

impress upon his most kind Führer, made the most of it. Wawel Castle was a beautiful place for him to lord his power in the most dreadful way over the land before him and so lord it he most gleefully did, with absolute terror for the Poles and extreme decadence for himself. The most wonderful and lavish parties were had, parties that were talked about with great hatred around Poland by those who wanted the Germans to leave. All who came listened to the enrapturing stories of the now Obergruppenführer Frank, a man of great power even now recognised by the terrifying SS, and a man who made it clear that he had the personal ear of the Führer himself. What was not to be in extreme awe over? Wealth and power dripped out of the walls of the buildings into the grounds, parties to match those of the Romans where nothing was out of bounds, no joy was too much or too extreme.

Added to these more carnal joys, Frank made the most of his love of chess, seeing the great intelligence of the game and in his own command of the board as something he could bring to the more enlightened people of Poland who wanted to learn from the Master race. He took great delight in welcoming masters of the game to his Wawel Castle and he established his own chess school under the chess legends of Efim Bogoljubow and Dr Alexander Alekhine. These wondrous joys filled him with a sense of nobility, that he, Frank, was doing some good in a world that had gone mad.

In his days Frank went about his job of extrapolation and annihilation with the same fervour, the earth stripped bare for his camps of extermination and anything of any value sent back for his beloved Führer to use as he saw fit. Heinrich Himmler, a man Frank despised, may have been responsible for running the camps, but he had to ensure all was in place for that evil butcher to do his business. The name of Doctor Hans Michael Frank quickly became one that was despised and hated and he, the man, revelled in the knowledge of the power he was wielding, the terror he was inflicting. Death never did stink so badly, arrive so coldly as here on the soiled land of Poland, the screaming voices of the wronged to be heard for all time.

Sadly for Frank his personal life during his reign of Poland had been littered with some hard fought battles behind the scenes, not least of which with his wife, the great battleaxe and self-proclaimed "Queen of Poland", Brigette. He had tried so hard to divorce her, to be rid of her constant attempts to bring him down, but she was having none of it. He swore that she was his greatest enemy yet in reality this was not true. Attempts on his life came and went far too frequently, the most serious of which had happened a year previously with a bomb on the train he was travelling on. Members of the Polish Secret State paid heavily for that and painfully too, but the fact remained that living in a country where people were constantly plotting how to kill you was no real joy at all.

Still, the installed Polish leader ploughed on, filling his days with the distraction of light and beauty to mitigate the darkness. Pretty and giving girls and boys were an ever-present at the castle and since the return of the beautiful works of art from the ever-increasingly bombed Berlin in the autumn of 1943, he had been able to dazzle his guests with three of the best, a Rembrandt, a Leonardo and a Raphael. Oh yes, he had much to be thankful for.

It was during the later months of 1944 it was becoming painfully clear that all was achingly falling apart. It wasn't so much what was being said by the Führer, a lot of which was becoming increasingly nonsensical, but rather the lack of clear leadership that was coming out of the Führer's command as to what to actually do to combat these setbacks. For too long now they had been on the back foot, fire-fighting and waiting. Brigette and the three children had long since fled back to the homeland, their safety at severe risk with hatred running at an all-time high and German resources to protect the now increasingly isolated Obergruppenführer becoming less and less able to cope. The initial hard-line troops that had stormed easily through Poland's streets had long since gone to fight elsewhere and were replaced by soldiers who Frank thought to be a disgrace to the uniform. He had raised the issue many times with his Führer only to be told to manage with what he had got. It was, it transpired, his responsibility to turn these boys into men but how could he do that? Warsaw was now once again a war zone and even the Poles had been able to drag together an army despite the fact that Frank thought they had just about killed all the able-bodied men they could find.

Even the bastard women and children were now taking arms against them! Add to this the fact that the Russians were now all over his eastern front and the case was simple; it was over.

And so, this miserable January morning as his car left for Berlin, the boot housing his three most precious and treasured paintings all wrapped up with great care and with all his other loot and baggage following in several lorries, Frank's heart dared to feel some ease at last returning. He would be much safer in Berlin and from there he could perhaps regain influence with his leader and help negotiate the end, because the end of the Nazi terror was now clearly coming, their golden dreams in tatters for all to see apart from, it seemed, his leader. As Hitler's once right-hand man on all matters legal, surely this was his time to negotiate peace, to save his Führer from total and utter humiliation. Yes, in this darkest hour, this could well be the time for Frank's brightest star to be born. History could write that it was he, Obergruppenführer Frank who had helped the Führer see sense and agree to world peace.

Doctor Frank had been advised against travel by road as he was subject to both the Polish freedom fighters and allied air attack and yet wasn't that also true of the trains where his life had so nearly been taken? The Polish High Commander had screamed to get the escape ready to his adviser, an unfortunate man from Leipzig who when he had got the position with the Obergruppenführer had thought himself the luckiest man on earth. He had already served time in the killing fields of France and a posting to Russia, the posting that nobody wanted, was next on the cards. Luckily his expert Polish gained from several years of working in an export business before the war that worked extensively within the Polish territories was picked up and he was taken mercifully out of the front line. Years of then being lectured at by both Frank and his mad wife had made him question his relief at being posted here and once again, in doing his best to protect his master, he had been subject to a threatening stream of abuse.

Hours later and the convoy of Frank and his precious belongings and several lorries full of the best of his troops made their way north to Lodz to round the danger of heading anywhere near the increasingly daring raids that the allied bombers were inflicting on the German heartlands. Winter made the journey even more depressing, the countryside bleaker than ever against a backdrop of years of bloody war. As they rounded the top of Radomski, Frank allowed himself to fall to the heat of the car and drift into a sleep that was calling him in to forget the terrors that he inflicted on others. The gunfire fight that woke him up was, therefore, a great shock and Spielman, his adviser who had worked tirelessly on the journey, met the gaze of a shocked Frank with a finger to his mouth to keep quiet and to keep down. With that the young German un-holstered his Walther P-38 and prepared for the worst. The Germans were holed down on what looked like a deserted road and they were clearly in trouble.

Outside, the exchange of violence intensified, the German troops having been caught by surprise, and being split equally between two truckloads at the back and two at the front, now tried to regroup. The troops at the front lost their lives very quickly and the initiative now belonged totally with the attackers. By the time the rear had responded they realised they were totally outflanked and now hopelessly outnumbered. The German soldiers were brave and efficient, but within fifteen minutes, they were dead.

Silence fell as Frank whispered urgently to the brave looking Spielman, bravery that Frank found was nowhere to be found in his own head.

'Where are we?'

'In woods north of Radomski.'

'Well, how on earth are we under such fire?'

It was a fair question. Brave Poles had been doing underground resistance work on an increasing scale but this was unprecedented. Spielman just shrugged his shoulders and motioned to Frank to remain low in the footwell. The adviser then nodded to the driver and the two of them slowly opened their doors and stepped out of the Mercedes staff car only to find twenty or more allied troops with machine guns pointing at them and smiles on their faces.

'Do you speak English?' asked Joshua Spearing in a most jovial and congenial voice.

'Yes,' answered Heinz Spielman cautiously, his voice

turning into steam that rose high into the now quiet sky that was filled with death.

'Oh, how absolutely marvellous!' Joshua replied in a tone that suggested he had just discovered a great artefact. 'Well, would you mind asking that clearly brave boss of yours to step out from his hiding place and join us? Thankyou so very much."

The question caused much hilarity to the allied troops, troops whose faces suggested they were British, though the one next to the speaking man was most definitely Russian which concerned Spielman immensely. Frank, who spoke perfect English and had been listening to the conversation with great fear, stepped out of the car with as much dignity as he could manage.

'Ah, Doctor Hans Michael Frank, murdering bastard of the most barbaric kind, how absolutely delightful to meet you, although I must apologize for the rather bloody circumstances of our arrival. Occupational hazard I am afraid. I can't seem to move nowadays without shooting some German or other.'

'I didn't catch your name?' Frank managed, pulling as much gravitas in his voice as he could muster, though it did sadly break slightly as he spoke the words.

'No, you didn't,' replied Joshua, 'Never mind. So, we are here, I should add at this point and to put your evil little mind to rest, not to kill you. Sadly I do have to kill all of your men.'

At this point the two remaining Germans received bullets to the head and died instantly. Frank turned wildly to his left and right where the two Germans had fallen.

'This is shocking and needless bloodshed!' he declared.

'Well, you would know all about that, would you not?' said Caspar Portichenko, quiet up to this point but now stepping forward causing the German to step back towards his car and, in turn, Caspar to laugh.

Joshua nodded to one of his men who promptly started issuing orders as fallen Germans and vehicles were removed from the woodland road. Joshua, Caspar and the extremely confused and fearful Frank got into the staff car together, Frank and Caspar in the back, Joshua in the front. They drove into the secrecy of a clearing as the troops went about the business of hiding their work and Joshua, turning off the engine, turned back to face the now terrified German.

'Right, I think it's fair to say we have your most avid attention, do we not?' Joshua asked, his voice now business-like and focussed, though still carrying a lace of amusement. Frank simply nodded.

'Well, let's begin', Joshua said, 'shall we?'

'Begin what?' asked a confused Frank.

'Your route to redemption,' replied a happy Caspar Portichenko, pleased to see a Nazi key figure in his grasp and squirming pathetically before them.

'Redemption?' asked a hapless Frank.

'Yes, redemption,' replied Caspar, 'after all you have murdered thousands and probably millions of innocent people including the most vulnerable that this planet has to offer and so I think you, of all people with your legal background, need to do some pretty quick work in filling that good deeds box, don't you agree?'

Frank thought of several things to say, all of which seemed fairly pointless. He simply managed, 'Get on with it, then.'

'Super,' replied Joshua who got out a folder and gave it to him. 'Your homework for later, Doctor Frank. You see, we have been watching you for a long time as you built your power base back up again, proving to your dear Führer that he was wrong to neglect you for so long during the rise of terror when it was you, loyal you, who had been one of his key men during those early important days. This was not the way you and your father imagined things was it when you followed him into the ranks of the law and climbed up your dirty rotten ladder?'

Frank's eyes lit up at this. How did they know so much?

'You must have felt rather used, giving your Führer everything only to be tossed off to the shadows. Tell me, how did that feel?'

Frank didn't know what to say.

'It felt bad, didn't it?' Joshua added.

'Yes,' mumbled Frank before he could stop the word coming out. Joshua went on.

'And yet then, and somewhat magnificently, you get given a huge job. Have you never really considered why this might have been, your rise from being sent back to the background to suddenly being accelerated to the world stage?'

'Well, I …' Frank stumbled, Joshua's words opening up a line of thought he had often started and allowed his pride to block their course, 'You tell me why!' he added with defiance mixed with obvious pain.

'Poisoned chalice, dear boy, poisoned chalice. You will forever be known as the man who slaughtered those who could do nothing but lie down and die, and in particular, slaughtering God's chosen people.'

'But I have not!' shouted Frank in immediate riposte only to find Caspar begin to place photo after photo of inhumanity on his lap.

'How did you…?' The question from Frank hung limp in the air as each shocking image, images he could never remove from his brain, shot back at him a look of defiance.

'You still have Germans with moral fibre, Doctor Frank,' replied Caspar who purposely left a photograph of a rotting human carcass under the German's eyes. Frank instinctively looked away and Caspar, his big, strong Russian hand, pushed the German's gaze back down to the photograph.

'You did that,' said Joshua, all humour now gone, 'you and your, what's the phrase, the "Master Race"? Really? Do you really think that is what you are, given what you have done and how you have done it? Your bloodthirsty appetite has lost you this war, you know that don't you? All that time spent murdering the innocent when many would have fought for you as they did in the First World War. You are about to lose the war in utter and absolute humiliation and your big plan, your "Final Solution", well, what good is that now? You are to lose and it is your filth that will forever litter history and in so doing you have made the Jews cause stronger than ever. You utter and absolute fools.'

Now Caspar produced more photos and the dirt of their content made Frank more and more uncomfortable until he cracked.

'Enough!'

They waited. The woods around them had now returned to silence and the allied captains waited for their words to sit in the Germans brain.

'What do you want from me?' asked Frank, his voice finding some humility as the terror of what he had witnessed both in the killing of his comrades and in the photographs placed down before him filled his body with a most horrid broth.

'You were there at the beginning,' began Joshua, tipping out the purpose of their mission before the hapless German, 'and you will now be there at the end. We will make use of that. We are here from the leaders of the free world to offer your soul a way out.'

'My soul? What about my life?'

'Ah yes, your life too.'

'How will you do this?' asked Frank, fear still present but interest clearly in his voice now.

'You will do it, Herr Frank. You go back now to a Berlin on its knees and you will discover a city with virtually nothing left. It will get far worse in the coming months unless your leader is brought down or he capitulates. We both know both eventualities will come but that both will not be easy, after all enough people have tried to kill him to show this to be true.'

Frank nodded at that. Hitler's ability to keep himself alive was legend amongst the leadership. The Führer had been untouchable and yet, and yet. Joshua continued.

'Eventually he will fall and when he does we need to not only crush him but we need to crush his name too, the power, the influence of the name "Adolf Hitler". This, Doctor Frank, is where your work will bring him down to his knees and you will have your redemption.'

'Go on,' nodded Frank, interest unable to be hidden in his voice.

'In this file is the story that you will release of Hitler's lineage. For all we know it could be true. You will say that in 1930 one of his nephew's, a William Patrick Hitler, sort to let the truth of Hitler's family line out through you, Hitler's legal adviser. You will say that you covered it up as what else could you do, but you will say that now, for the good of the world, the time is ripe to tell the truth. You will reveal that his father, Alois Hitler, was born out of wedlock to a Jewish man, the son of Leopold Frankenberger for whom Hitler's grandmother, Maria, worked as a cook. You will prove that a very healthy income was forthcoming from Leopold for his son's indiscretion to Hitler's grandmother for many years and that she, and the Hitler family, had happily lived and indeed prospered on this money from this Jewish family. Your work will prove that Adolf Hitler was, therefore, himself of Jewish hereditary, and that his lie, the lie of his life, will truly be exposed for all time.'

Frank laughed.

'You cannot be serious?'

'Oh, but we are,' said Caspar, 'we have done our work and the dates could all fit.'

'But Hitler, a Jew?' spluttered Frank.

'Yes indeed and a Jew that will save your life, Doctor Frank, and save the reputation of your family,' replied Caspar.

'I will be murdered for saying this!' spluttered out Frank.

'Possibly,' said Caspar, 'but you will be murdered anyway by a war trial and forever held up as a man of butchery so why not try this way instead?'

'Look,' said Joshua, 'we have to go now. You will appreciate that your dear German colleagues will be on their way to rescue you and that my men and I do not wish to die here, so for one last time, this is the deal. You will deliver this news when we say so. We will be in touch with you when the time is right. Your job for now is just to go on with overseeing the demise of your country. There is nothing you can do about this save for your own life to stay close to your Führer.'

'What if I refuse?'

'You will die along with all the others and your name will forever be dirt. We offer you redemption. It is your choice whether you take it.'

'What if I tell him of your plan?'

Joshua laughed.

'We both know that if you tell him of this plan he will kill you. This is so preposterous that it could never be spoken of while he is in power. You will say nothing.'

Frank nodded. He knew this to be true.

At this Caspar and Joshua opened the car doors and stepped out into the still winter air, leaving Frank confused and alone. As he sat there the boot was opened, alarm filling Frank once more as his precious cargo of historic paintings was in there. Then, after a few seconds, the door was mercifully shut.

Joshua reappeared at the open door by Frank's side.

'One more thing, Hans, you don't mind if I call you Hans do you? We have a little insurance.'

Frank lifted his face to meet that of the Englishman.

'One of your stolen paintings, no doubt incredibly valuable and no doubt one that you were hoping to ensure your income into retirement, well, you can have it back when you do what we need you to do. OK?'

Frank began to utter an insult but he was just met by laughter.

With that the car door was slammed and the Special Air Service troops made their getaway, their play made, the future to decide what fate would do with history.